THE PATHFINDERS SOCIETY

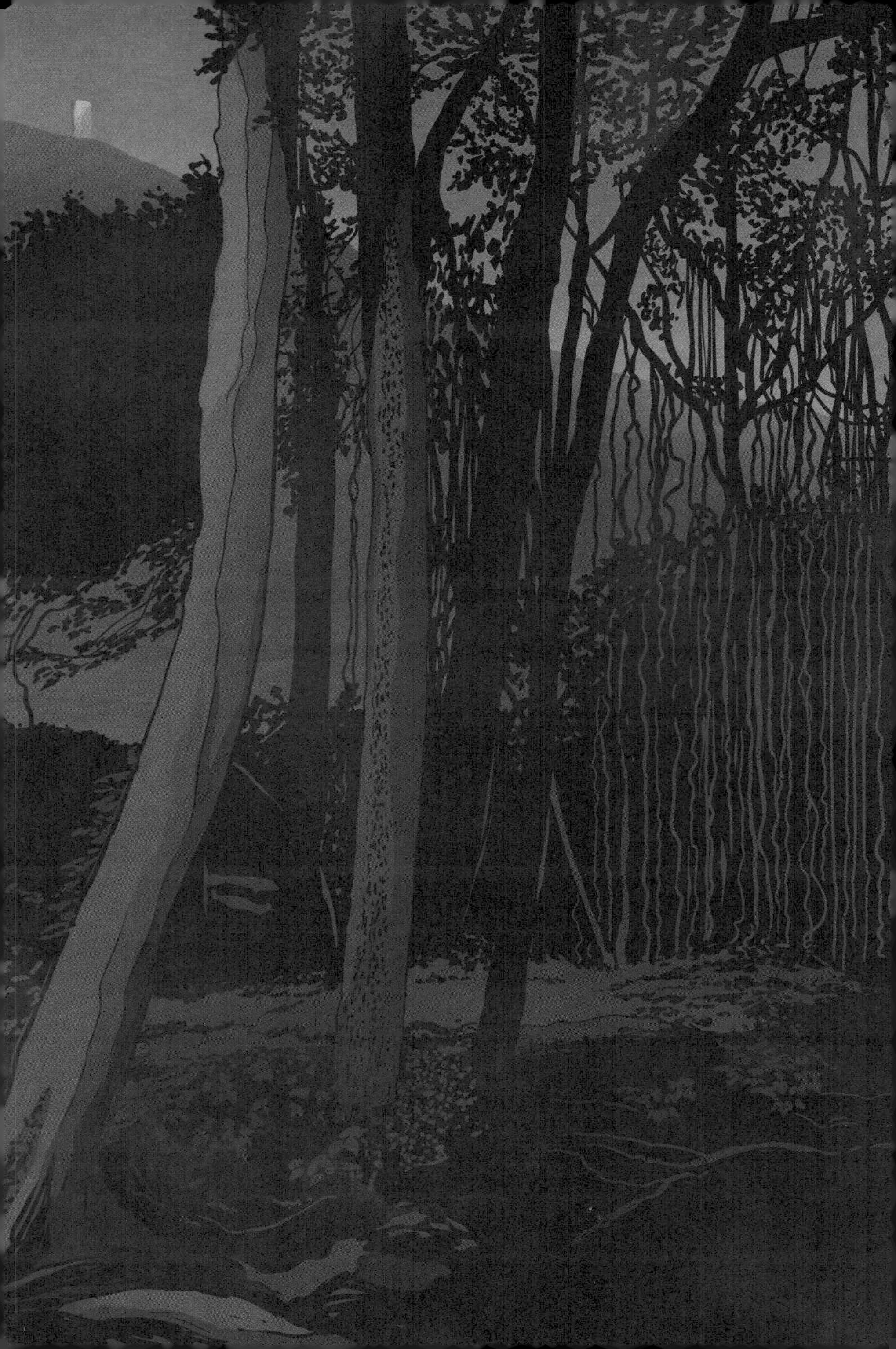

THE PATHFINDERS SOCIETY

The Mystery of the Moon Tower

Francesco Sedita &
Prescott Seraydarian

illustrated by
Steve Hamaker

VIKING

VIKING
An imprint of Penguin Random House LLC, New York

First published in the United States of America by Viking,
an imprint of Penguin Random House LLC, 2020

Photo credit: page 171, Library of Congress

Visit us online at penguinrandomhouse.com

LIBRARY OF CONGRESS CATALOGING-IN-PUBLICATION DATA IS AVAILABLE
ISBN 9780425291863 (hardcover)
ISBN 9780425291870 (paperback)

Manufactured in China
Book design by Steve Hamaker and Jim Hoover

1 3 5 7 9 10 8 6 4 2

Dedications

For Doug,

who makes so much seem possible,

and who keeps me on the path. —FS

For C., B., and G.,

for giving purpose to my path. —PS

For my son, Alexander. —SH

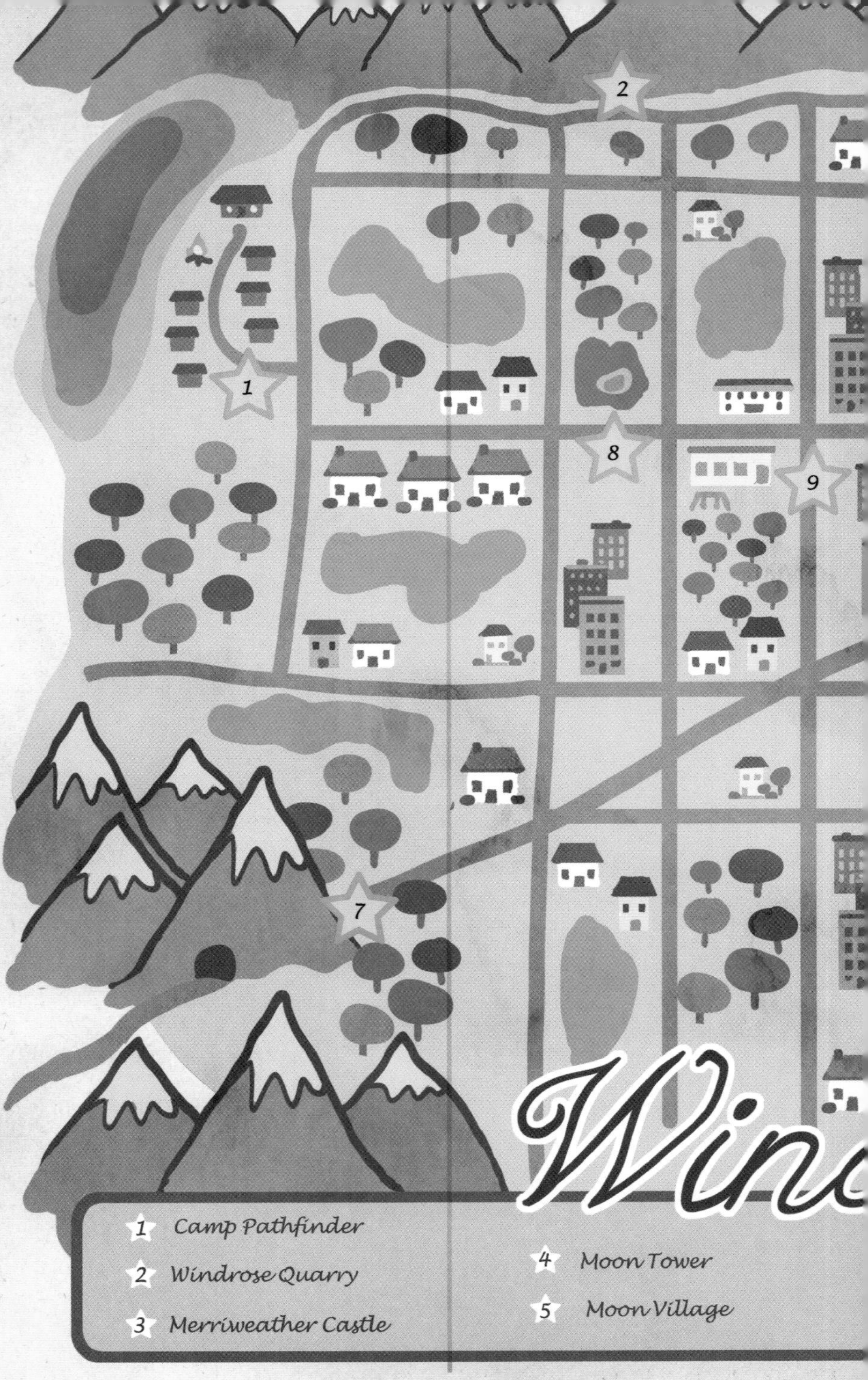
2
1
8
9
7
Win
1 Camp Pathfinder
2 Windrose Quarry
3 Merriweather Castle
4 Moon Tower
5 Moon Village

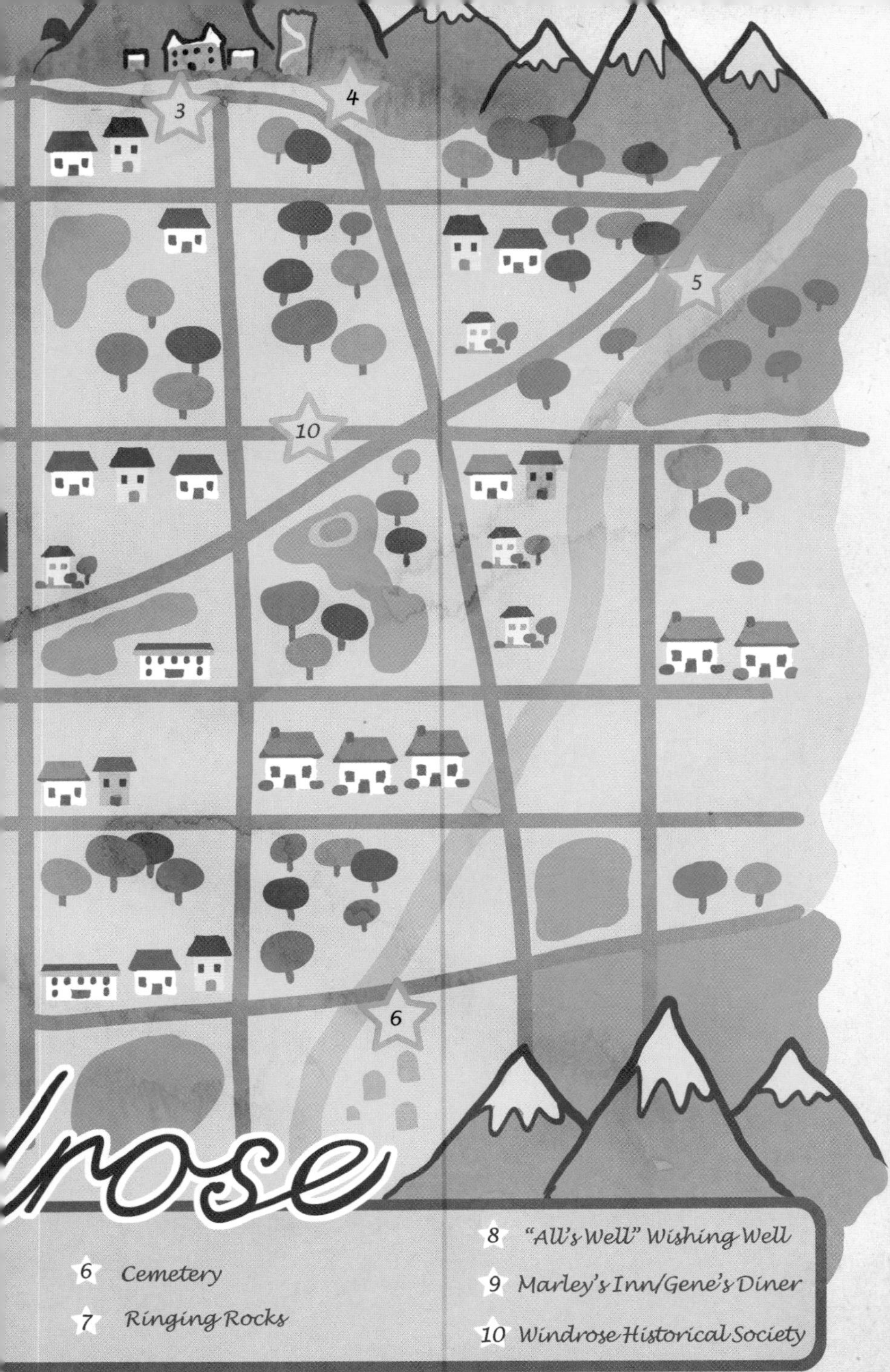

3
4
5
10
6
rose
6 Cemetery
7 Ringing Rocks
8 "All's Well" Wishing Well
9 Marley's Inn/Gene's Diner
10 Windrose Historical Society

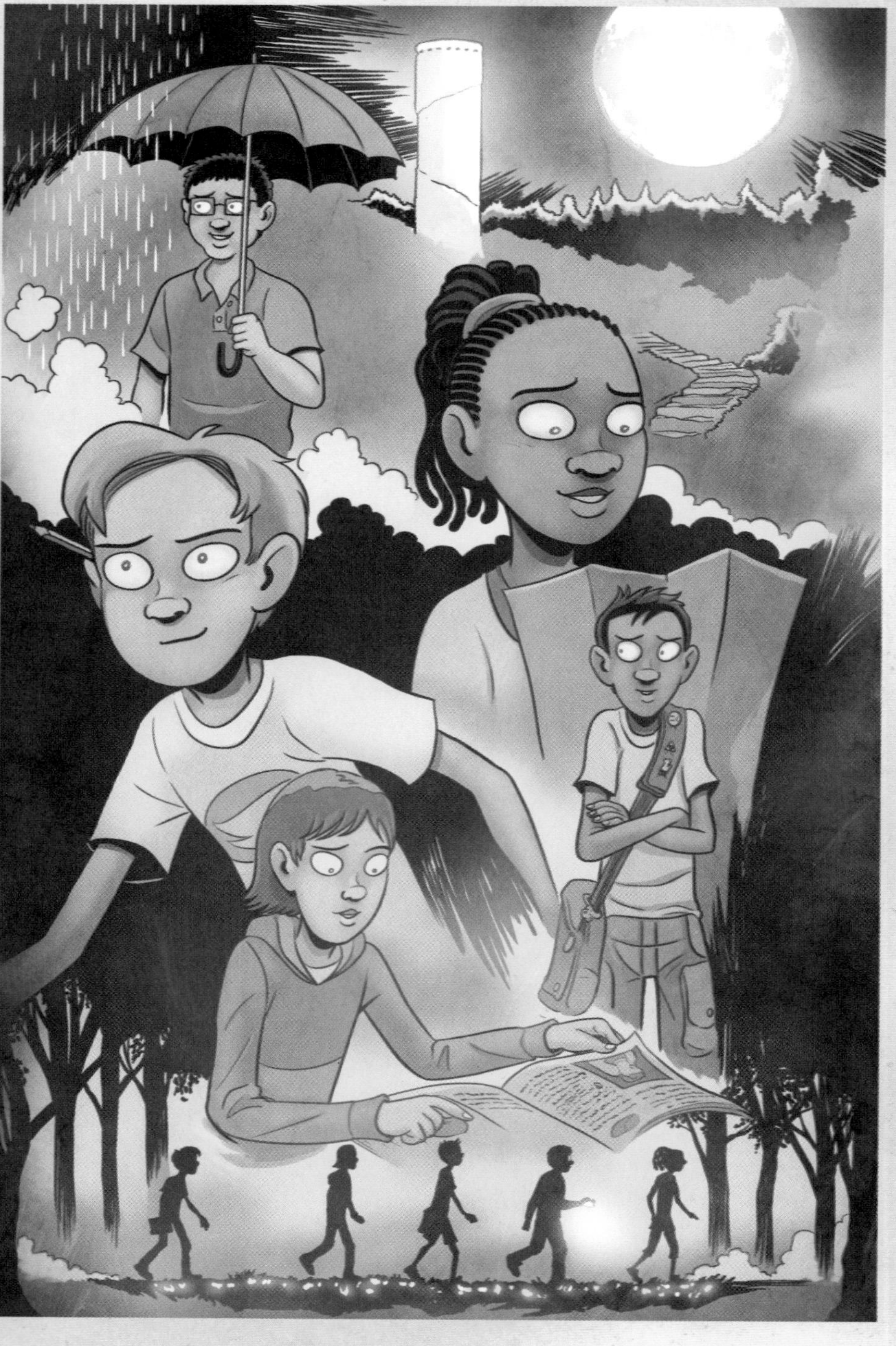

Meet the Pathfinders

KYLE is the new kid in town. He's always got a sketchbook in his pocket—and drawing is a very useful tool when you're connecting the dots on a treasure hunt!

BETH is super-organized and a bit of a history nerd. Need to go forward following a map? Or backward in time to solve a mystery? She's your girl.

HARRY is a goofball whose mouth sometimes moves faster than his brain. But his love of magic means he spots what's hidden in a tricky situation.

VICTORIA (VIC) is a popular cheerleader— and a secret math whiz. She figures out numbers and patterns along the path before anybody else even sees them.

NATE likes to invent stuff. His motto? A.B.R.: *Always Be Ready.* He's the guy you want on your team when you need solutions . . . *fast!*

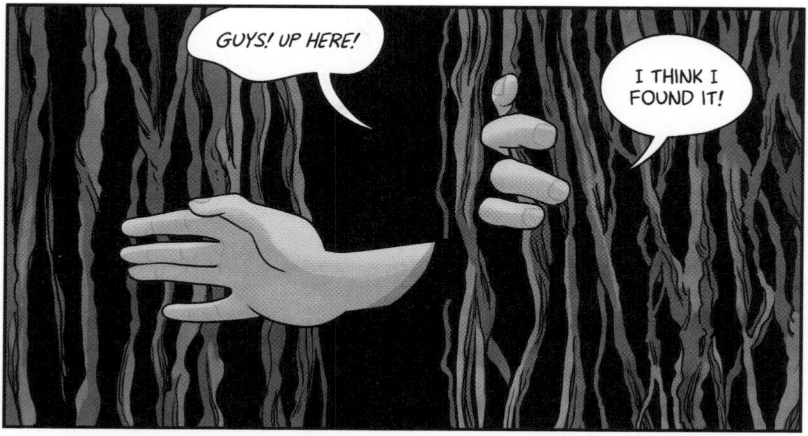
GUYS! UP HERE!
I THINK I FOUND IT!

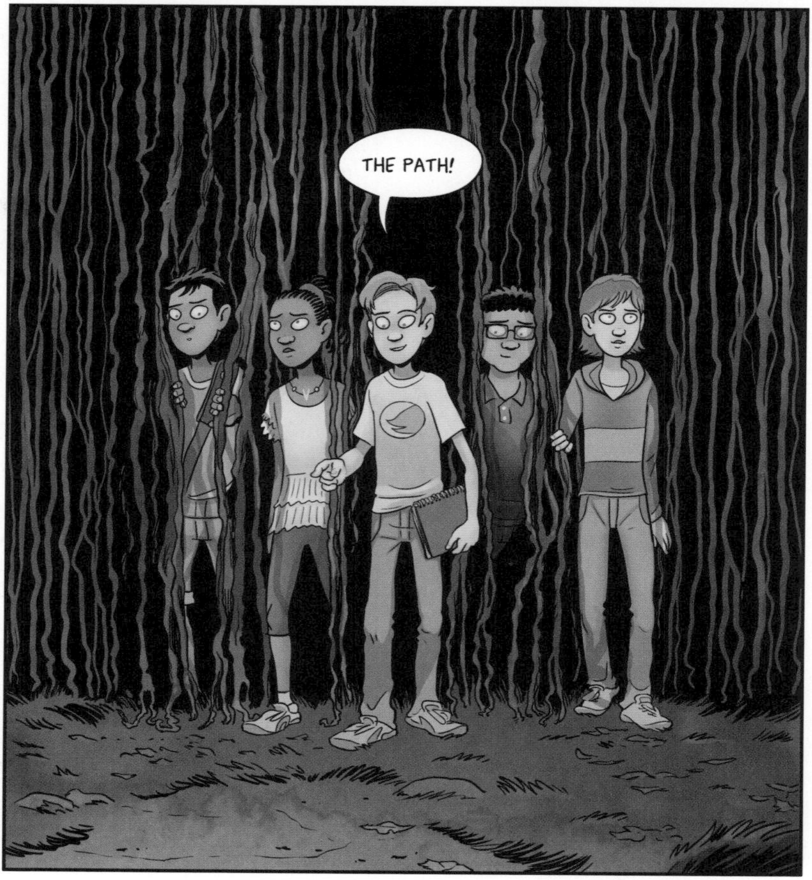
THE PATH!

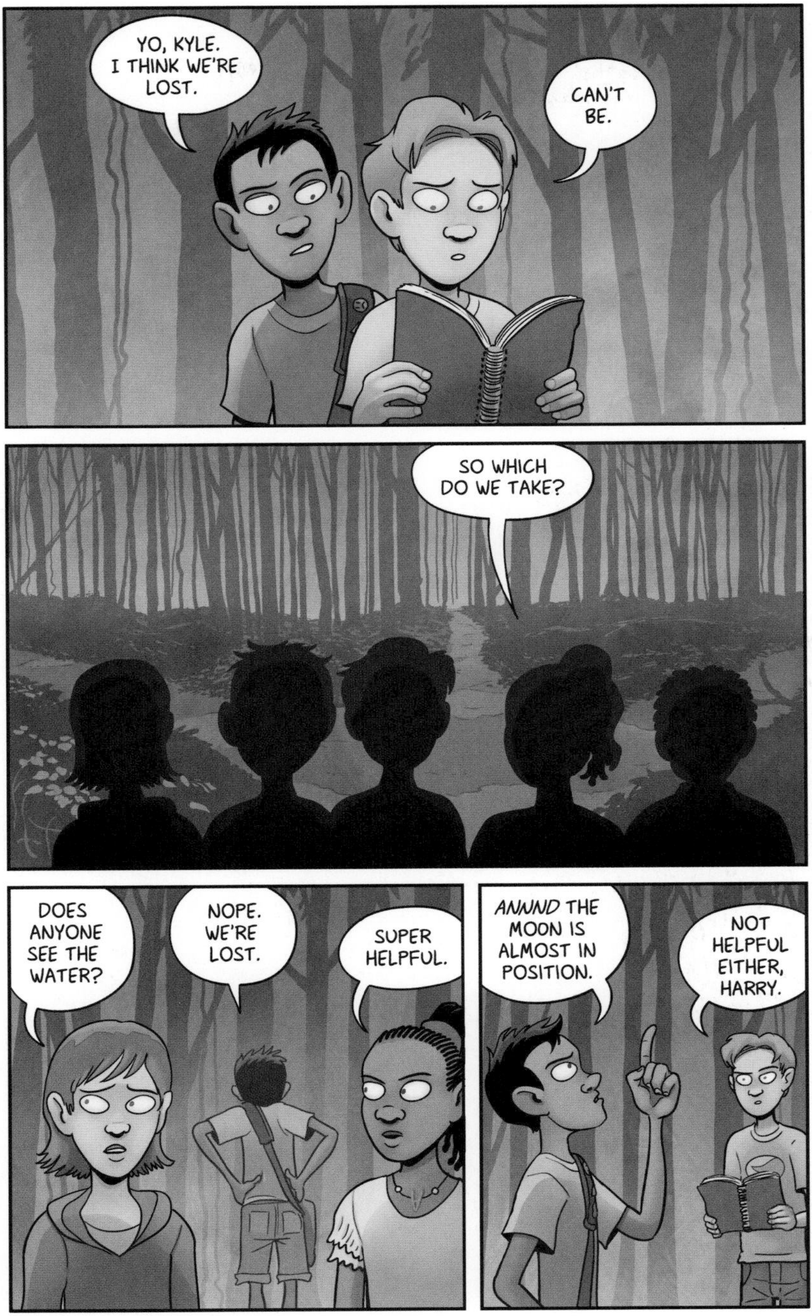
YO, KYLE. I THINK WE'RE LOST.
CAN'T BE.
SO WHICH DO WE TAKE?
DOES ANYONE SEE THE WATER?
NOPE. WE'RE LOST.
SUPER HELPFUL.
ANNND THE MOON IS ALMOST IN POSITION.
NOT HELPFUL EITHER, HARRY.

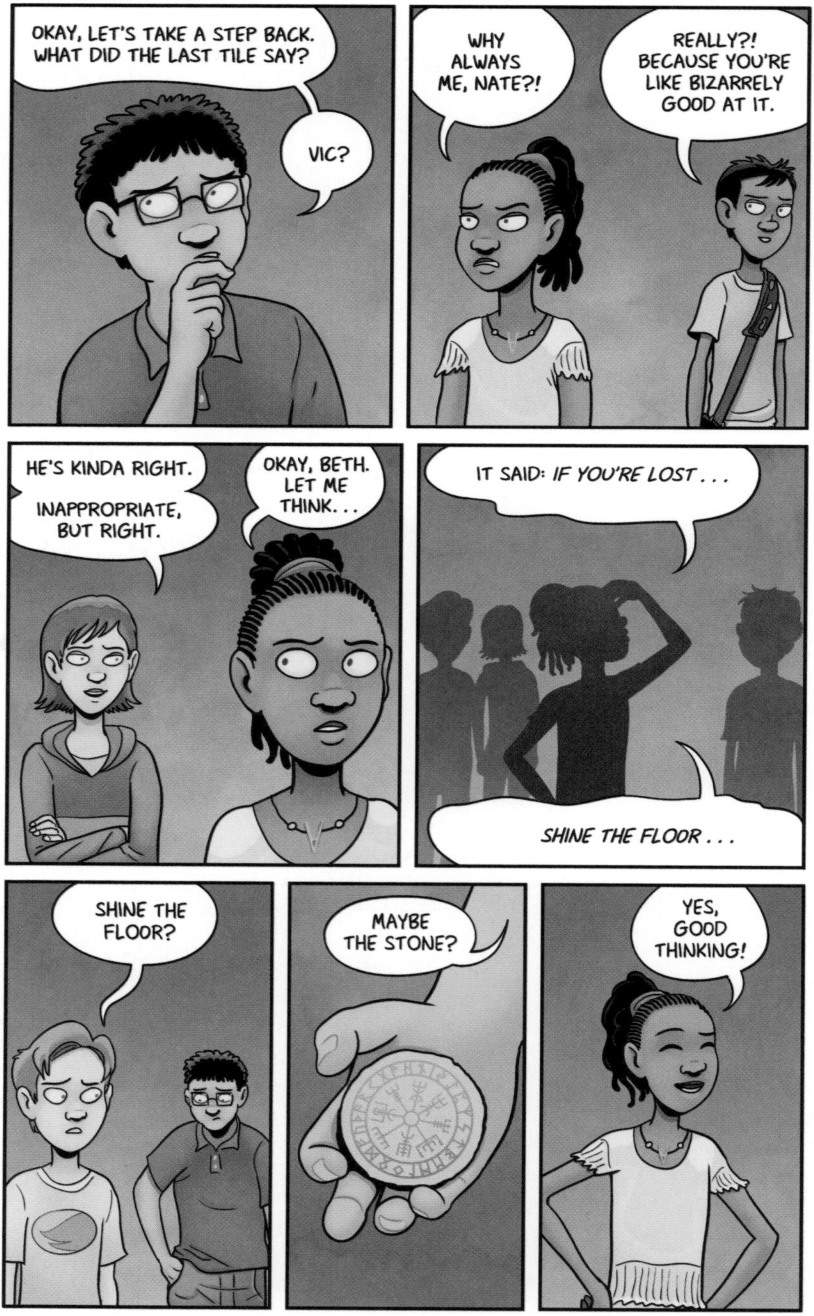
OKAY, LET'S TAKE A STEP BACK. WHAT DID THE LAST TILE SAY?
VIC?
WHY ALWAYS ME, NATE?!
REALLY?! BECAUSE YOU'RE LIKE BIZARRELY GOOD AT IT.
HE'S KINDA RIGHT.
INAPPROPRIATE, BUT RIGHT.
OKAY, BETH. LET ME THINK. . .
IT SAID: *IF YOU'RE LOST . . .*
SHINE THE FLOOR . . .
SHINE THE FLOOR?
MAYBE THE STONE?
YES, GOOD THINKING!

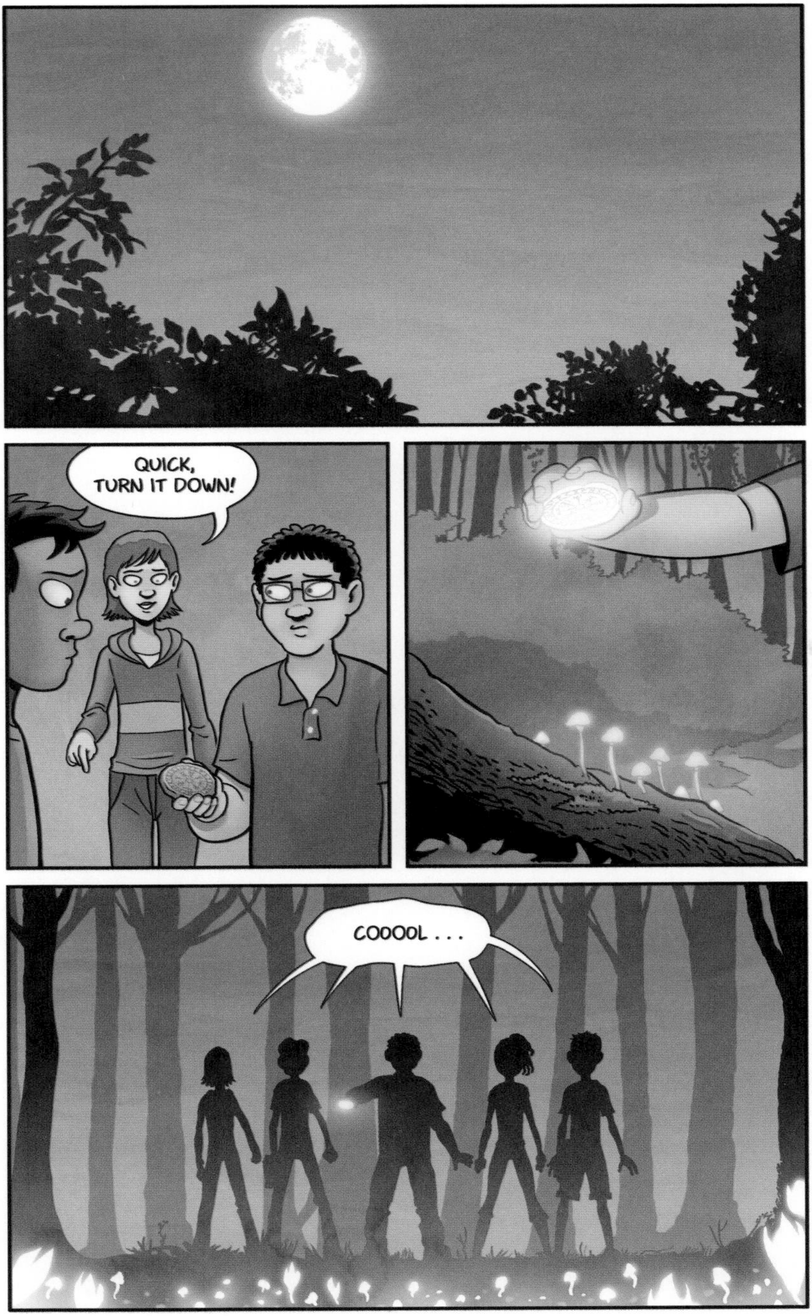
QUICK, TURN IT DOWN!
COOOOL . . .

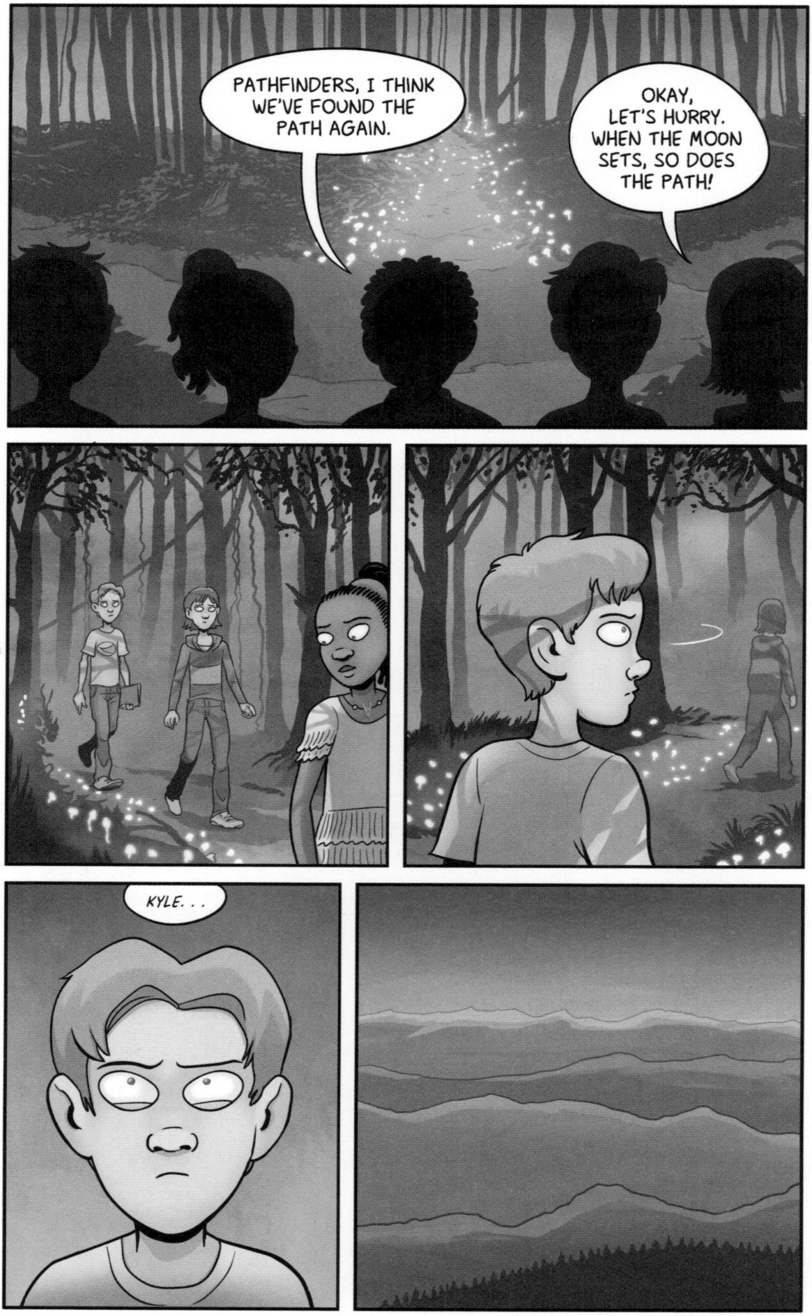
PATHFINDERS, I THINK WE'VE FOUND THE PATH AGAIN.
OKAY, LET'S HURRY. WHEN THE MOON SETS, SO DOES THE PATH!
KYLE. . .

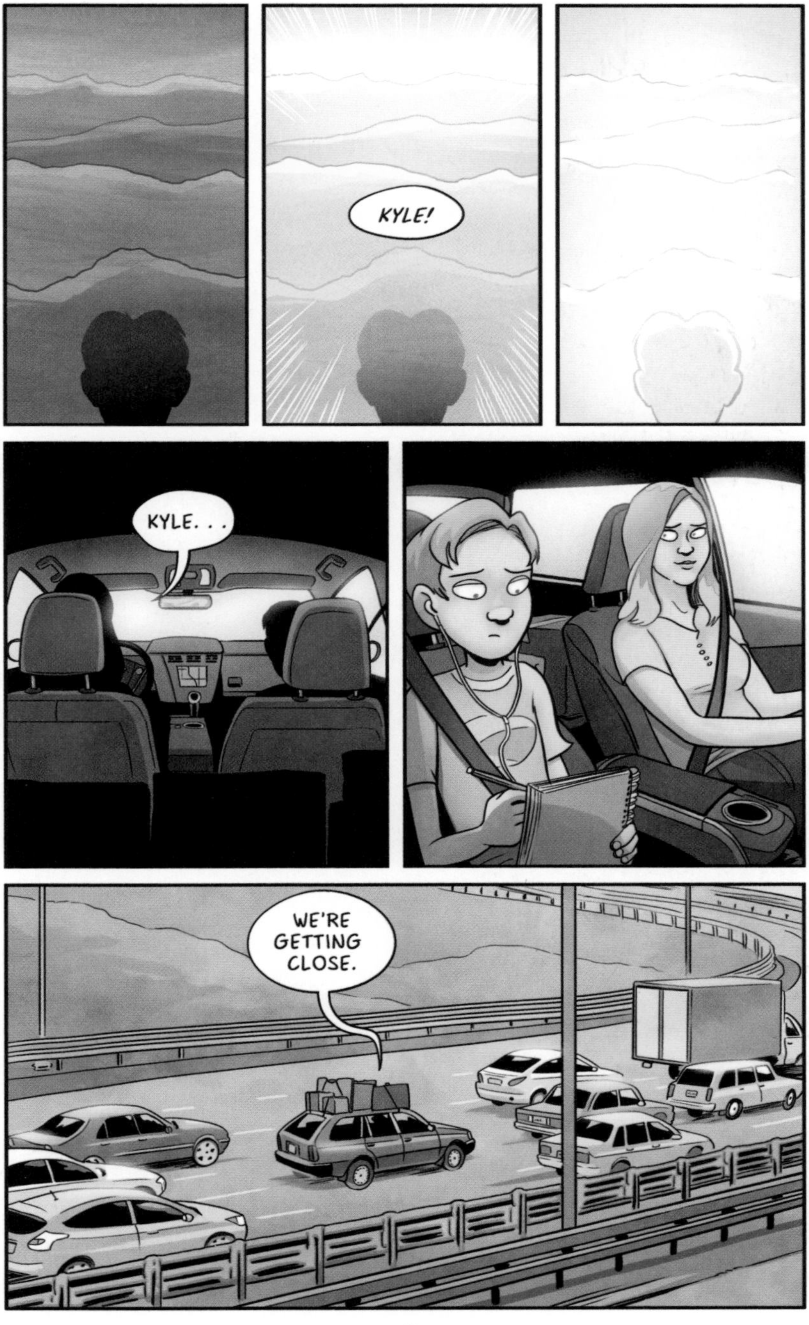
KYLE!
KYLE. . .
WE'RE GETTING CLOSE.

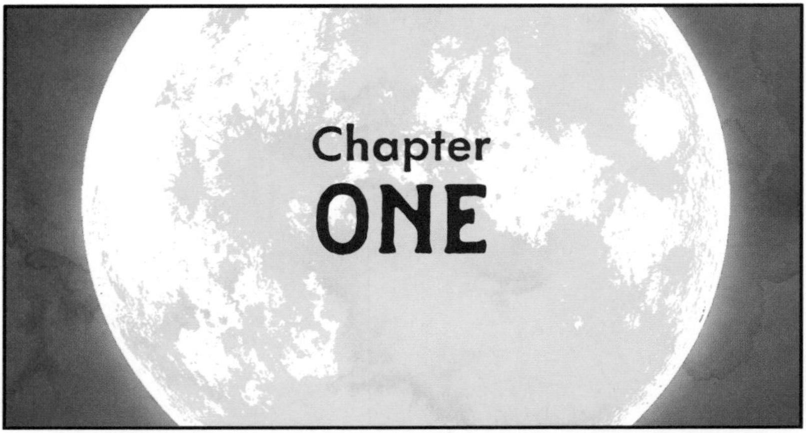
Chapter
ONE

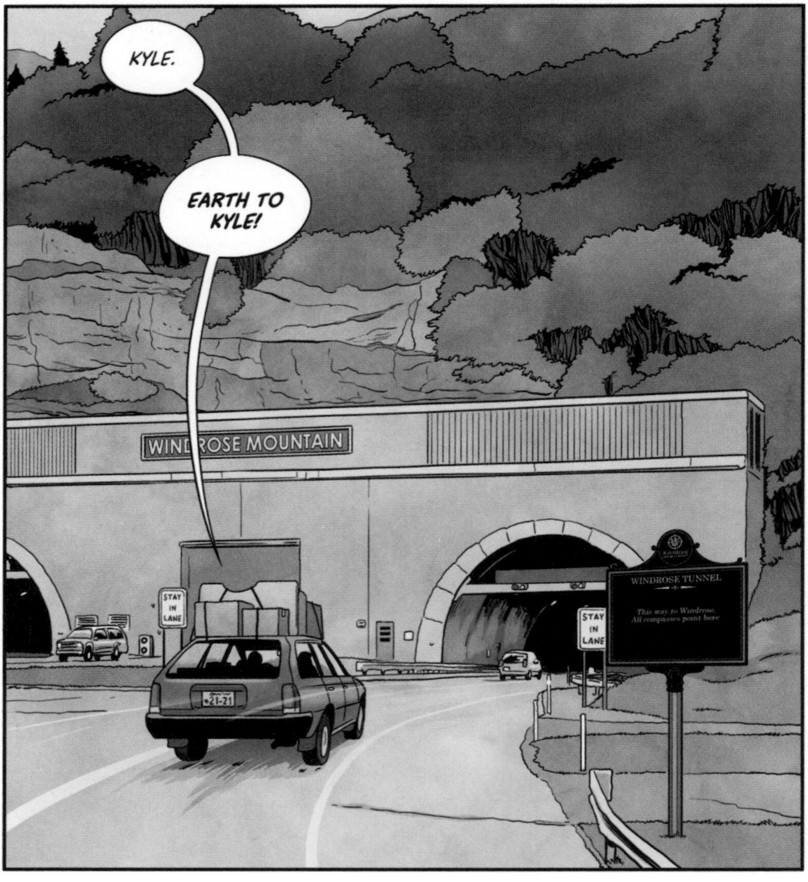
KYLE.
EARTH TO KYLE!
WINDROSE MOUNTAIN
STAY IN LANE
STAY IN LANE
WINDROSE TUNNEL
This way to Windrose.
All compasses point here

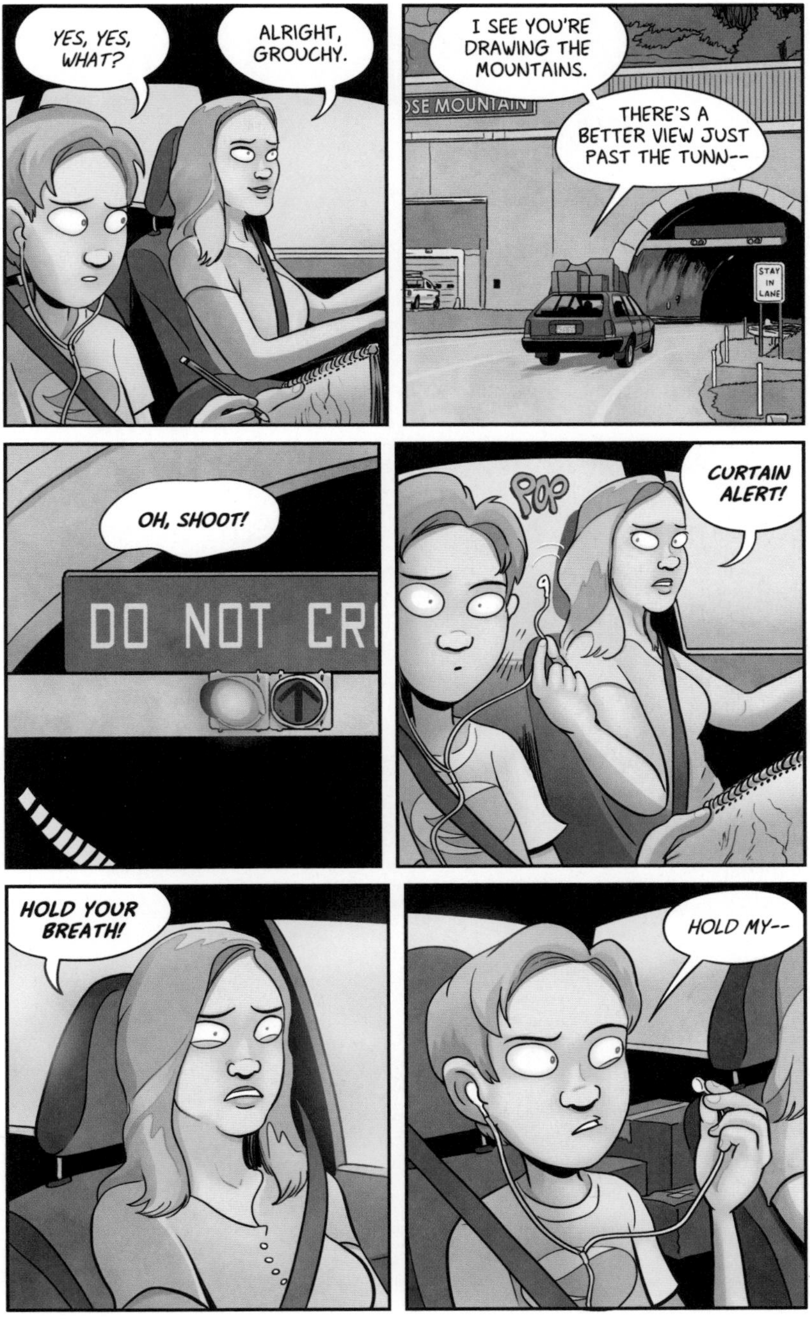
YES, YES, WHAT?
ALRIGHT, GROUCHY.
I SEE YOU'RE DRAWING THE MOUNTAINS.
OSE MOUNTAIN
THERE'S A BETTER VIEW JUST PAST THE TUNN--
STAY IN LANE
OH, SHOOT!
DO NOT CR
POP
CURTAIN ALERT!
HOLD YOUR BREATH!
HOLD MY--

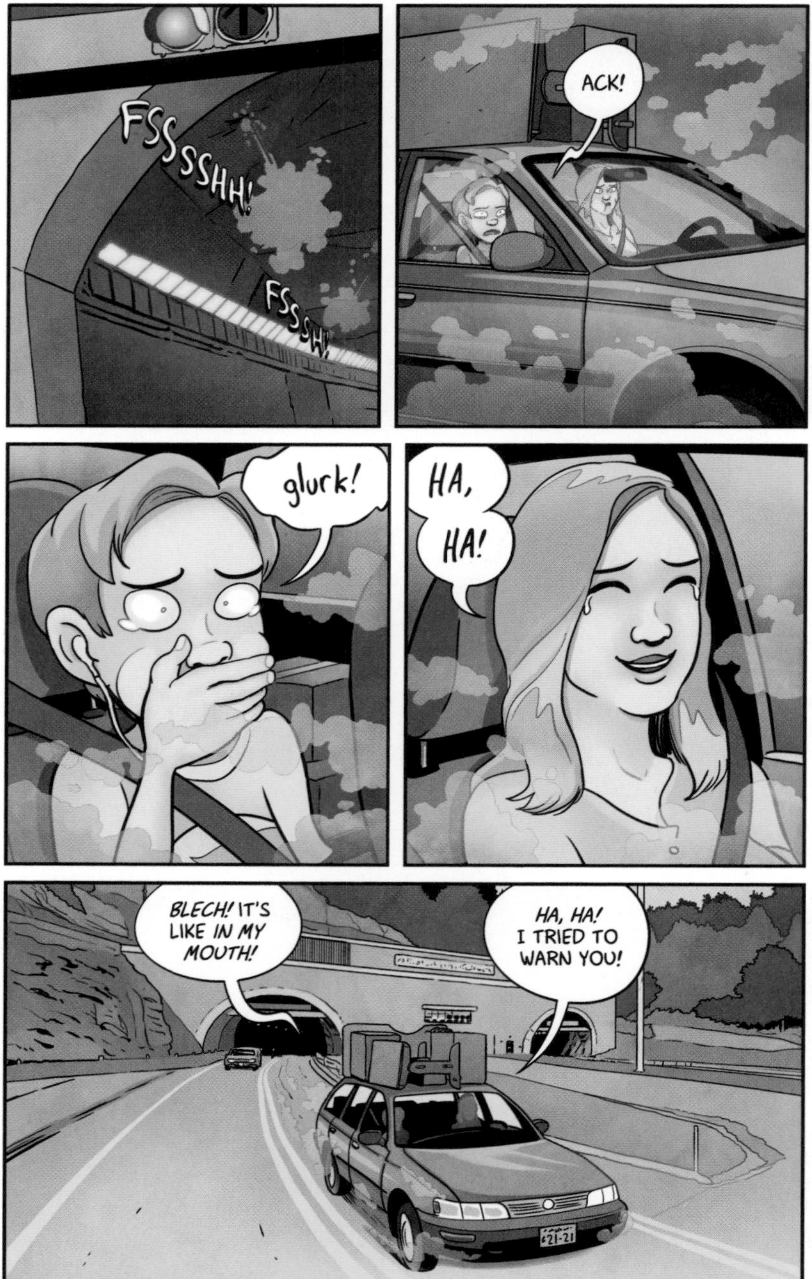
FSSSSHH!
FSSSH!
ACK!
glurk!
HA,
HA!
BLECH! IT'S LIKE IN MY MOUTH!
HA, HA! I TRIED TO WARN YOU!

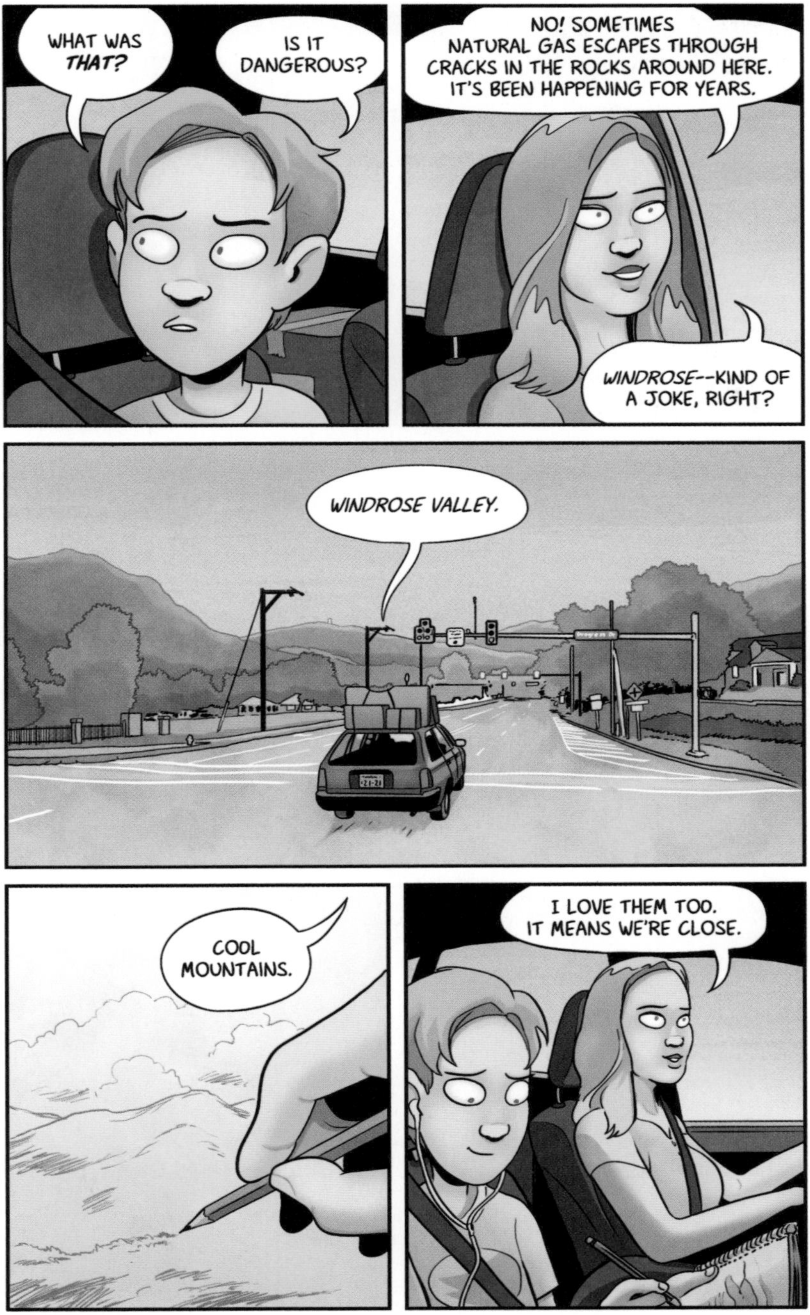
WHAT WAS THAT?
IS IT DANGEROUS?
NO! SOMETIMES NATURAL GAS ESCAPES THROUGH CRACKS IN THE ROCKS AROUND HERE. IT'S BEEN HAPPENING FOR YEARS.
WINDROSE--KIND OF A JOKE, RIGHT?
WINDROSE VALLEY.
COOL MOUNTAINS.
I LOVE THEM TOO. IT MEANS WE'RE CLOSE.

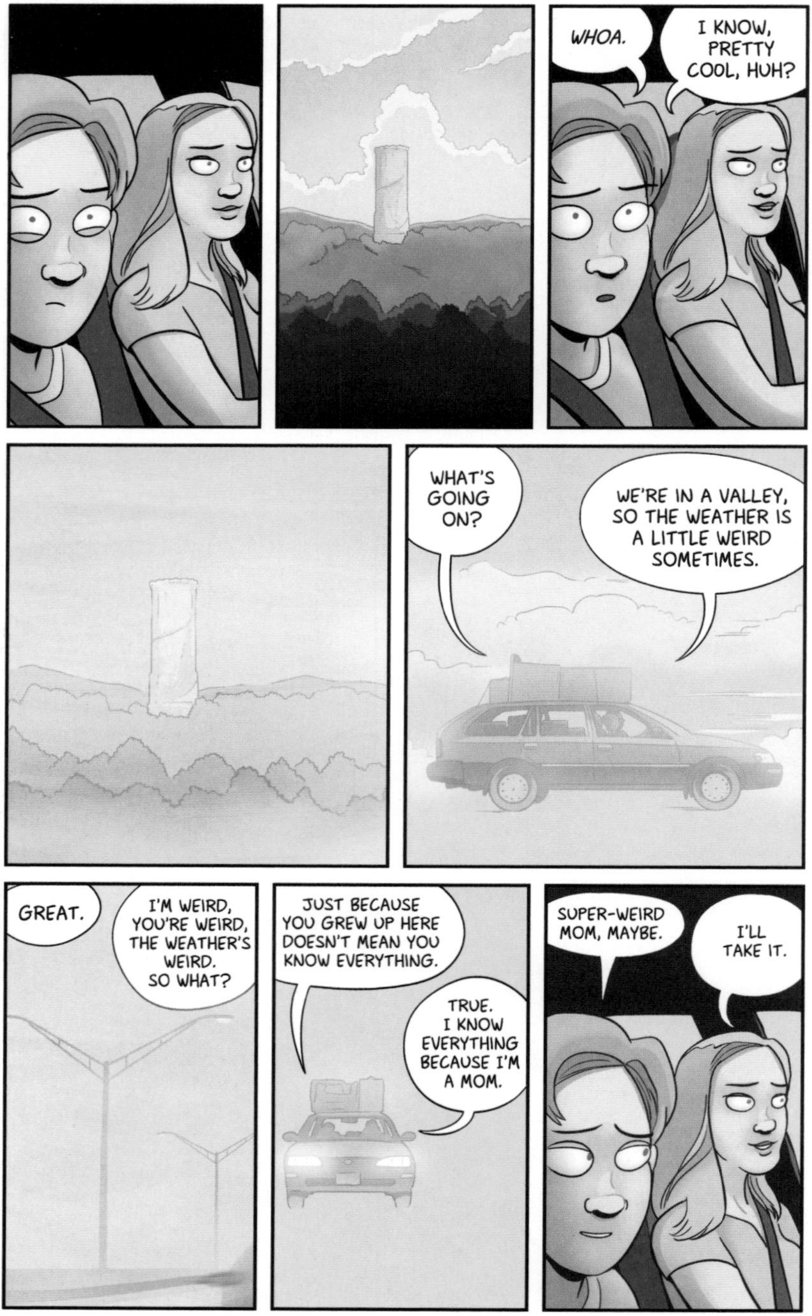
WHOA.
I KNOW, PRETTY COOL, HUH?
WHAT'S GOING ON?
WE'RE IN A VALLEY, SO THE WEATHER IS A LITTLE WEIRD SOMETIMES.
GREAT.
I'M WEIRD, YOU'RE WEIRD, THE WEATHER'S WEIRD. SO WHAT?
JUST BECAUSE YOU GREW UP HERE DOESN'T MEAN YOU KNOW EVERYTHING.
TRUE. I KNOW EVERYTHING BECAUSE I'M A MOM.
SUPER-WEIRD MOM, MAYBE.
I'LL TAKE IT.

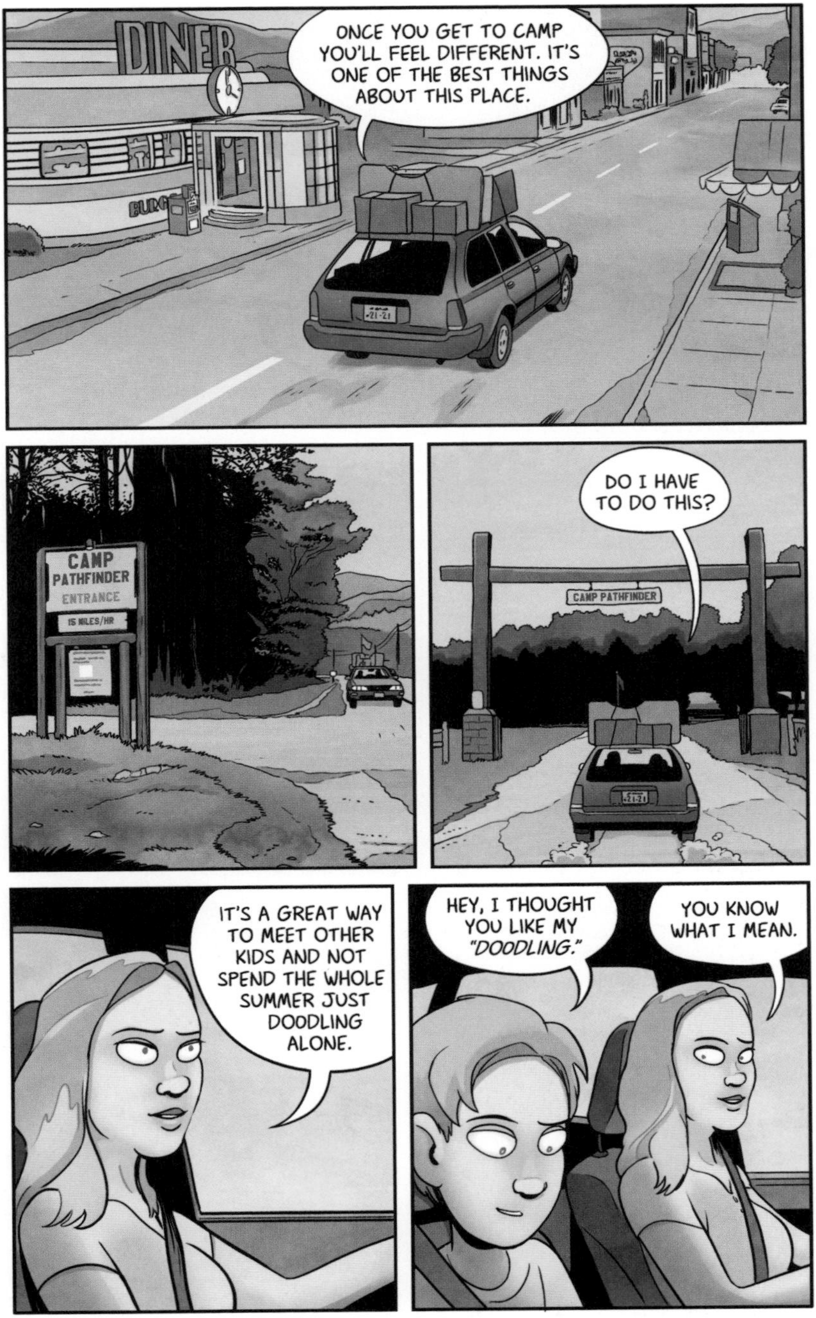
DINER
ONCE YOU GET TO CAMP YOU'LL FEEL DIFFERENT. IT'S ONE OF THE BEST THINGS ABOUT THIS PLACE.
CAMP PATHFINDER ENTRANCE
15 MILES/HR
DO I HAVE TO DO THIS?
CAMP PATHFINDER
IT'S A GREAT WAY TO MEET OTHER KIDS AND NOT SPEND THE WHOLE SUMMER JUST DOODLING ALONE.
HEY, I THOUGHT YOU LIKE MY *"DOODLING."*
YOU KNOW WHAT I MEAN.

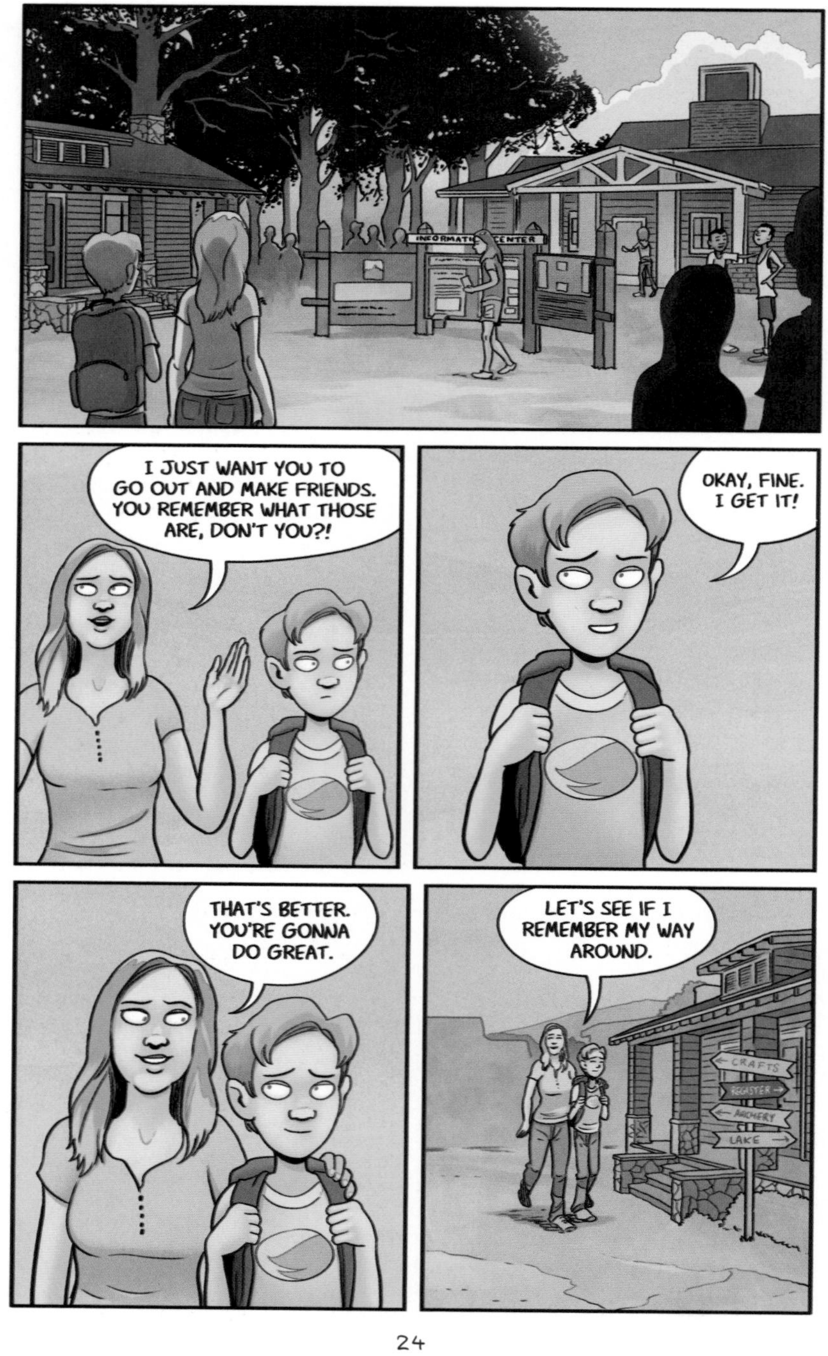
I JUST WANT YOU TO GO OUT AND MAKE FRIENDS. YOU REMEMBER WHAT THOSE ARE, DON'T YOU?!
OKAY, FINE. I GET IT!
THAT'S BETTER. YOU'RE GONNA DO GREAT.
LET'S SEE IF I REMEMBER MY WAY AROUND.
CRAFTS
REGISTER
ARCHERY
LAKE

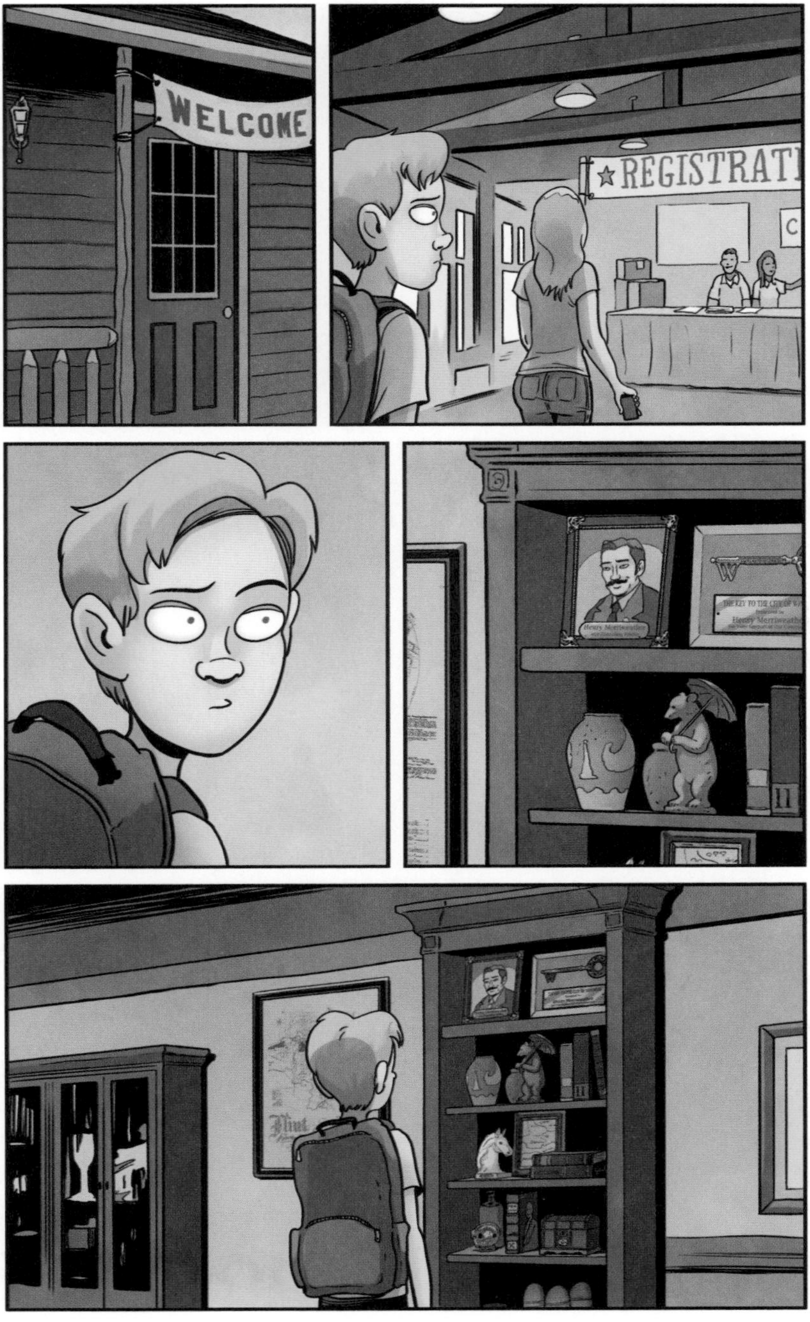
WELCOME
REGISTRATI
Henry Merriweather

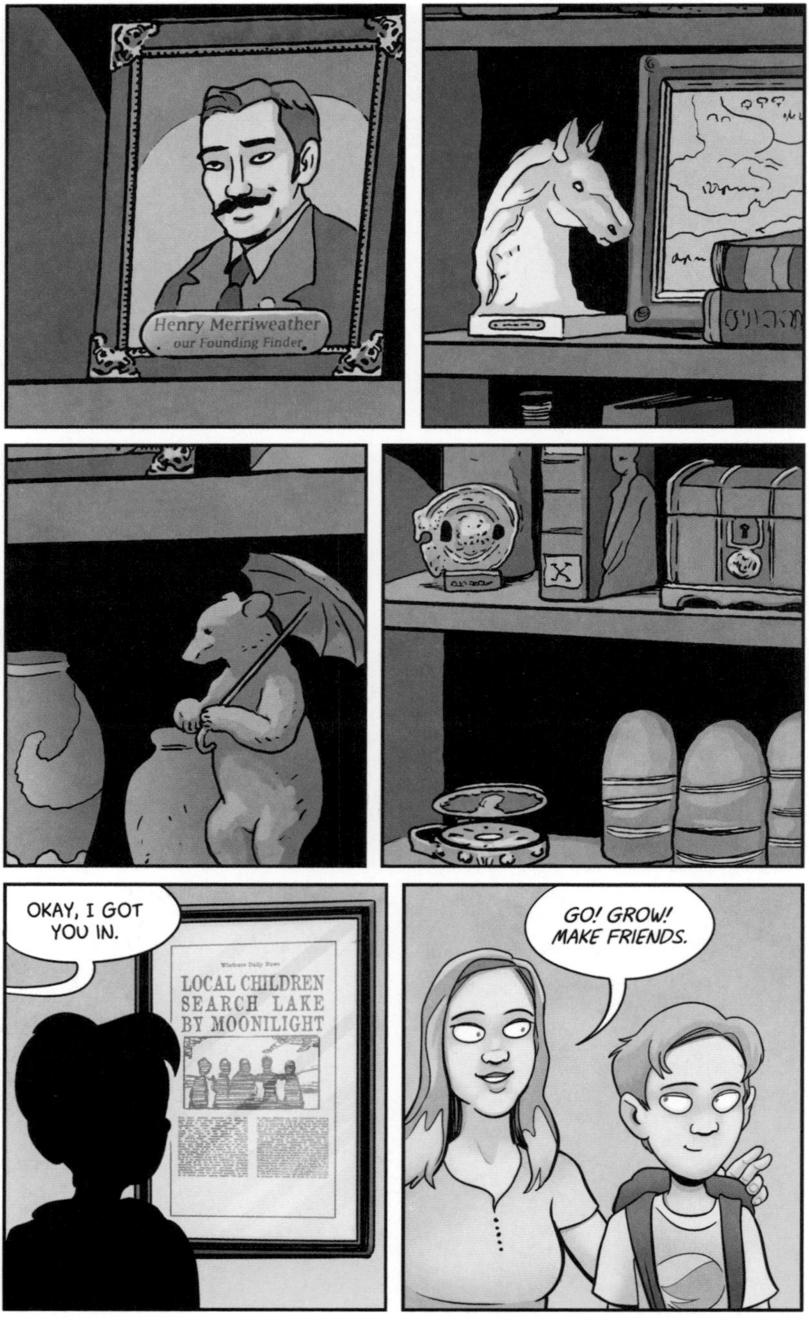
Henry Merriweather
our Founding Finder
OKAY, I GOT YOU IN.
LOCAL CHILDREN SEARCH LAKE BY MOONLIGHT
GO! GROW! MAKE FRIENDS.

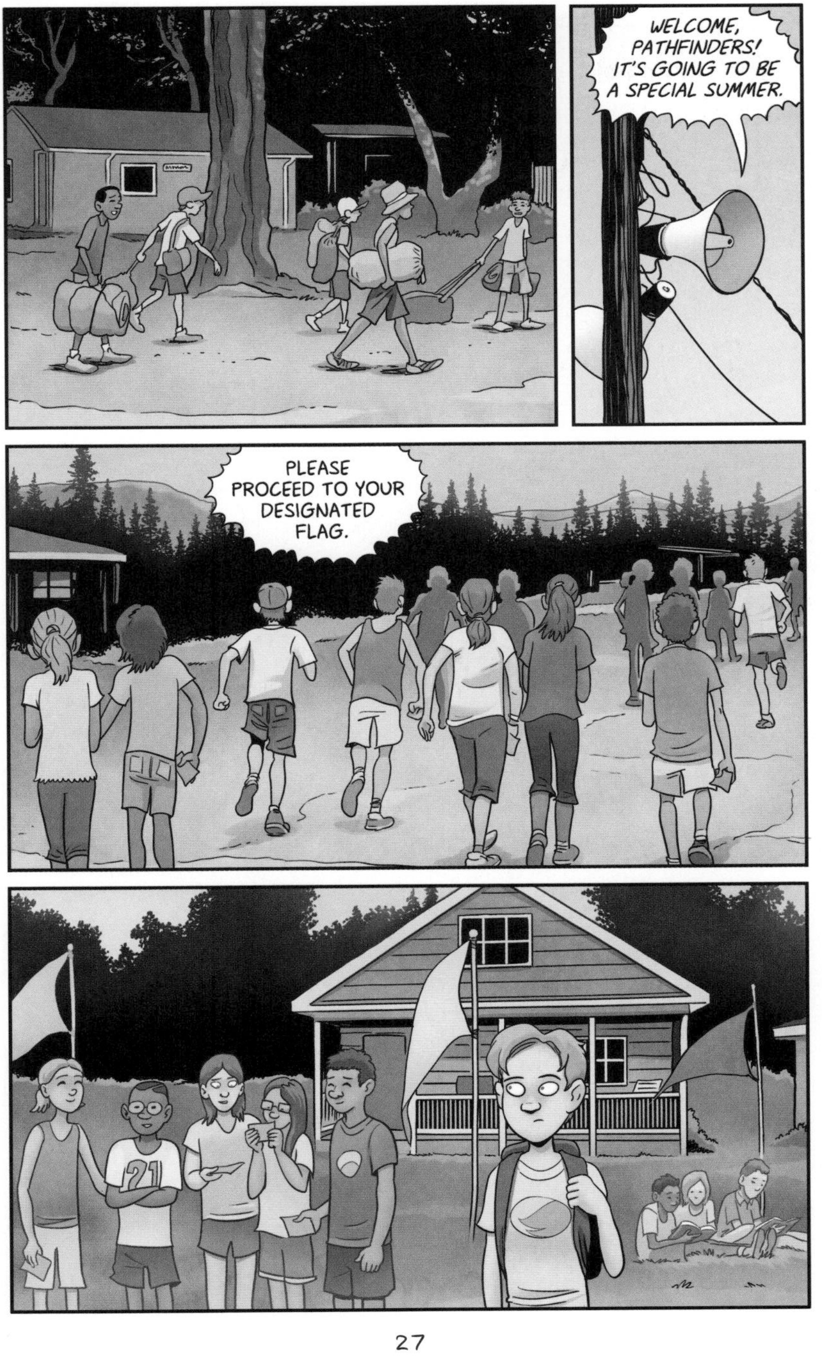
WELCOME, PATHFINDERS! IT'S GOING TO BE A SPECIAL SUMMER.
PLEASE PROCEED TO YOUR DESIGNATED FLAG.
21

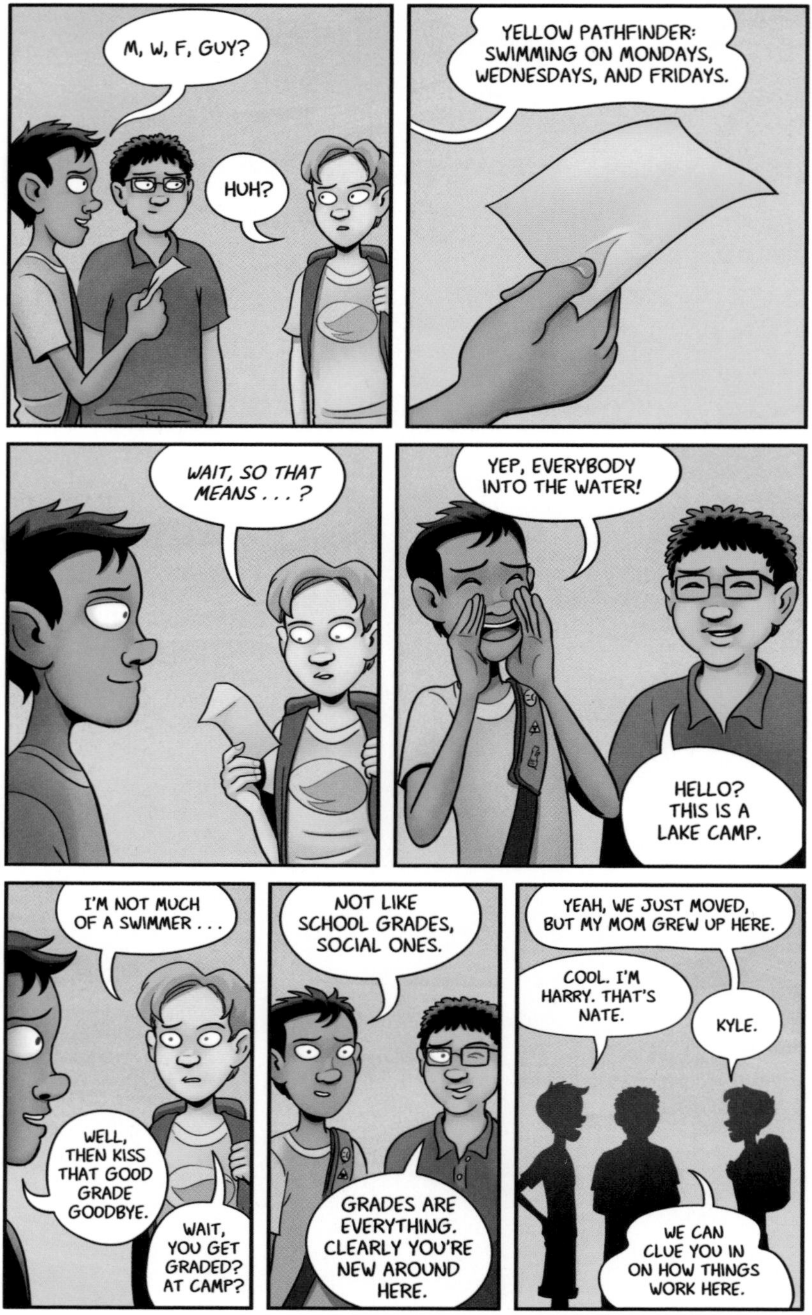
M, W, F, GUY?
HUH?
YELLOW PATHFINDER: SWIMMING ON MONDAYS, WEDNESDAYS, AND FRIDAYS.
WAIT, SO THAT MEANS . . . ?
YEP, EVERYBODY INTO THE WATER!
HELLO? THIS IS A LAKE CAMP.
I'M NOT MUCH OF A SWIMMER . . .
WELL, THEN KISS THAT GOOD GRADE GOODBYE.
WAIT, YOU GET GRADED? AT CAMP?
NOT LIKE SCHOOL GRADES, SOCIAL ONES.
GRADES ARE EVERYTHING. CLEARLY YOU'RE NEW AROUND HERE.
YEAH, WE JUST MOVED, BUT MY MOM GREW UP HERE.
COOL. I'M HARRY. THAT'S NATE.
KYLE.
WE CAN CLUE YOU IN ON HOW THINGS WORK HERE.

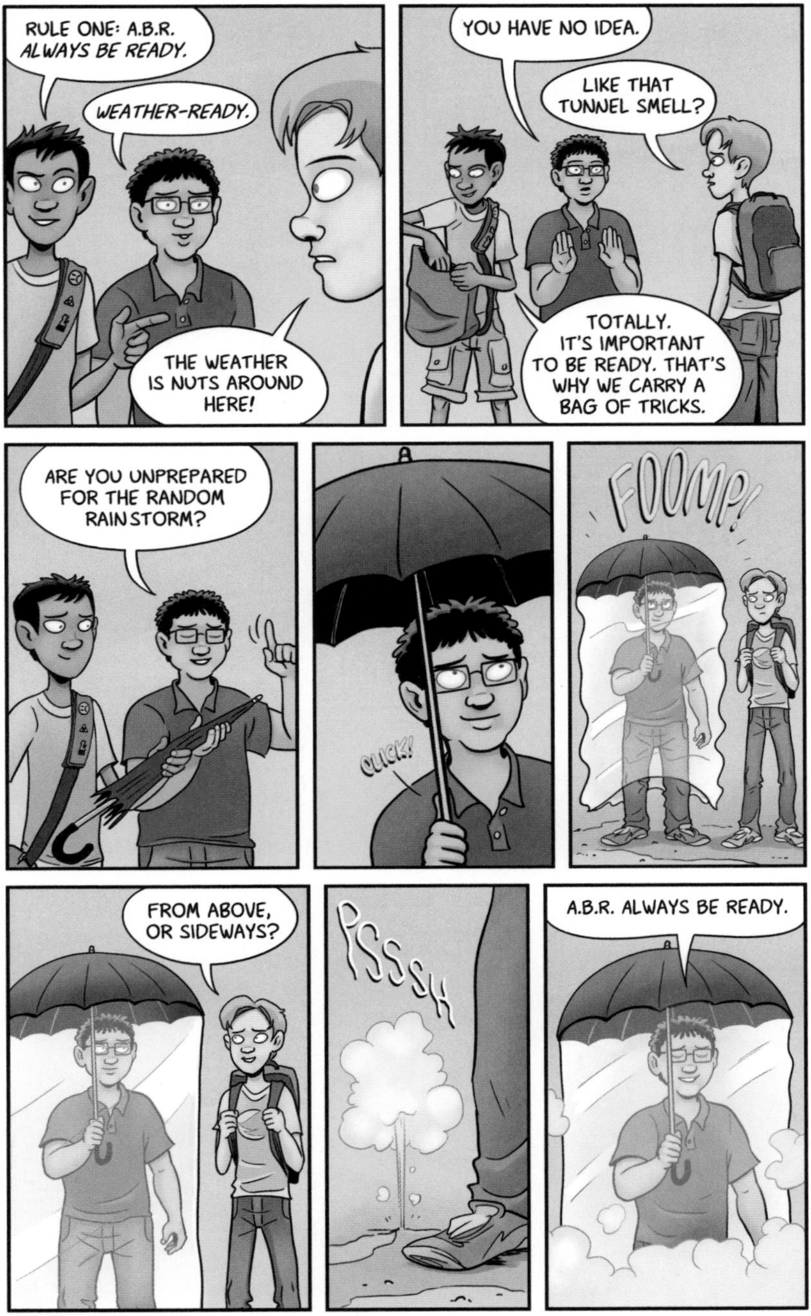
RULE ONE: A.B.R. ALWAYS BE READY.
WEATHER-READY.
THE WEATHER IS NUTS AROUND HERE!
YOU HAVE NO IDEA.
LIKE THAT TUNNEL SMELL?
TOTALLY. IT'S IMPORTANT TO BE READY. THAT'S WHY WE CARRY A BAG OF TRICKS.
ARE YOU UNPREPARED FOR THE RANDOM RAINSTORM?
CLICK!
FOOMP!
FROM ABOVE, OR SIDEWAYS?
PSSSSH
A.B.R. ALWAYS BE READY.

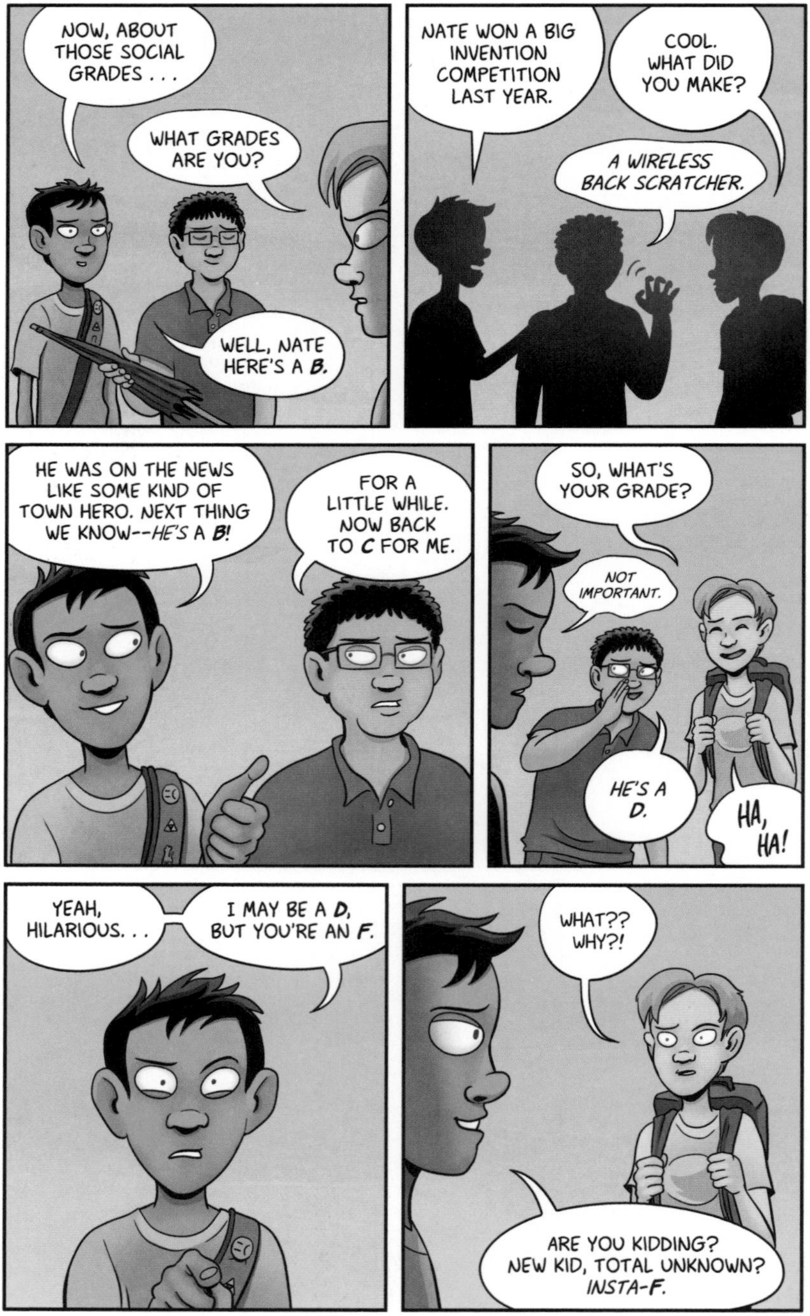
NOW, ABOUT THOSE SOCIAL GRADES . . .
WHAT GRADES ARE YOU?
WELL, NATE HERE'S A ***B.***
NATE WON A BIG INVENTION COMPETITION LAST YEAR.
COOL. WHAT DID YOU MAKE?
A WIRELESS BACK SCRATCHER.
HE WAS ON THE NEWS LIKE SOME KIND OF TOWN HERO. NEXT THING WE KNOW--*HE'S* A ***B!***
FOR A LITTLE WHILE. NOW BACK TO ***C*** FOR ME.
SO, WHAT'S YOUR GRADE?
NOT IMPORTANT.
HE'S A ***D.***
HA, HA!
YEAH, HILARIOUS. . .
I MAY BE A ***D,*** BUT YOU'RE AN ***F.***
WHAT?? WHY?!
ARE YOU KIDDING? NEW KID, TOTAL UNKNOWN? *INSTA-****F.***

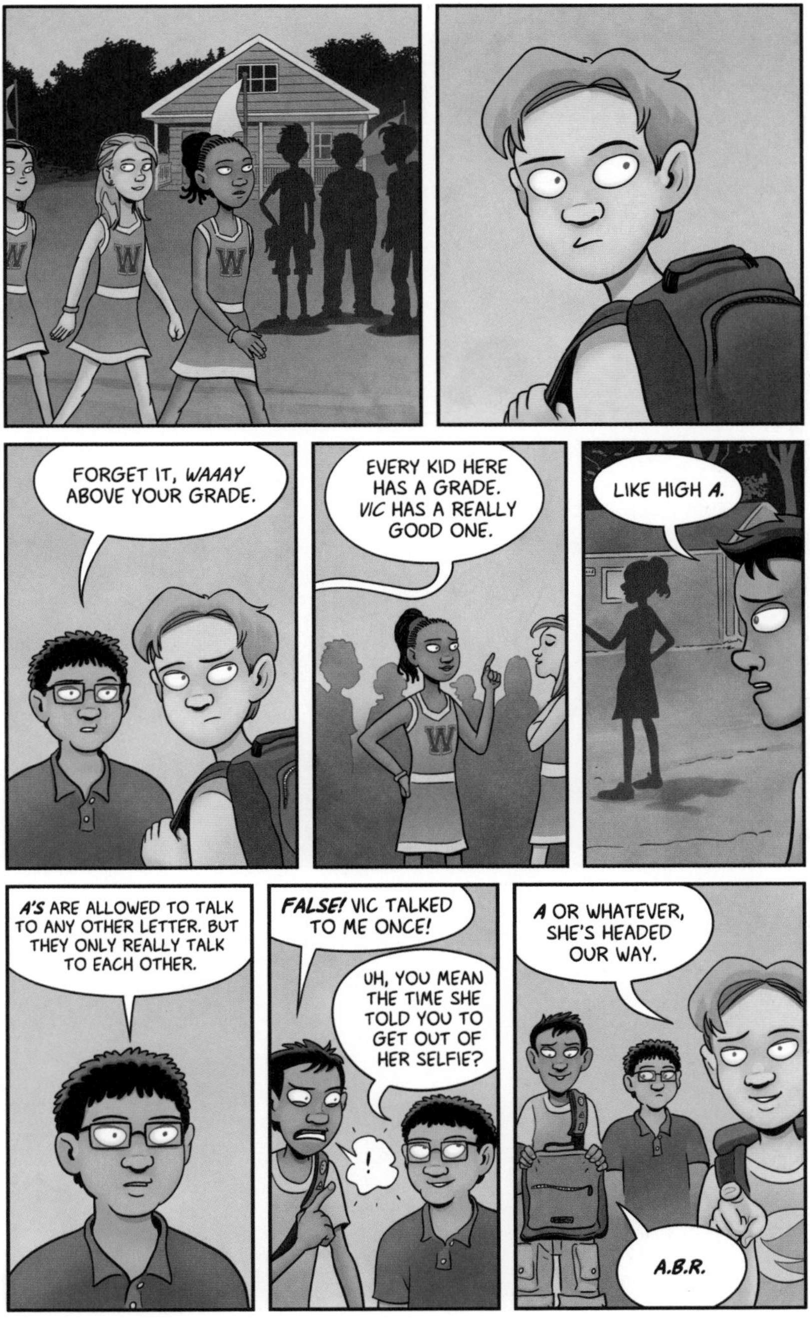
FORGET IT, *WAAAY* ABOVE YOUR GRADE.
EVERY KID HERE HAS A GRADE. *VIC* HAS A REALLY GOOD ONE.
LIKE HIGH *A*.
A'S ARE ALLOWED TO TALK TO ANY OTHER LETTER. BUT THEY ONLY REALLY TALK TO EACH OTHER.
FALSE! VIC TALKED TO ME ONCE!
UH, YOU MEAN THE TIME SHE TOLD YOU TO GET OUT OF HER SELFIE?
!
A OR WHATEVER, SHE'S HEADED OUR WAY.
A.B.R.

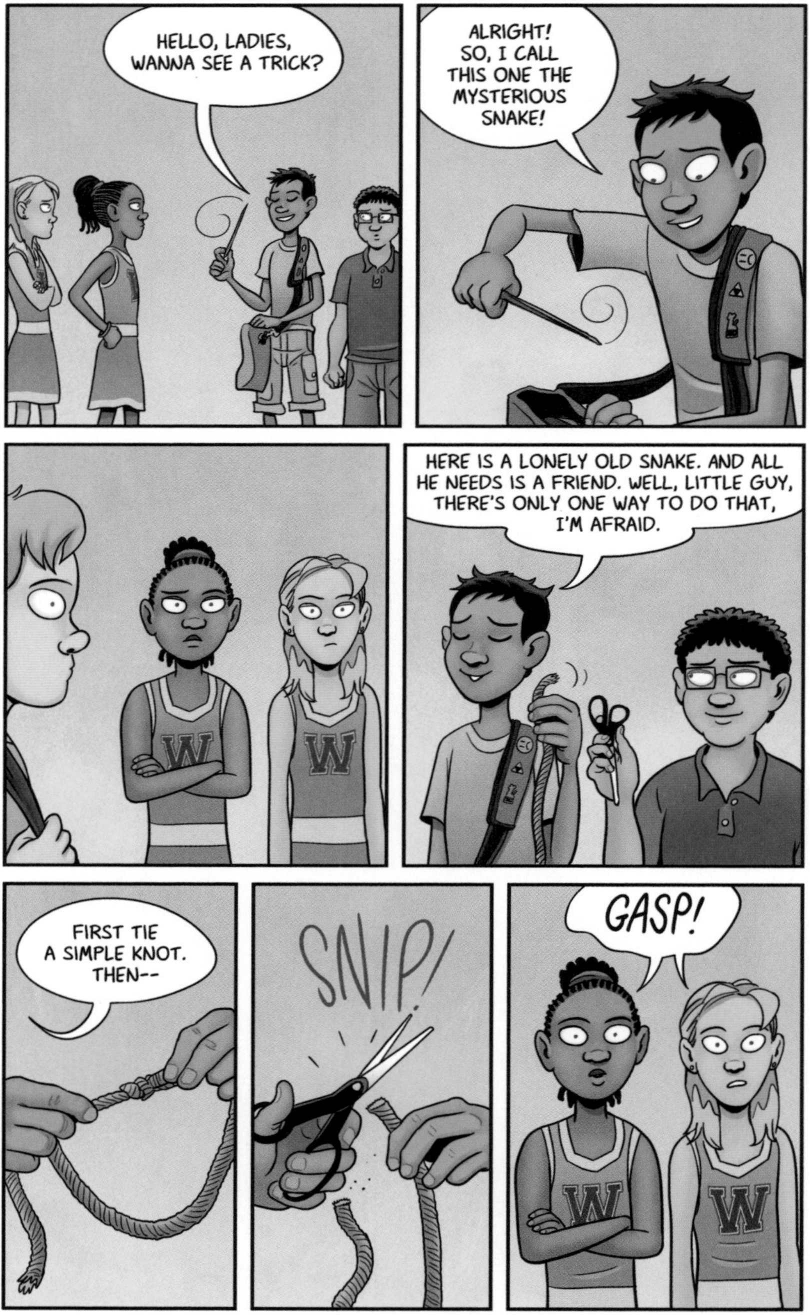
HELLO, LADIES, WANNA SEE A TRICK?
ALRIGHT! SO, I CALL THIS ONE THE MYSTERIOUS SNAKE!
HERE IS A LONELY OLD SNAKE. AND ALL HE NEEDS IS A FRIEND. WELL, LITTLE GUY, THERE'S ONLY ONE WAY TO DO THAT, I'M AFRAID.
FIRST TIE A SIMPLE KNOT. THEN--
SNIP!
GASP!

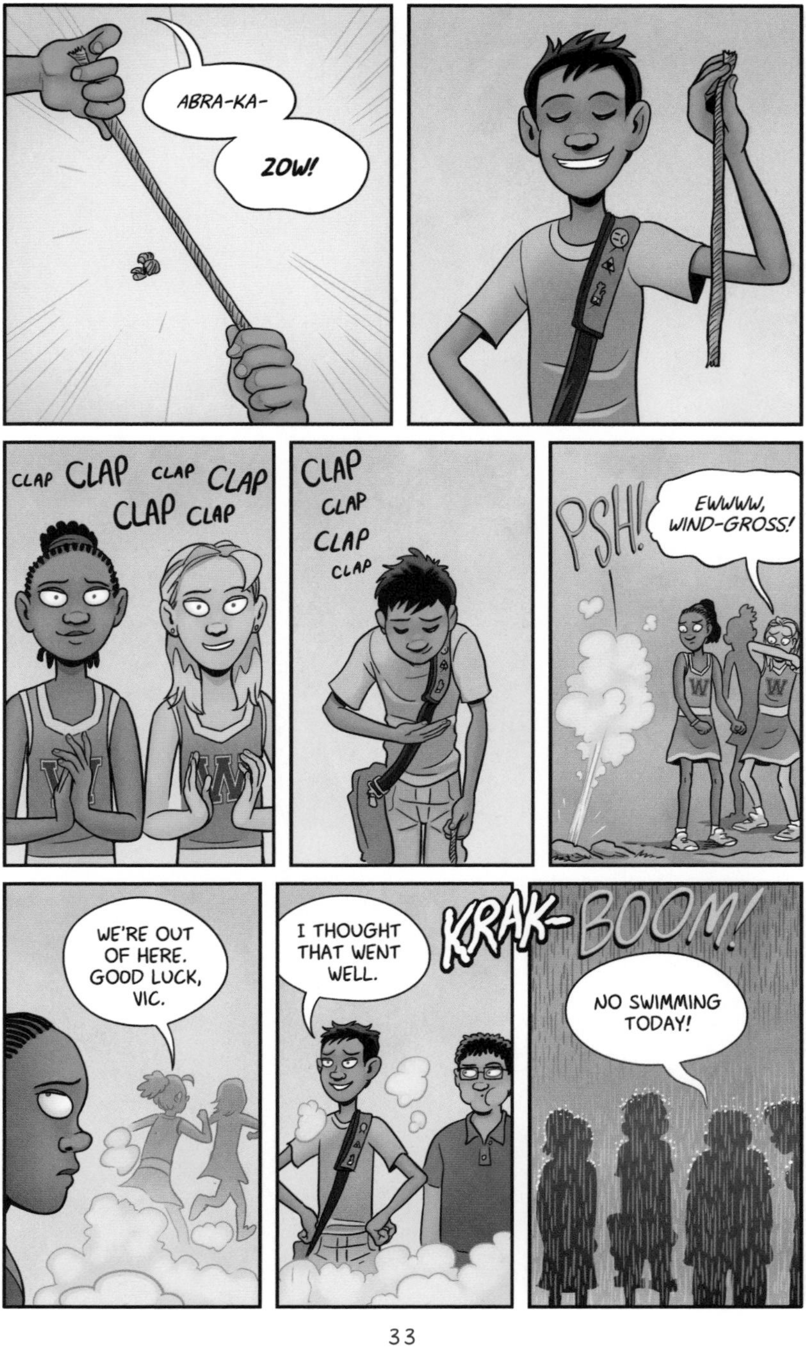
ABRA-KA-
ZOW!
CLAP CLAP CLAP CLAP
CLAP CLAP
CLAP
CLAP
CLAP
CLAP
PSH!
EWWWW, WIND-GROSS!
WE'RE OUT OF HERE. GOOD LUCK, VIC.
I THOUGHT THAT WENT WELL.
KRAK-BOOM!
NO SWIMMING TODAY!

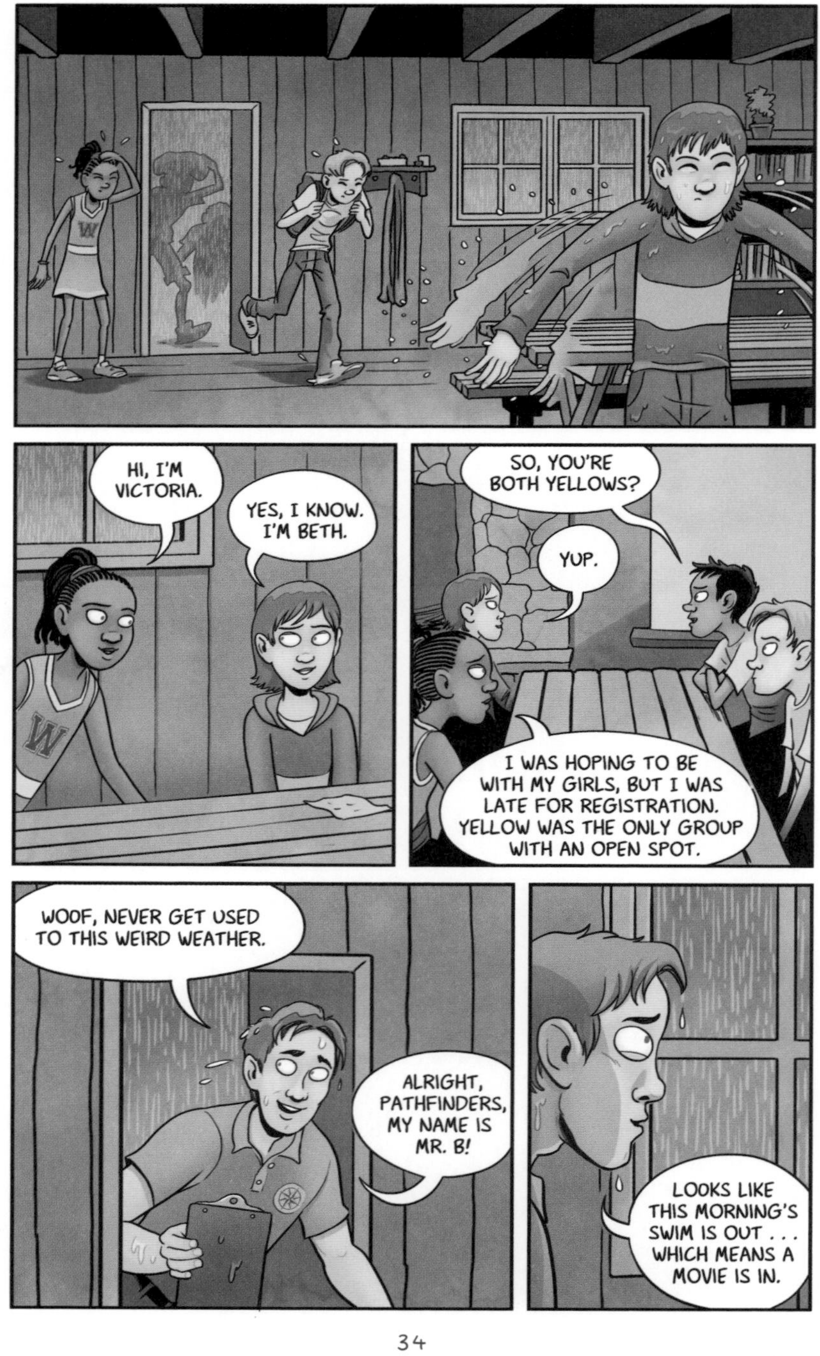
HI, I'M VICTORIA.
YES, I KNOW. I'M BETH.
SO, YOU'RE BOTH YELLOWS?
YUP.
I WAS HOPING TO BE WITH MY GIRLS, BUT I WAS LATE FOR REGISTRATION. YELLOW WAS THE ONLY GROUP WITH AN OPEN SPOT.
WOOF, NEVER GET USED TO THIS WEIRD WEATHER.
ALRIGHT, PATHFINDERS, MY NAME IS MR. B!
LOOKS LIKE THIS MORNING'S SWIM IS OUT . . . WHICH MEANS A MOVIE IS IN.

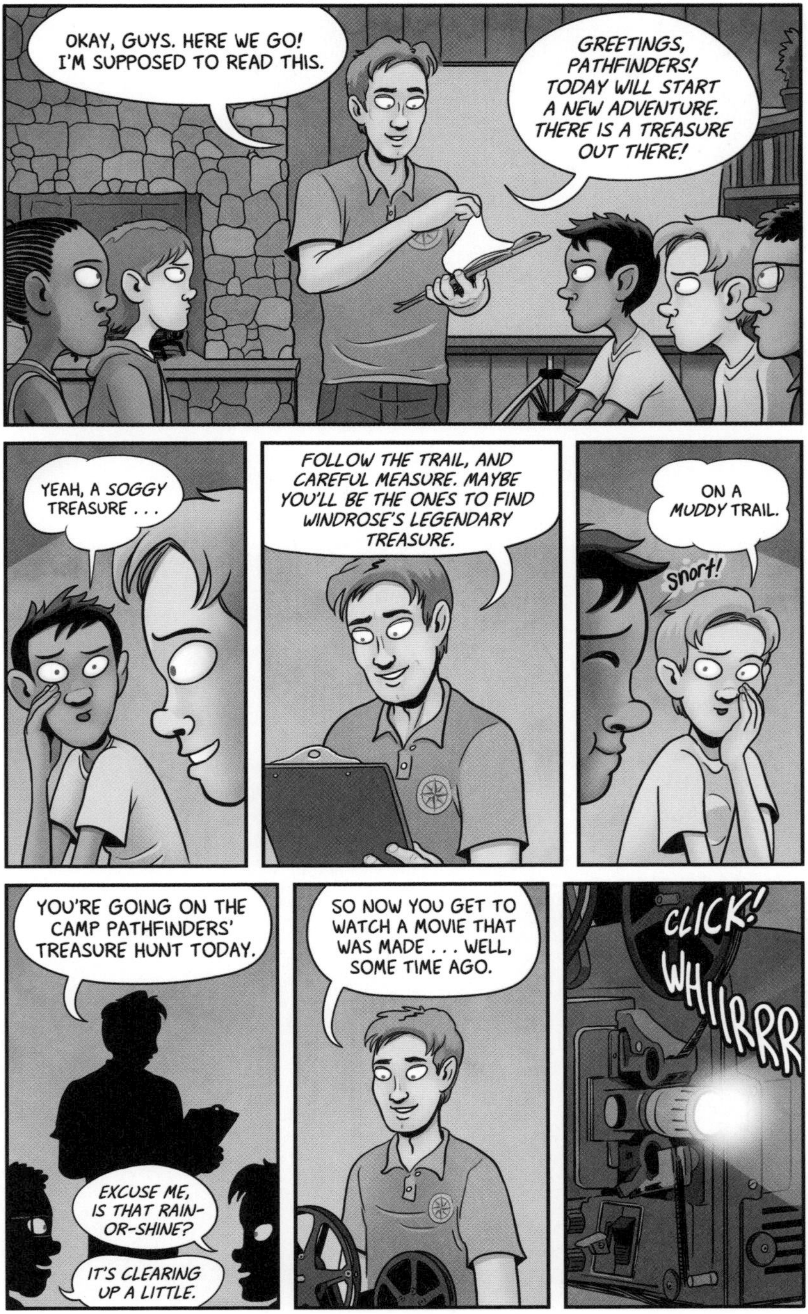
OKAY, GUYS. HERE WE GO! I'M SUPPOSED TO READ THIS.
GREETINGS, PATHFINDERS! TODAY WILL START A NEW ADVENTURE. THERE IS A TREASURE OUT THERE!
YEAH, A SOGGY TREASURE . . .
FOLLOW THE TRAIL, AND CAREFUL MEASURE. MAYBE YOU'LL BE THE ONES TO FIND WINDROSE'S LEGENDARY TREASURE.
ON A MUDDY TRAIL.
Snort!
YOU'RE GOING ON THE CAMP PATHFINDERS' TREASURE HUNT TODAY.
EXCUSE ME, IS THAT RAIN-OR-SHINE?
IT'S CLEARING UP A LITTLE.
SO NOW YOU GET TO WATCH A MOVIE THAT WAS MADE . . . WELL, SOME TIME AGO.
CLICK!
WHIIRRR

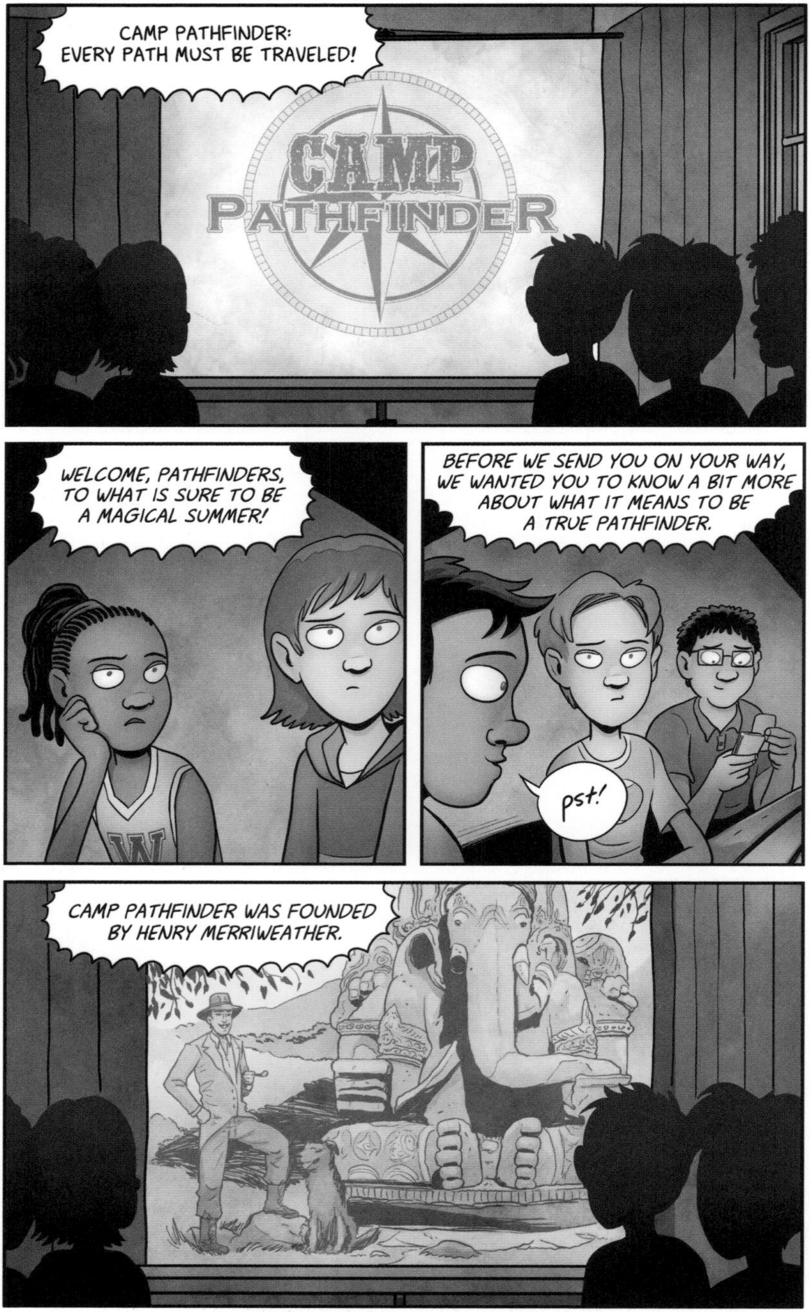
CAMP PATHFINDER: EVERY PATH MUST BE TRAVELED!
CAMP PATHFINDER
WELCOME, PATHFINDERS, TO WHAT IS SURE TO BE A MAGICAL SUMMER!
W
BEFORE WE SEND YOU ON YOUR WAY, WE WANTED YOU TO KNOW A BIT MORE ABOUT WHAT IT MEANS TO BE A TRUE PATHFINDER.
pst!
CAMP PATHFINDER WAS FOUNDED BY HENRY MERRIWEATHER.

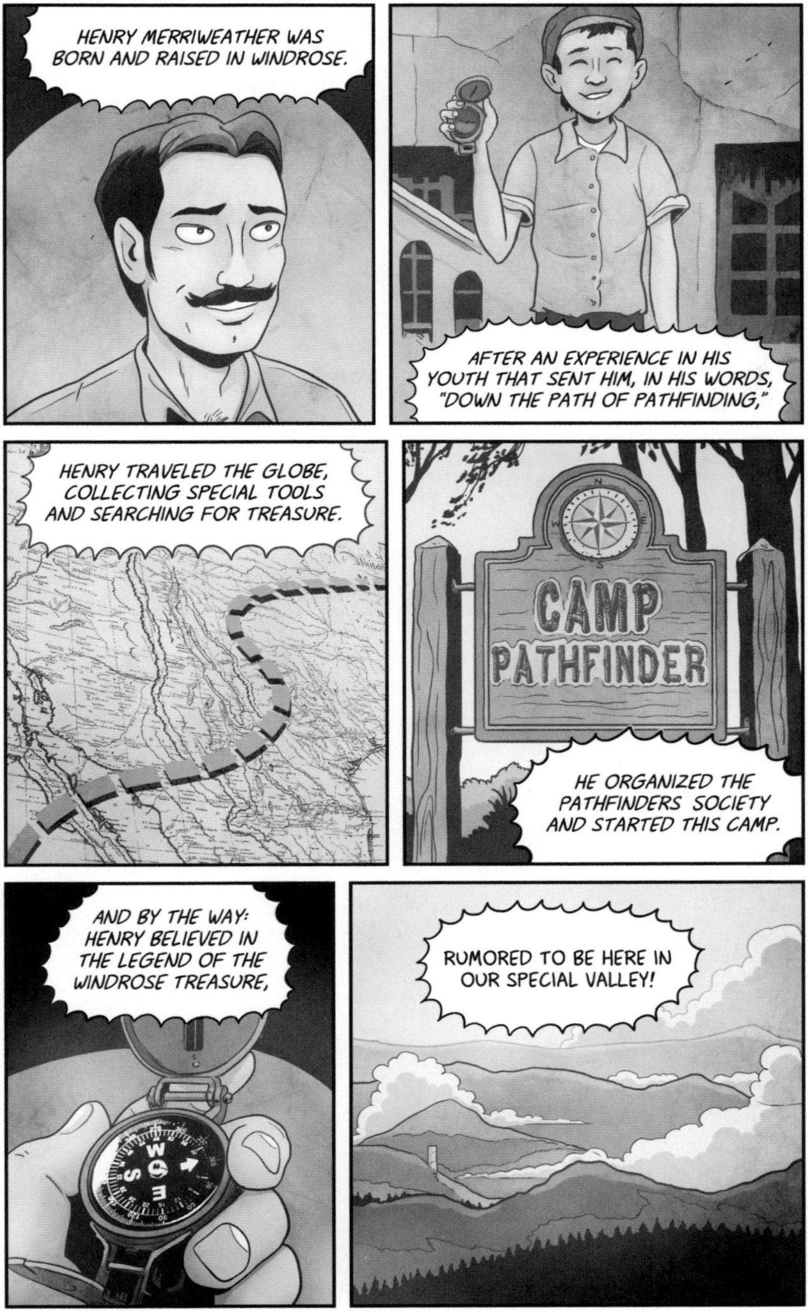
HENRY MERRIWEATHER WAS BORN AND RAISED IN WINDROSE.
AFTER AN EXPERIENCE IN HIS YOUTH THAT SENT HIM, IN HIS WORDS, "DOWN THE PATH OF PATHFINDING,"
HENRY TRAVELED THE GLOBE, COLLECTING SPECIAL TOOLS AND SEARCHING FOR TREASURE.
CAMP PATHFINDER
HE ORGANIZED THE PATHFINDERS SOCIETY AND STARTED THIS CAMP.
AND BY THE WAY: HENRY BELIEVED IN THE LEGEND OF THE WINDROSE TREASURE,
RUMORED TO BE HERE IN OUR SPECIAL VALLEY!

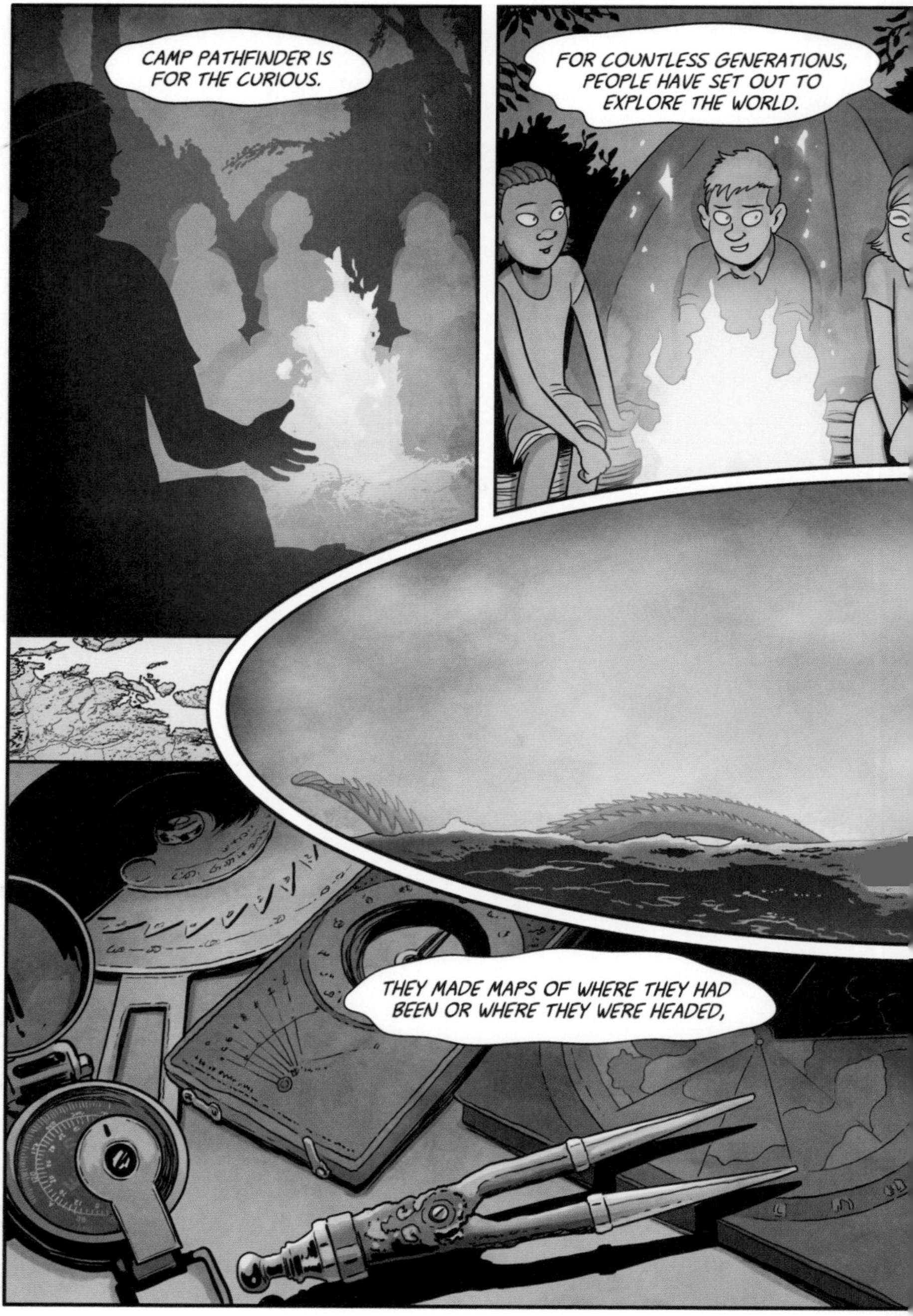
CAMP PATHFINDER IS FOR THE CURIOUS.
FOR COUNTLESS GENERATIONS, PEOPLE HAVE SET OUT TO EXPLORE THE WORLD.
THEY MADE MAPS OF WHERE THEY HAD BEEN OR WHERE THEY WERE HEADED,

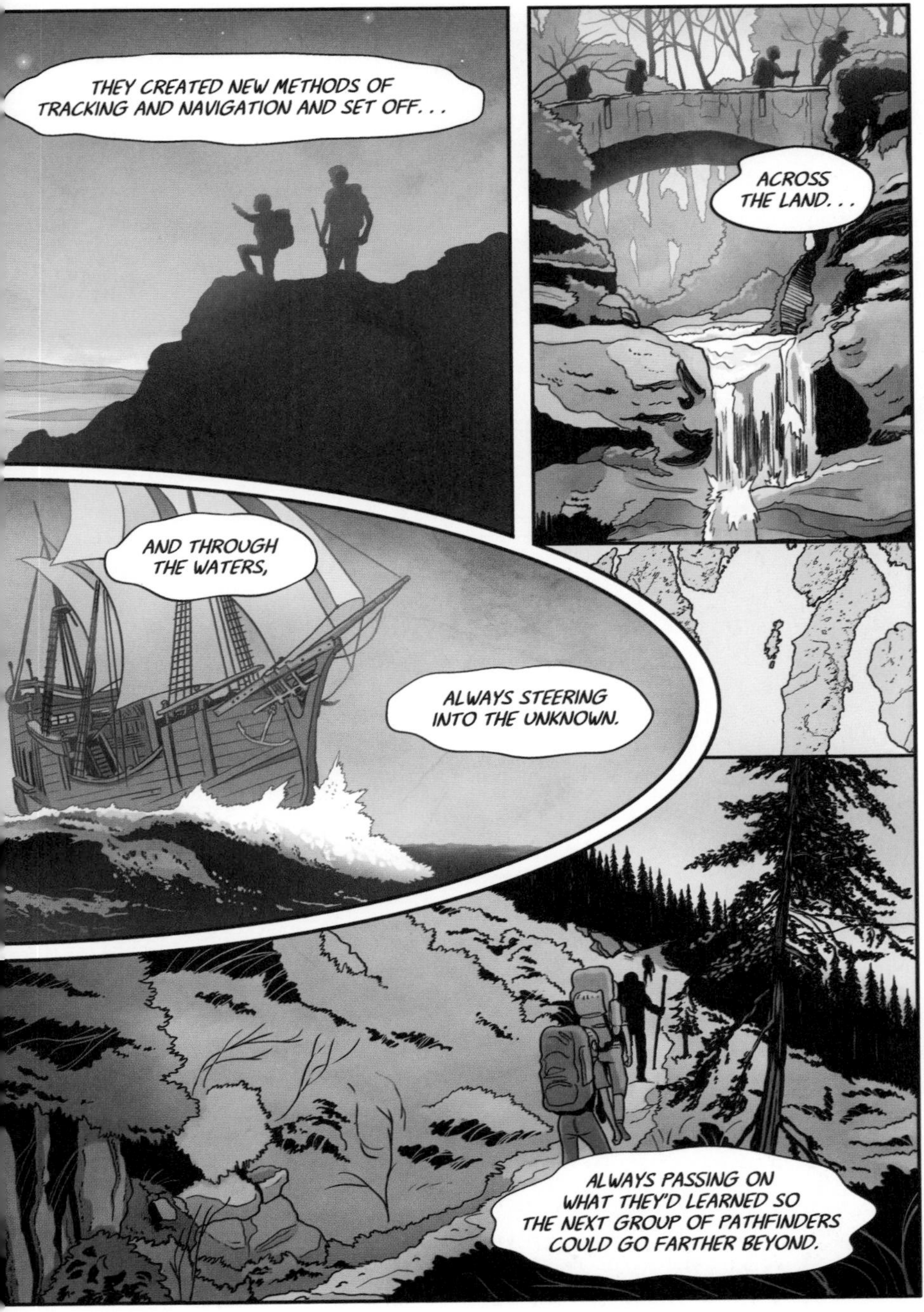
THEY CREATED NEW METHODS OF TRACKING AND NAVIGATION AND SET OFF. . .
ACROSS THE LAND. . .
AND THROUGH THE WATERS,
ALWAYS STEERING INTO THE UNKNOWN.
ALWAYS PASSING ON WHAT THEY'D LEARNED SO THE NEXT GROUP OF PATHFINDERS COULD GO FARTHER BEYOND.

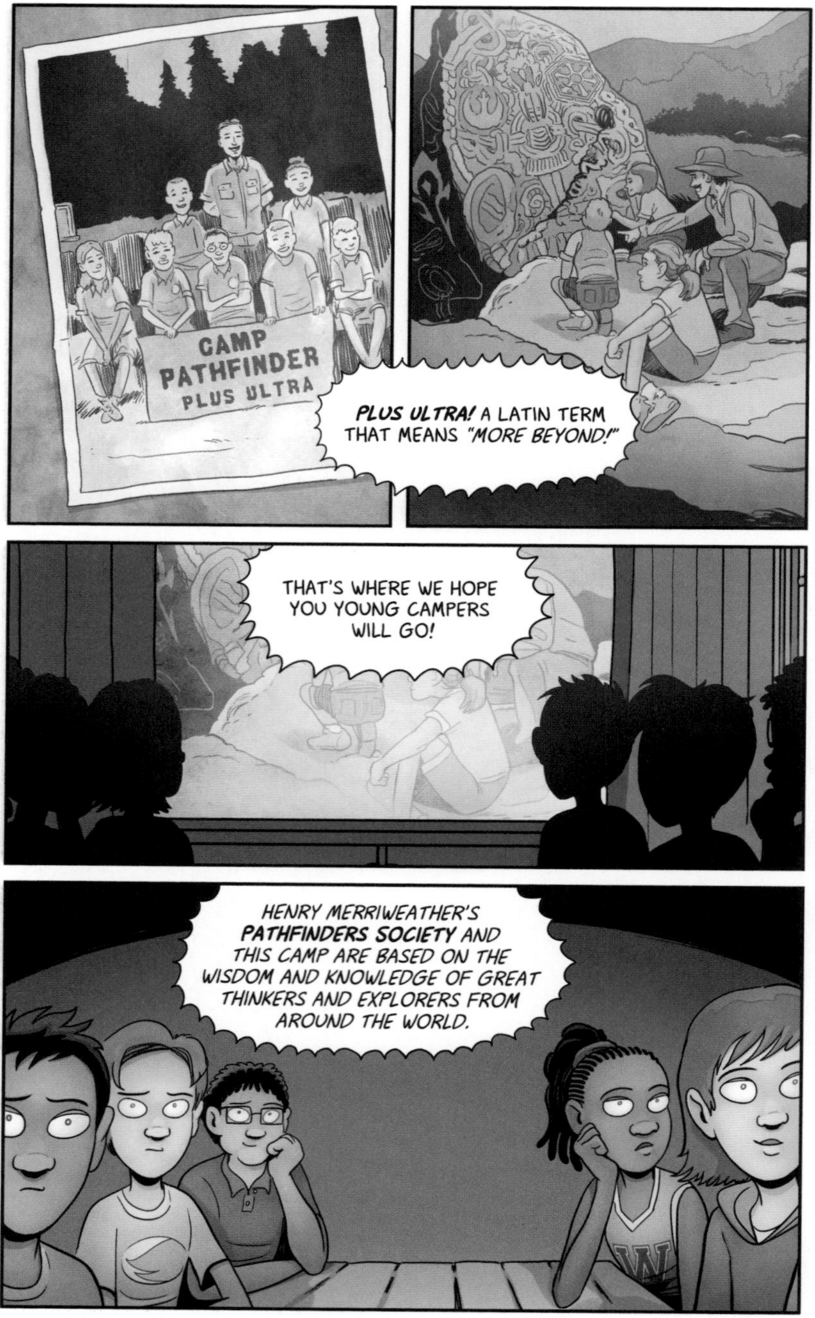
CAMP PATHFINDER PLUS ULTRA
PLUS ULTRA! A LATIN TERM THAT MEANS "MORE BEYOND!"
THAT'S WHERE WE HOPE YOU YOUNG CAMPERS WILL GO!
HENRY MERRIWEATHER'S PATHFINDERS SOCIETY AND THIS CAMP ARE BASED ON THE WISDOM AND KNOWLEDGE OF GREAT THINKERS AND EXPLORERS FROM AROUND THE WORLD.

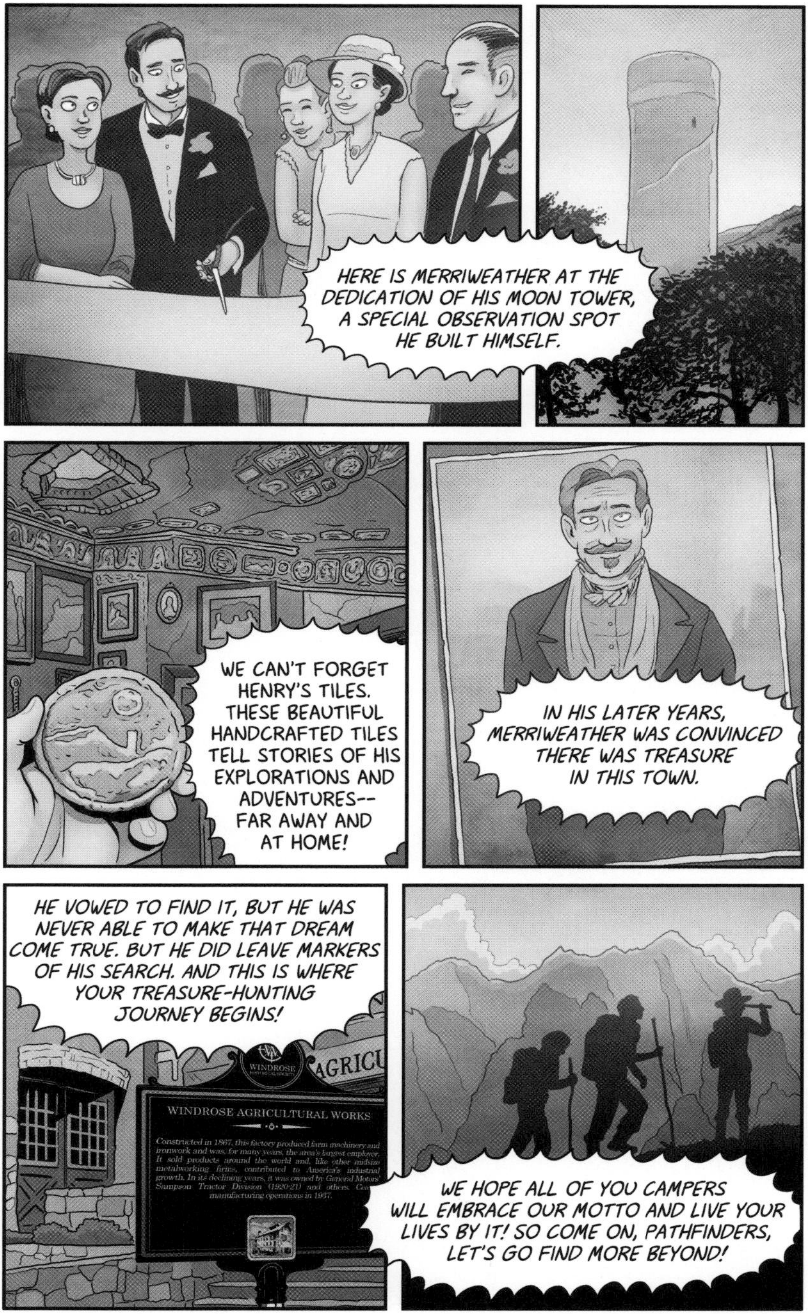
HERE IS MERRIWEATHER AT THE DEDICATION OF HIS MOON TOWER, A SPECIAL OBSERVATION SPOT HE BUILT HIMSELF.
WE CAN'T FORGET HENRY'S TILES. THESE BEAUTIFUL HANDCRAFTED TILES TELL STORIES OF HIS EXPLORATIONS AND ADVENTURES--FAR AWAY AND AT HOME!
IN HIS LATER YEARS, MERRIWEATHER WAS CONVINCED THERE WAS TREASURE IN THIS TOWN.
HE VOWED TO FIND IT, BUT HE WAS NEVER ABLE TO MAKE THAT DREAM COME TRUE. BUT HE DID LEAVE MARKERS OF HIS SEARCH. AND THIS IS WHERE YOUR TREASURE-HUNTING JOURNEY BEGINS!
WINDROSE
AGRICU
WINDROSE AGRICULTURAL WORKS
Constructed in 1867, this factory produced farm machinery and ironwork and was, for many years, the area's largest employer. It sold products around the world and, like other midsize metalworking firms, contributed to America's industrial growth. In its declining years, it was owned by General Motors' Sampson Tractor Division (1920-21) and others. Co manufacturing operations in 1937.
WE HOPE ALL OF YOU CAMPERS WILL EMBRACE OUR MOTTO AND LIVE YOUR LIVES BY IT! SO COME ON, PATHFINDERS, LET'S GO FIND MORE BEYOND!

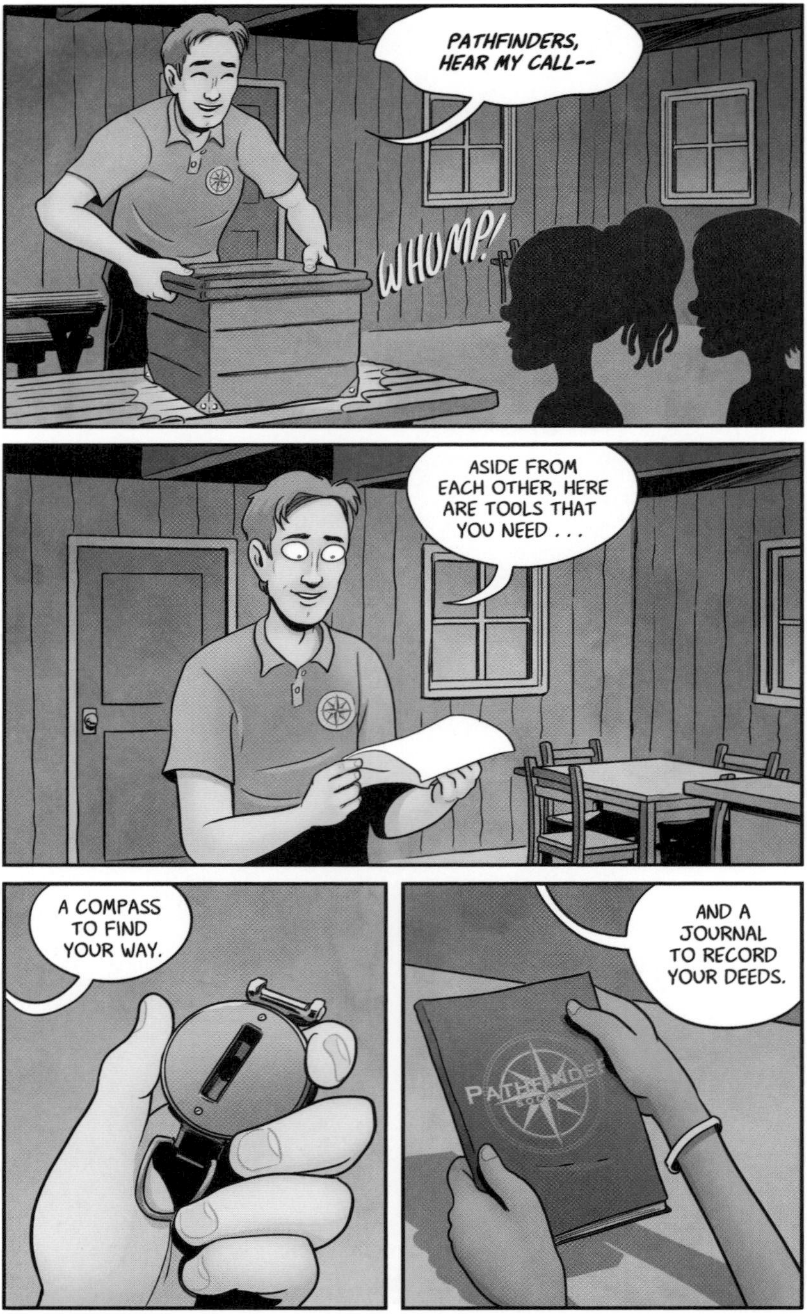
PATHFINDERS, HEAR MY CALL--
WHUMP!
ASIDE FROM EACH OTHER, HERE ARE TOOLS THAT YOU NEED . . .
A COMPASS TO FIND YOUR WAY.
AND A JOURNAL TO RECORD YOUR DEEDS.
PATHFINDER

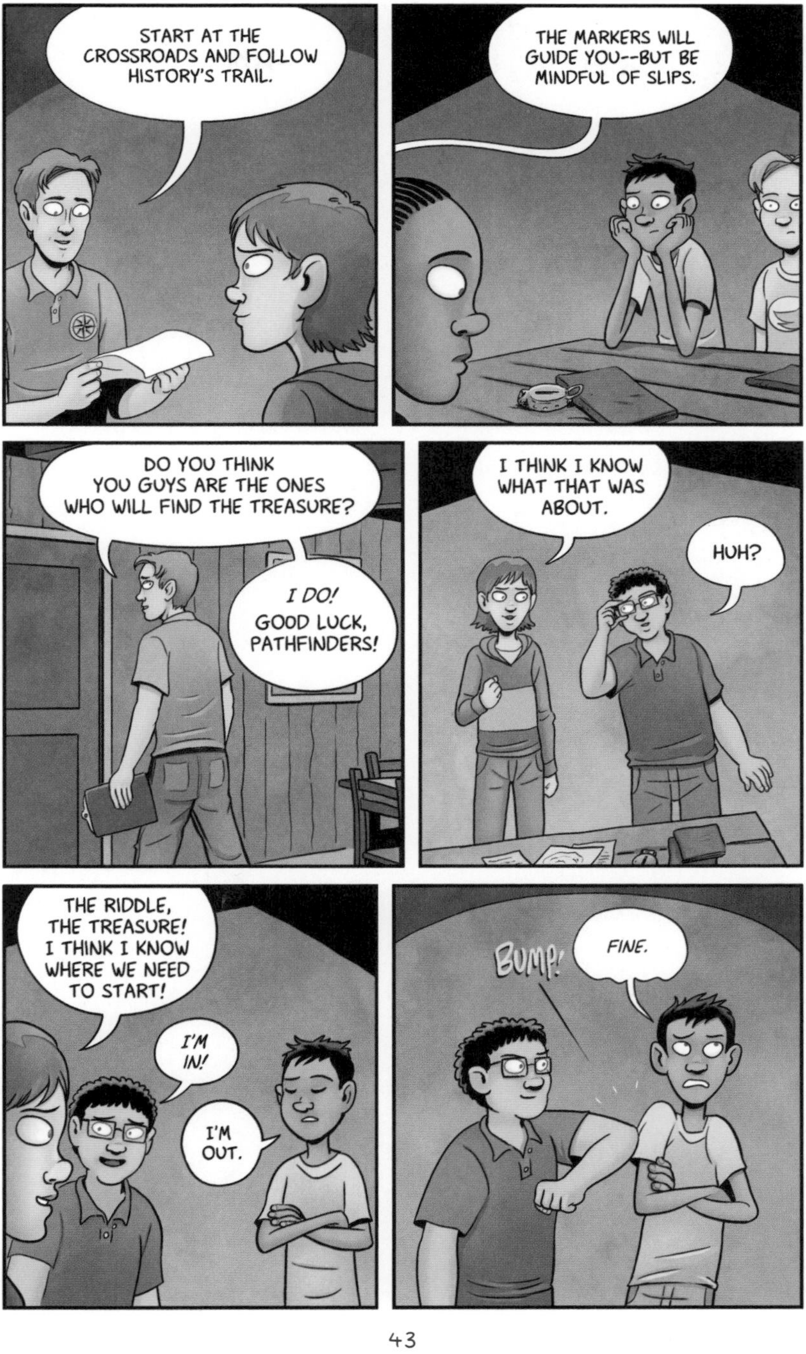
START AT THE CROSSROADS AND FOLLOW HISTORY'S TRAIL.
THE MARKERS WILL GUIDE YOU--BUT BE MINDFUL OF SLIPS.
DO YOU THINK YOU GUYS ARE THE ONES WHO WILL FIND THE TREASURE?
I DO! GOOD LUCK, PATHFINDERS!
I THINK I KNOW WHAT THAT WAS ABOUT.
HUH?
THE RIDDLE, THE TREASURE! I THINK I KNOW WHERE WE NEED TO START!
I'M IN!
I'M OUT.
BUMP!
FINE.

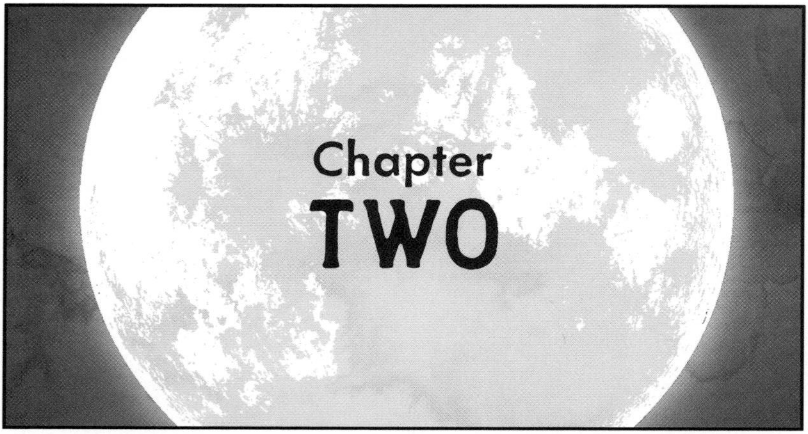
Chapter
TWO

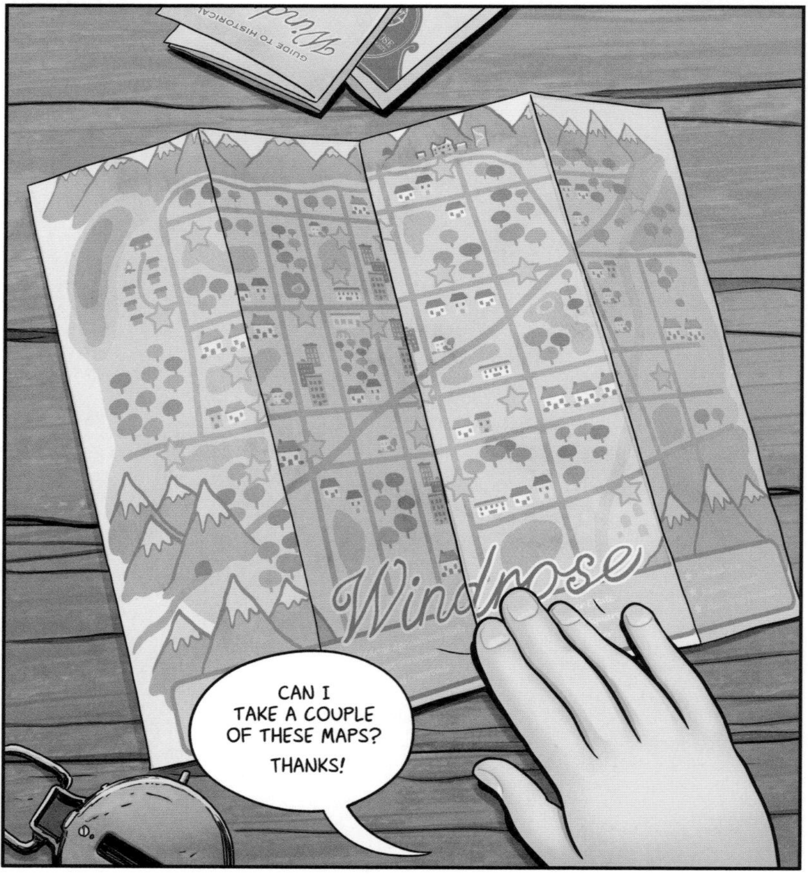
Windrose
CAN I TAKE A COUPLE OF THESE MAPS?
THANKS!

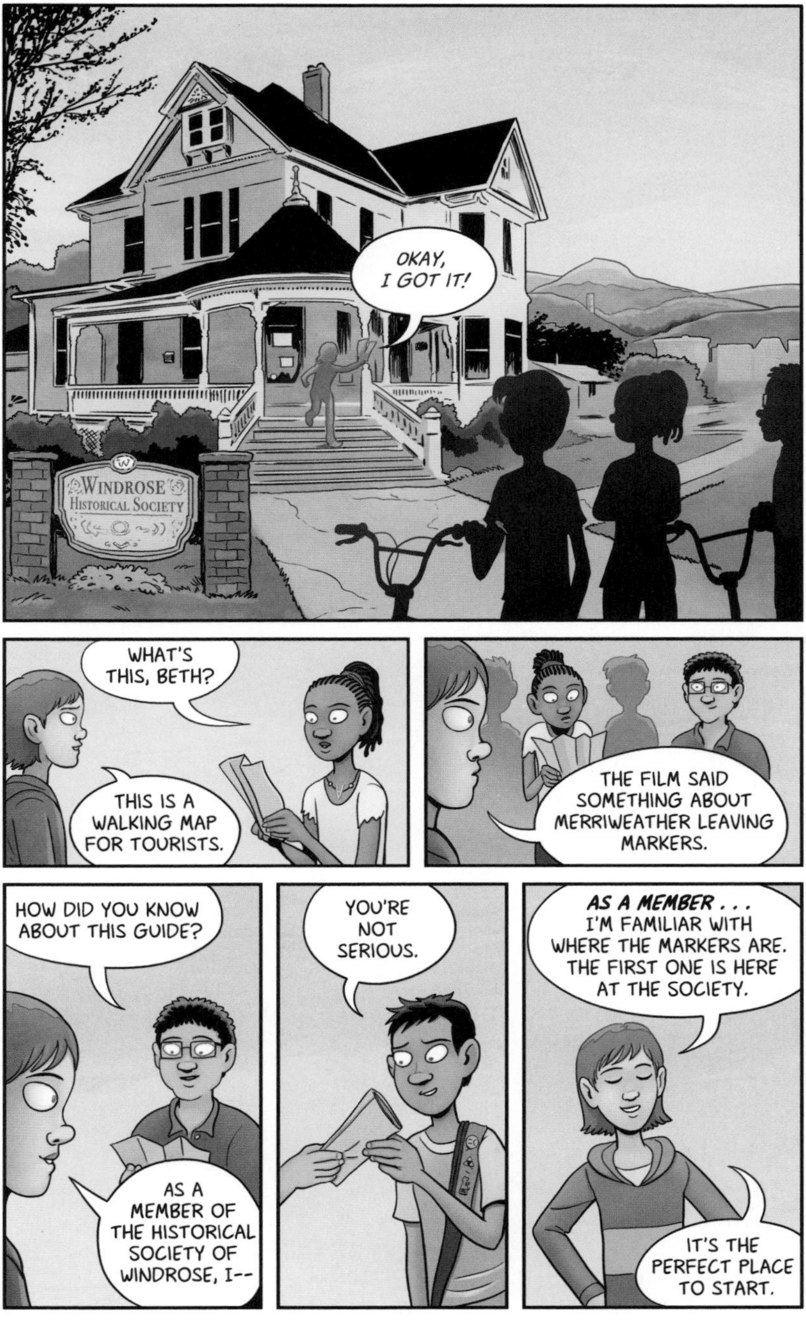
OKAY, I GOT IT!
WINDROSE HISTORICAL SOCIETY
WHAT'S THIS, BETH?
THIS IS A WALKING MAP FOR TOURISTS.
THE FILM SAID SOMETHING ABOUT MERRIWEATHER LEAVING MARKERS.
HOW DID YOU KNOW ABOUT THIS GUIDE?
AS A MEMBER OF THE HISTORICAL SOCIETY OF WINDROSE, I--
YOU'RE NOT SERIOUS.
AS A MEMBER . . . I'M FAMILIAR WITH WHERE THE MARKERS ARE. THE FIRST ONE IS HERE AT THE SOCIETY.
IT'S THE PERFECT PLACE TO START.

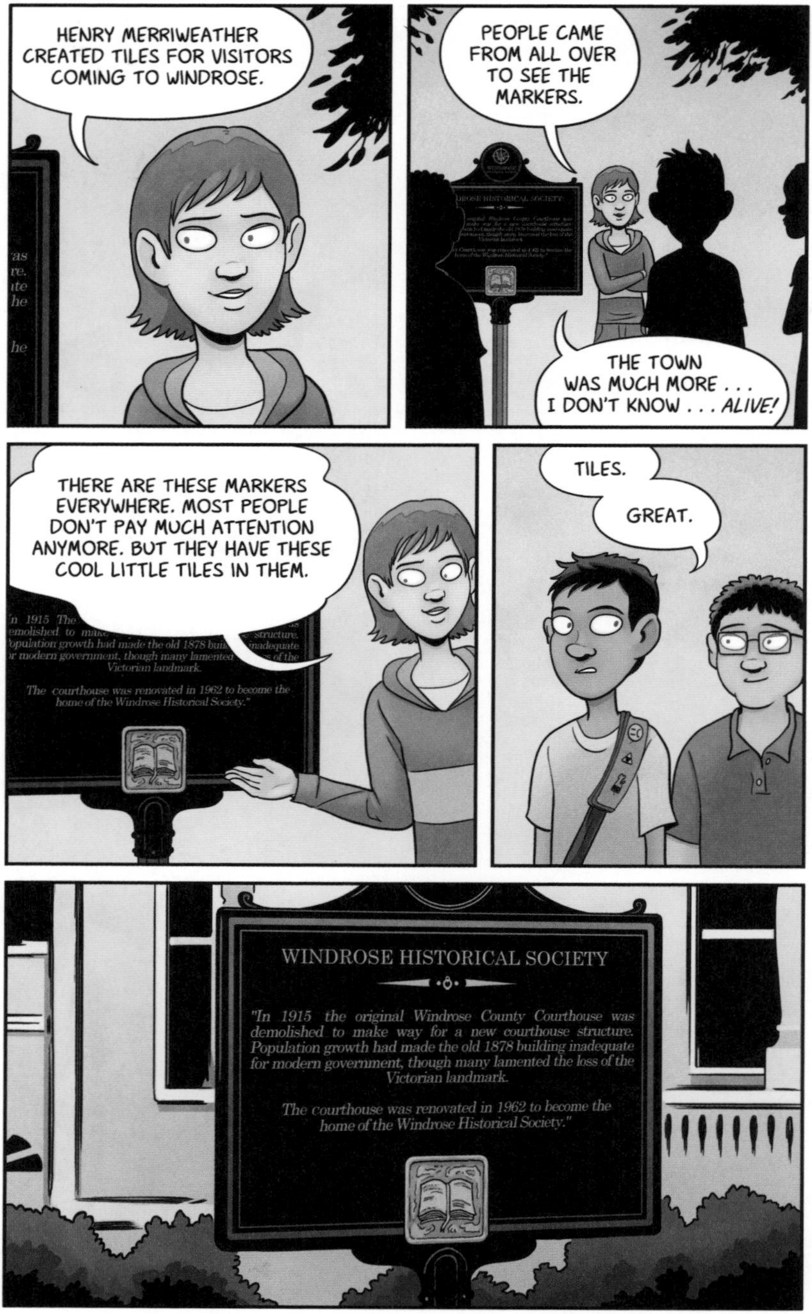
HENRY MERRIWEATHER CREATED TILES FOR VISITORS COMING TO WINDROSE.
PEOPLE CAME FROM ALL OVER TO SEE THE MARKERS.
THE TOWN WAS MUCH MORE . . . I DON'T KNOW . . . *ALIVE!*
THERE ARE THESE MARKERS EVERYWHERE. MOST PEOPLE DON'T PAY MUCH ATTENTION ANYMORE. BUT THEY HAVE THESE COOL LITTLE TILES IN THEM.
TILES.
GREAT.
WINDROSE HISTORICAL SOCIETY
"In 1915 the original Windrose County Courthouse was demolished to make way for a new courthouse structure. Population growth had made the old 1878 building inadequate for modern government, though many lamented the loss of the Victorian landmark.
The courthouse was renovated in 1962 to become the home of the Windrose Historical Society."

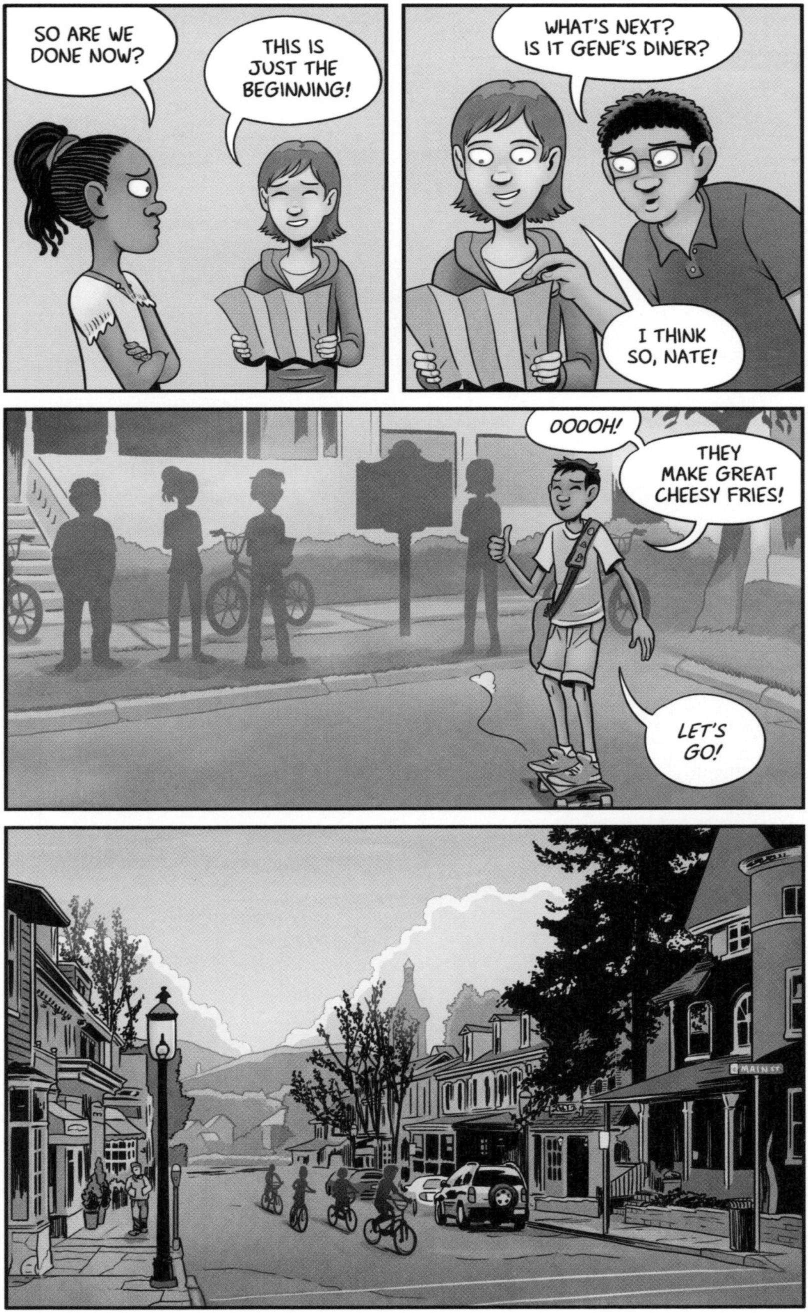
SO ARE WE DONE NOW?
THIS IS JUST THE BEGINNING!
WHAT'S NEXT? IS IT GENE'S DINER?
I THINK SO, NATE!
OOOOH!
THEY MAKE GREAT CHEESY FRIES!
LET'S GO!
MAIN ST

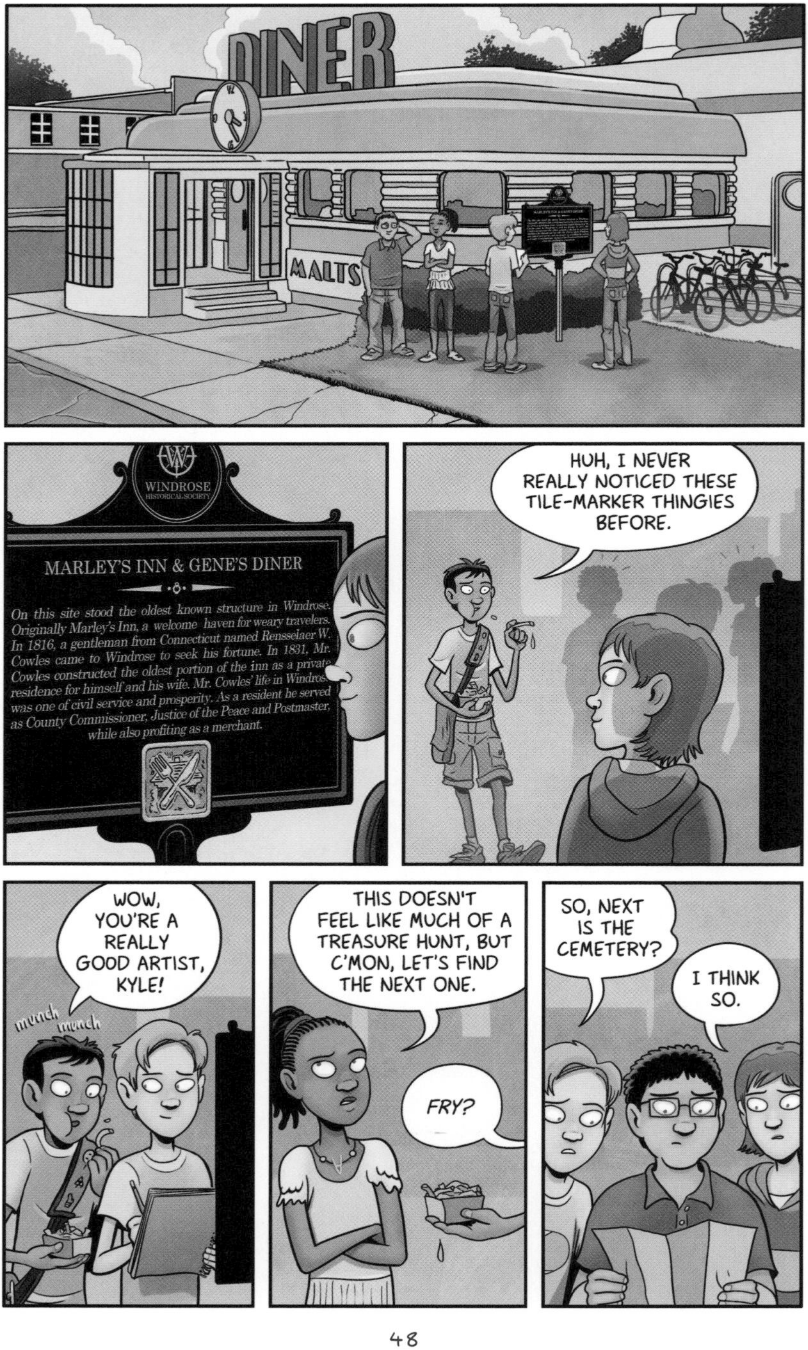
DINER
MALTS
WINDROSE HISTORICAL SOCIETY
MARLEY'S INN & GENE'S DINER
On this site stood the oldest known structure in Windrose. Originally Marley's Inn, a welcome haven for weary travelers. In 1816, a gentleman from Connecticut named Rensselaer W. Cowles came to Windrose to seek his fortune. In 1831, Mr. Cowles constructed the oldest portion of the inn as a private residence for himself and his wife. Mr. Cowles' life in Windros was one of civil service and prosperity. As a resident he served as County Commissioner, Justice of the Peace and Postmaster, while also profiting as a merchant.
HUH, I NEVER REALLY NOTICED THESE TILE-MARKER THINGIES BEFORE.
WOW, YOU'RE A REALLY GOOD ARTIST, KYLE!
munch munch
THIS DOESN'T FEEL LIKE MUCH OF A TREASURE HUNT, BUT C'MON, LET'S FIND THE NEXT ONE.
FRY?
SO, NEXT IS THE CEMETERY?
I THINK SO.

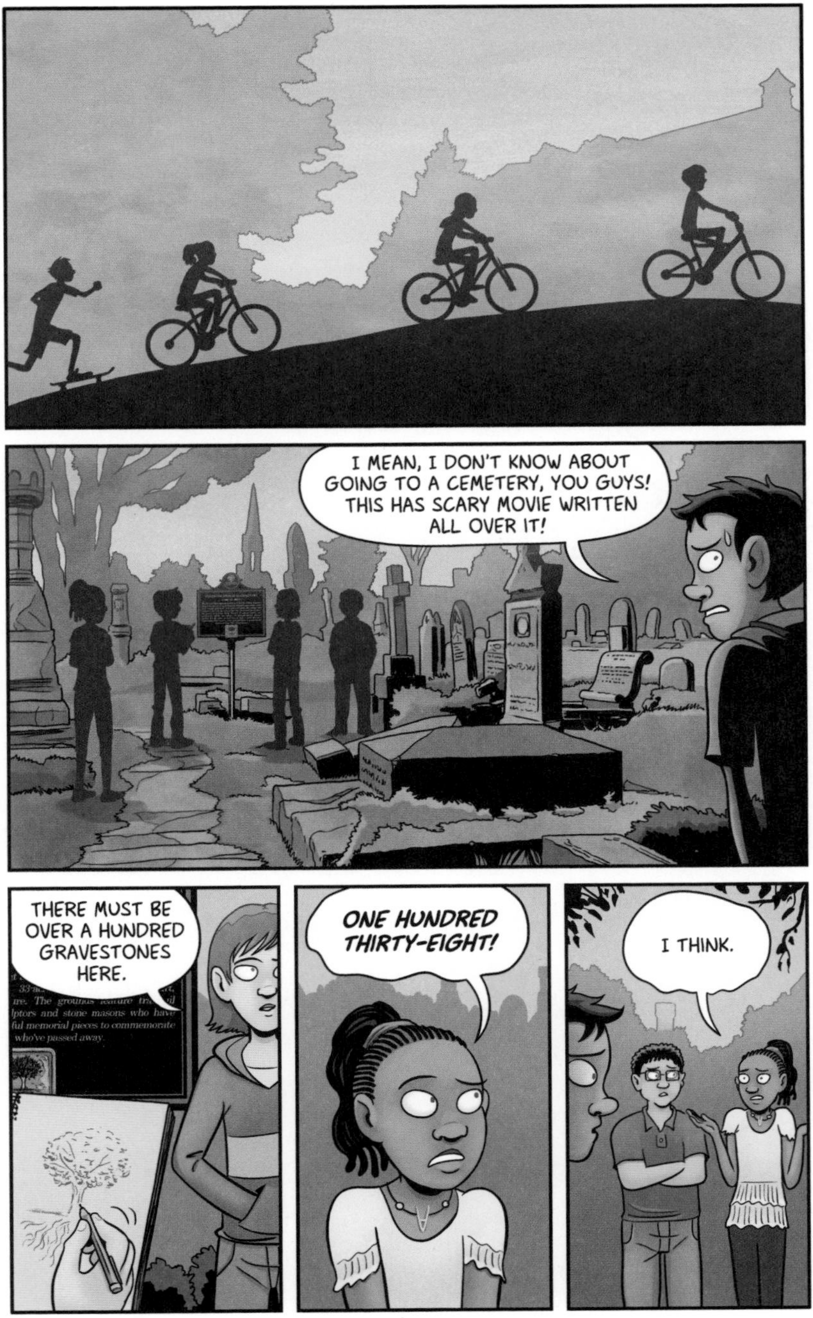

I MEAN, I DON'T KNOW ABOUT GOING TO A CEMETERY, YOU GUYS! THIS HAS SCARY MOVIE WRITTEN ALL OVER IT!
THERE MUST BE OVER A HUNDRED GRAVESTONES HERE.
ONE HUNDRED THIRTY-EIGHT!
I THINK.

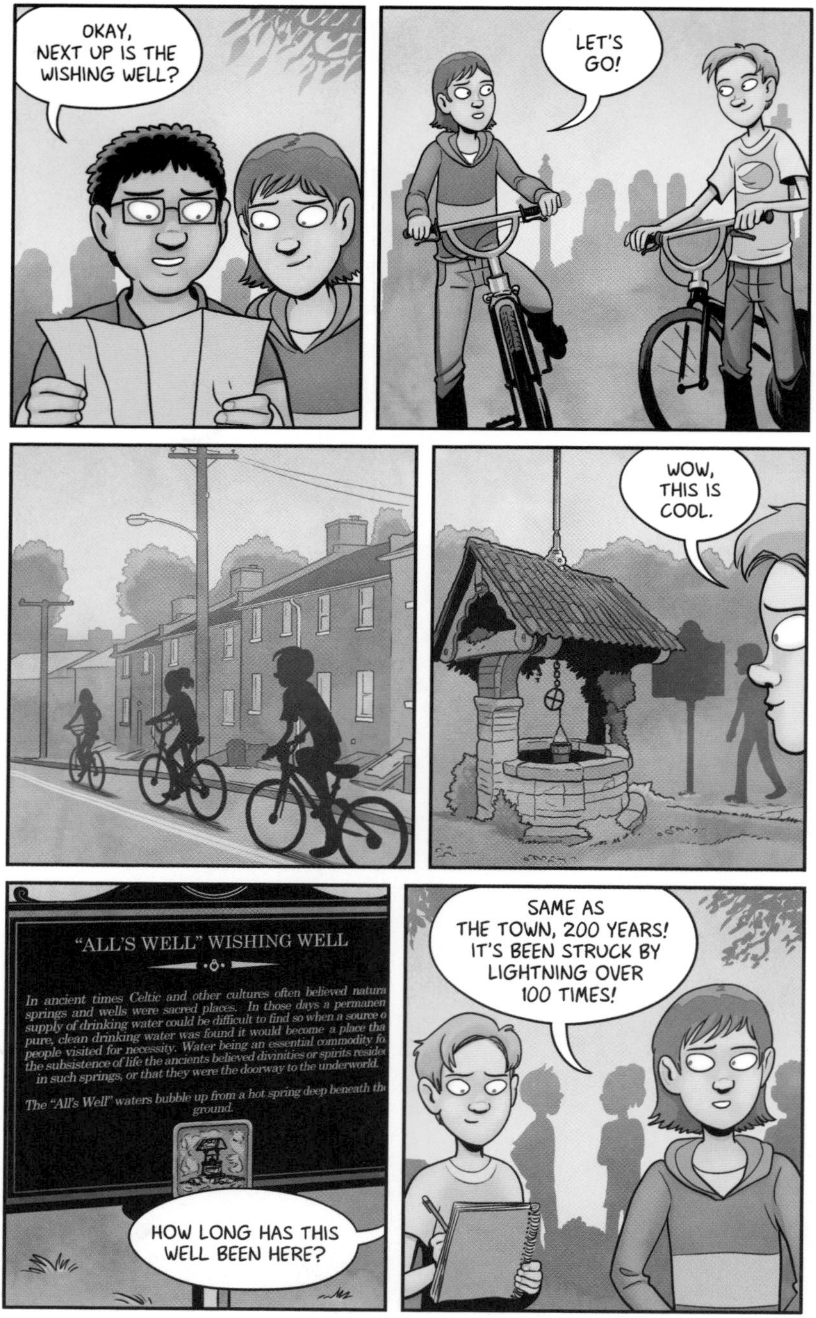
OKAY, NEXT UP IS THE WISHING WELL?
LET'S GO!
WOW, THIS IS COOL.
"ALL'S WELL" WISHING WELL
In ancient times Celtic and other cultures often believed natura
springs and wells were sacred places. In those days a permanen
supply of drinking water could be difficult to find so when a source o
pure, clean drinking water was found it would become a place tha
people visited for necessity. Water being an essential commodity fo
the subsistence of life the ancients believed divinities or spirits reside
in such springs, or that they were the doorway to the underworld.
The "All's Well" waters bubble up from a hot spring deep beneath th
ground.
HOW LONG HAS THIS WELL BEEN HERE?
SAME AS THE TOWN, 200 YEARS! IT'S BEEN STRUCK BY LIGHTNING OVER 100 TIMES!

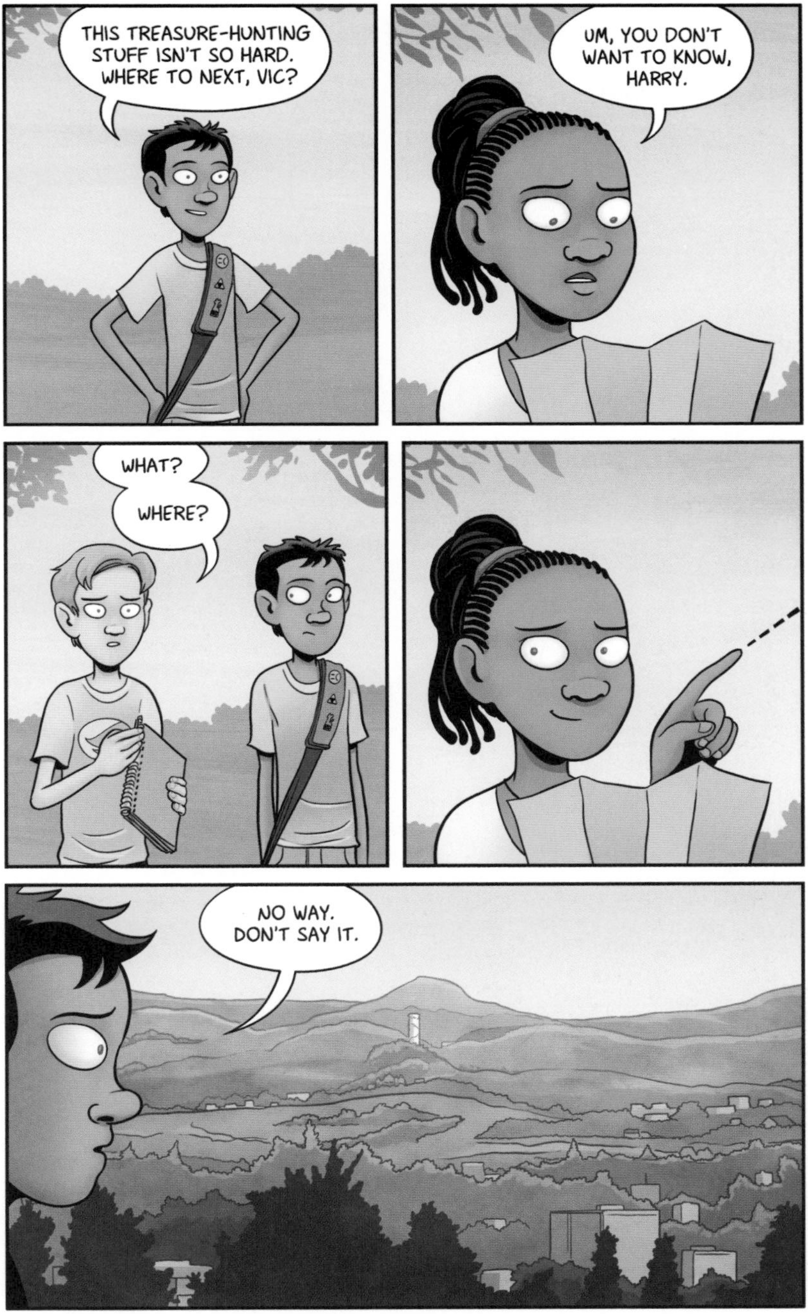
THIS TREASURE-HUNTING STUFF ISN'T SO HARD. WHERE TO NEXT, VIC?
UM, YOU DON'T WANT TO KNOW, HARRY.
WHAT?
WHERE?
NO WAY. DON'T SAY IT.

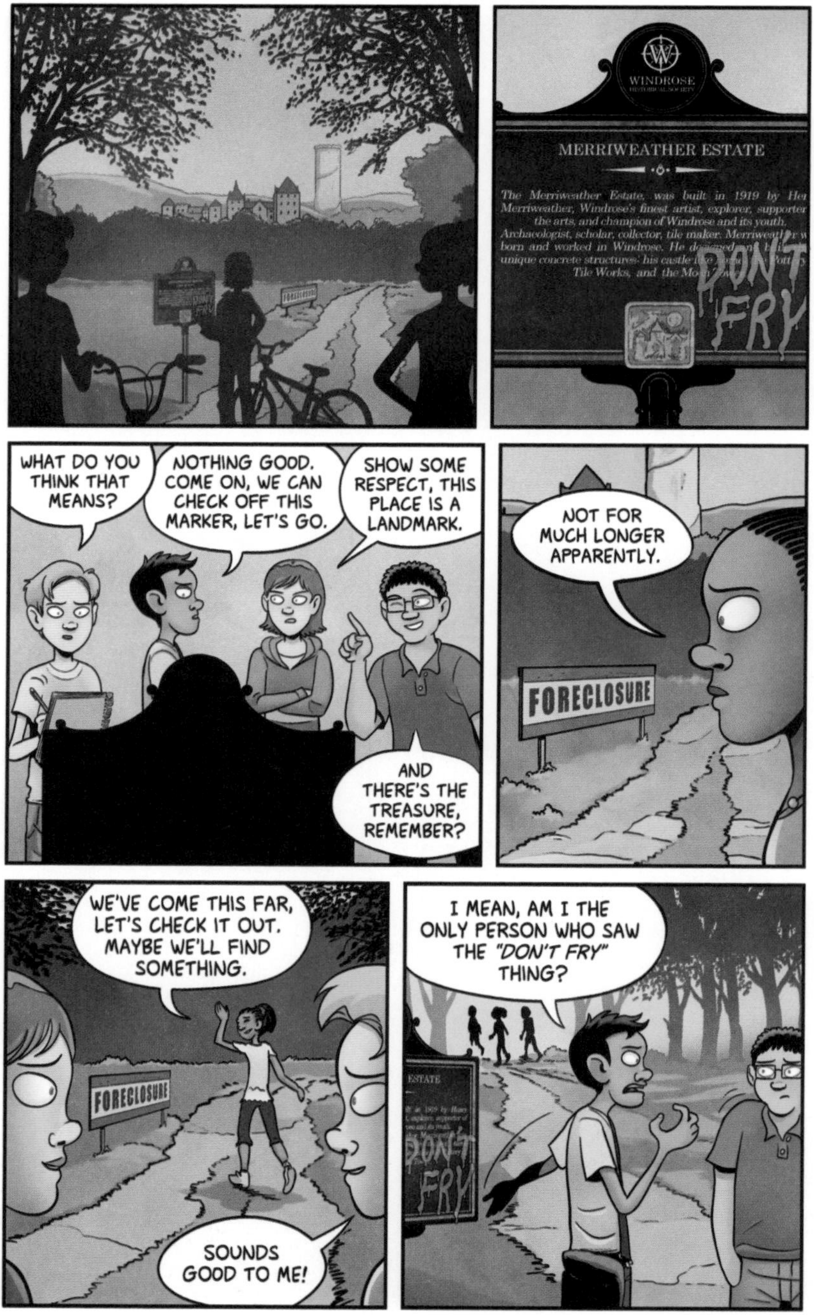
WINDROSE
HISTORICAL SOCIETY
MERRIWEATHER ESTATE
DON'T FRY
WHAT DO YOU THINK THAT MEANS?
NOTHING GOOD. COME ON, WE CAN CHECK OFF THIS MARKER, LET'S GO.
SHOW SOME RESPECT, THIS PLACE IS A LANDMARK.
AND THERE'S THE TREASURE, REMEMBER?
NOT FOR MUCH LONGER APPARENTLY.
FORECLOSURE
WE'VE COME THIS FAR, LET'S CHECK IT OUT. MAYBE WE'LL FIND SOMETHING.
SOUNDS GOOD TO ME!
FORECLOSURE
I MEAN, AM I THE ONLY PERSON WHO SAW THE *"DON'T FRY"* THING?
DON'T FRY

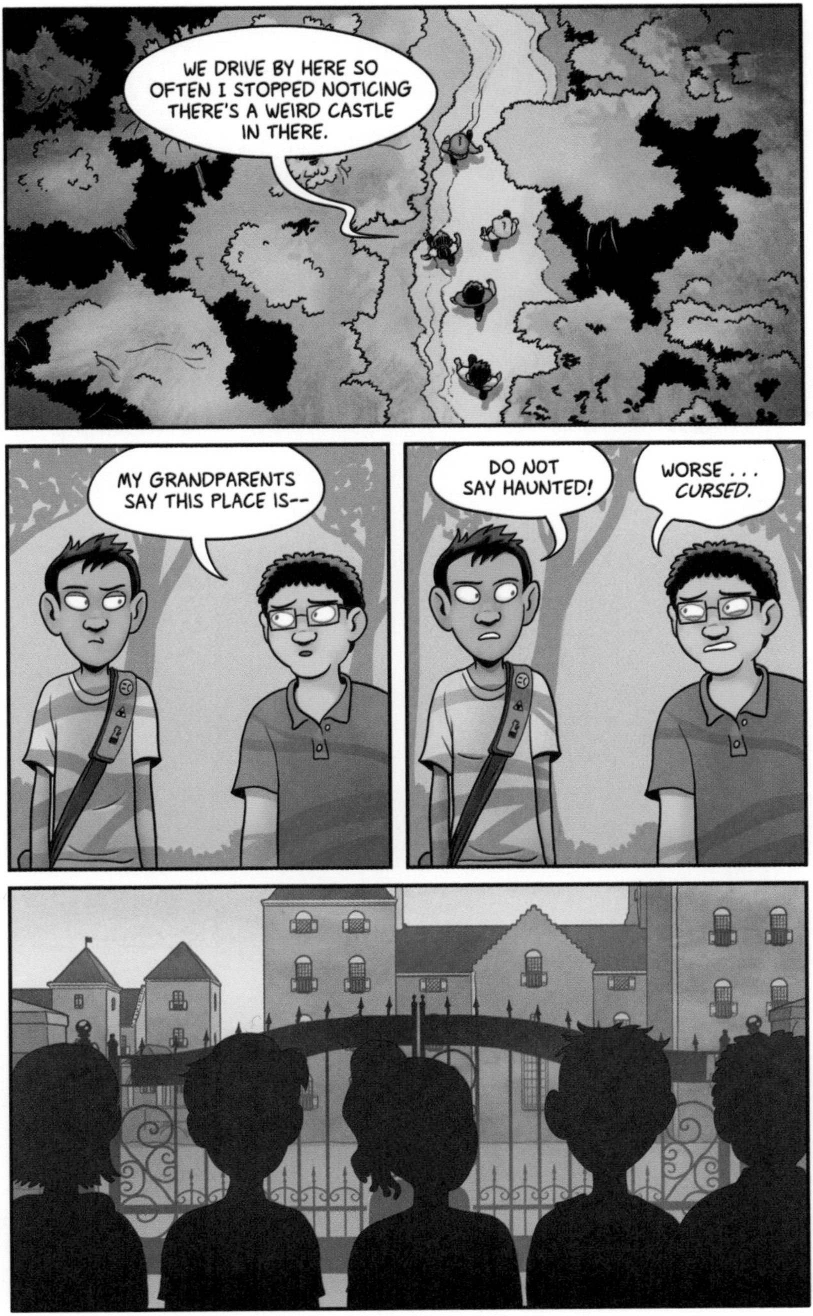

WE DRIVE BY HERE SO OFTEN I STOPPED NOTICING THERE'S A WEIRD CASTLE IN THERE.
MY GRANDPARENTS SAY THIS PLACE IS--
DO NOT SAY HAUNTED!
WORSE . . . CURSED.

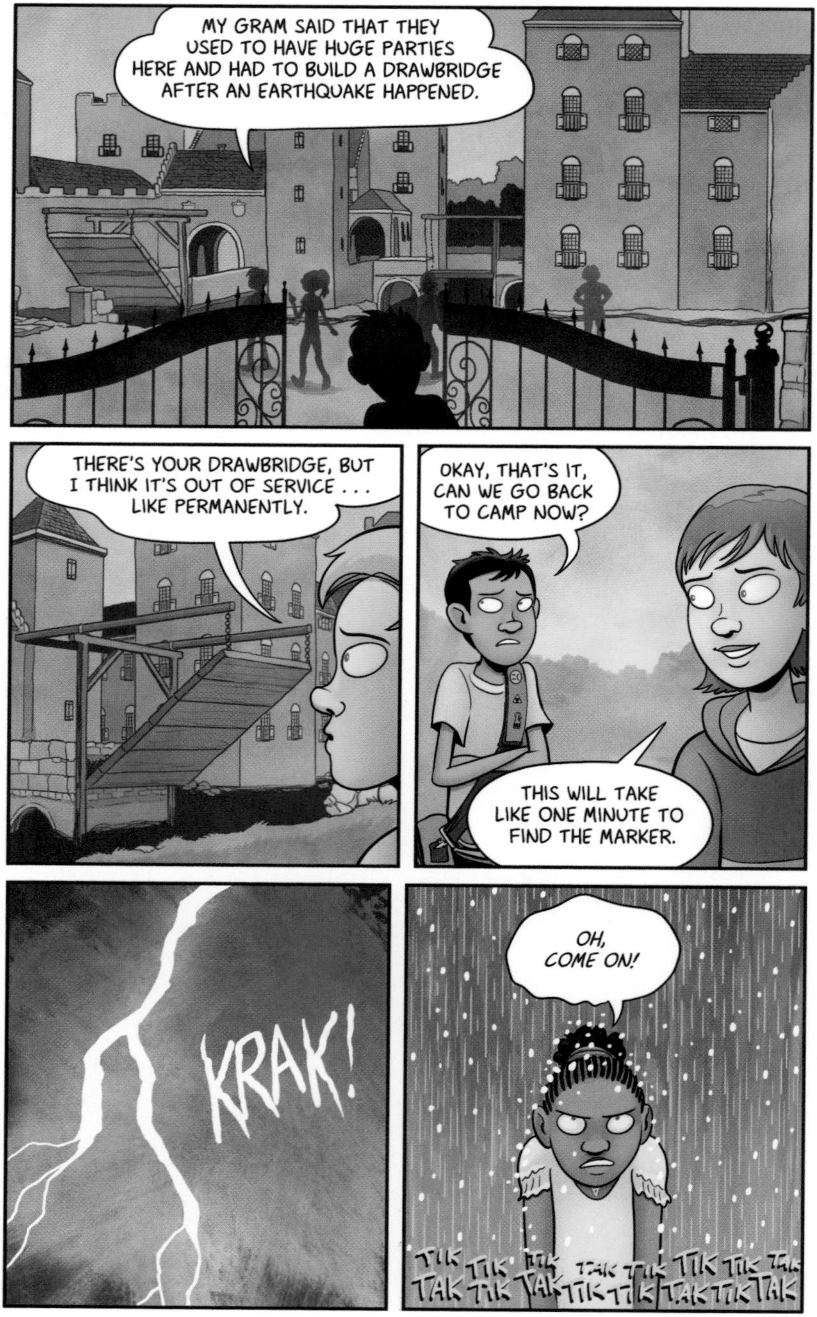
MY GRAM SAID THAT THEY USED TO HAVE HUGE PARTIES HERE AND HAD TO BUILD A DRAWBRIDGE AFTER AN EARTHQUAKE HAPPENED.
THERE'S YOUR DRAWBRIDGE, BUT I THINK IT'S OUT OF SERVICE . . . LIKE PERMANENTLY.
OKAY, THAT'S IT, CAN WE GO BACK TO CAMP NOW?
THIS WILL TAKE LIKE ONE MINUTE TO FIND THE MARKER.
KRAK!
OH, COME ON!
TIK TIK TIK TAK TIK TIK TIK TAK
TAK TIK TAK TIK TIK TAK TIK TAK

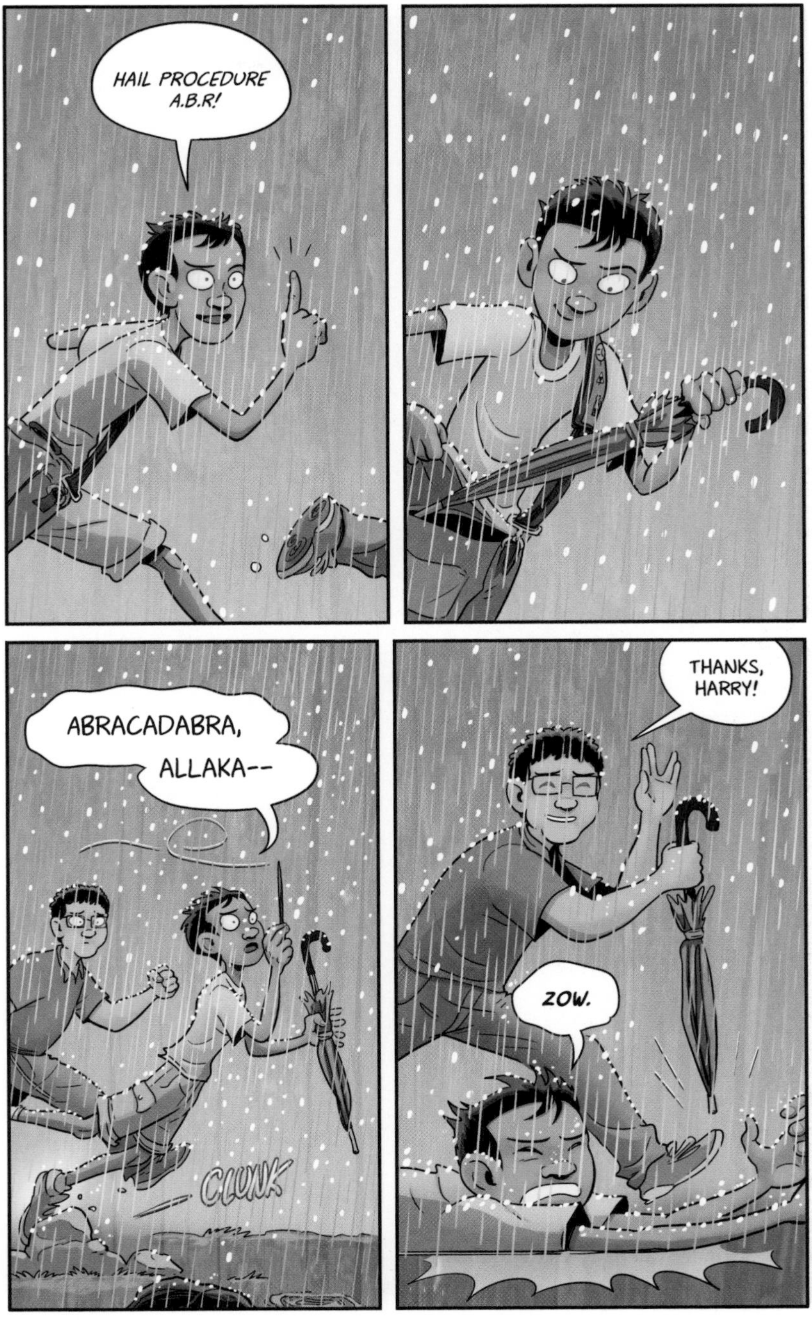
HAIL PROCEDURE A.B.R!
ABRACADABRA,
ALLAKA--
CLUNK
THANKS, HARRY!
ZOW.

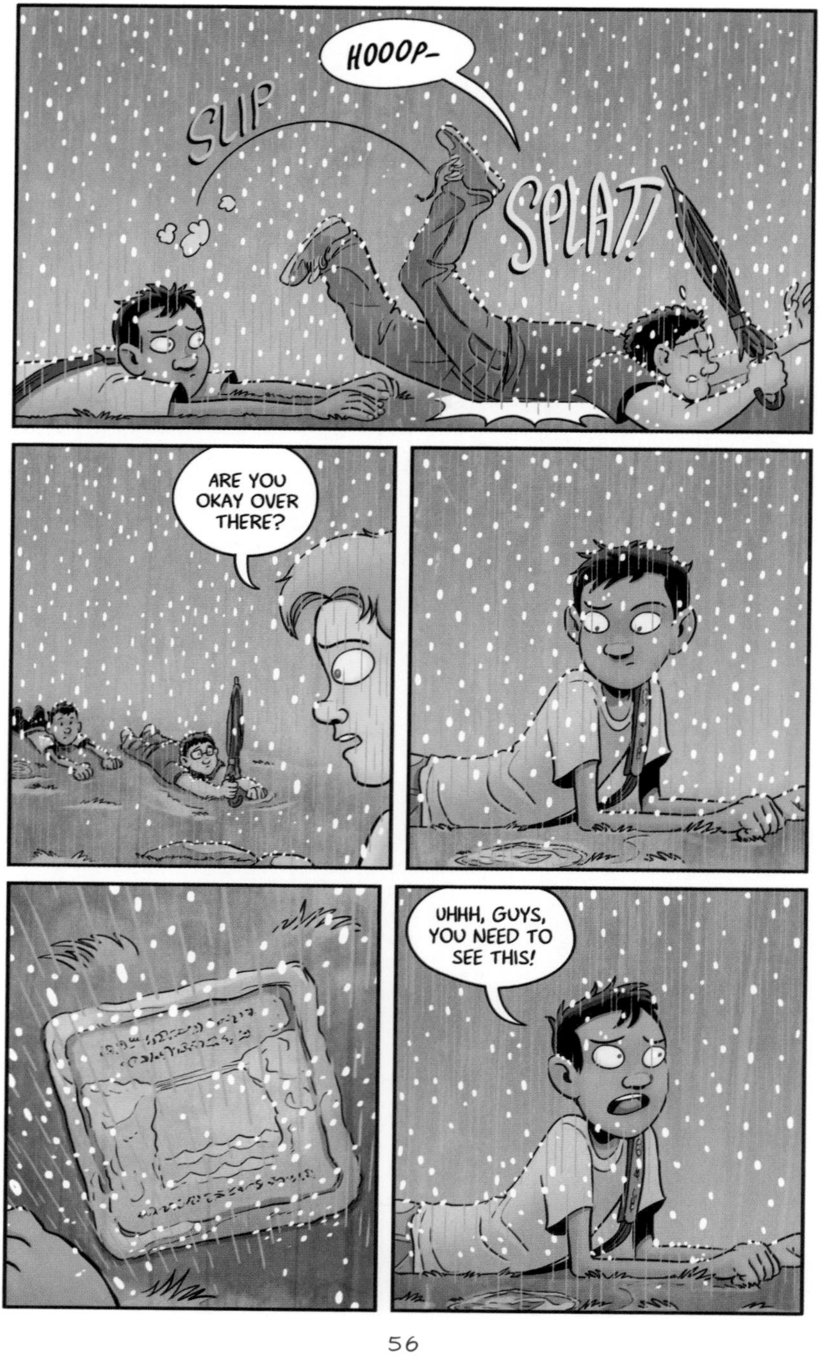
SLIP
HOOOP-
SPLAT!
ARE YOU OKAY OVER THERE?
UHHH, GUYS, YOU NEED TO SEE THIS!

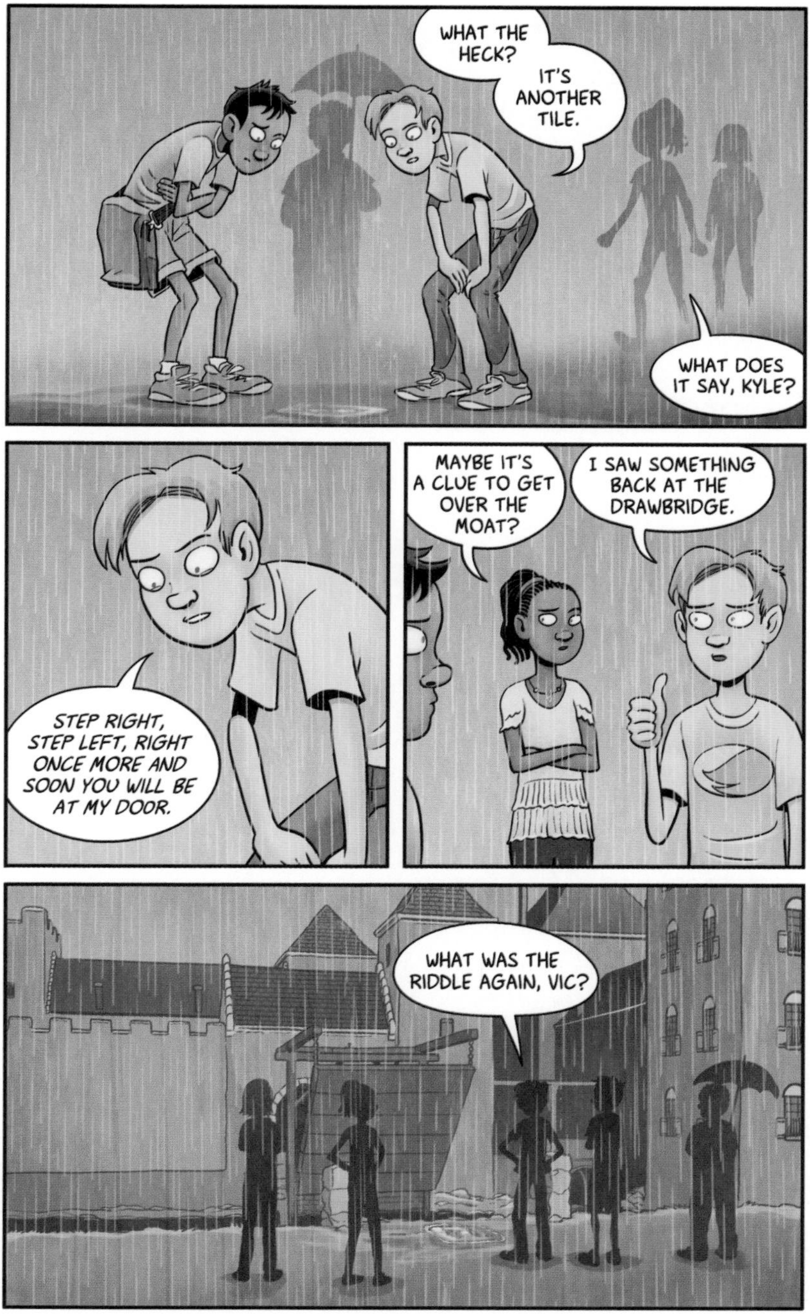
WHAT THE HECK?
IT'S ANOTHER TILE.
WHAT DOES IT SAY, KYLE?
STEP RIGHT, STEP LEFT, RIGHT ONCE MORE AND SOON YOU WILL BE AT MY DOOR.
MAYBE IT'S A CLUE TO GET OVER THE MOAT?
I SAW SOMETHING BACK AT THE DRAWBRIDGE.
WHAT WAS THE RIDDLE AGAIN, VIC?

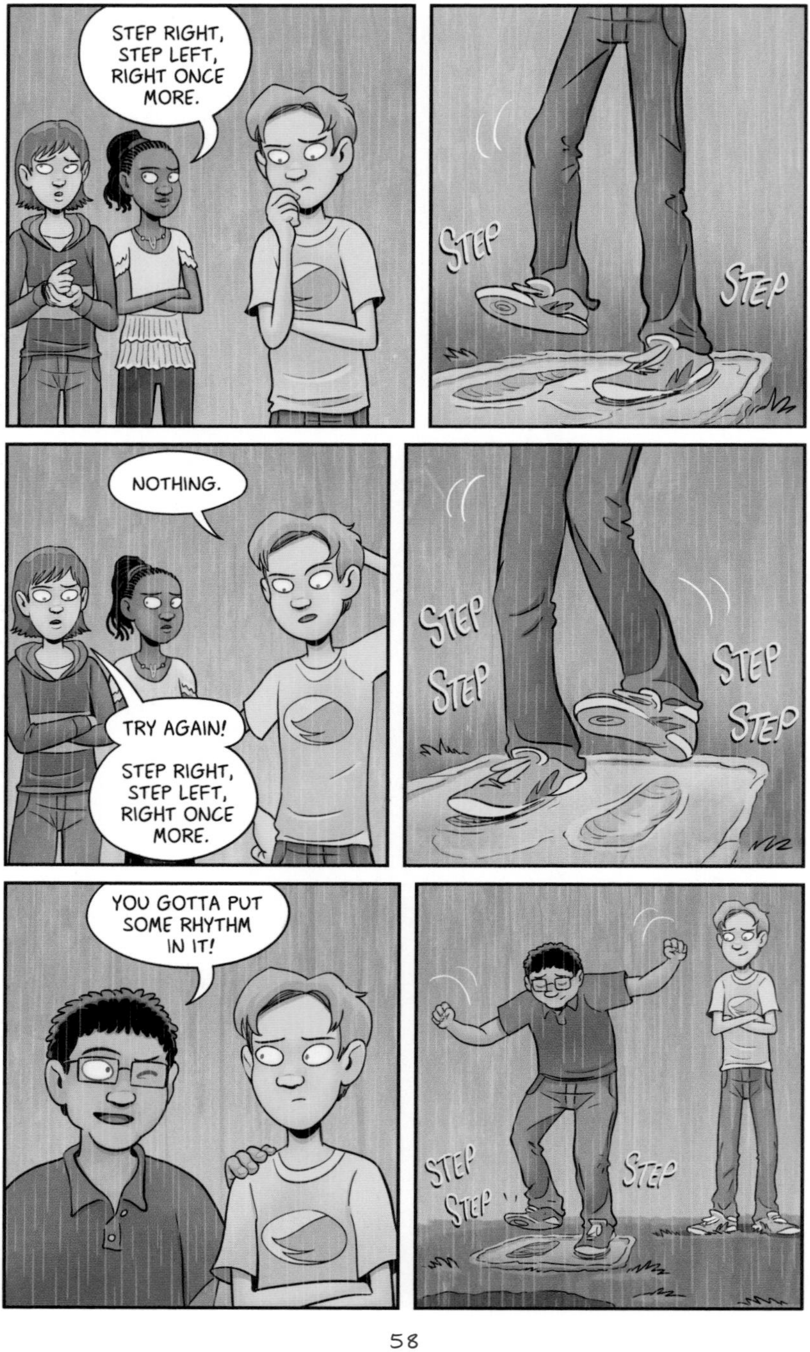
STEP RIGHT, STEP LEFT, RIGHT ONCE MORE.
STEP
STEP
NOTHING.
TRY AGAIN!
STEP RIGHT, STEP LEFT, RIGHT ONCE MORE.
STEP
STEP
STEP
STEP
YOU GOTTA PUT SOME RHYTHM IN IT!
STEP
STEP
STEP

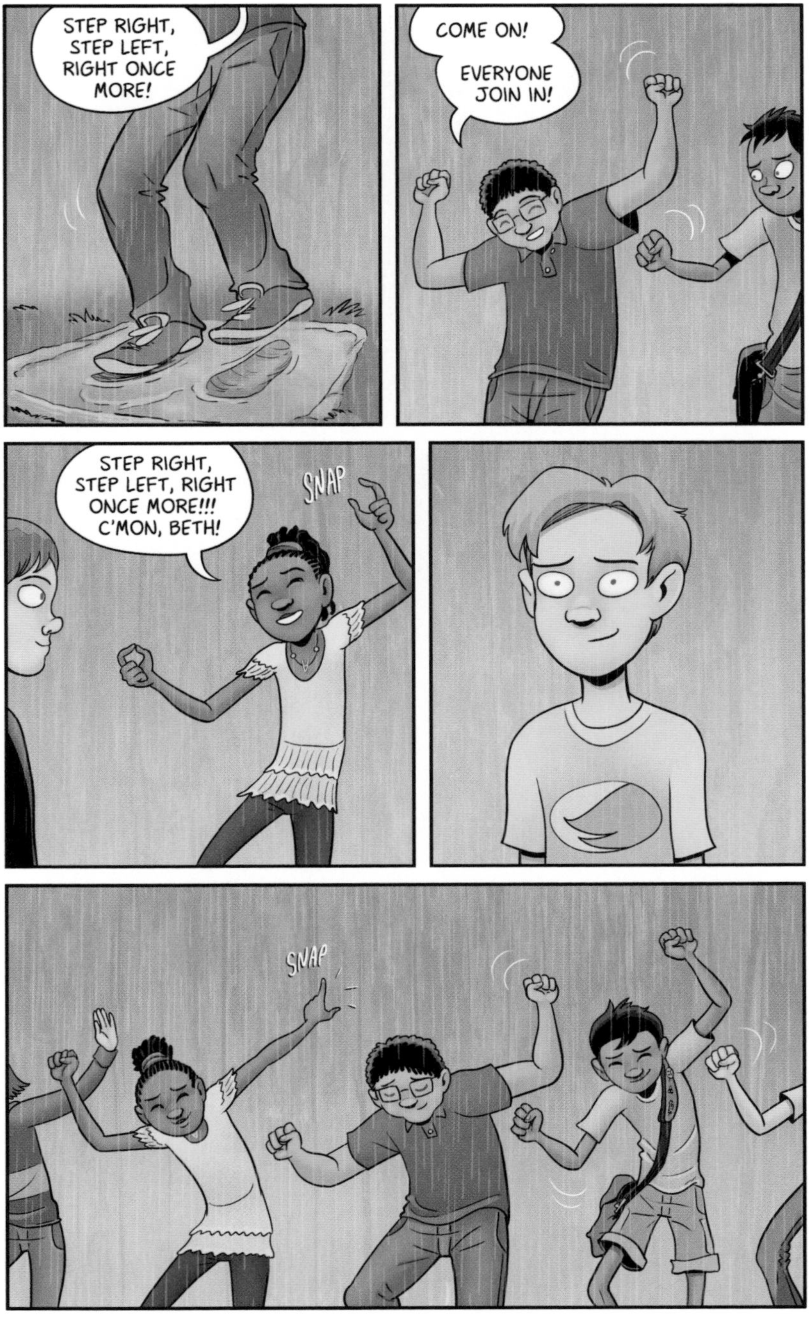
STEP RIGHT, STEP LEFT, RIGHT ONCE MORE!
COME ON!
EVERYONE JOIN IN!
STEP RIGHT, STEP LEFT, RIGHT ONCE MORE!!! C'MON, BETH!
SNAP
SNAP

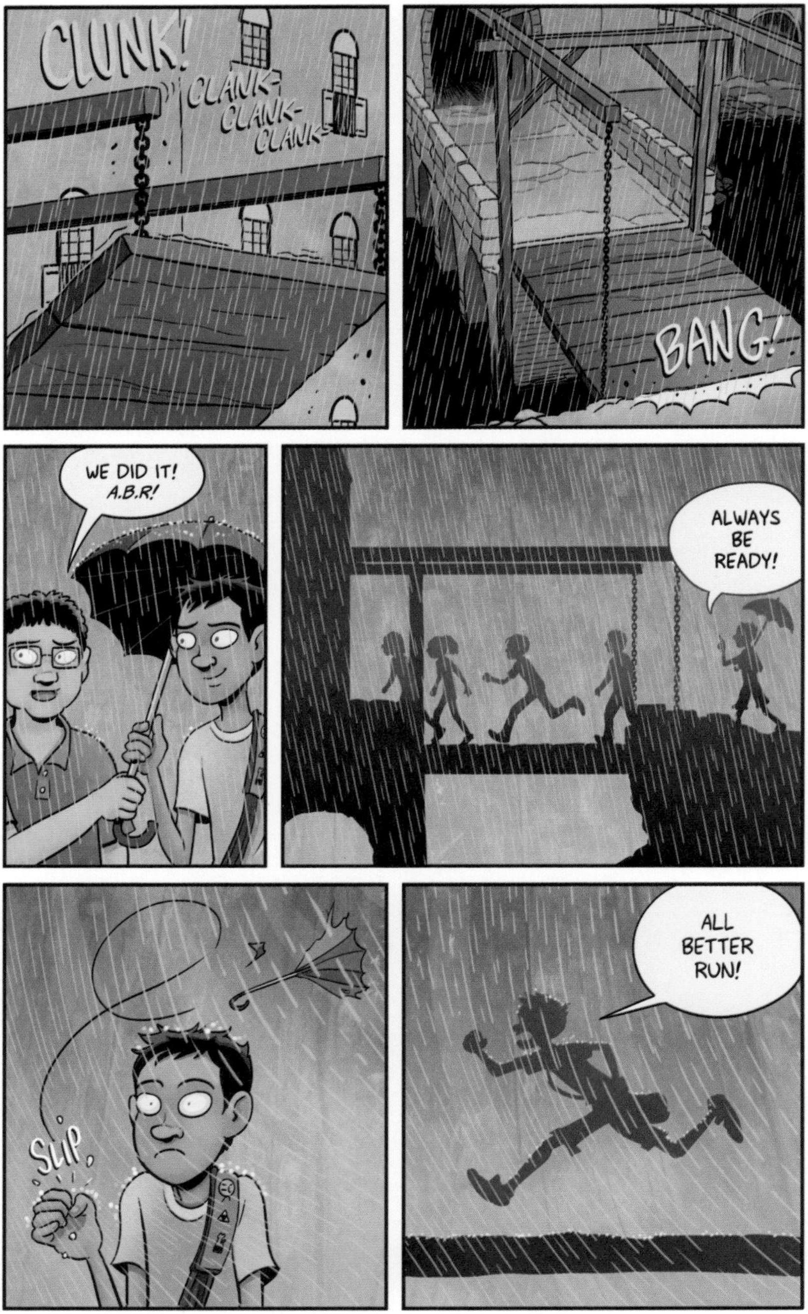
CLUNK!
CLANK-CLANK-CLANK-
BANG!
WE DID IT! A.B.R!
ALWAYS BE READY!
SLIP
ALL BETTER RUN!

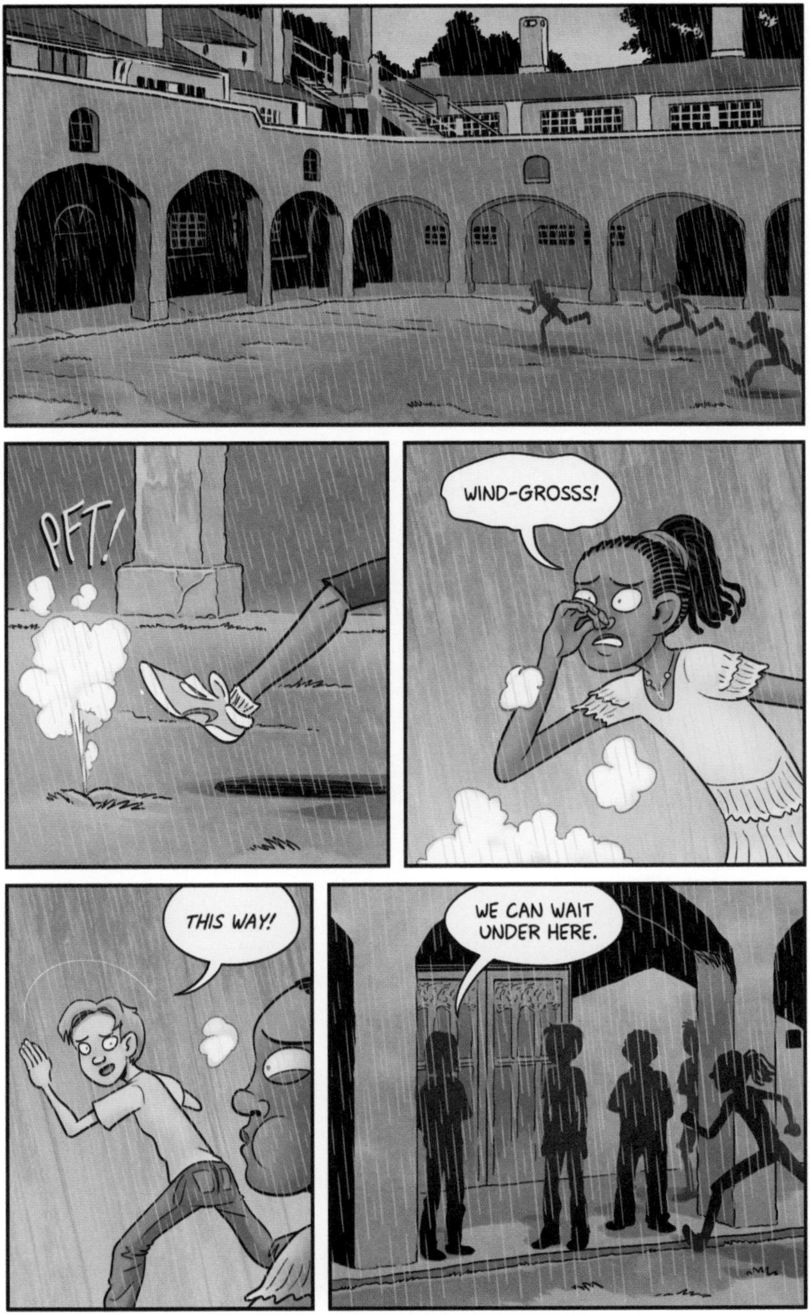
PFT!
WIND-GROSSS!
THIS WAY!
WE CAN WAIT UNDER HERE.

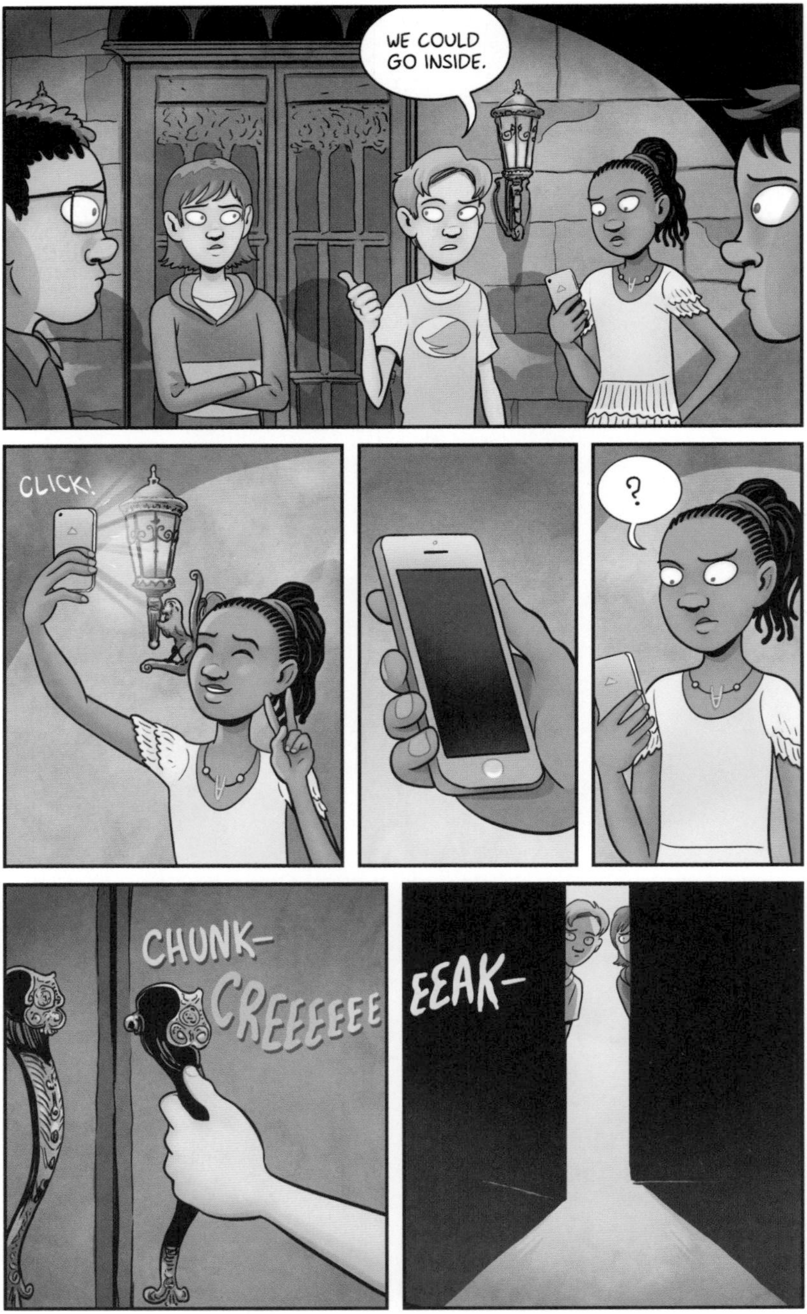
WE COULD GO INSIDE.
CLICK!
?
CHUNK-
CREEEEEEE
EEAK-

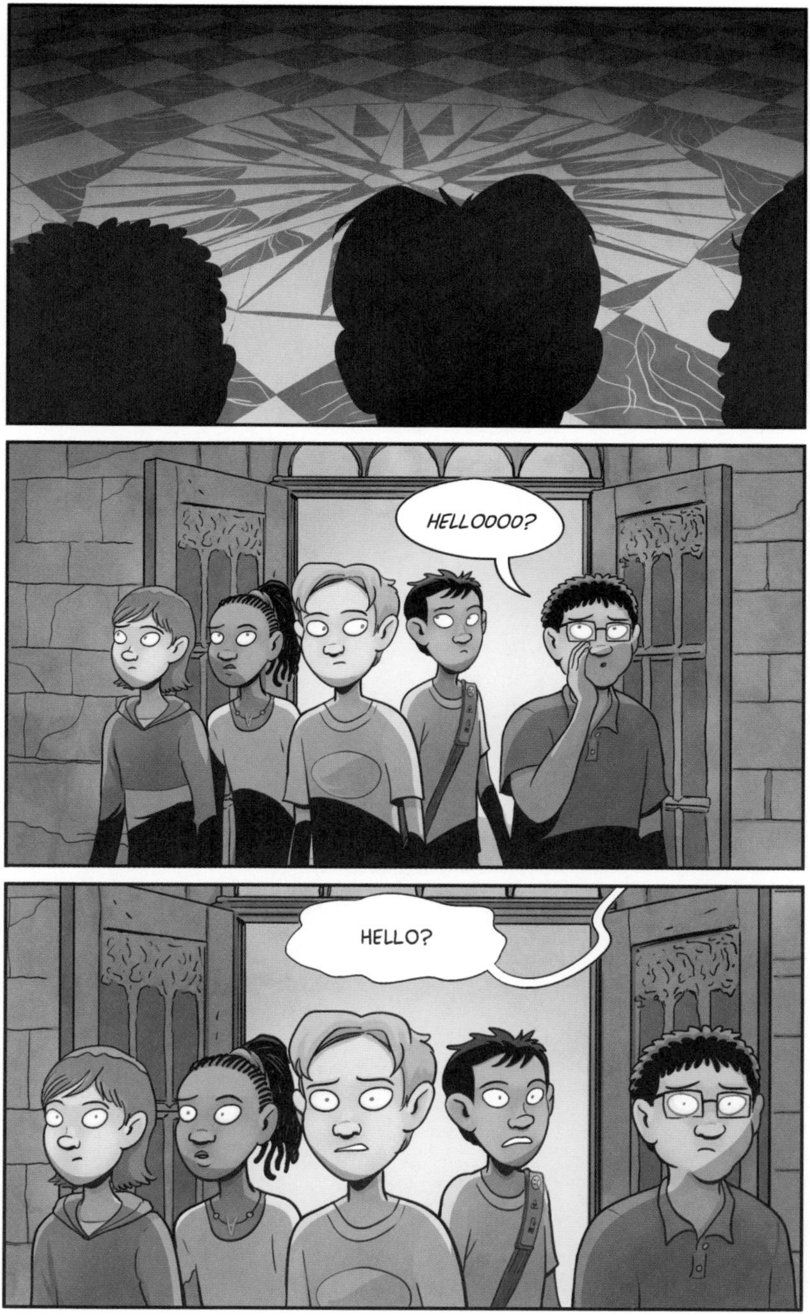
HELLOOOO?
HELLO?

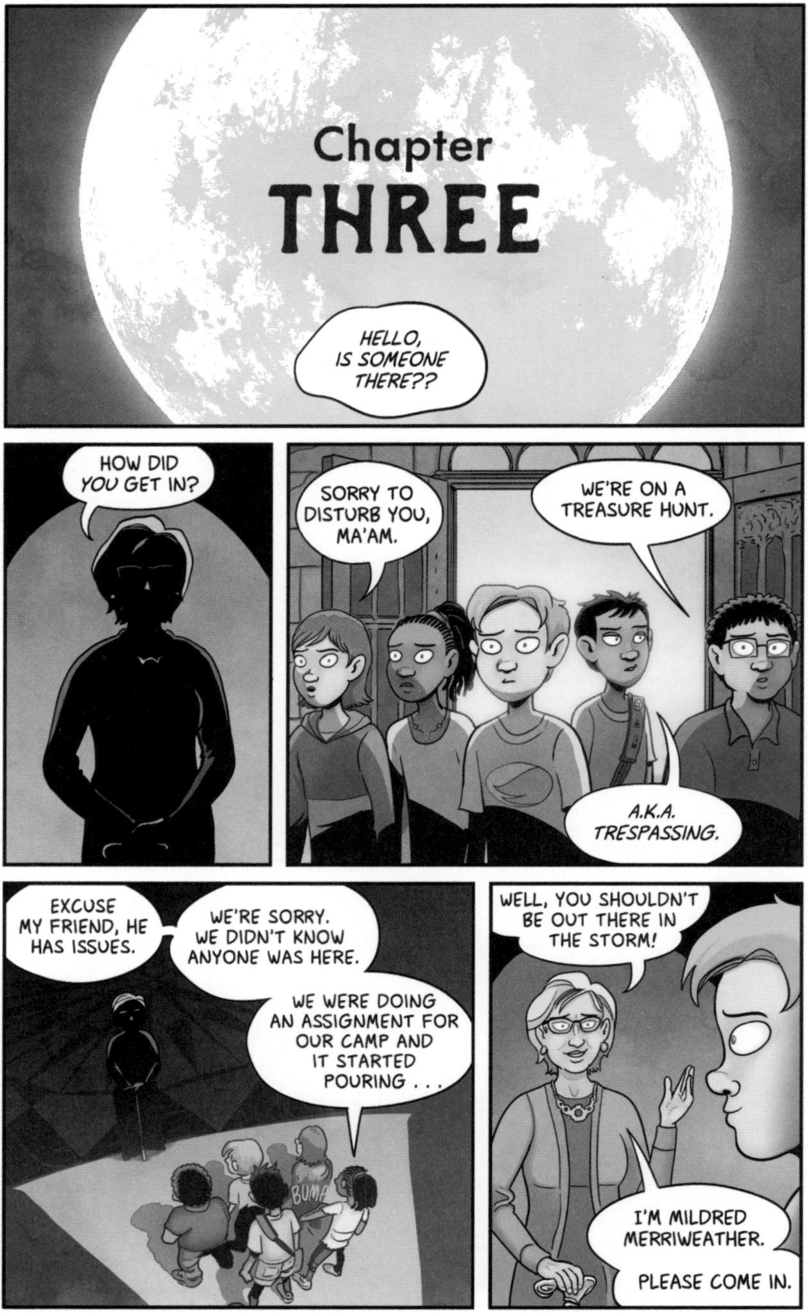
Chapter
THREE
HELLO, IS SOMEONE THERE??
HOW DID YOU GET IN?
SORRY TO DISTURB YOU, MA'AM.
WE'RE ON A TREASURE HUNT.
A.K.A. TRESPASSING.
EXCUSE MY FRIEND, HE HAS ISSUES.
WE'RE SORRY. WE DIDN'T KNOW ANYONE WAS HERE.
WE WERE DOING AN ASSIGNMENT FOR OUR CAMP AND IT STARTED POURING . . .
WELL, YOU SHOULDN'T BE OUT THERE IN THE STORM!
I'M MILDRED MERRIWEATHER.
PLEASE COME IN.

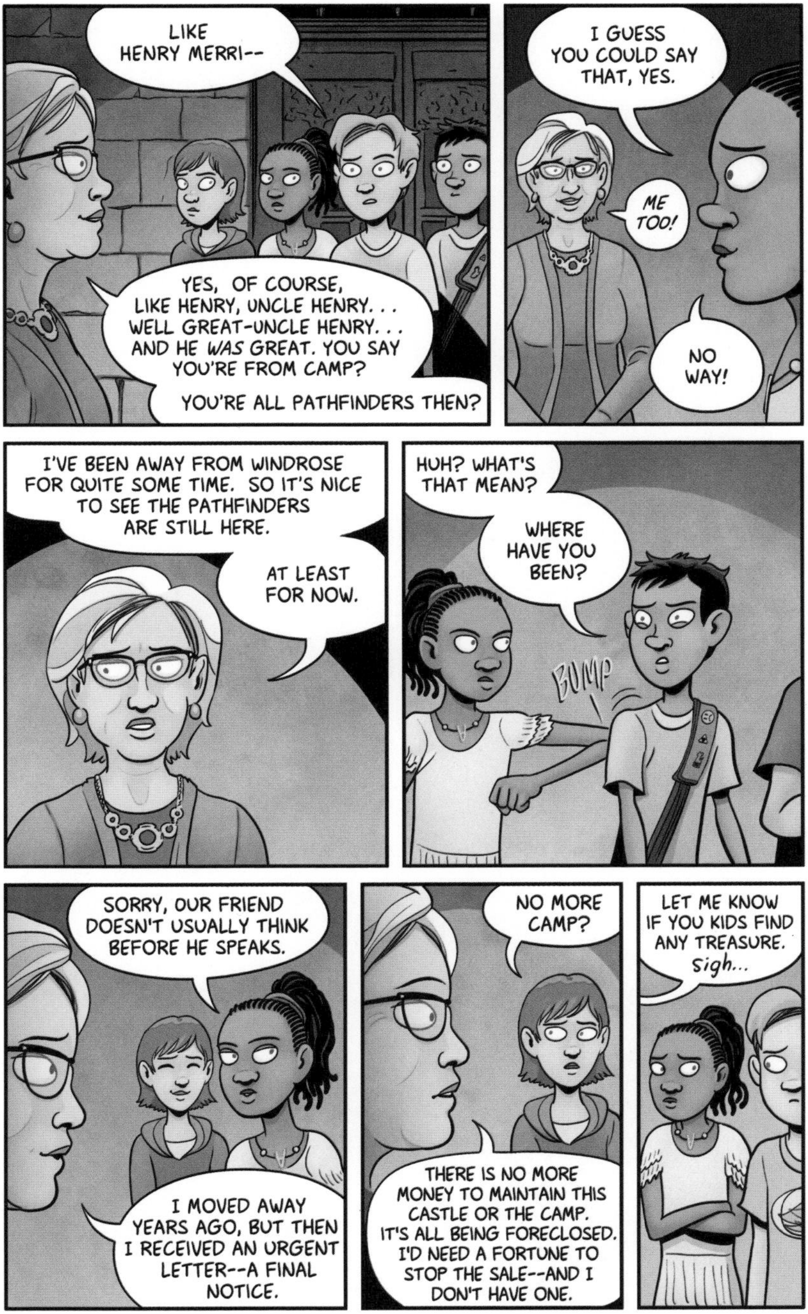
LIKE HENRY MERRI--
YES, OF COURSE, LIKE HENRY, UNCLE HENRY. . . WELL GREAT-UNCLE HENRY. . . AND HE *WAS* GREAT. YOU SAY YOU'RE FROM CAMP?
YOU'RE ALL PATHFINDERS THEN?
I GUESS YOU COULD SAY THAT, YES.
ME TOO!
NO WAY!
I'VE BEEN AWAY FROM WINDROSE FOR QUITE SOME TIME. SO IT'S NICE TO SEE THE PATHFINDERS ARE STILL HERE.
AT LEAST FOR NOW.
HUH? WHAT'S THAT MEAN?
WHERE HAVE YOU BEEN?
BUMP
SORRY, OUR FRIEND DOESN'T USUALLY THINK BEFORE HE SPEAKS.
I MOVED AWAY YEARS AGO, BUT THEN I RECEIVED AN URGENT LETTER--A FINAL NOTICE.
NO MORE CAMP?
THERE IS NO MORE MONEY TO MAINTAIN THIS CASTLE OR THE CAMP. IT'S ALL BEING FORECLOSED. I'D NEED A FORTUNE TO STOP THE SALE--AND I DON'T HAVE ONE.
LET ME KNOW IF YOU KIDS FIND ANY TREASURE.
Sigh...

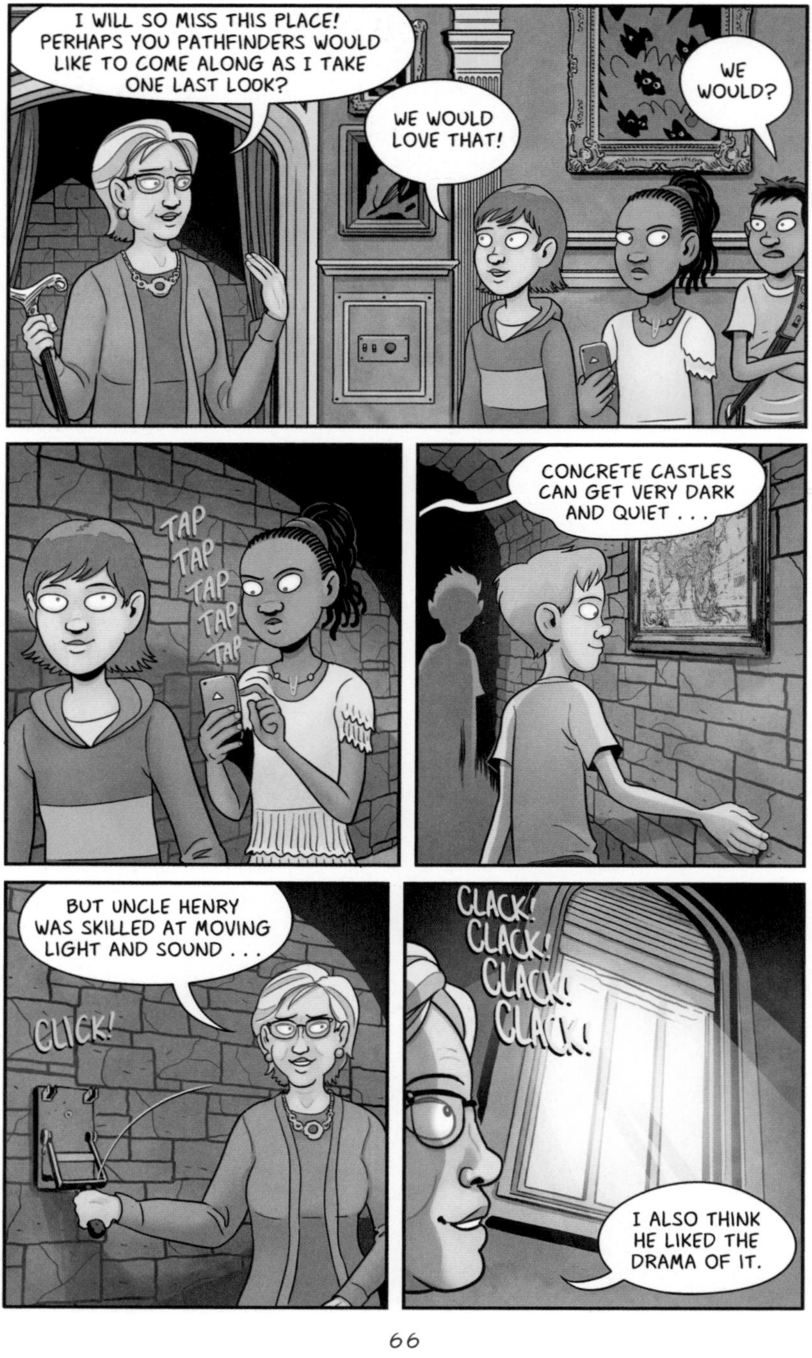
I WILL SO MISS THIS PLACE! PERHAPS YOU PATHFINDERS WOULD LIKE TO COME ALONG AS I TAKE ONE LAST LOOK?
WE WOULD LOVE THAT!
WE WOULD?
TAP TAP TAP TAP TAP
CONCRETE CASTLES CAN GET VERY DARK AND QUIET . . .
BUT UNCLE HENRY WAS SKILLED AT MOVING LIGHT AND SOUND . . .
CLICK!
CLACK! CLACK! CLACK! CLACK!
I ALSO THINK HE LIKED THE DRAMA OF IT.

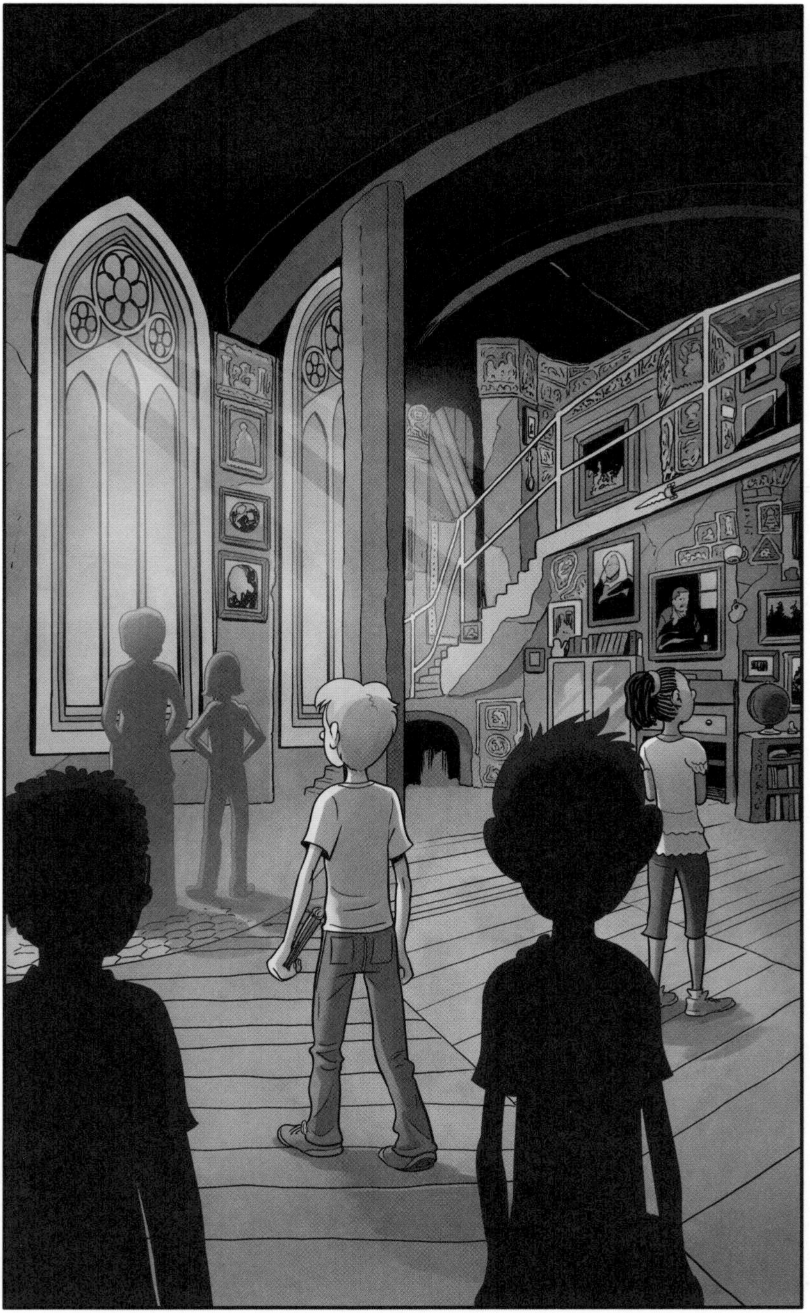

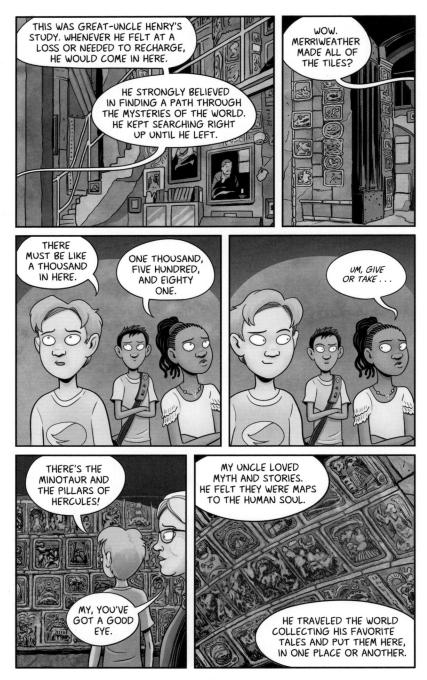

THIS WAS GREAT-UNCLE HENRY'S STUDY. WHENEVER HE FELT AT A LOSS OR NEEDED TO RECHARGE, HE WOULD COME IN HERE.

HE STRONGLY BELIEVED IN FINDING A PATH THROUGH THE MYSTERIES OF THE WORLD. HE KEPT SEARCHING RIGHT UP UNTIL HE LEFT.

WOW. MERRIWEATHER MADE ALL OF THE TILES?

THERE MUST BE LIKE A THOUSAND IN HERE.

ONE THOUSAND, FIVE HUNDRED, AND EIGHTY ONE.

UM, GIVE OR TAKE . . .

THERE'S THE MINOTAUR AND THE PILLARS OF HERCULES!

MY, YOU'VE GOT A GOOD EYE.

MY UNCLE LOVED MYTH AND STORIES. HE FELT THEY WERE MAPS TO THE HUMAN SOUL.

HE TRAVELED THE WORLD COLLECTING HIS FAVORITE TALES AND PUT THEM HERE, IN ONE PLACE OR ANOTHER.

68

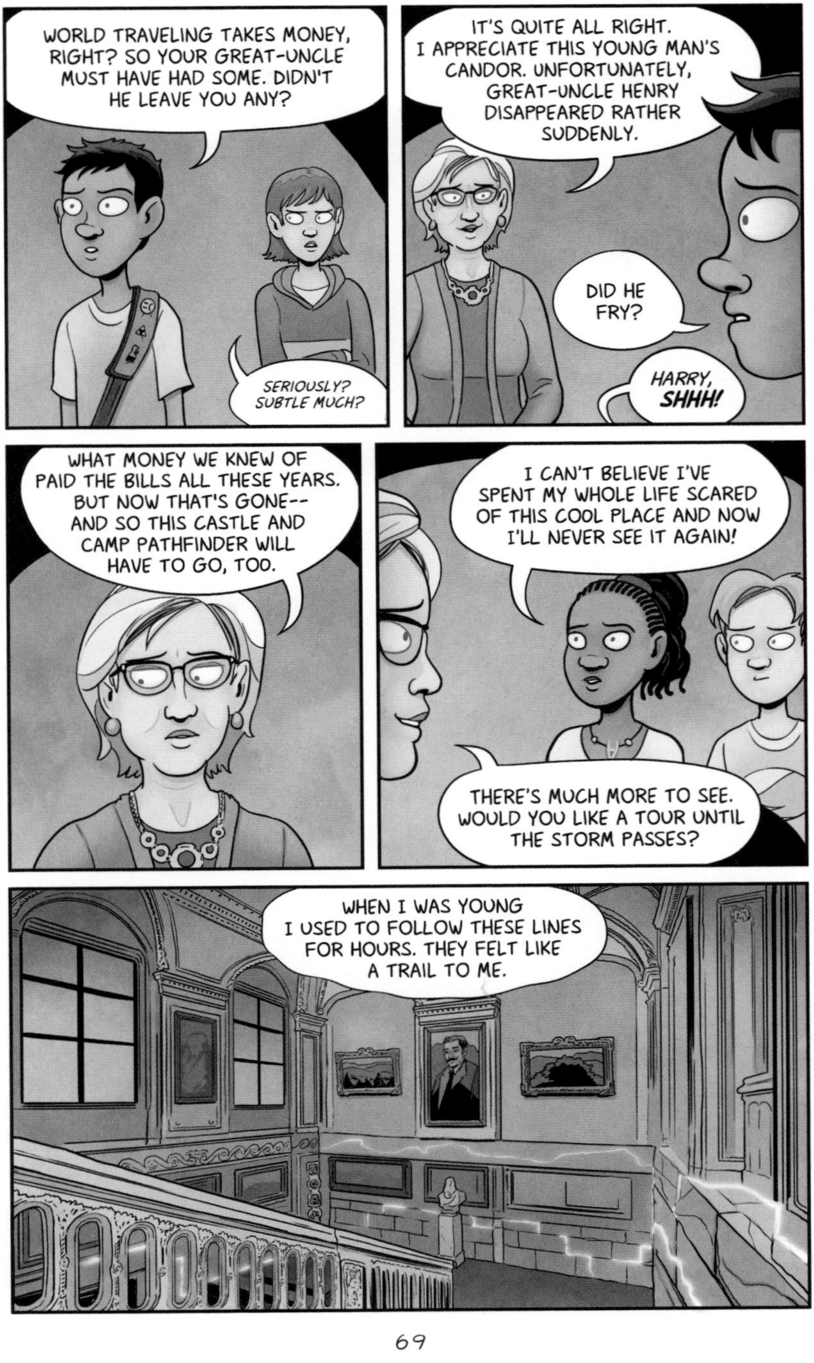
WORLD TRAVELING TAKES MONEY, RIGHT? SO YOUR GREAT-UNCLE MUST HAVE HAD SOME. DIDN'T HE LEAVE YOU ANY?
SERIOUSLY? SUBTLE MUCH?
IT'S QUITE ALL RIGHT. I APPRECIATE THIS YOUNG MAN'S CANDOR. UNFORTUNATELY, GREAT-UNCLE HENRY DISAPPEARED RATHER SUDDENLY.
DID HE FRY?
HARRY, SHHH!
WHAT MONEY WE KNEW OF PAID THE BILLS ALL THESE YEARS. BUT NOW THAT'S GONE--AND SO THIS CASTLE AND CAMP PATHFINDER WILL HAVE TO GO, TOO.
I CAN'T BELIEVE I'VE SPENT MY WHOLE LIFE SCARED OF THIS COOL PLACE AND NOW I'LL NEVER SEE IT AGAIN!
THERE'S MUCH MORE TO SEE. WOULD YOU LIKE A TOUR UNTIL THE STORM PASSES?
WHEN I WAS YOUNG I USED TO FOLLOW THESE LINES FOR HOURS. THEY FELT LIKE A TRAIL TO ME.

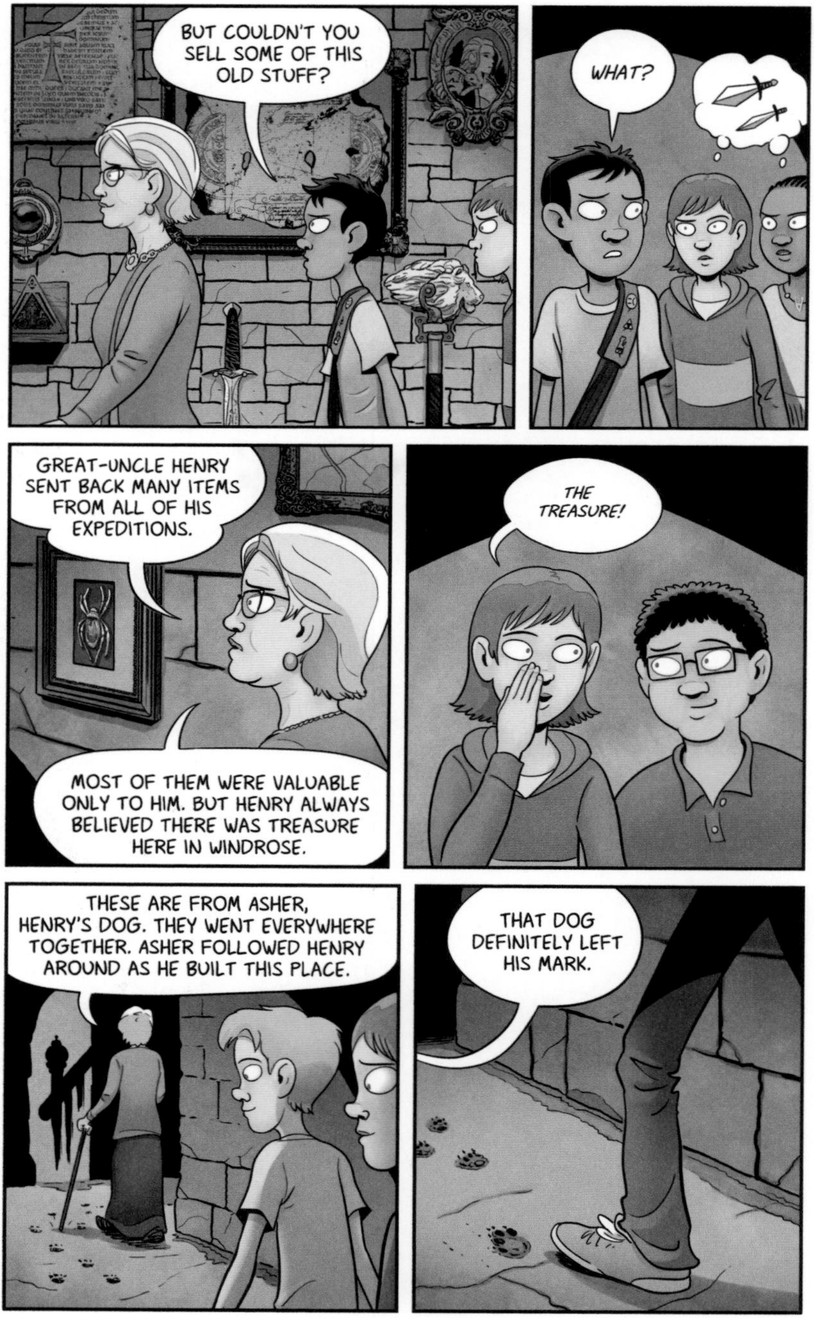
BUT COULDN'T YOU SELL SOME OF THIS OLD STUFF?
WHAT?
GREAT-UNCLE HENRY SENT BACK MANY ITEMS FROM ALL OF HIS EXPEDITIONS.
MOST OF THEM WERE VALUABLE ONLY TO HIM. BUT HENRY ALWAYS BELIEVED THERE WAS TREASURE HERE IN WINDROSE.
THE TREASURE!
THESE ARE FROM ASHER, HENRY'S DOG. THEY WENT EVERYWHERE TOGETHER. ASHER FOLLOWED HENRY AROUND AS HE BUILT THIS PLACE.
THAT DOG DEFINITELY LEFT HIS MARK.

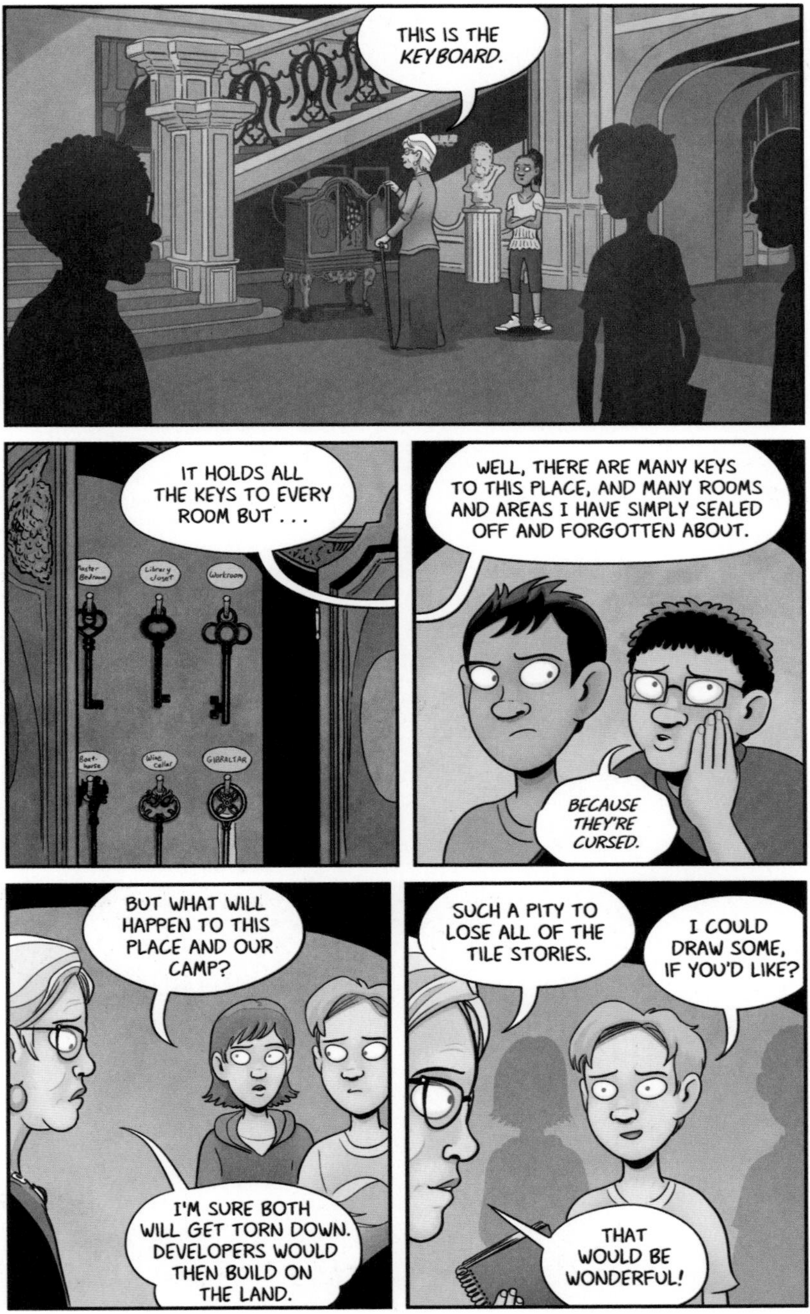

THIS IS THE *KEYBOARD.*
IT HOLDS ALL THE KEYS TO EVERY ROOM BUT . . .
Workroom
GIBRALTAR
WELL, THERE ARE MANY KEYS TO THIS PLACE, AND MANY ROOMS AND AREAS I HAVE SIMPLY SEALED OFF AND FORGOTTEN ABOUT.
BECAUSE THEY'RE CURSED.
BUT WHAT WILL HAPPEN TO THIS PLACE AND OUR CAMP?
I'M SURE BOTH WILL GET TORN DOWN. DEVELOPERS WOULD THEN BUILD ON THE LAND.
SUCH A PITY TO LOSE ALL OF THE TILE STORIES.
I COULD DRAW SOME, IF YOU'D LIKE?
THAT WOULD BE WONDERFUL!

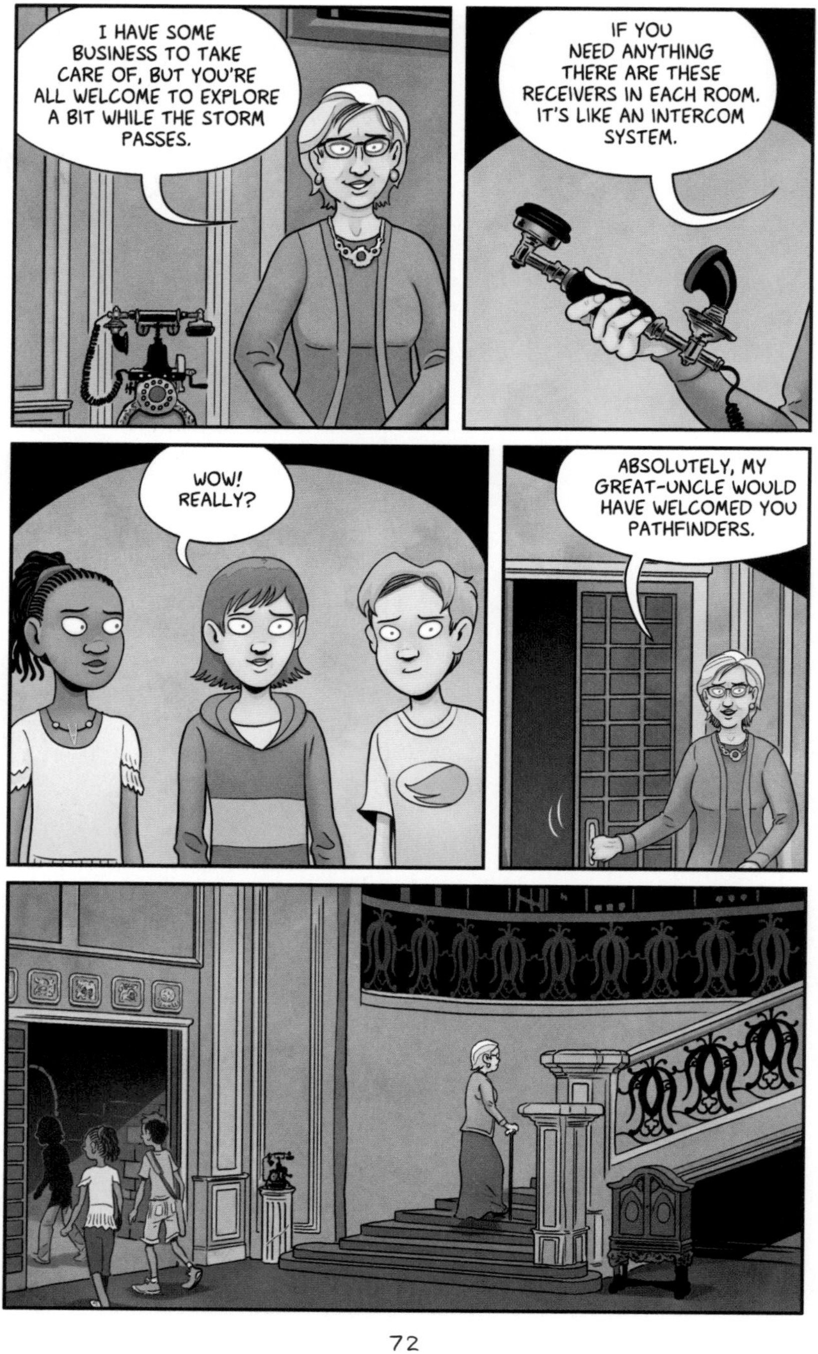
I HAVE SOME BUSINESS TO TAKE CARE OF, BUT YOU'RE ALL WELCOME TO EXPLORE A BIT WHILE THE STORM PASSES.
IF YOU NEED ANYTHING THERE ARE THESE RECEIVERS IN EACH ROOM. IT'S LIKE AN INTERCOM SYSTEM.
WOW! REALLY?
ABSOLUTELY, MY GREAT-UNCLE WOULD HAVE WELCOMED YOU PATHFINDERS.

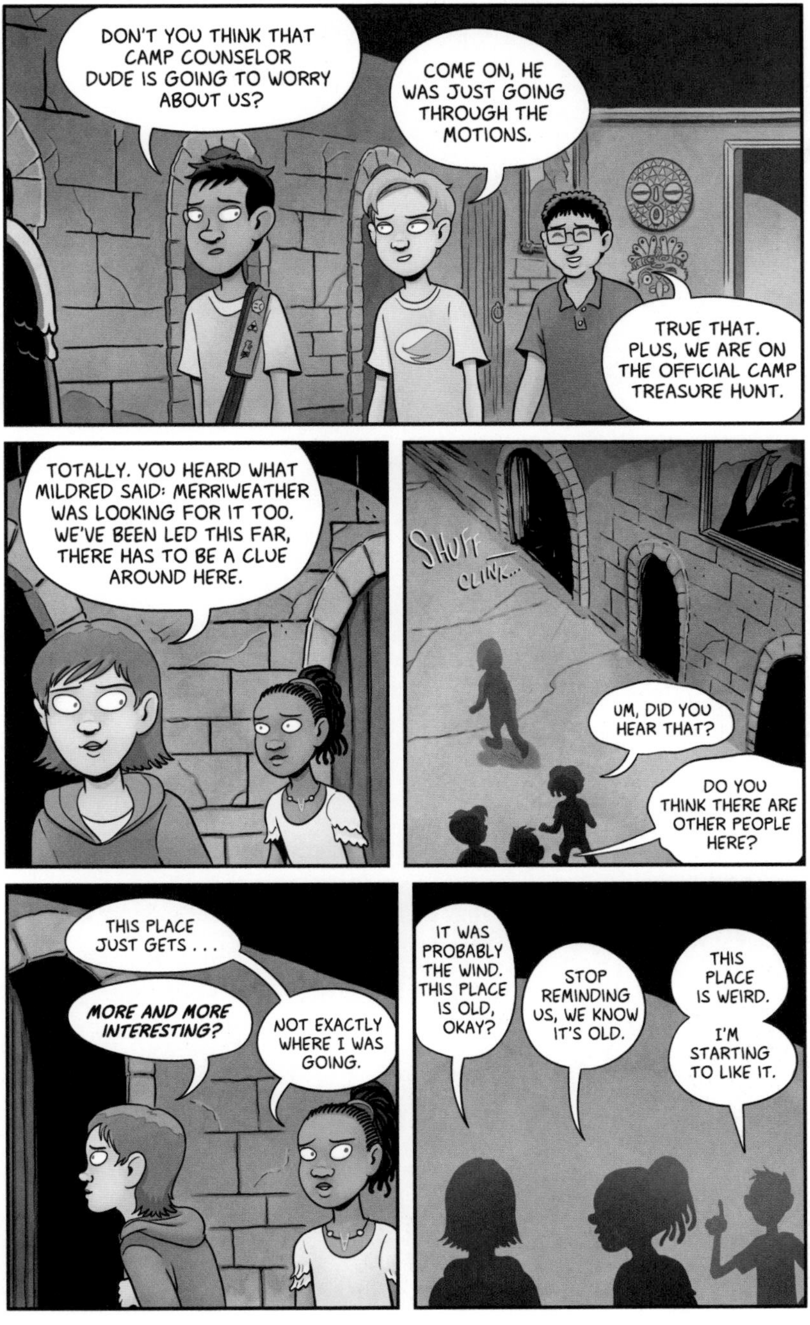
DON'T YOU THINK THAT CAMP COUNSELOR DUDE IS GOING TO WORRY ABOUT US?
COME ON, HE WAS JUST GOING THROUGH THE MOTIONS.
TRUE THAT. PLUS, WE ARE ON THE OFFICIAL CAMP TREASURE HUNT.
TOTALLY. YOU HEARD WHAT MILDRED SAID: MERRIWEATHER WAS LOOKING FOR IT TOO. WE'VE BEEN LED THIS FAR, THERE HAS TO BE A CLUE AROUND HERE.
SHUFF
CLINK...
UM, DID YOU HEAR THAT?
DO YOU THINK THERE ARE OTHER PEOPLE HERE?
THIS PLACE JUST GETS . . .
MORE AND MORE INTERESTING?
NOT EXACTLY WHERE I WAS GOING.
IT WAS PROBABLY THE WIND. THIS PLACE IS OLD, OKAY?
STOP REMINDING US, WE KNOW IT'S OLD.
THIS PLACE IS WEIRD.
I'M STARTING TO LIKE IT.

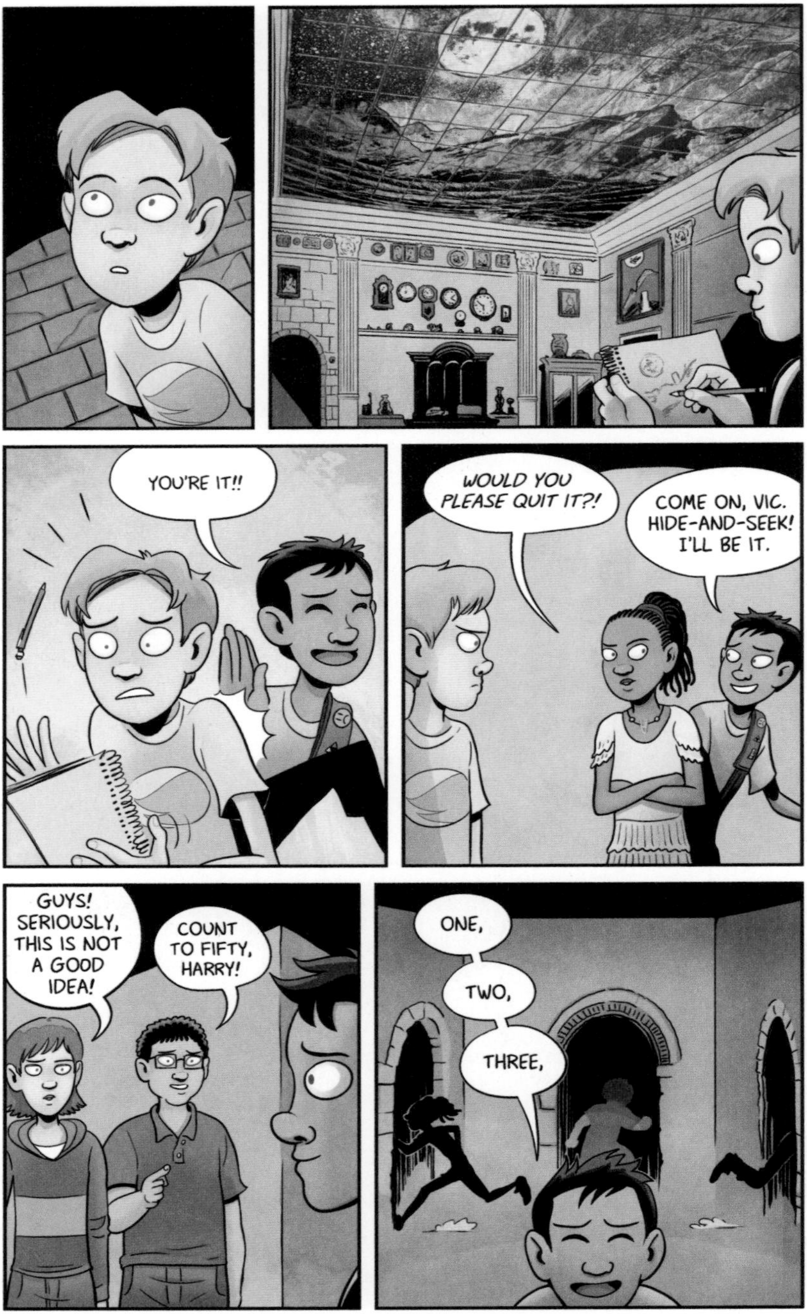
YOU'RE IT!!
WOULD YOU PLEASE QUIT IT?!
COME ON, VIC. HIDE-AND-SEEK! I'LL BE IT.
GUYS! SERIOUSLY, THIS IS NOT A GOOD IDEA!
COUNT TO FIFTY, HARRY!
ONE,
TWO,
THREE,

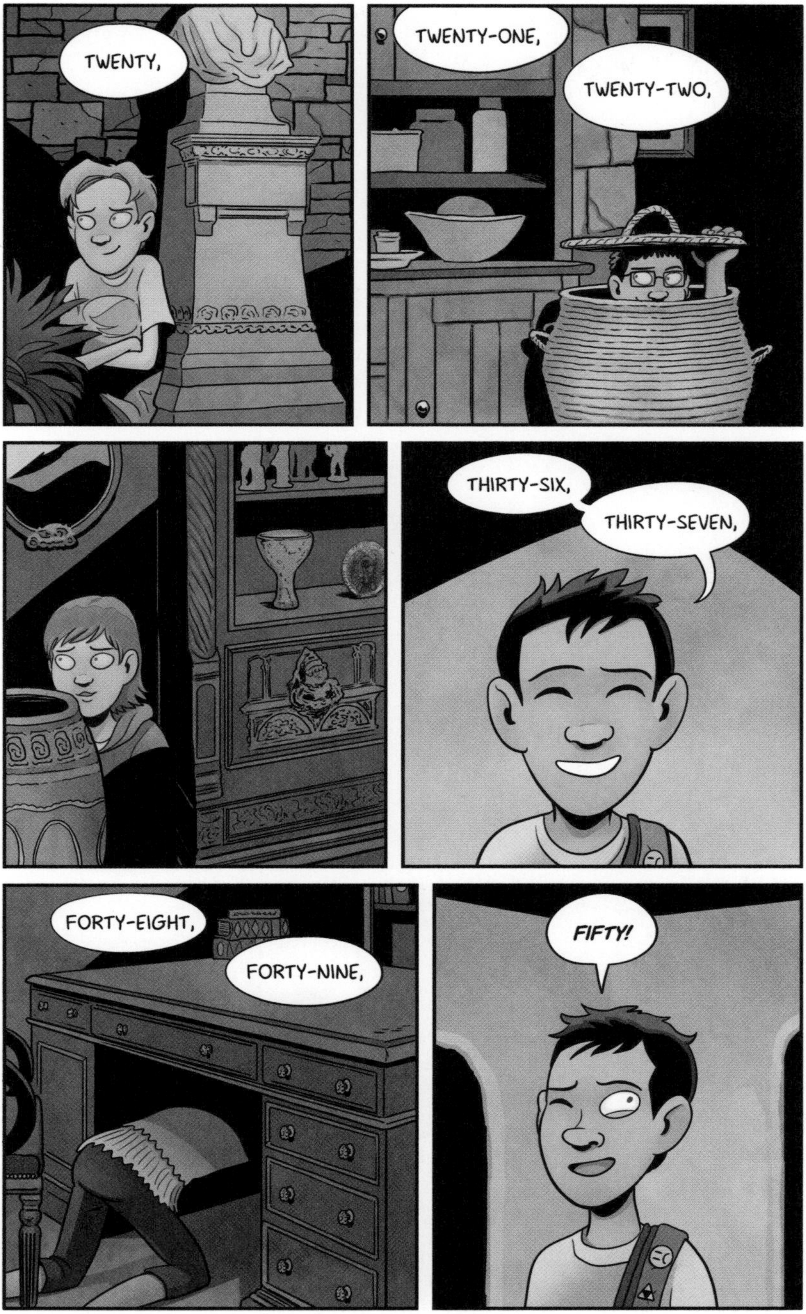
TWENTY,
TWENTY-ONE,
TWENTY-TWO,
THIRTY-SIX,
THIRTY-SEVEN,
FORTY-EIGHT,
FORTY-NINE,
FIFTY!

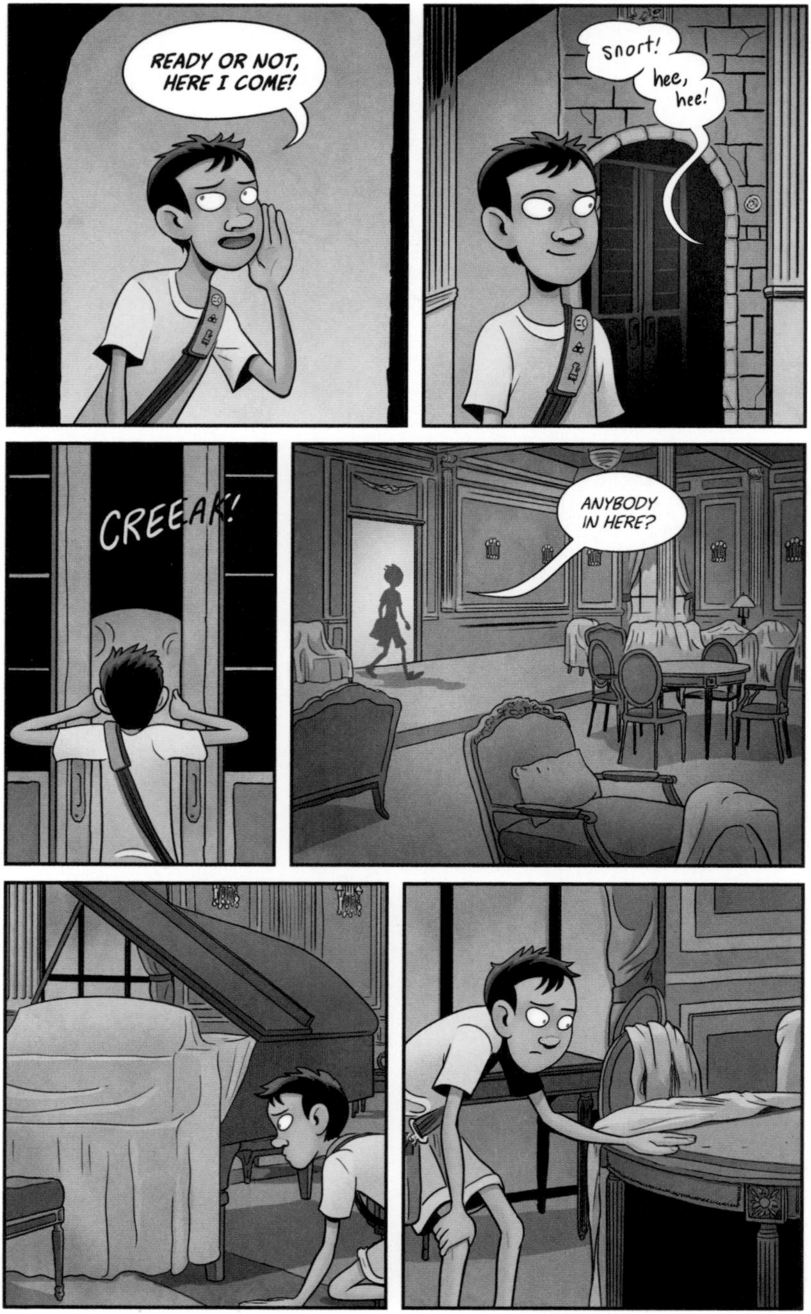
READY OR NOT, HERE I COME!
snort!
hee, hee!
CREEAK!
ANYBODY IN HERE?

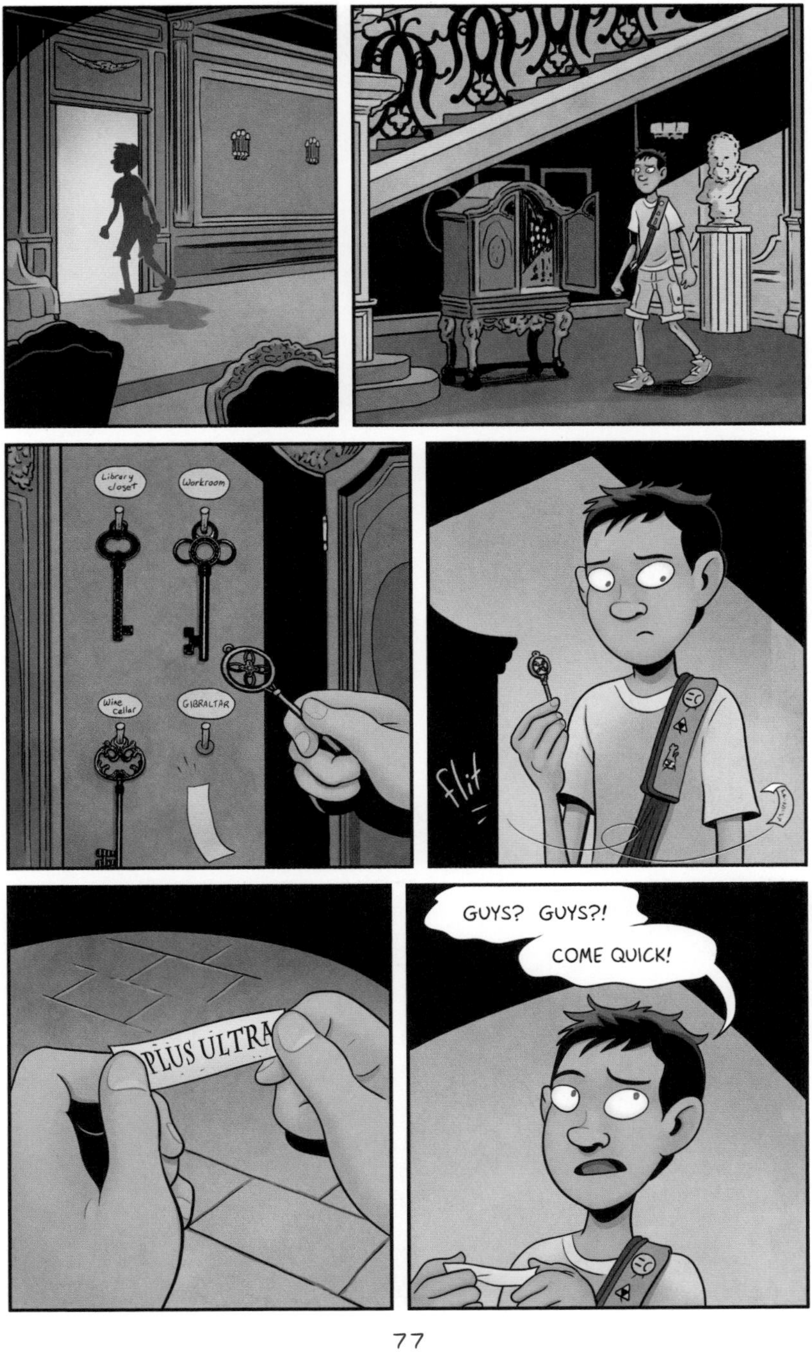
Library closet
Workroom
Wine cellar
GIBRALTAR
flit
PLUS ULTRA
GUYS? GUYS?!
COME QUICK!

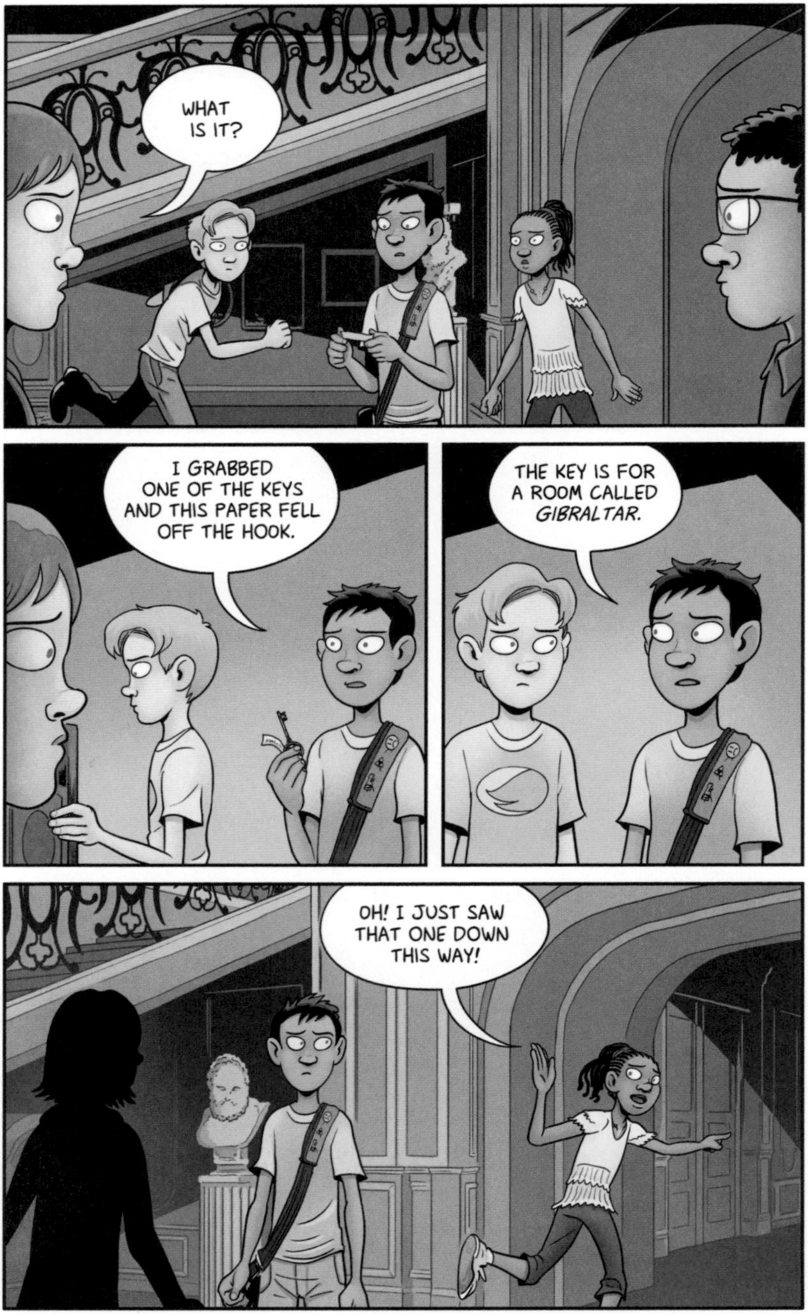
WHAT IS IT?
I GRABBED ONE OF THE KEYS AND THIS PAPER FELL OFF THE HOOK.
THE KEY IS FOR A ROOM CALLED *GIBRALTAR*.
OH! I JUST SAW THAT ONE DOWN THIS WAY!

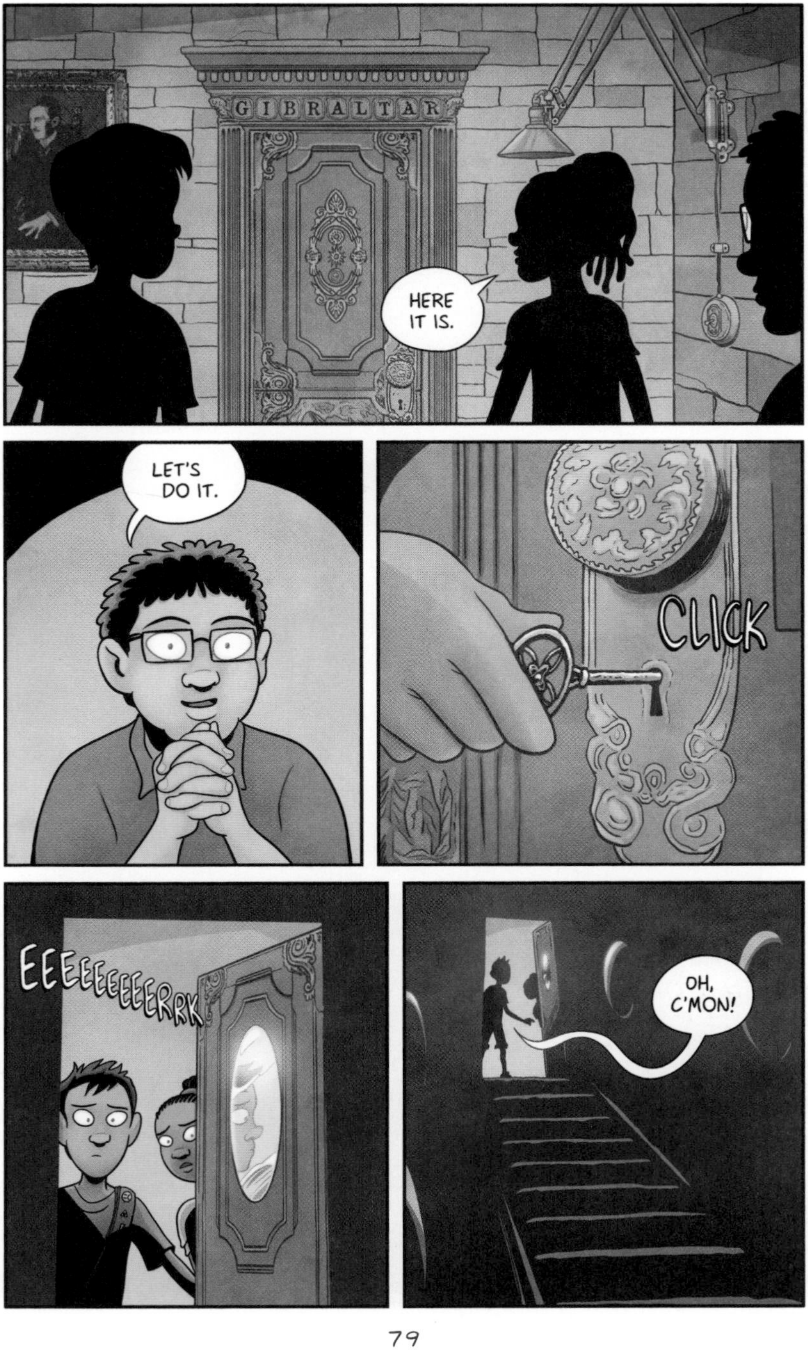
GIBRALTAR
HERE IT IS.
LET'S DO IT.
CLICK
EEEEEEEEEERRK
OH, C'MON!

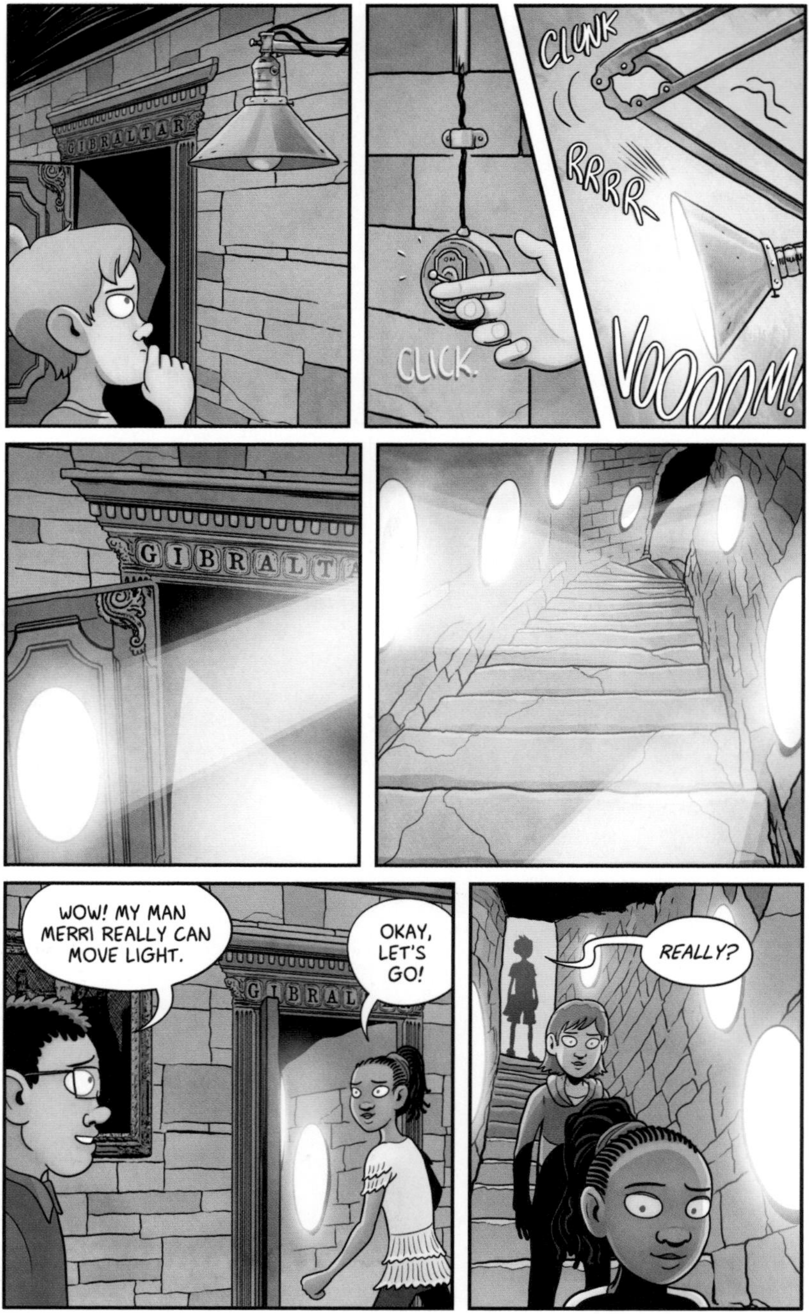
GIBRALTAR
CLICK.
CLUNK
RRRR-
VOOOOOM!
GIBRALTA
WOW! MY MAN MERRI REALLY CAN MOVE LIGHT.
OKAY, LET'S GO!
REALLY?

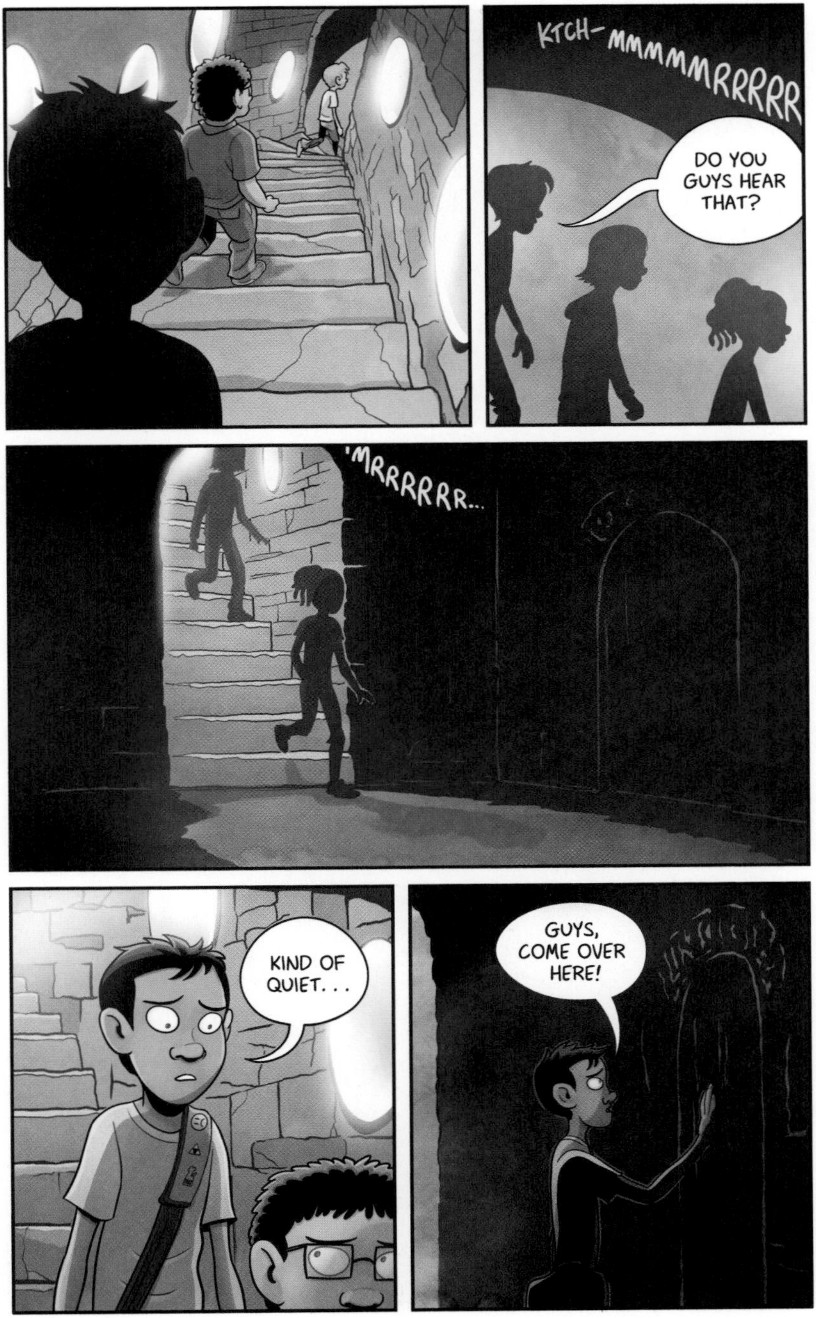
KTCH-MMMMMRRRRR
DO YOU GUYS HEAR THAT?
'MRRRRRR...
KIND OF QUIET. . .
GUYS, COME OVER HERE!

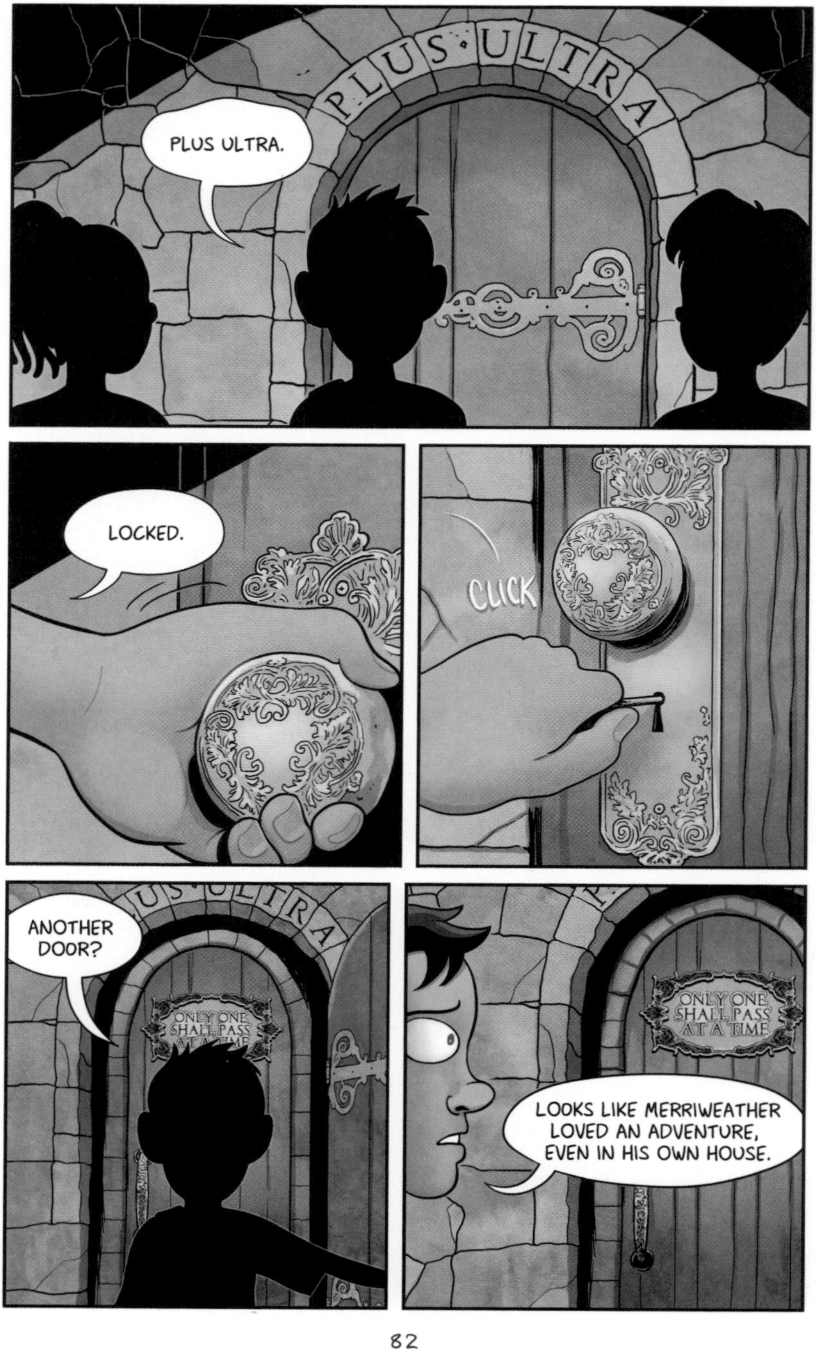
PLUS ULTRA
PLUS ULTRA.
LOCKED.
CLICK
PLUS ULTRA
ANOTHER DOOR?
ONLY ONE SHALL PASS AT A TIME
ONLY ONE SHALL PASS AT A TIME
LOOKS LIKE MERRIWEATHER LOVED AN ADVENTURE, EVEN IN HIS OWN HOUSE.

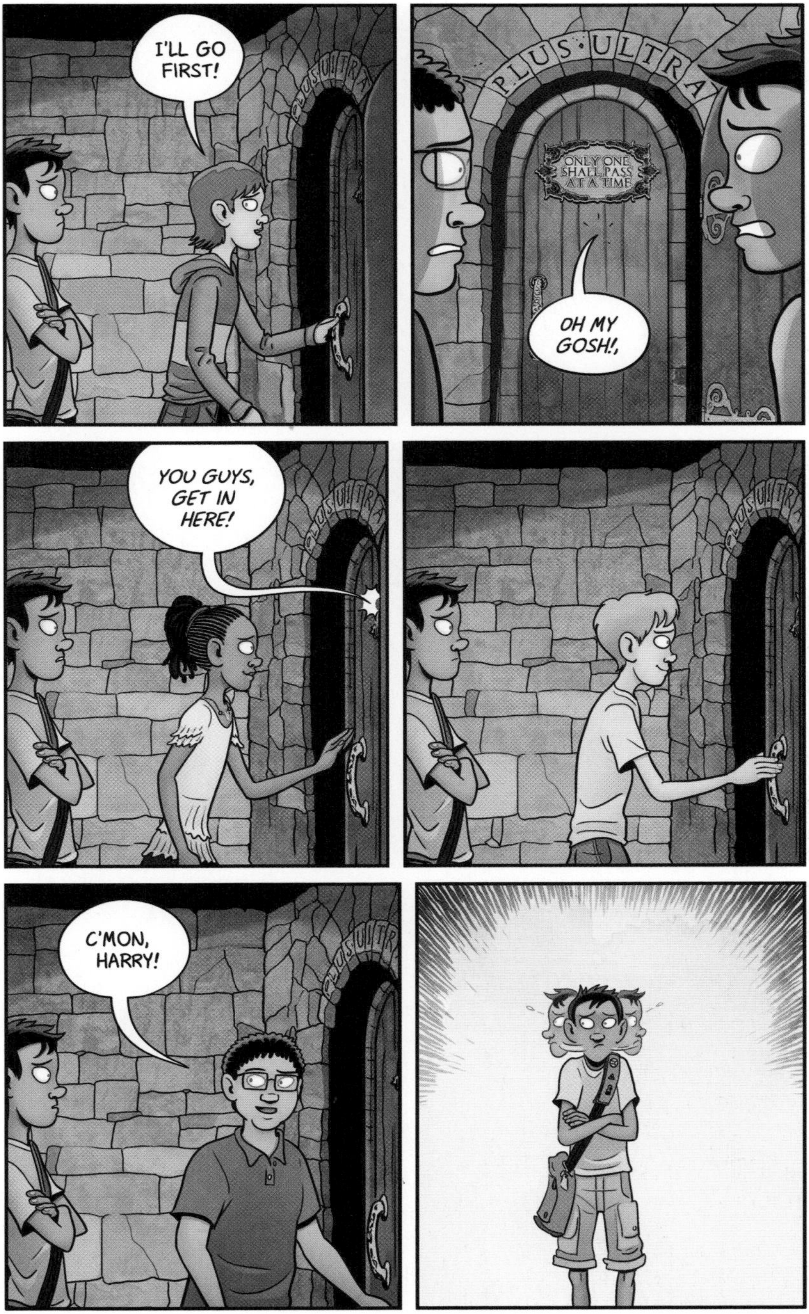
I'LL GO FIRST!
PLUS ULTRA
ONLY ONE SHALL PASS AT A TIME
OH MY GOSH!,
YOU GUYS, GET IN HERE!
C'MON, HARRY!

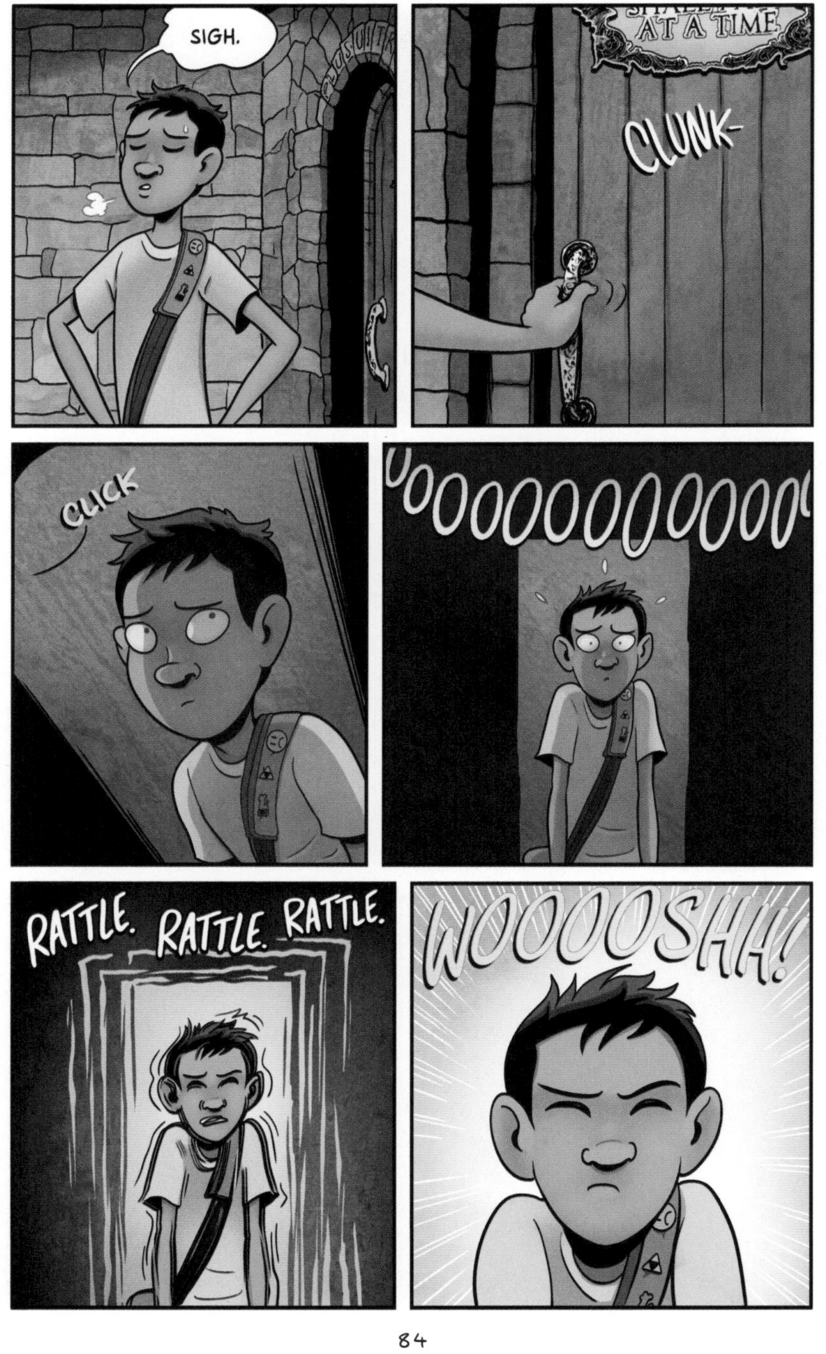
SIGH.
AT A TIME
CLUNK-
CLICK
OOOOOOOOOOOOO
RATTLE. RATTLE. RATTLE.
WOOOOSHH!

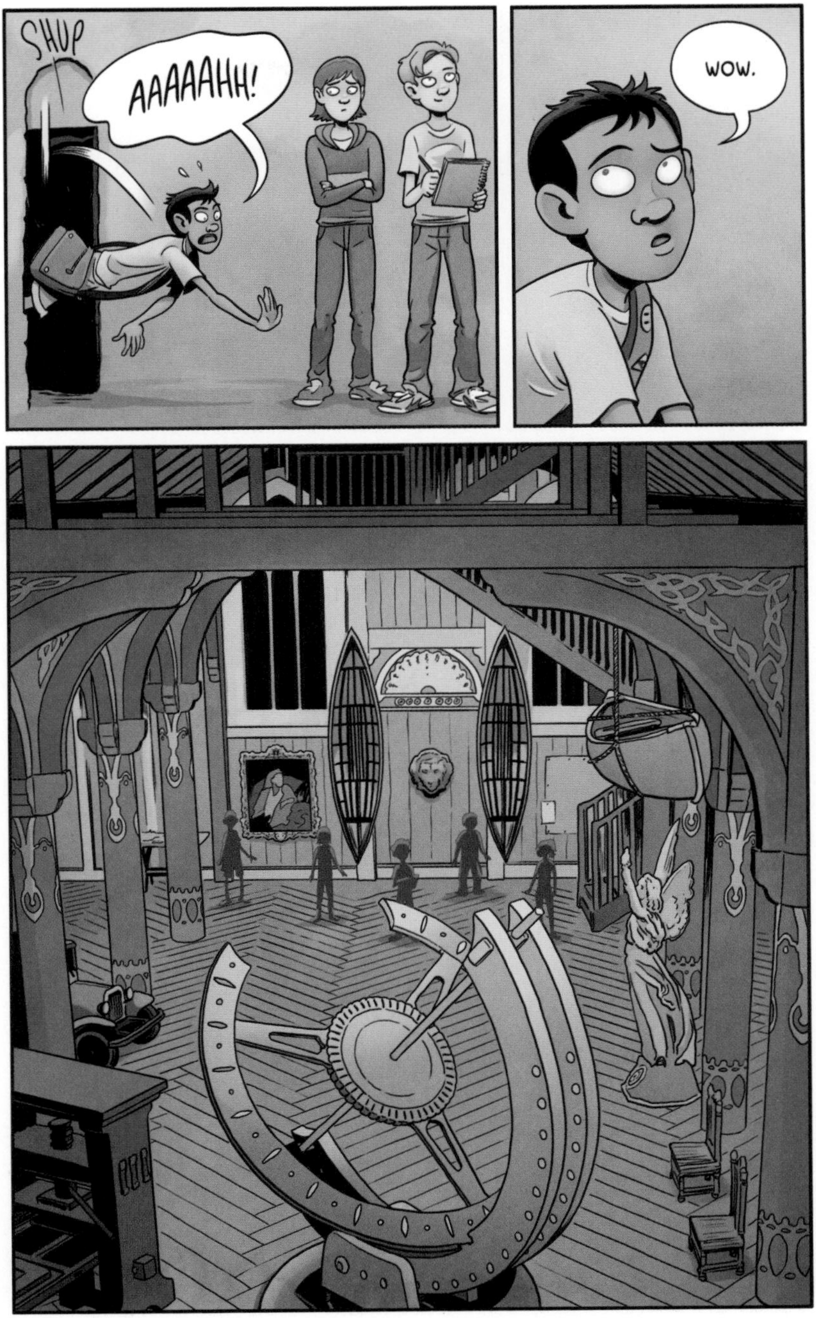
SHUP
AAAAAHH!
WOW.

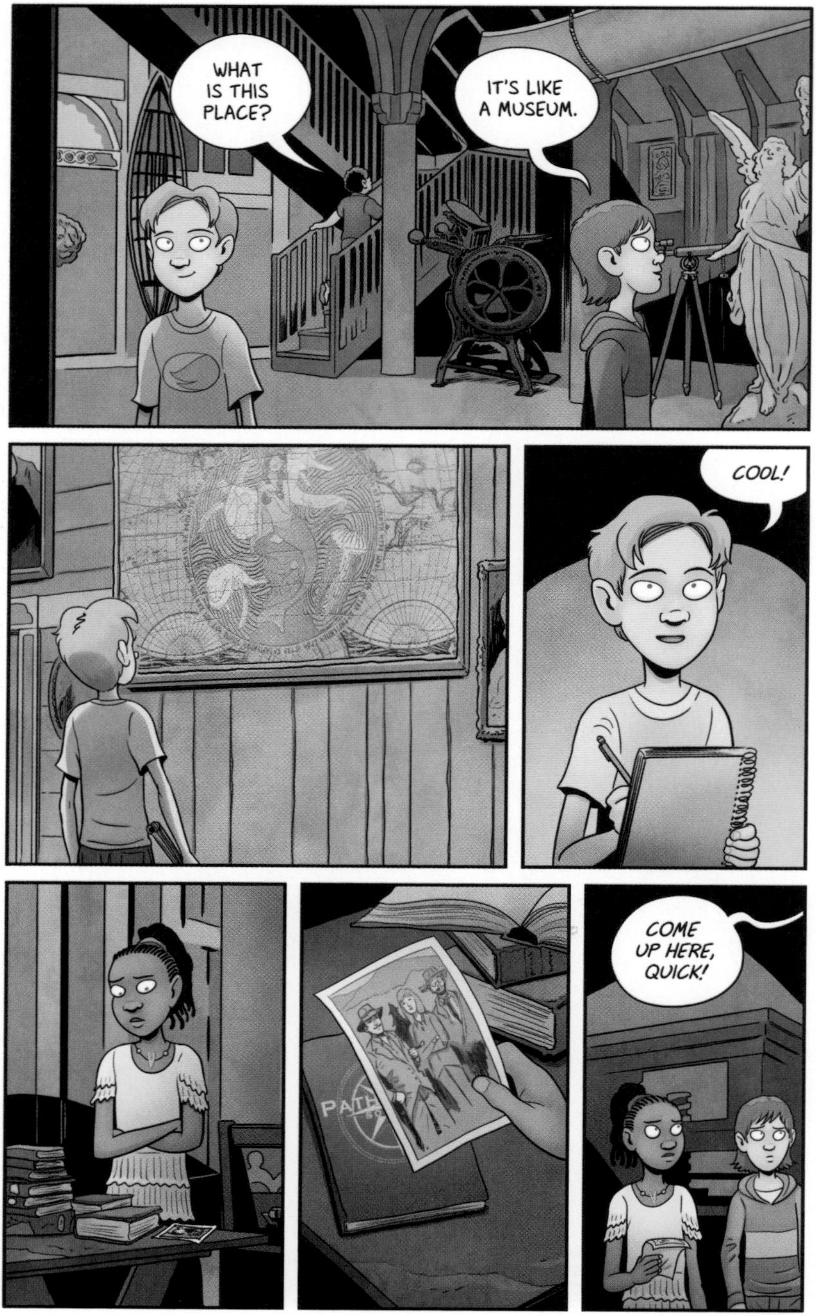
WHAT IS THIS PLACE?
IT'S LIKE A MUSEUM.
COOL!
COME UP HERE, QUICK!

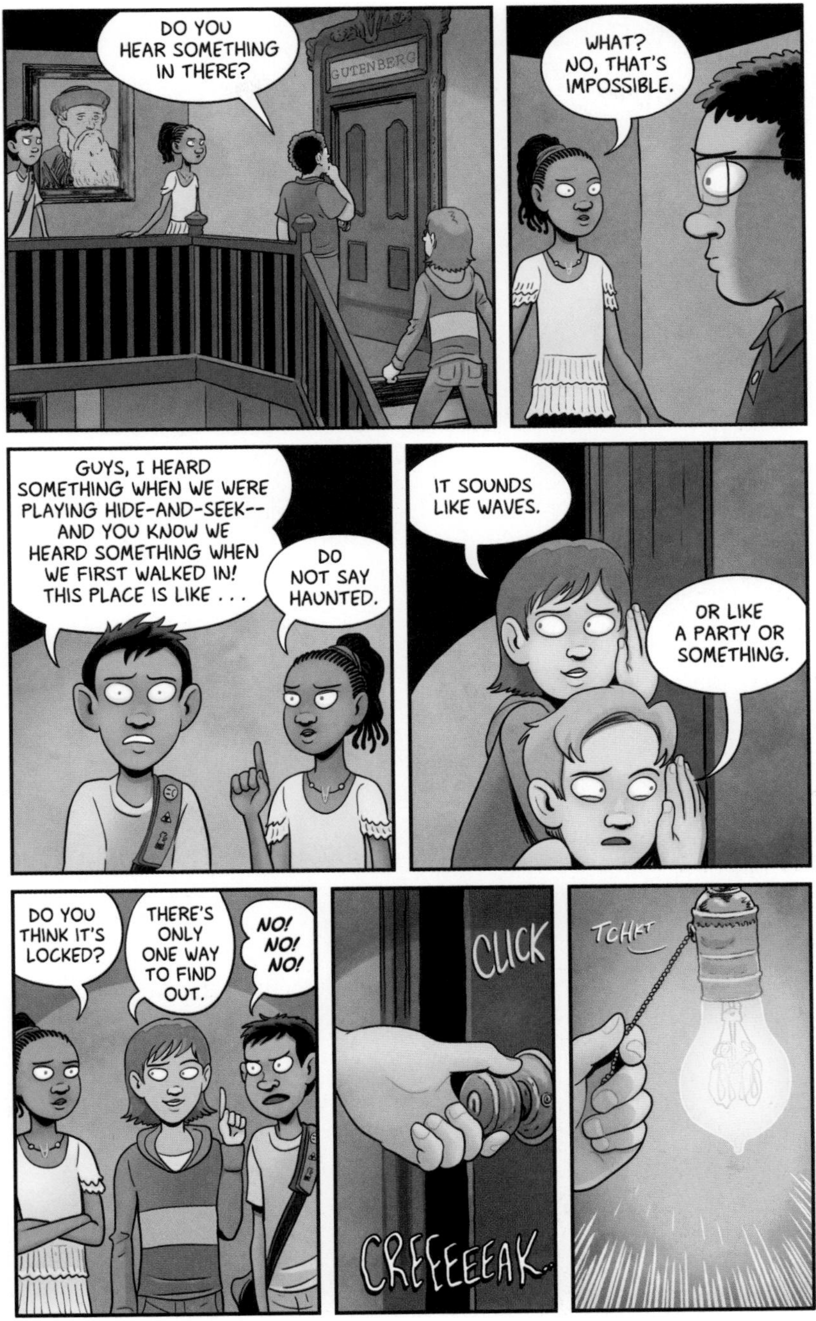
GUTENBERG
DO YOU HEAR SOMETHING IN THERE?
WHAT? NO, THAT'S IMPOSSIBLE.
GUYS, I HEARD SOMETHING WHEN WE WERE PLAYING HIDE-AND-SEEK-- AND YOU KNOW WE HEARD SOMETHING WHEN WE FIRST WALKED IN! THIS PLACE IS LIKE . . .
DO NOT SAY HAUNTED.
IT SOUNDS LIKE WAVES.
OR LIKE A PARTY OR SOMETHING.
DO YOU THINK IT'S LOCKED?
THERE'S ONLY ONE WAY TO FIND OUT.
NO! NO! NO!
CLICK
CREEEEEAK..
TCHKT

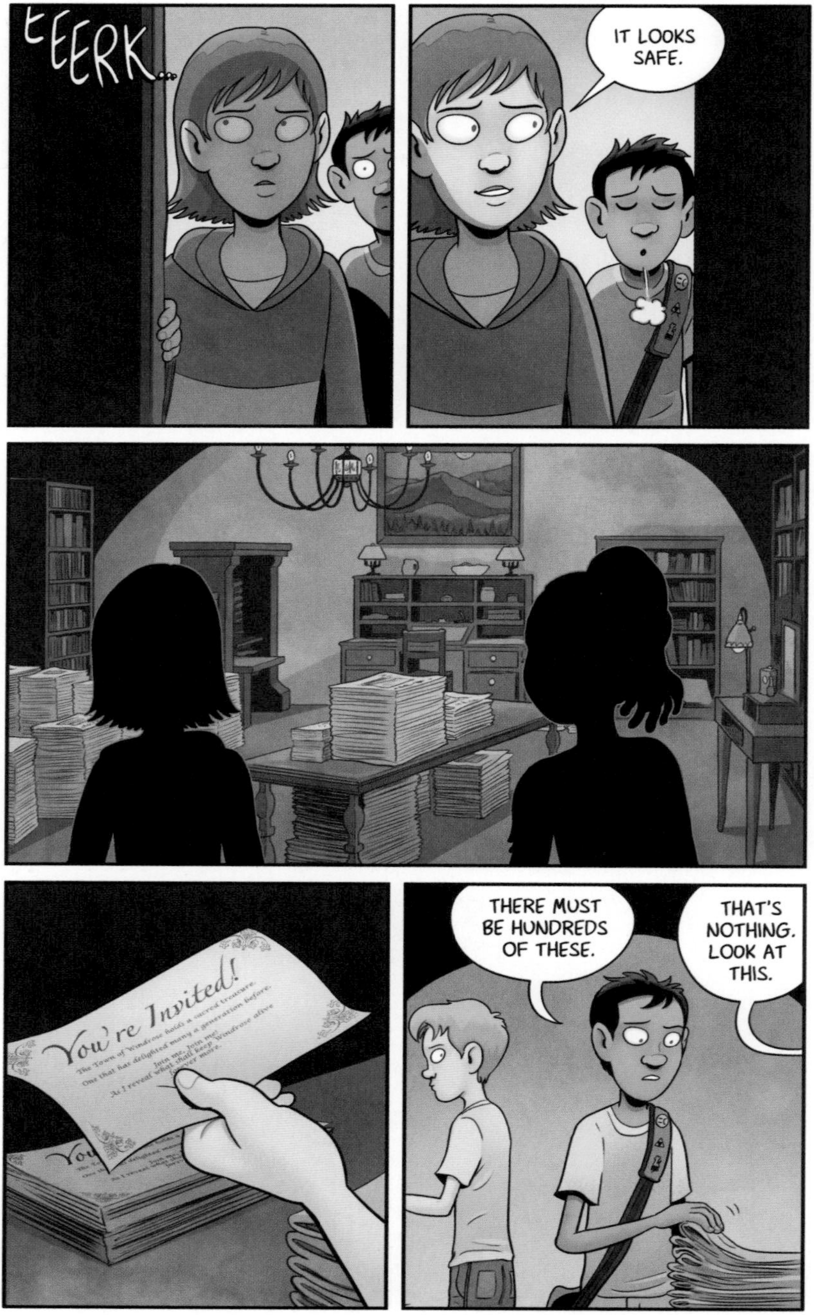
EEERK...
IT LOOKS SAFE.
You're Invited!
The Town of Windrose holds a sacred treasure,
One that has delighted many a generation before.
Join me, join me!
As I reveal what shall keep Windrose alive
forever more.
THERE MUST BE HUNDREDS OF THESE.
THAT'S NOTHING. LOOK AT THIS.

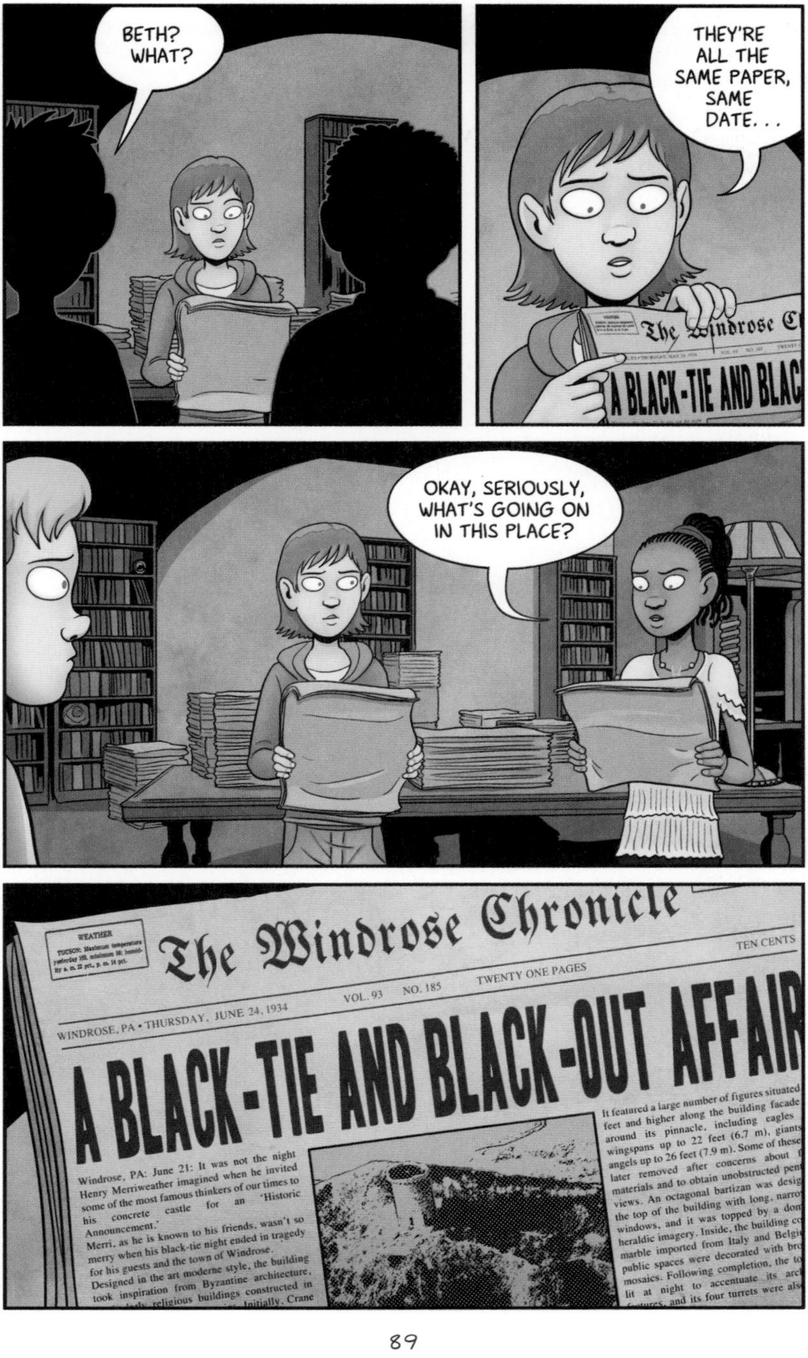
BETH? WHAT?
THEY'RE ALL THE SAME PAPER, SAME DATE. . .
The Windrose Ch
A BLACK-TIE AND BLAC
OKAY, SERIOUSLY, WHAT'S GOING ON IN THIS PLACE?
WEATHER
The Windrose Chronicle
TEN CENTS
TWENTY ONE PAGES
VOL. 93 NO. 185
WINDROSE, PA • THURSDAY, JUNE 24, 1934
A BLACK-TIE AND BLACK-OUT AFFAIR
Windrose, PA: June 21: It was not the night Henry Merriweather imagined when he invited some of the most famous thinkers of our times to his concrete castle for an 'Historic Announcement.'
Merri, as he is known to his friends, wasn't so merry when his black-tie night ended in tragedy for his guests and the town of Windrose.
Designed in the art moderne style, the building took inspiration from Byzantine architecture, religious buildings constructed in Initially, Crane
It featured a large number of figures situated feet and higher along the building facade around its pinnacle, including eagles wingspans up to 22 feet (6.7 m), giants angels up to 26 feet (7.9 m). Some of these later removed after concerns about materials and to obtain unobstructed views. An octagonal bartizan was the top of the building with long, windows, and it was topped by a heraldic imagery. Inside, the building marble imported from Italy and public spaces were decorated with mosaics. Following completion, the lit at night to accentuate its and its four turrets were

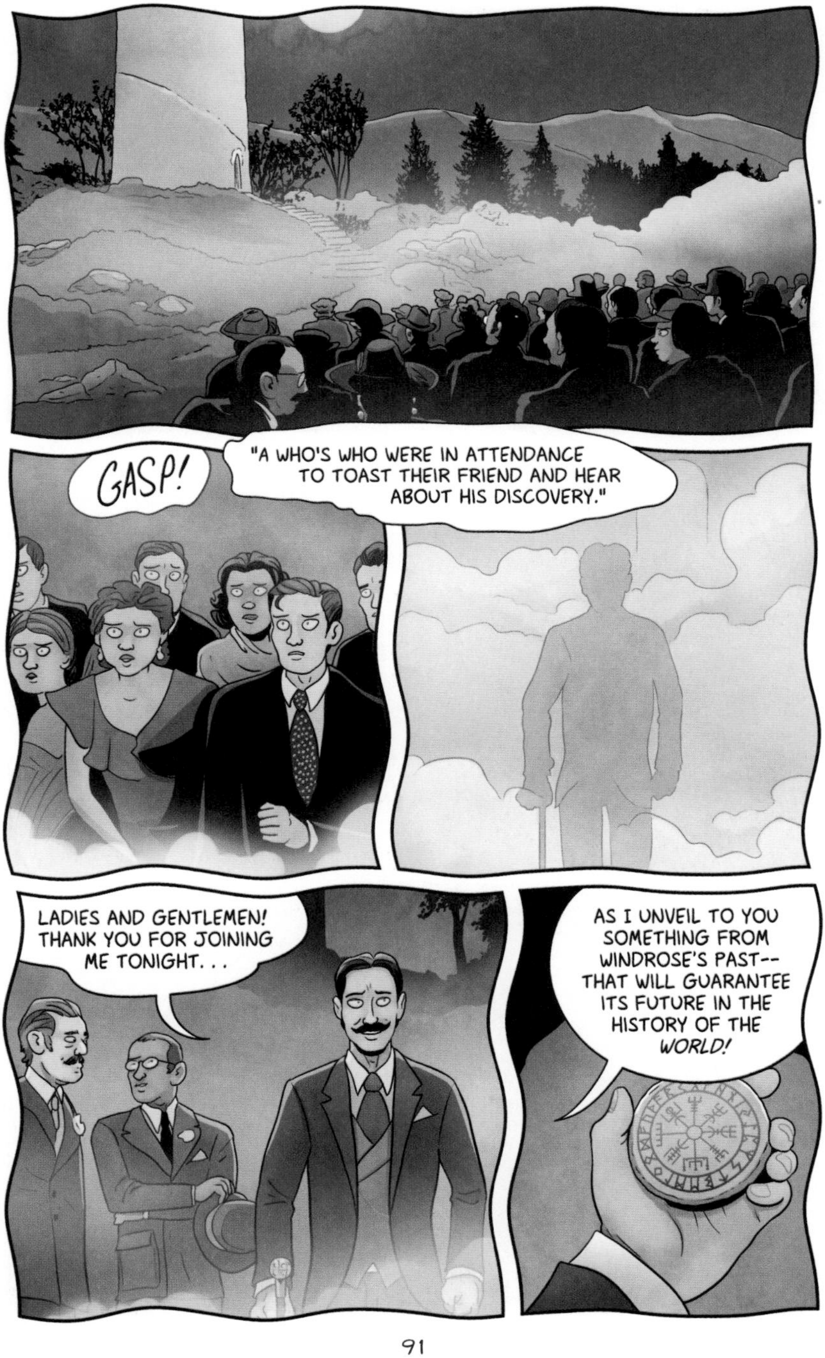
GASP!
"A WHO'S WHO WERE IN ATTENDANCE TO TOAST THEIR FRIEND AND HEAR ABOUT HIS DISCOVERY."
LADIES AND GENTLEMEN! THANK YOU FOR JOINING ME TONIGHT. . .
AS I UNVEIL TO YOU SOMETHING FROM WINDROSE'S PAST-- THAT WILL GUARANTEE ITS FUTURE IN THE HISTORY OF THE *WORLD!*

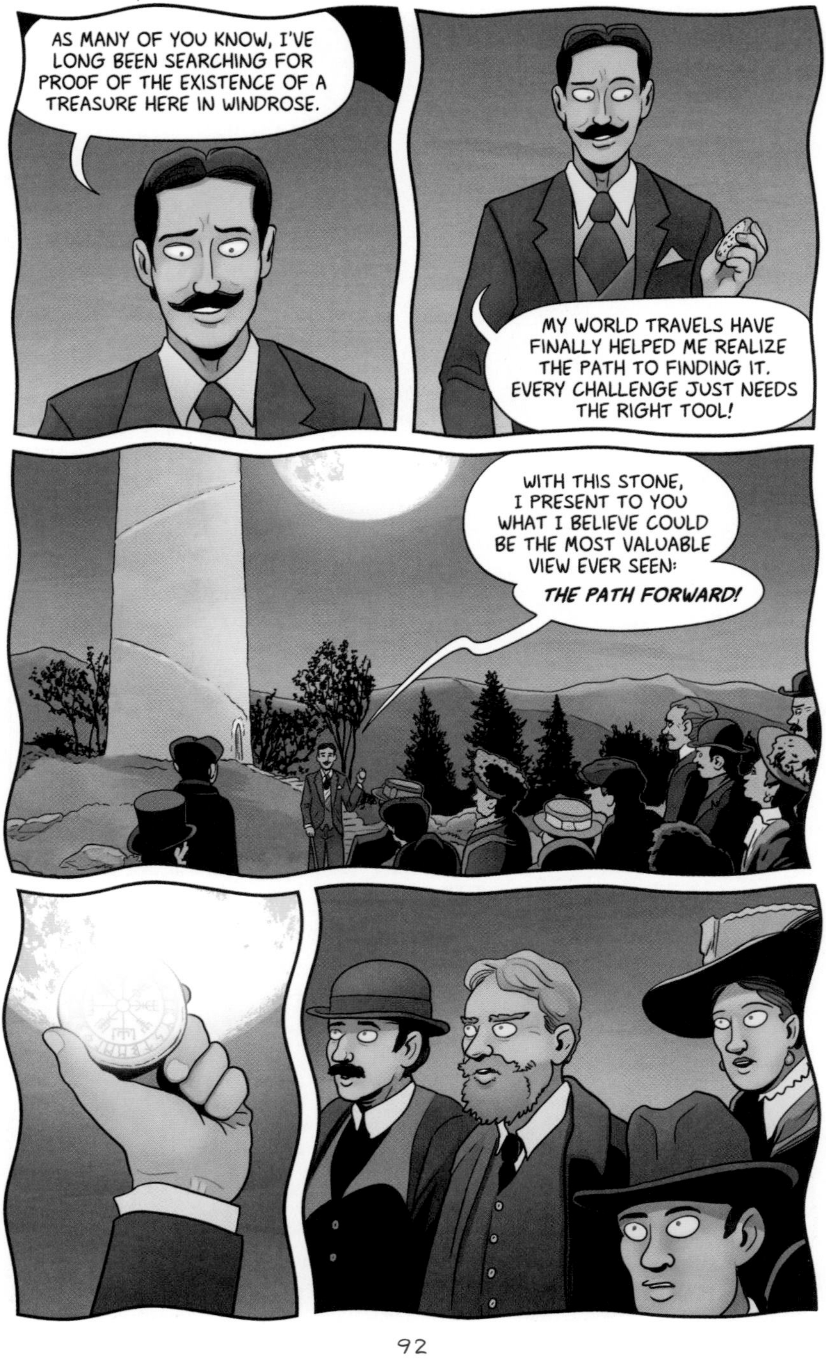
AS MANY OF YOU KNOW, I'VE LONG BEEN SEARCHING FOR PROOF OF THE EXISTENCE OF A TREASURE HERE IN WINDROSE.
MY WORLD TRAVELS HAVE FINALLY HELPED ME REALIZE THE PATH TO FINDING IT. EVERY CHALLENGE JUST NEEDS THE RIGHT TOOL!
WITH THIS STONE, I PRESENT TO YOU WHAT I BELIEVE COULD BE THE MOST VALUABLE VIEW EVER SEEN: *THE PATH FORWARD!*

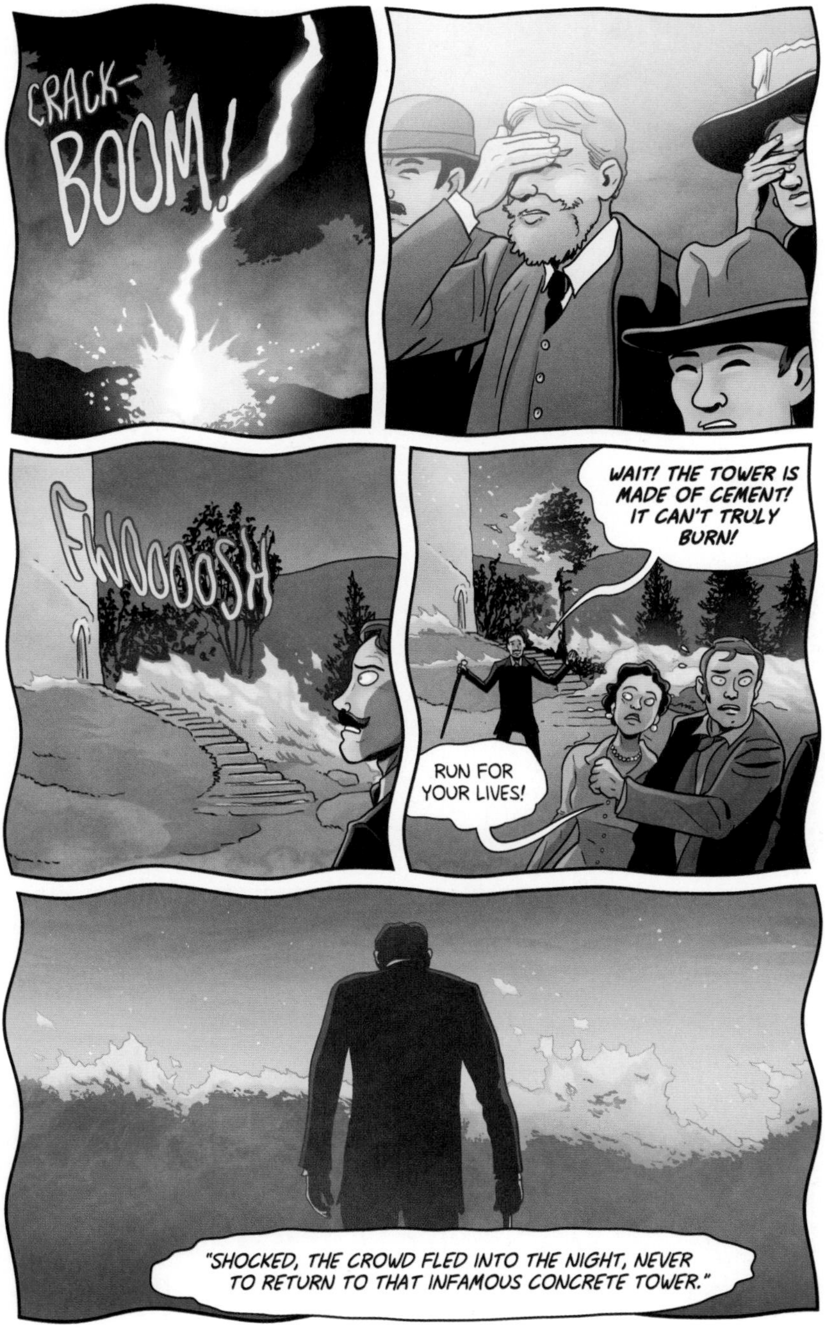
CRACK-
BOOM!
FWOOOOSH
WAIT! THE TOWER IS MADE OF CEMENT! IT CAN'T TRULY BURN!
RUN FOR YOUR LIVES!
"SHOCKED, THE CROWD FLED INTO THE NIGHT, NEVER TO RETURN TO THAT INFAMOUS CONCRETE TOWER."

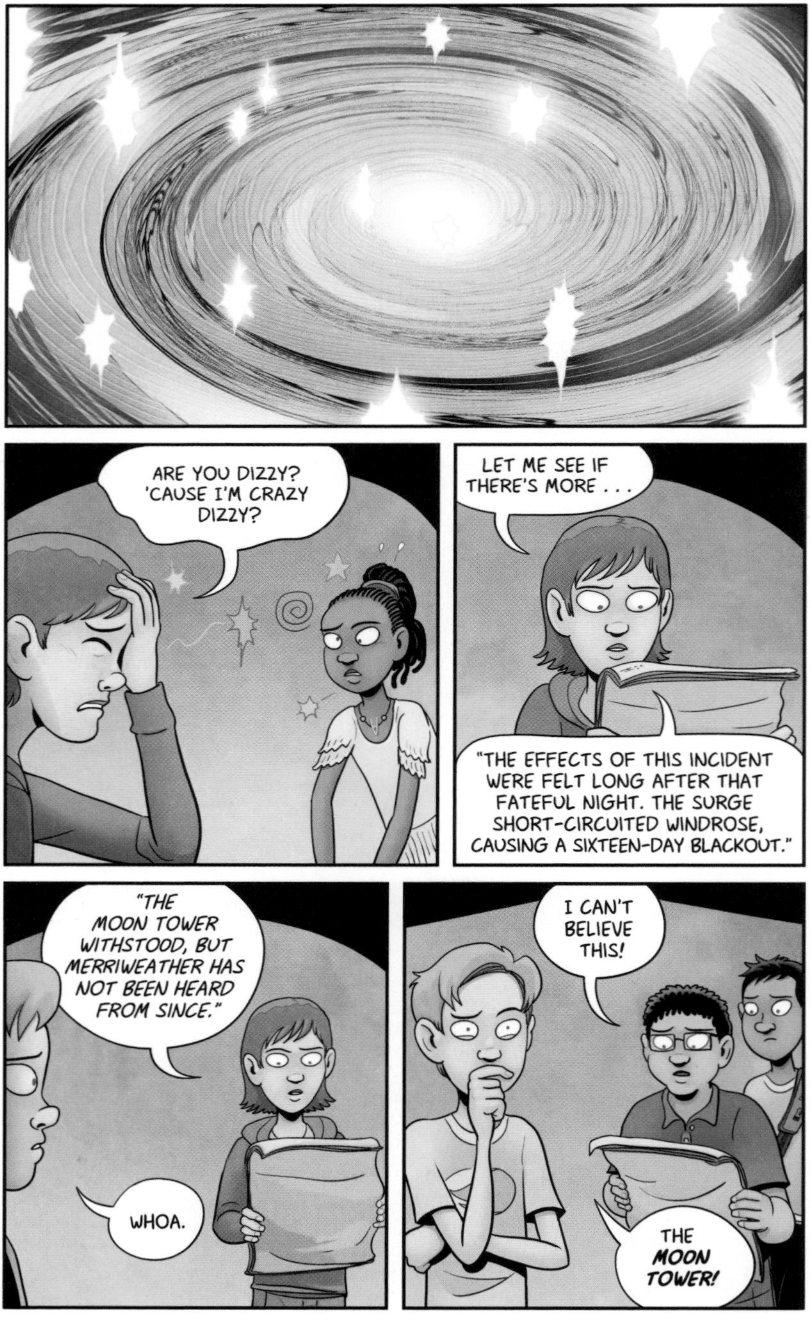
ARE YOU DIZZY? 'CAUSE I'M CRAZY DIZZY?
LET ME SEE IF THERE'S MORE . . .
"THE EFFECTS OF THIS INCIDENT WERE FELT LONG AFTER THAT FATEFUL NIGHT. THE SURGE SHORT-CIRCUITED WINDROSE, CAUSING A SIXTEEN-DAY BLACKOUT."
"THE MOON TOWER WITHSTOOD, BUT MERRIWEATHER HAS NOT BEEN HEARD FROM SINCE."
WHOA.
I CAN'T BELIEVE THIS!
THE MOON TOWER!

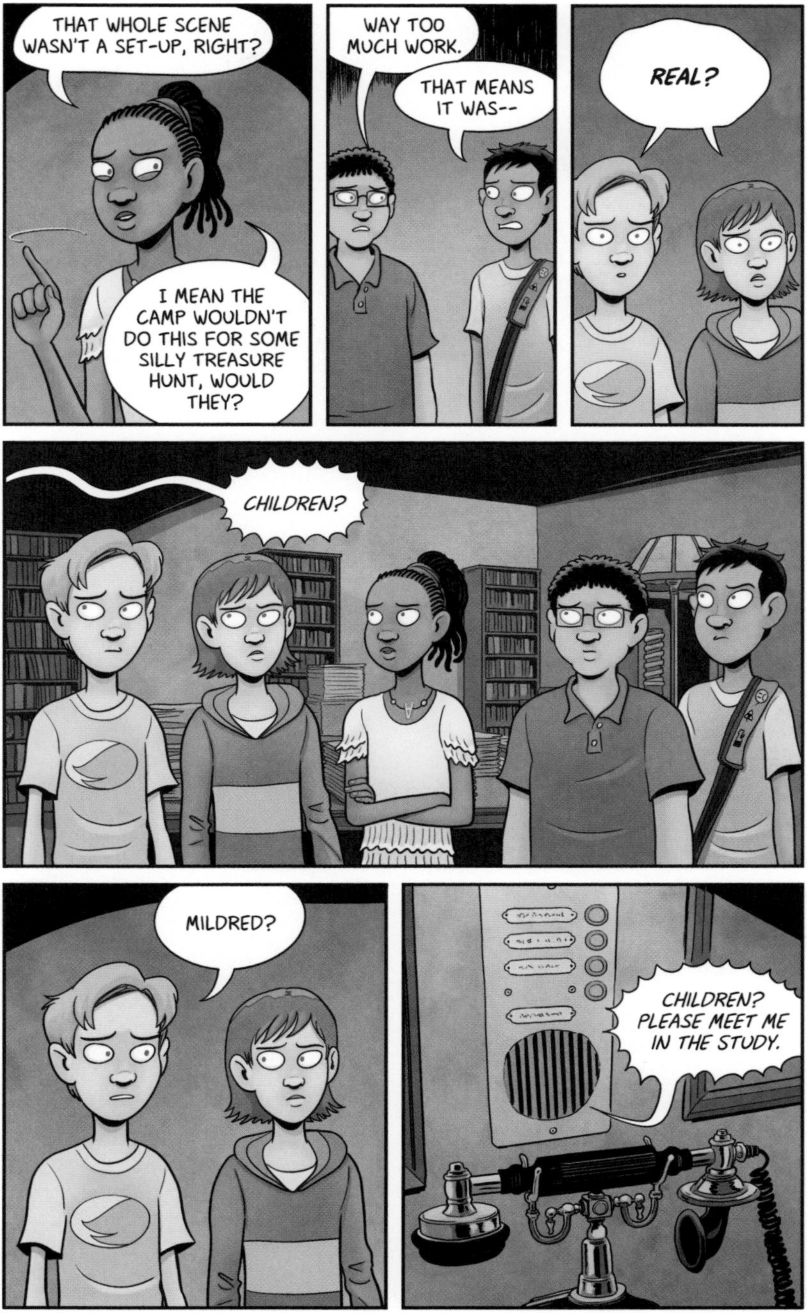
THAT WHOLE SCENE WASN'T A SET-UP, RIGHT?
I MEAN THE CAMP WOULDN'T DO THIS FOR SOME SILLY TREASURE HUNT, WOULD THEY?
WAY TOO MUCH WORK.
THAT MEANS IT WAS--
REAL?
CHILDREN?
MILDRED?
CHILDREN? PLEASE MEET ME IN THE STUDY.

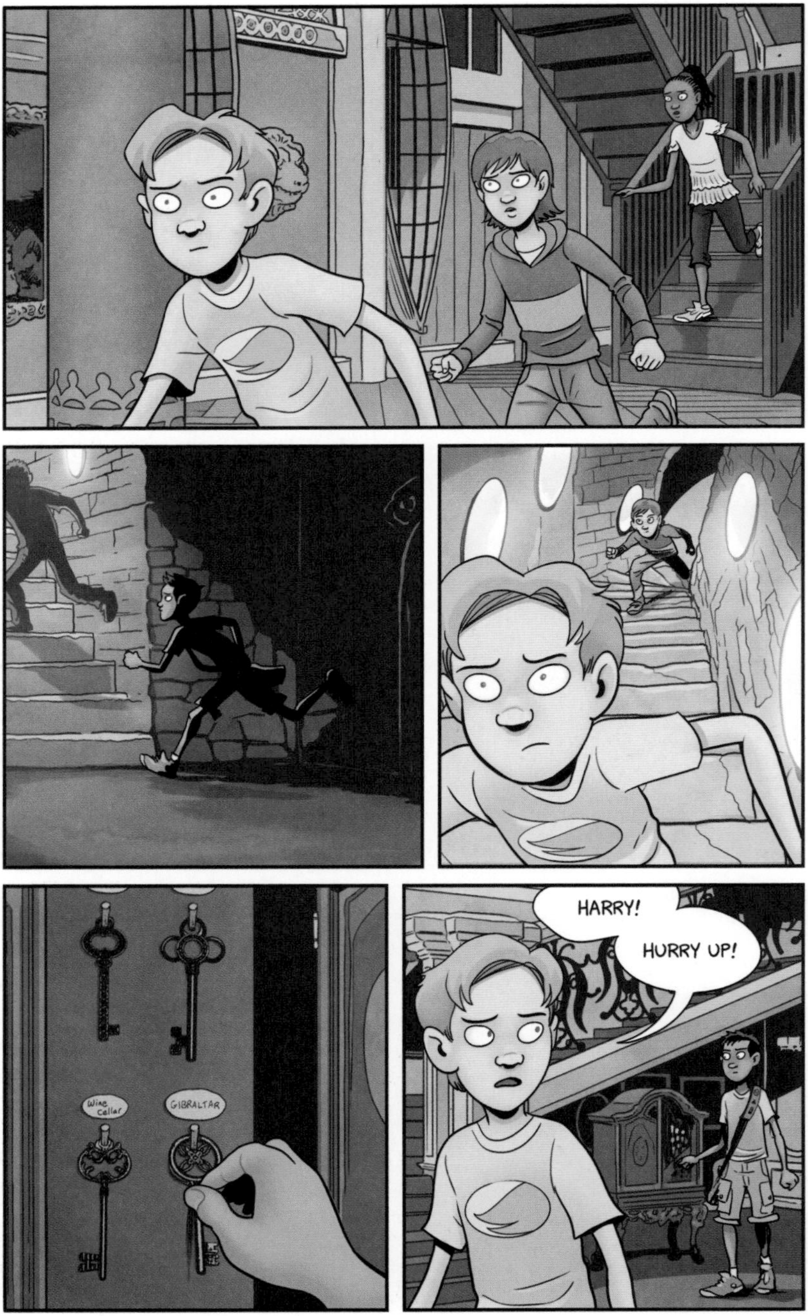
Wine Cellar
GIBRALTAR
HARRY!
HURRY UP!

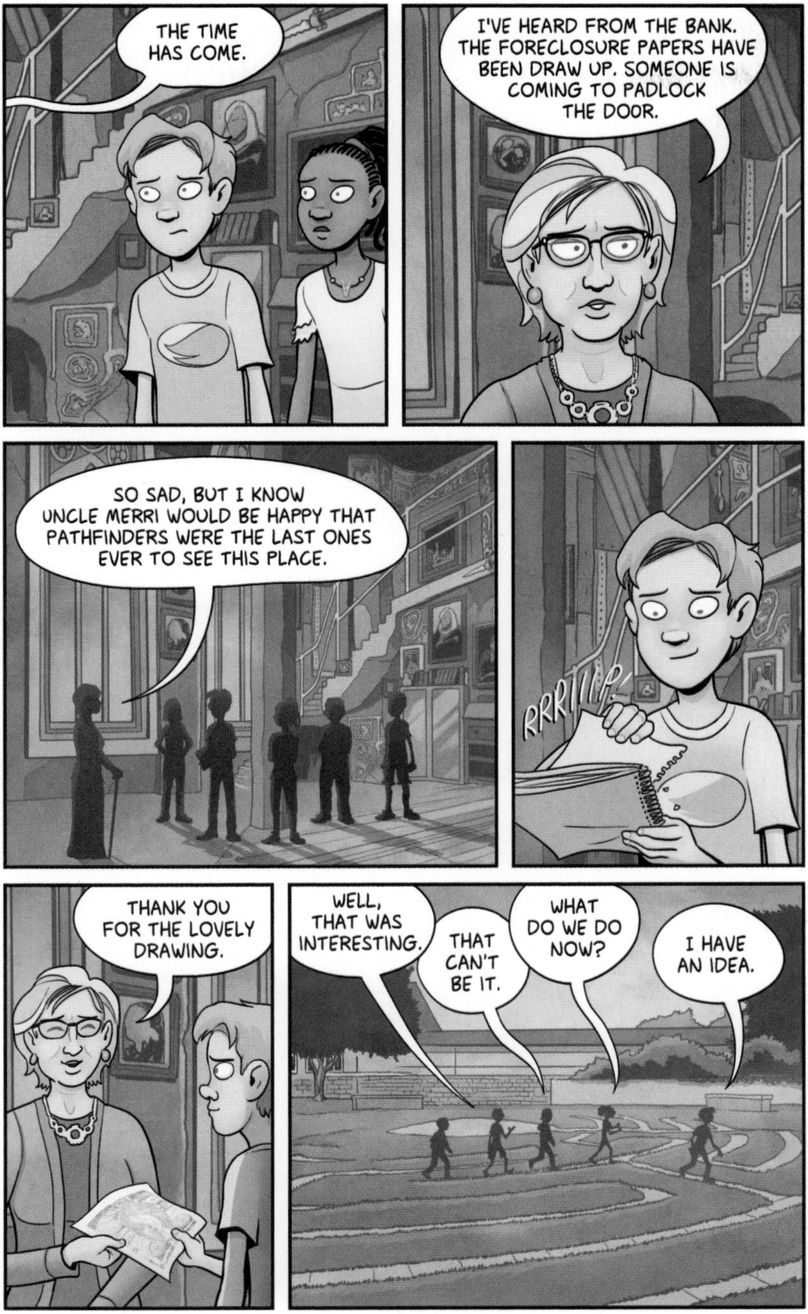
THE TIME HAS COME.
I'VE HEARD FROM THE BANK. THE FORECLOSURE PAPERS HAVE BEEN DRAW UP. SOMEONE IS COMING TO PADLOCK THE DOOR.
SO SAD, BUT I KNOW UNCLE MERRI WOULD BE HAPPY THAT PATHFINDERS WERE THE LAST ONES EVER TO SEE THIS PLACE.
RRRIIIP!
THANK YOU FOR THE LOVELY DRAWING.
WELL, THAT WAS INTERESTING.
THAT CAN'T BE IT.
WHAT DO WE DO NOW?
I HAVE AN IDEA.

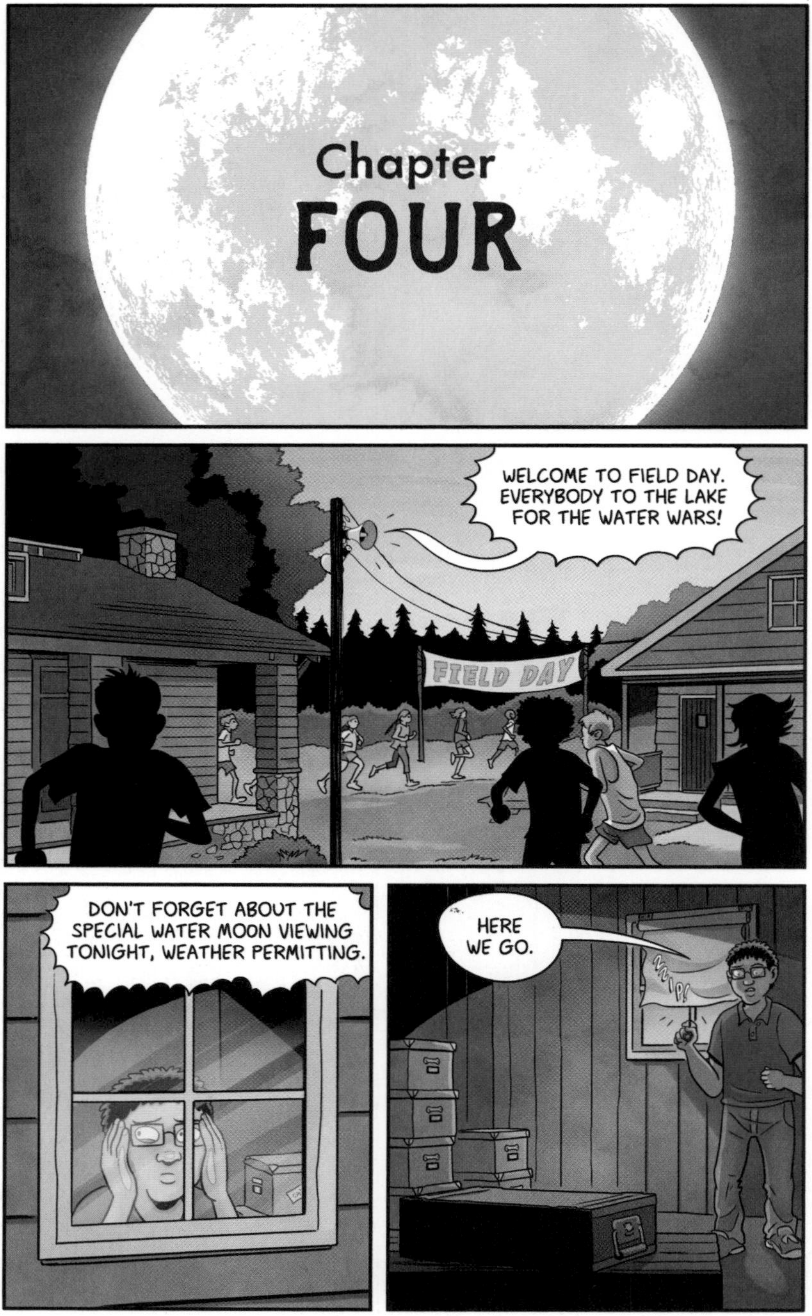
Chapter
FOUR
FIELD DAY
WELCOME TO FIELD DAY. EVERYBODY TO THE LAKE FOR THE WATER WARS!
DON'T FORGET ABOUT THE SPECIAL WATER MOON VIEWING TONIGHT, WEATHER PERMITTING.
HERE WE GO.
WHIP!

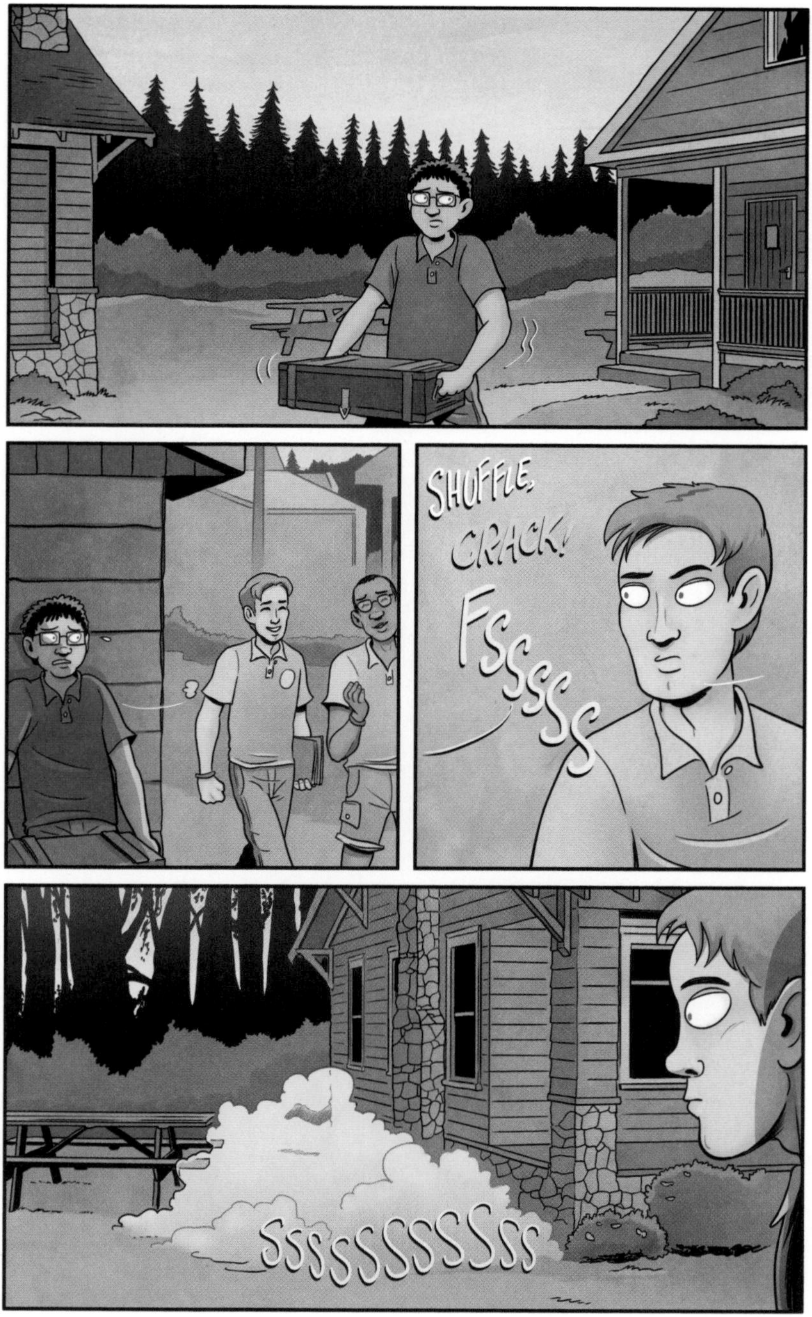
SHUFFLE,
CRACK!
FSSSSS
SSSSSSSSSSSS

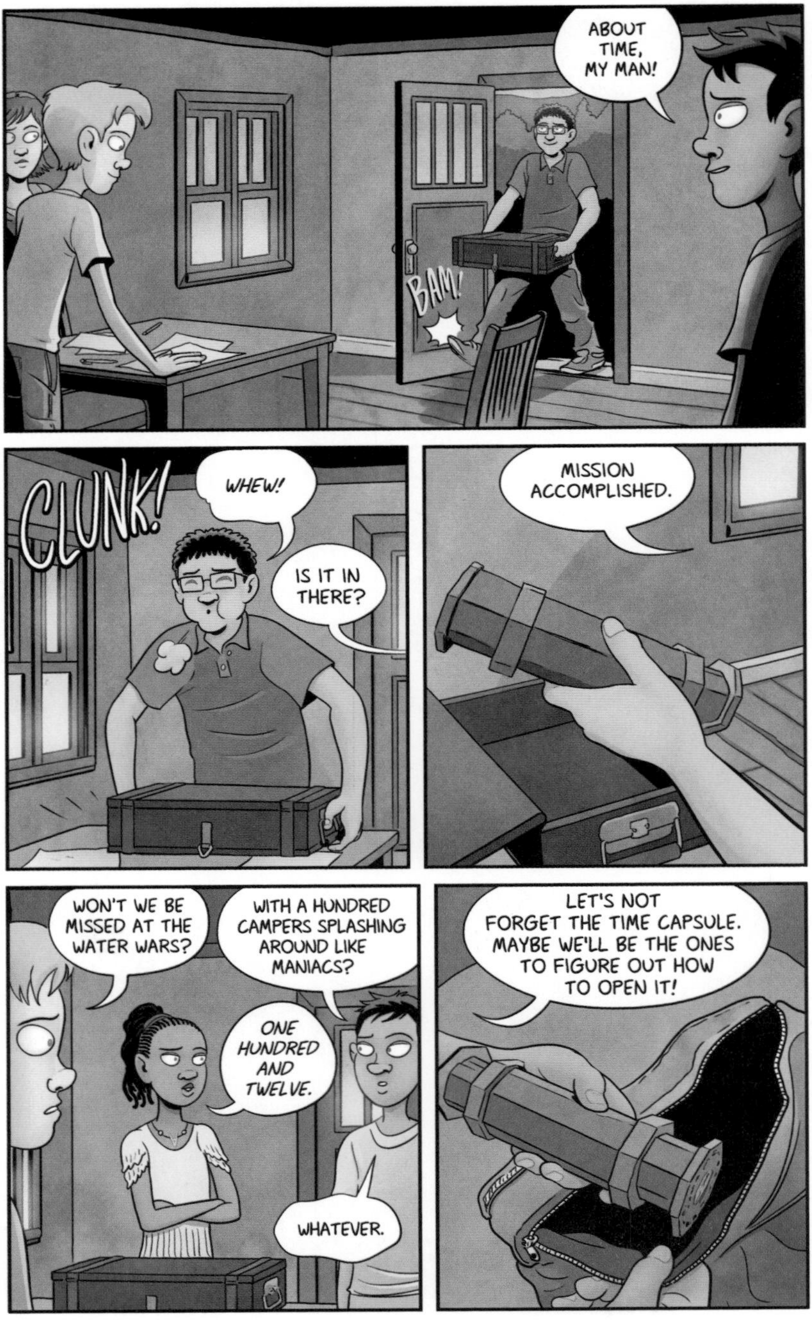
ABOUT TIME, MY MAN!
BAM!
CLUNK!
WHEW!
IS IT IN THERE?
MISSION ACCOMPLISHED.
WON'T WE BE MISSED AT THE WATER WARS?
WITH A HUNDRED CAMPERS SPLASHING AROUND LIKE MANIACS?
ONE HUNDRED AND TWELVE.
WHATEVER.
LET'S NOT FORGET THE TIME CAPSULE. MAYBE WE'LL BE THE ONES TO FIGURE OUT HOW TO OPEN IT!

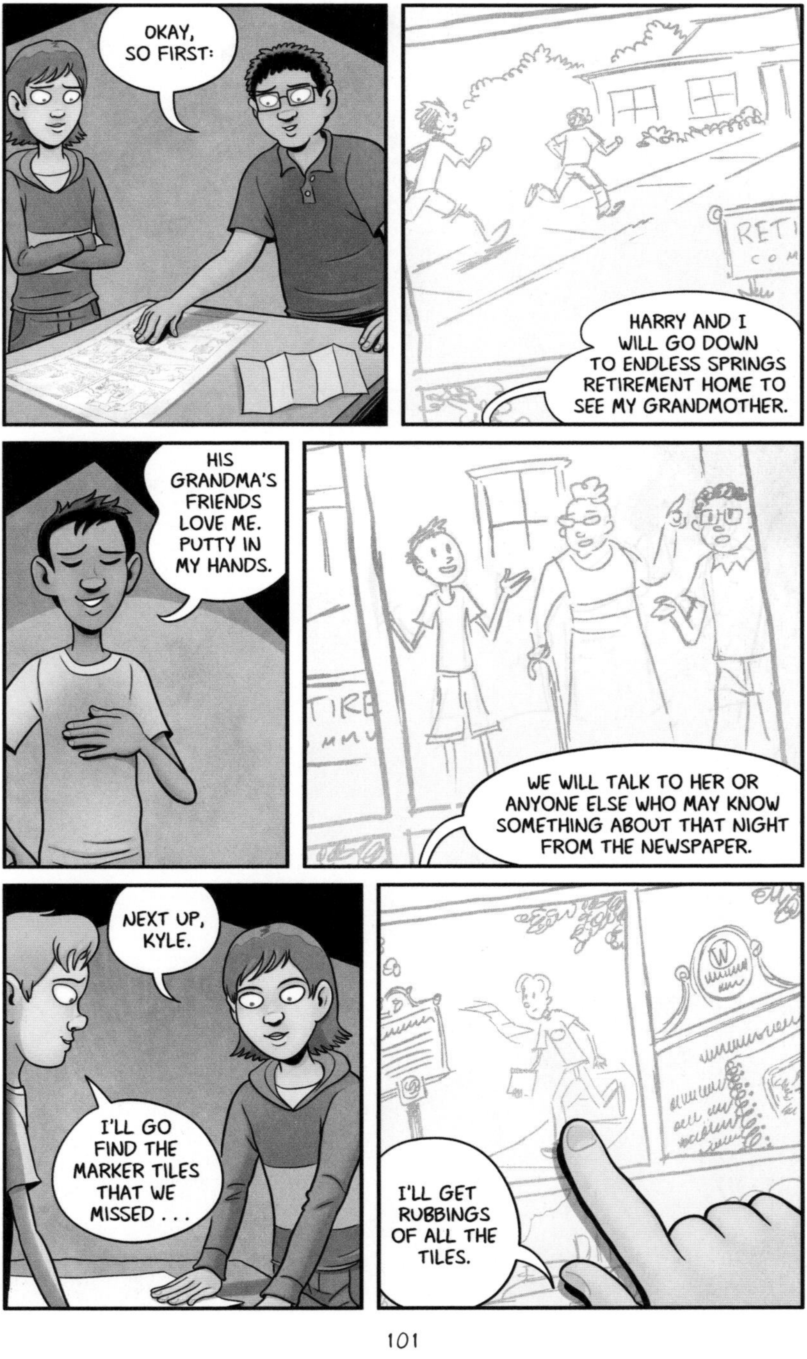
OKAY, SO FIRST:
HARRY AND I WILL GO DOWN TO ENDLESS SPRINGS RETIREMENT HOME TO SEE MY GRANDMOTHER.
RETI
COM
HIS GRANDMA'S FRIENDS LOVE ME. PUTTY IN MY HANDS.
TIRE
WE WILL TALK TO HER OR ANYONE ELSE WHO MAY KNOW SOMETHING ABOUT THAT NIGHT FROM THE NEWSPAPER.
NEXT UP, KYLE.
I'LL GO FIND THE MARKER TILES THAT WE MISSED . . .
I'LL GET RUBBINGS OF ALL THE TILES.

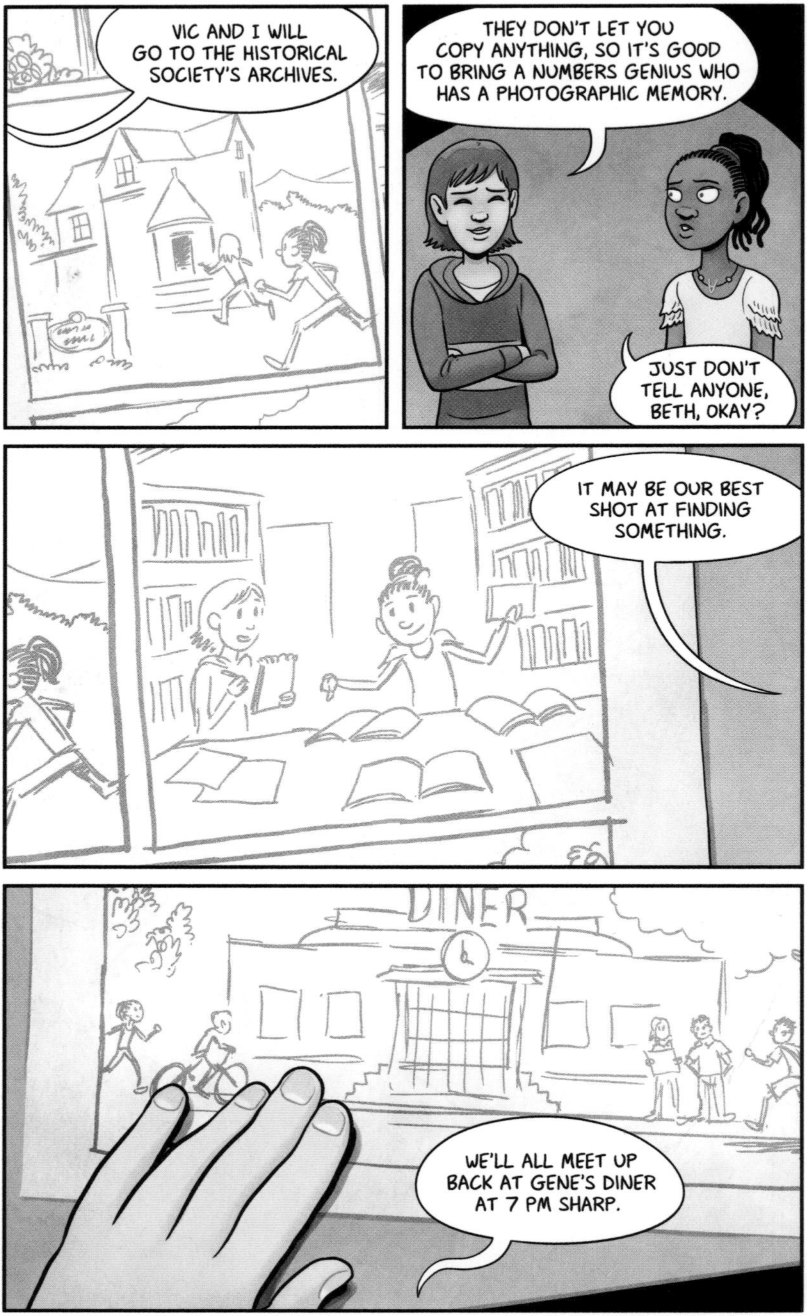
VIC AND I WILL GO TO THE HISTORICAL SOCIETY'S ARCHIVES.
THEY DON'T LET YOU COPY ANYTHING, SO IT'S GOOD TO BRING A NUMBERS GENIUS WHO HAS A PHOTOGRAPHIC MEMORY.
JUST DON'T TELL ANYONE, BETH, OKAY?
IT MAY BE OUR BEST SHOT AT FINDING SOMETHING.
DINER
WE'LL ALL MEET UP BACK AT GENE'S DINER AT 7 PM SHARP.

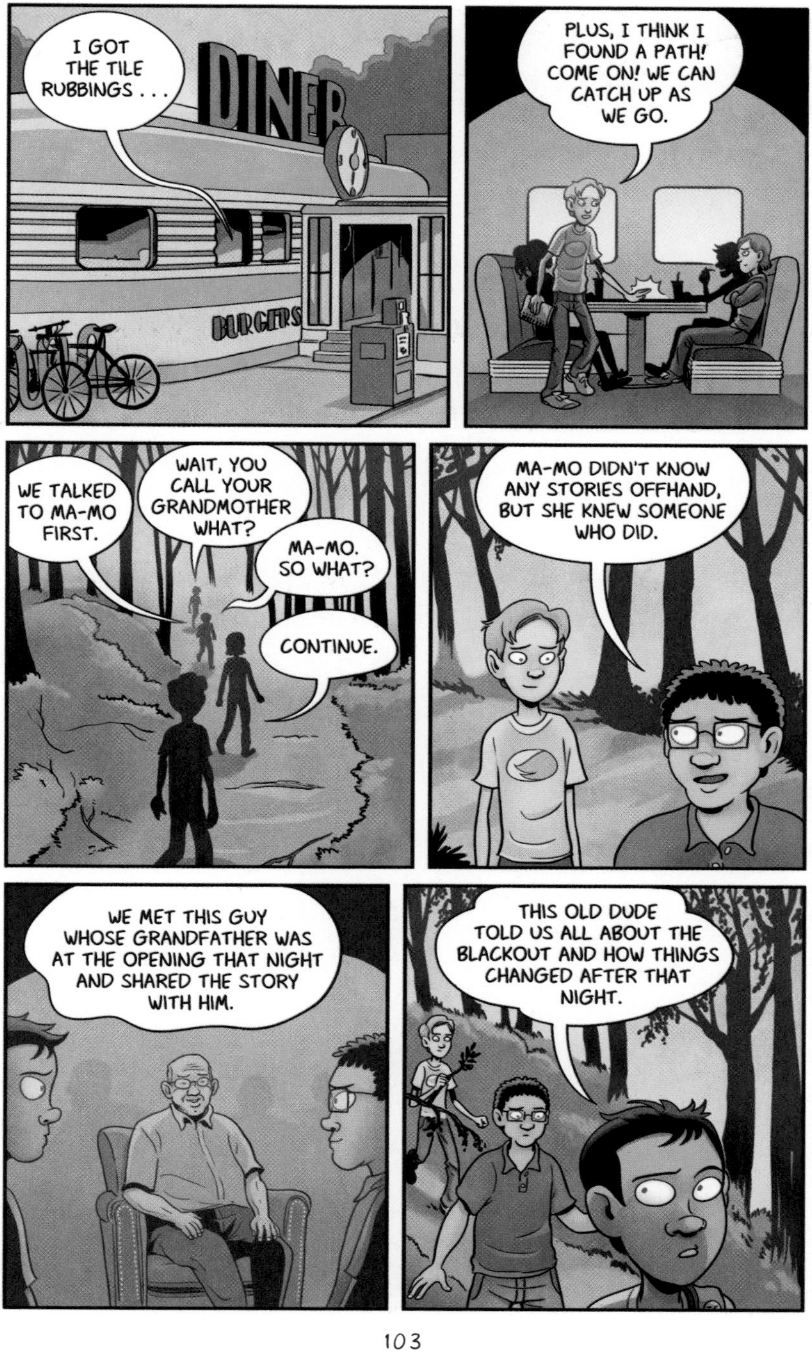

DINER
I GOT THE TILE RUBBINGS . . .
BURGERS
PLUS, I THINK I FOUND A PATH! COME ON! WE CAN CATCH UP AS WE GO.
WE TALKED TO MA-MO FIRST.
WAIT, YOU CALL YOUR GRANDMOTHER WHAT?
MA-MO. SO WHAT?
CONTINUE.
MA-MO DIDN'T KNOW ANY STORIES OFFHAND, BUT SHE KNEW SOMEONE WHO DID.
WE MET THIS GUY WHOSE GRANDFATHER WAS AT THE OPENING THAT NIGHT AND SHARED THE STORY WITH HIM.
THIS OLD DUDE TOLD US ALL ABOUT THE BLACKOUT AND HOW THINGS CHANGED AFTER THAT NIGHT.

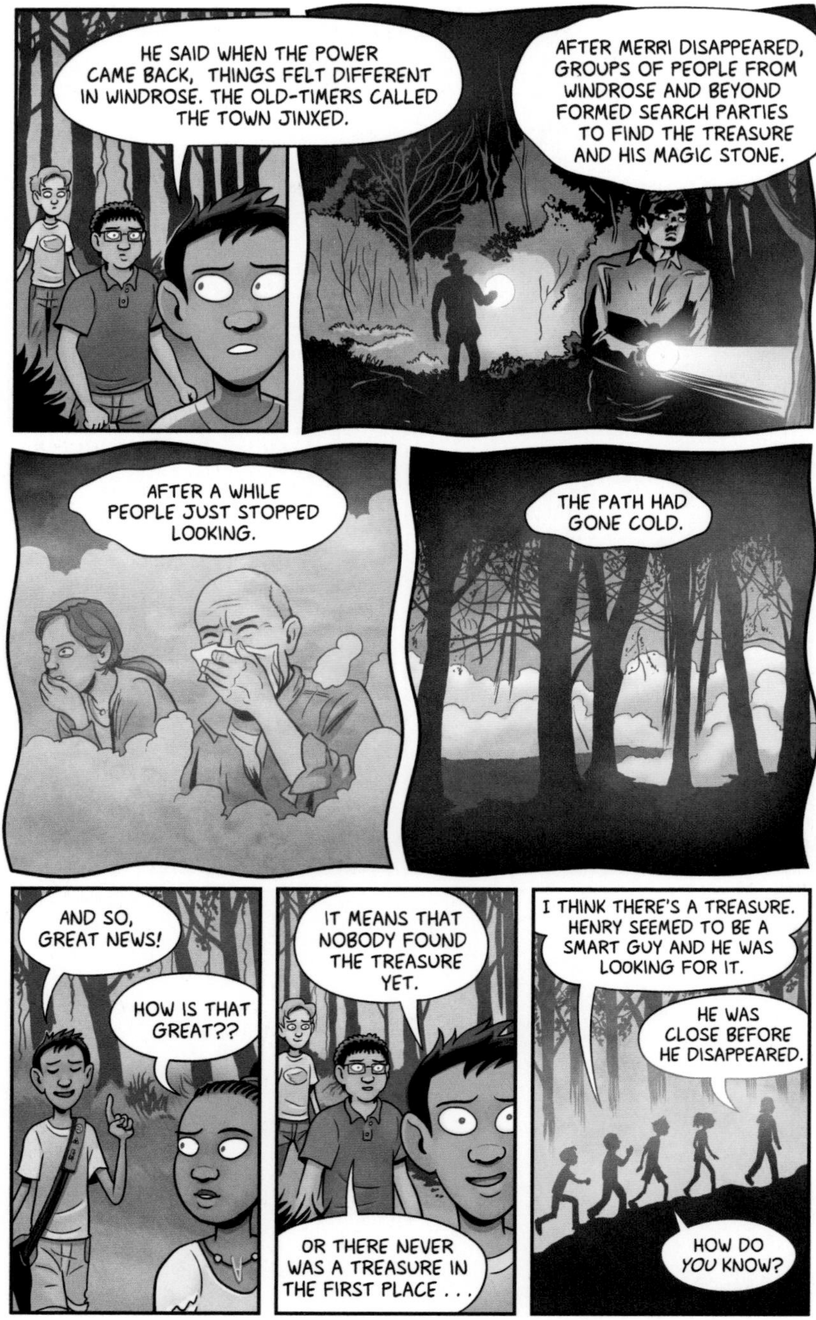
HE SAID WHEN THE POWER CAME BACK, THINGS FELT DIFFERENT IN WINDROSE. THE OLD-TIMERS CALLED THE TOWN JINXED.
AFTER MERRI DISAPPEARED, GROUPS OF PEOPLE FROM WINDROSE AND BEYOND FORMED SEARCH PARTIES TO FIND THE TREASURE AND HIS MAGIC STONE.
AFTER A WHILE PEOPLE JUST STOPPED LOOKING.
THE PATH HAD GONE COLD.
AND SO, GREAT NEWS!
HOW IS THAT GREAT??
IT MEANS THAT NOBODY FOUND THE TREASURE YET.
OR THERE NEVER WAS A TREASURE IN THE FIRST PLACE . . .
I THINK THERE'S A TREASURE. HENRY SEEMED TO BE A SMART GUY AND HE WAS LOOKING FOR IT.
HE WAS CLOSE BEFORE HE DISAPPEARED.
HOW DO *YOU* KNOW?

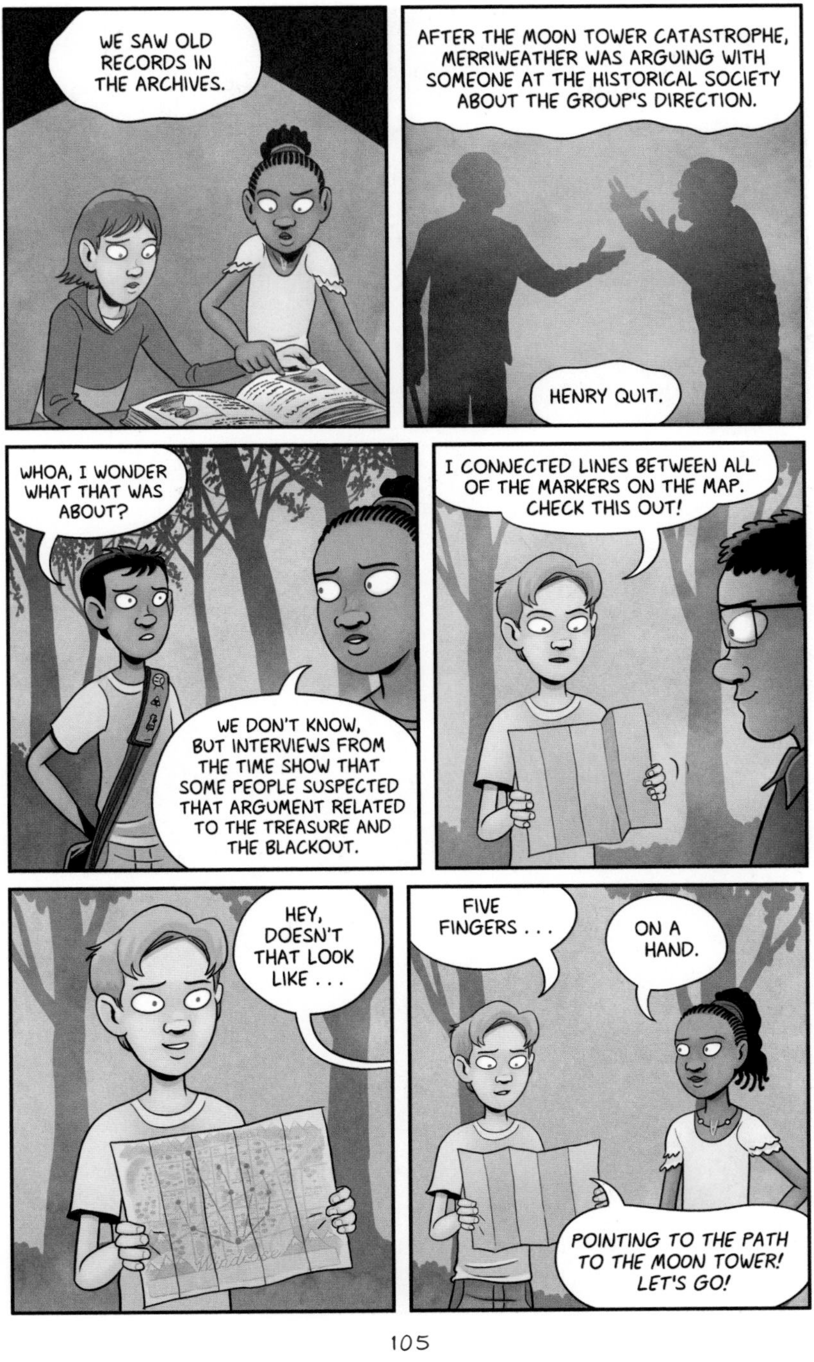

WE SAW OLD RECORDS IN THE ARCHIVES.
AFTER THE MOON TOWER CATASTROPHE, MERRIWEATHER WAS ARGUING WITH SOMEONE AT THE HISTORICAL SOCIETY ABOUT THE GROUP'S DIRECTION.
HENRY QUIT.
WHOA, I WONDER WHAT THAT WAS ABOUT?
WE DON'T KNOW, BUT INTERVIEWS FROM THE TIME SHOW THAT SOME PEOPLE SUSPECTED THAT ARGUMENT RELATED TO THE TREASURE AND THE BLACKOUT.
I CONNECTED LINES BETWEEN ALL OF THE MARKERS ON THE MAP. CHECK THIS OUT!
HEY, DOESN'T THAT LOOK LIKE . . .
FIVE FINGERS . . .
ON A HAND.
POINTING TO THE PATH TO THE MOON TOWER! LET'S GO!

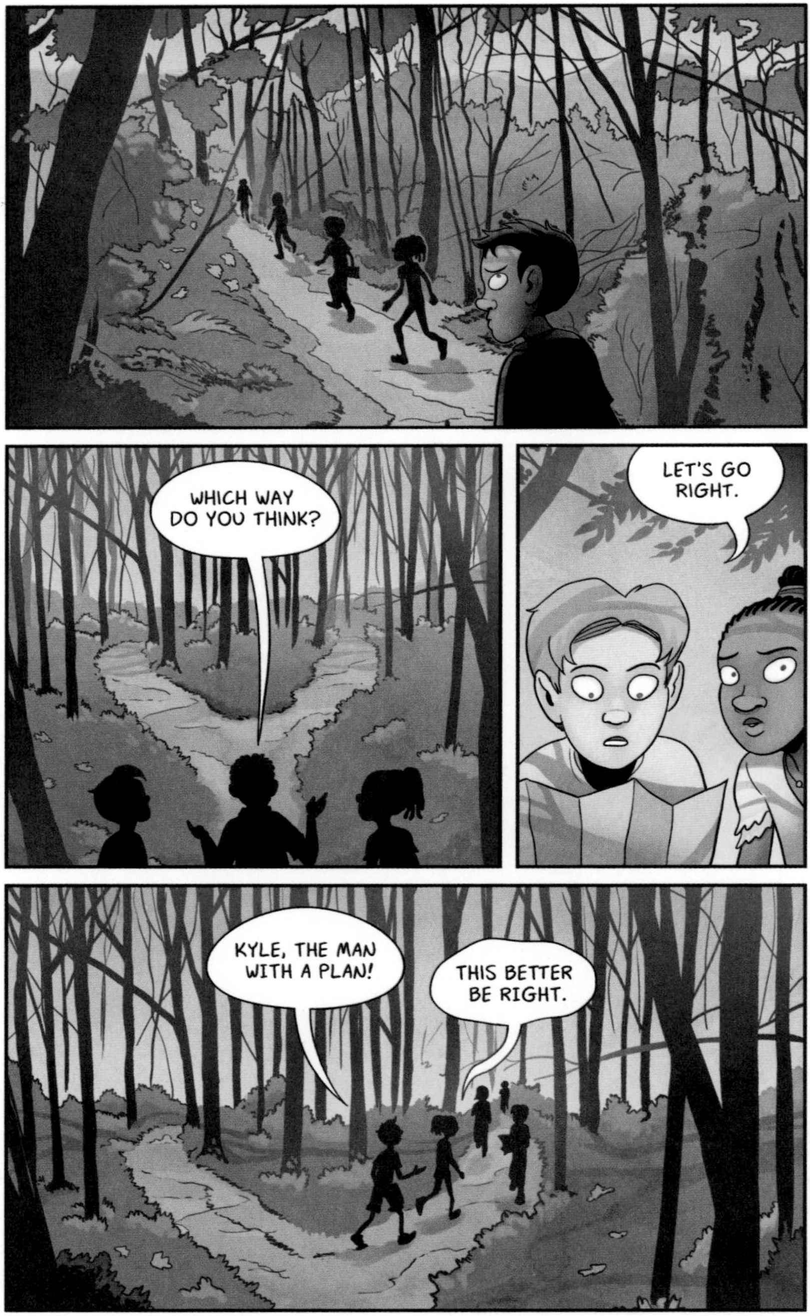
WHICH WAY DO YOU THINK?
LET'S GO RIGHT.
KYLE, THE MAN WITH A PLAN!
THIS BETTER BE RIGHT.

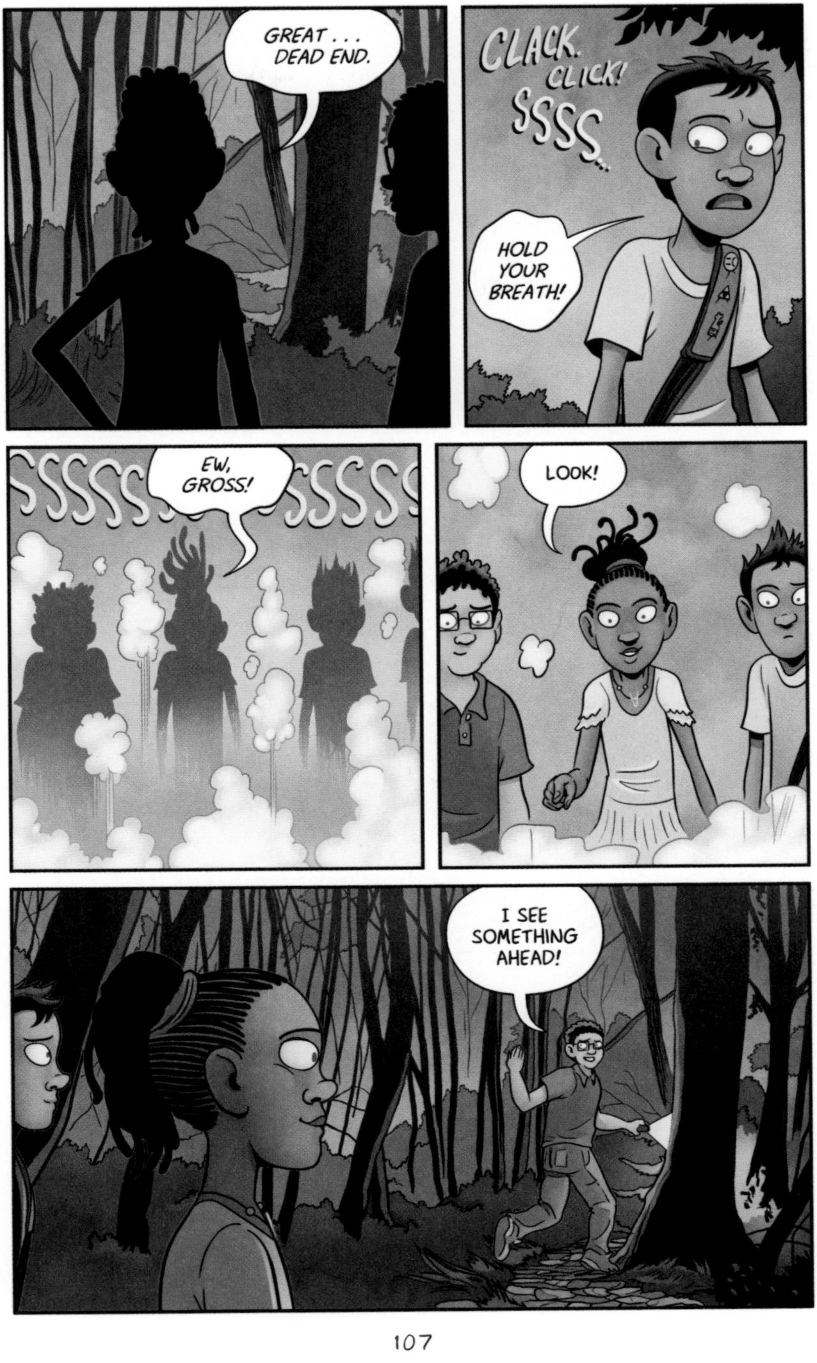
GREAT . . . DEAD END.
CLACK.
CLICK!
SSSS...
HOLD YOUR BREATH!
EW, GROSS!
LOOK!
I SEE SOMETHING AHEAD!

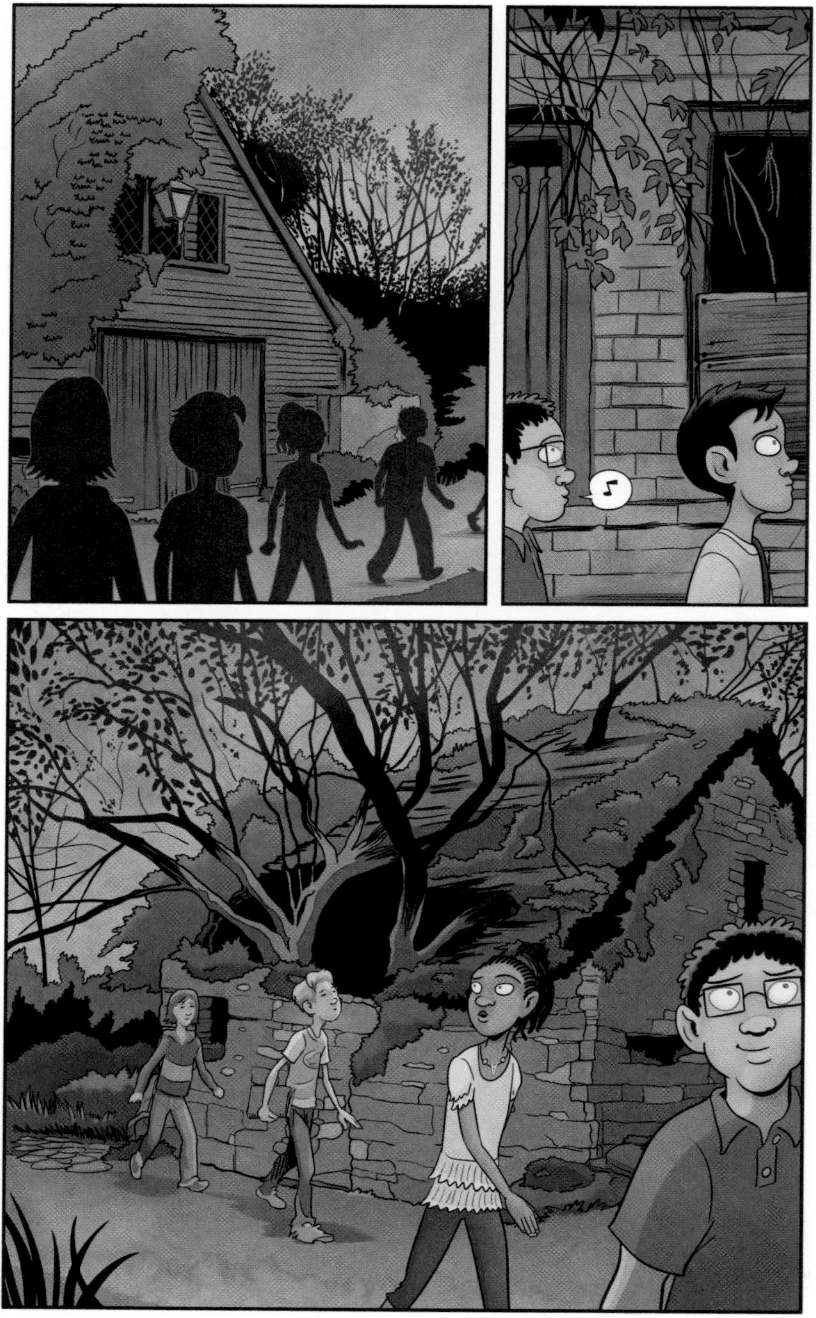
♪

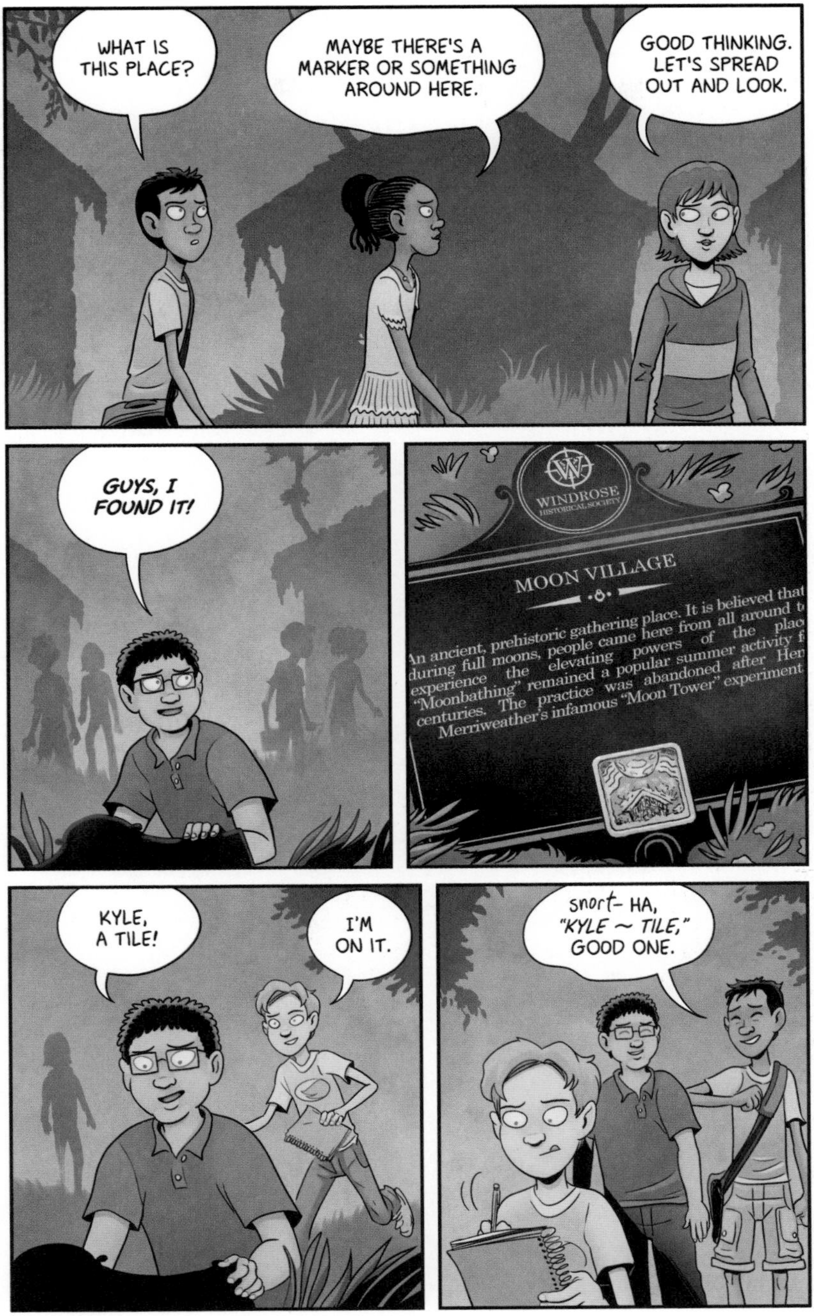
WHAT IS THIS PLACE?
MAYBE THERE'S A MARKER OR SOMETHING AROUND HERE.
GOOD THINKING. LET'S SPREAD OUT AND LOOK.
GUYS, I FOUND IT!
WINDROSE HISTORICAL SOCIETY
MOON VILLAGE
An ancient, prehistoric gathering place. It is believed that during full moons, people came here from all around t experience the elevating powers of the plac "Moonbathing" remained a popular summer activity f centuries. The practice was abandoned after Her Merriweather's infamous "Moon Tower" experiment.
KYLE, A TILE!
I'M ON IT.
snort- HA, "KYLE ~ TILE," GOOD ONE.

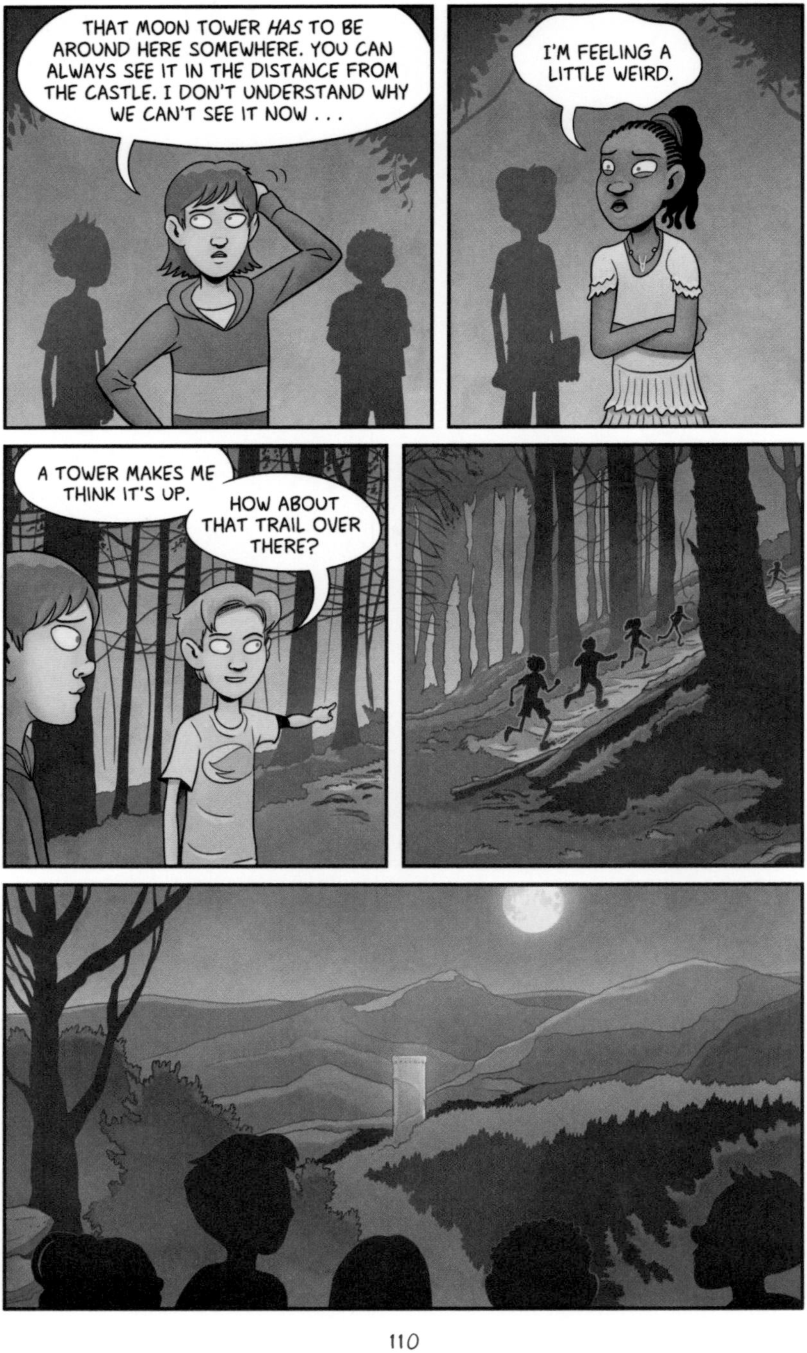
THAT MOON TOWER *HAS* TO BE AROUND HERE SOMEWHERE. YOU CAN ALWAYS SEE IT IN THE DISTANCE FROM THE CASTLE. I DON'T UNDERSTAND WHY WE CAN'T SEE IT NOW . . .
I'M FEELING A LITTLE WEIRD.
A TOWER MAKES ME THINK IT'S UP.
HOW ABOUT THAT TRAIL OVER THERE?

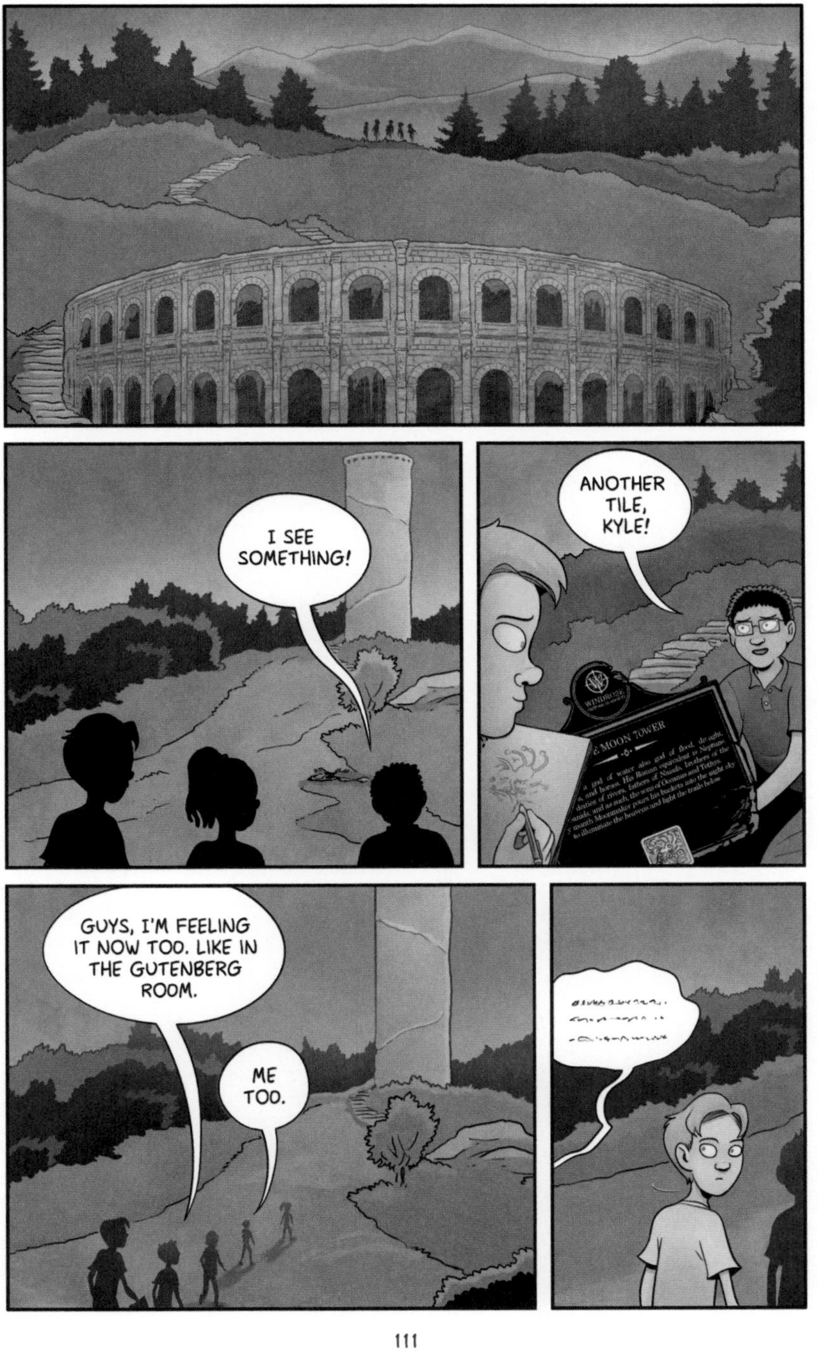
I SEE SOMETHING!
ANOTHER TILE, KYLE!
GUYS, I'M FEELING IT NOW TOO. LIKE IN THE GUTENBERG ROOM.
ME TOO.

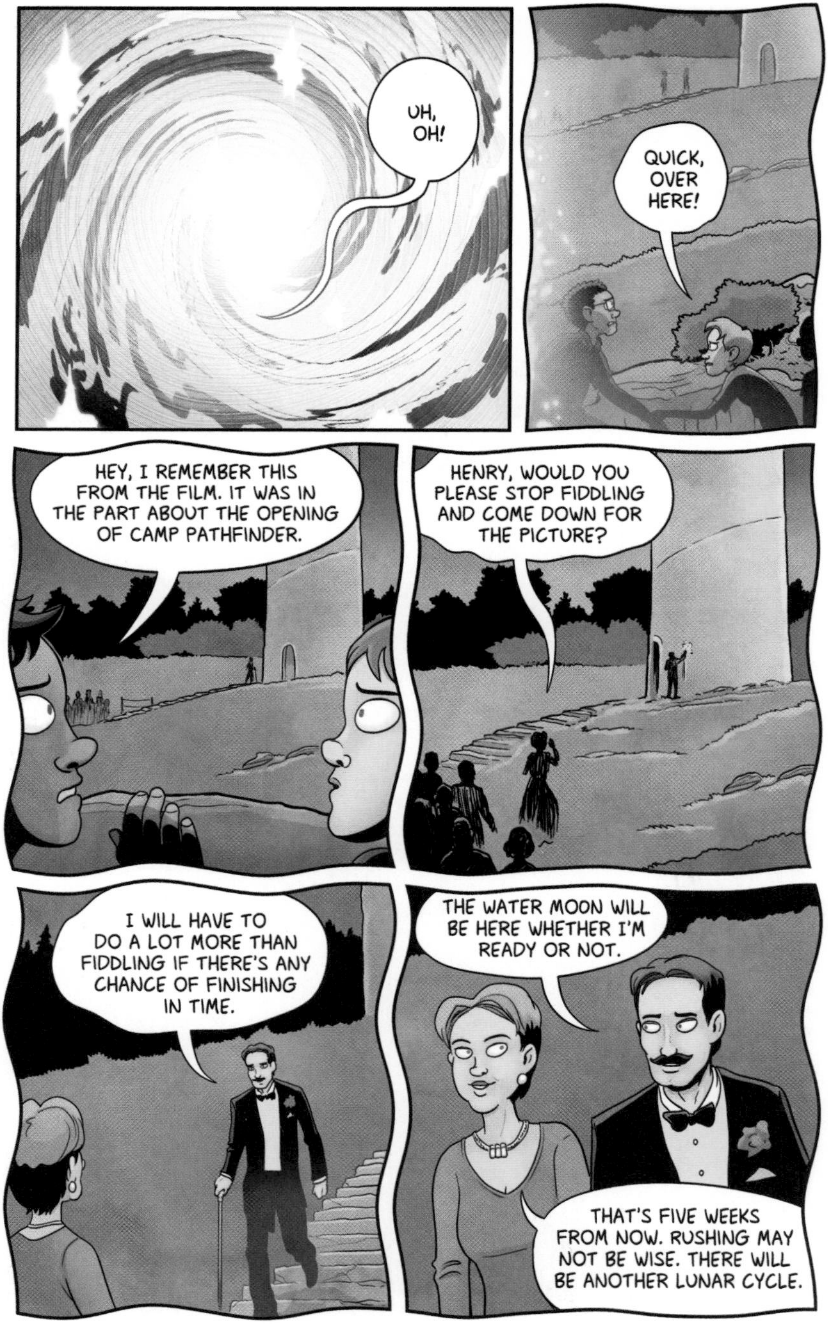
UH, OH!
QUICK, OVER HERE!
HEY, I REMEMBER THIS FROM THE FILM. IT WAS IN THE PART ABOUT THE OPENING OF CAMP PATHFINDER.
HENRY, WOULD YOU PLEASE STOP FIDDLING AND COME DOWN FOR THE PICTURE?
I WILL HAVE TO DO A LOT MORE THAN FIDDLING IF THERE'S ANY CHANCE OF FINISHING IN TIME.
THE WATER MOON WILL BE HERE WHETHER I'M READY OR NOT.
THAT'S FIVE WEEKS FROM NOW. RUSHING MAY NOT BE WISE. THERE WILL BE ANOTHER LUNAR CYCLE.

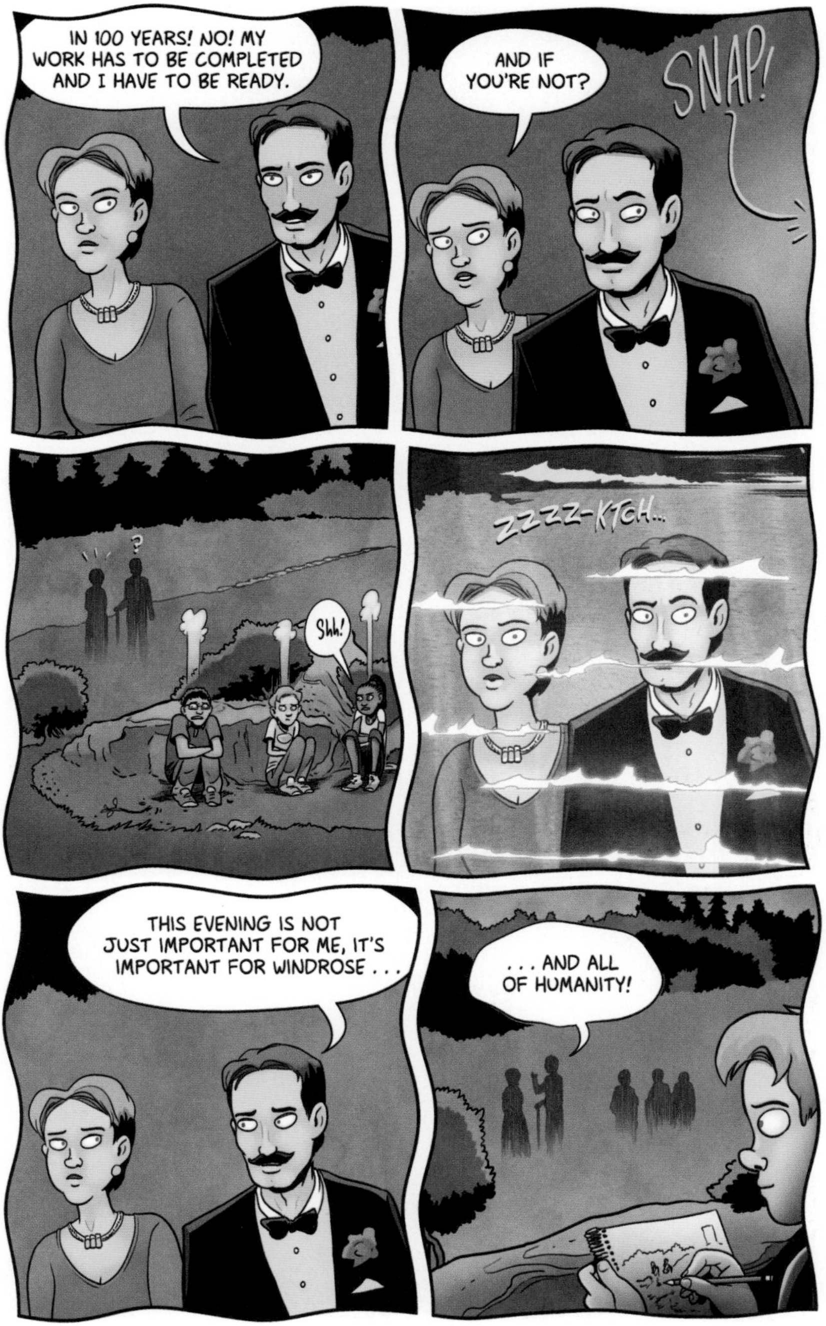
IN 100 YEARS! NO! MY WORK HAS TO BE COMPLETED AND I HAVE TO BE READY.
AND IF YOU'RE NOT?
SNAP!
Shh!
ZZZZ-KTCH...
THIS EVENING IS NOT JUST IMPORTANT FOR ME, IT'S IMPORTANT FOR WINDROSE . . .
. . . AND ALL OF HUMANITY!

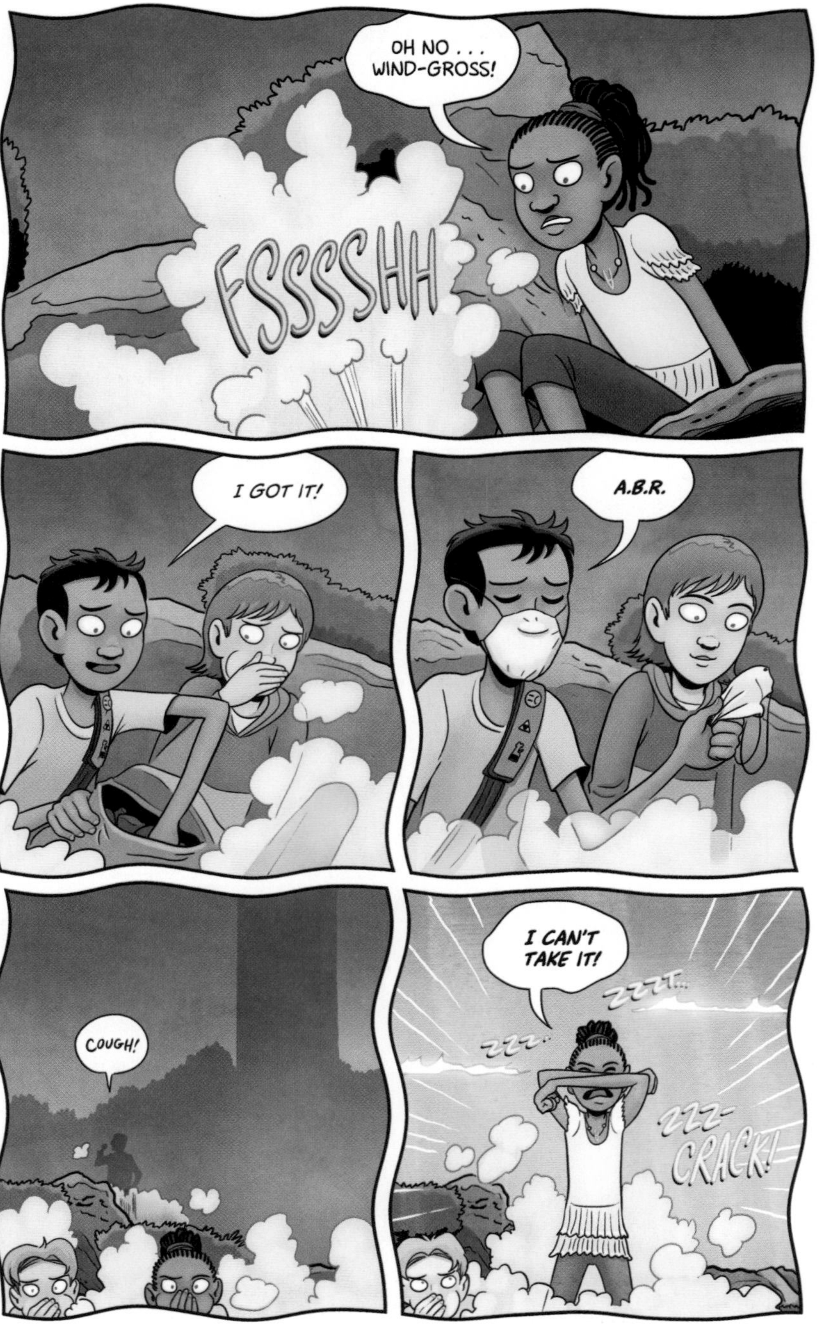
OH NO . . . WIND-GROSS!
FSSSSHH
I GOT IT!
A.B.R.
COUGH!
I CAN'T TAKE IT!
ZZZT...
ZZZ-
ZZZ-CRACK!

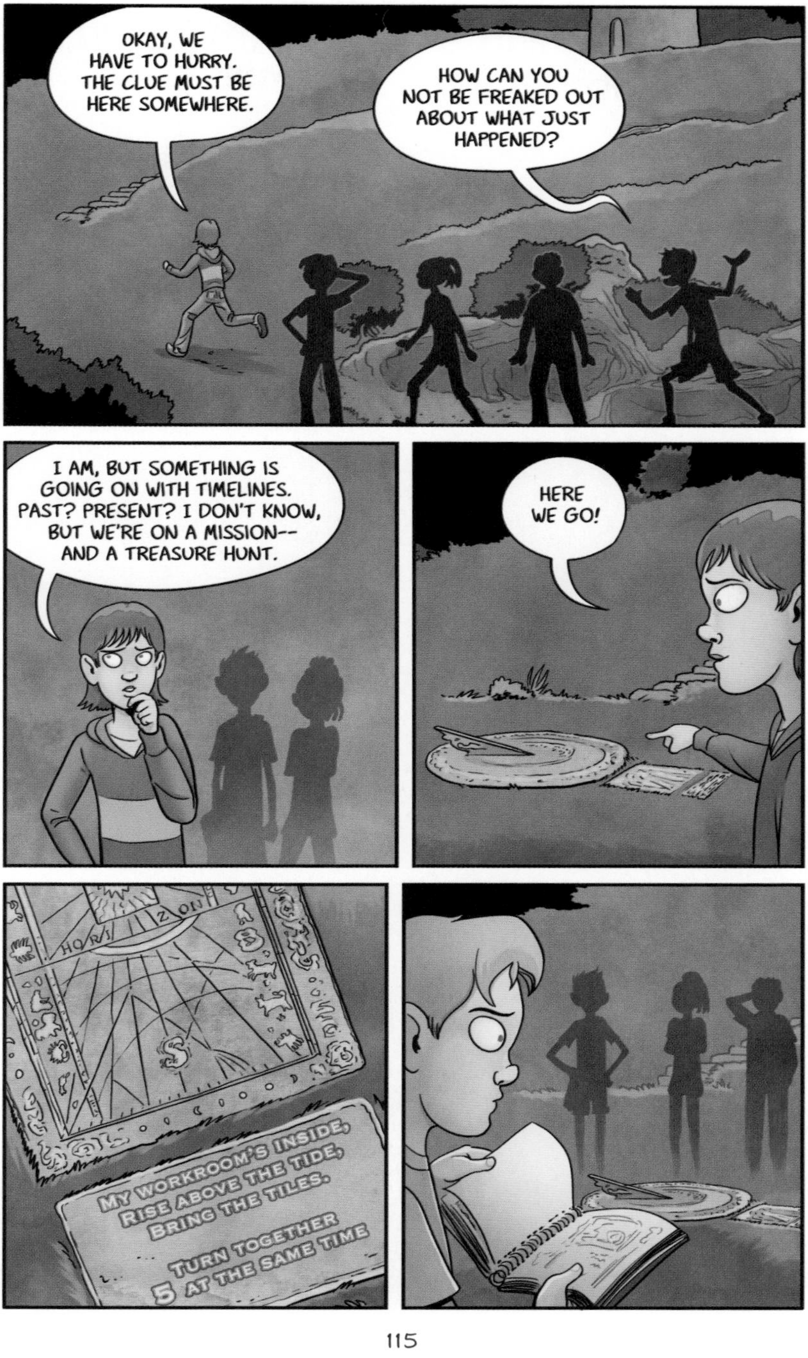
OKAY, WE HAVE TO HURRY. THE CLUE MUST BE HERE SOMEWHERE.
HOW CAN YOU NOT BE FREAKED OUT ABOUT WHAT JUST HAPPENED?
I AM, BUT SOMETHING IS GOING ON WITH TIMELINES. PAST? PRESENT? I DON'T KNOW, BUT WE'RE ON A MISSION-- AND A TREASURE HUNT.
HERE WE GO!
MY WORKROOM'S INSIDE,
RISE ABOVE THE TIDE,
BRING THE TILES.
TURN TOGETHER
5 AT THE SAME TIME

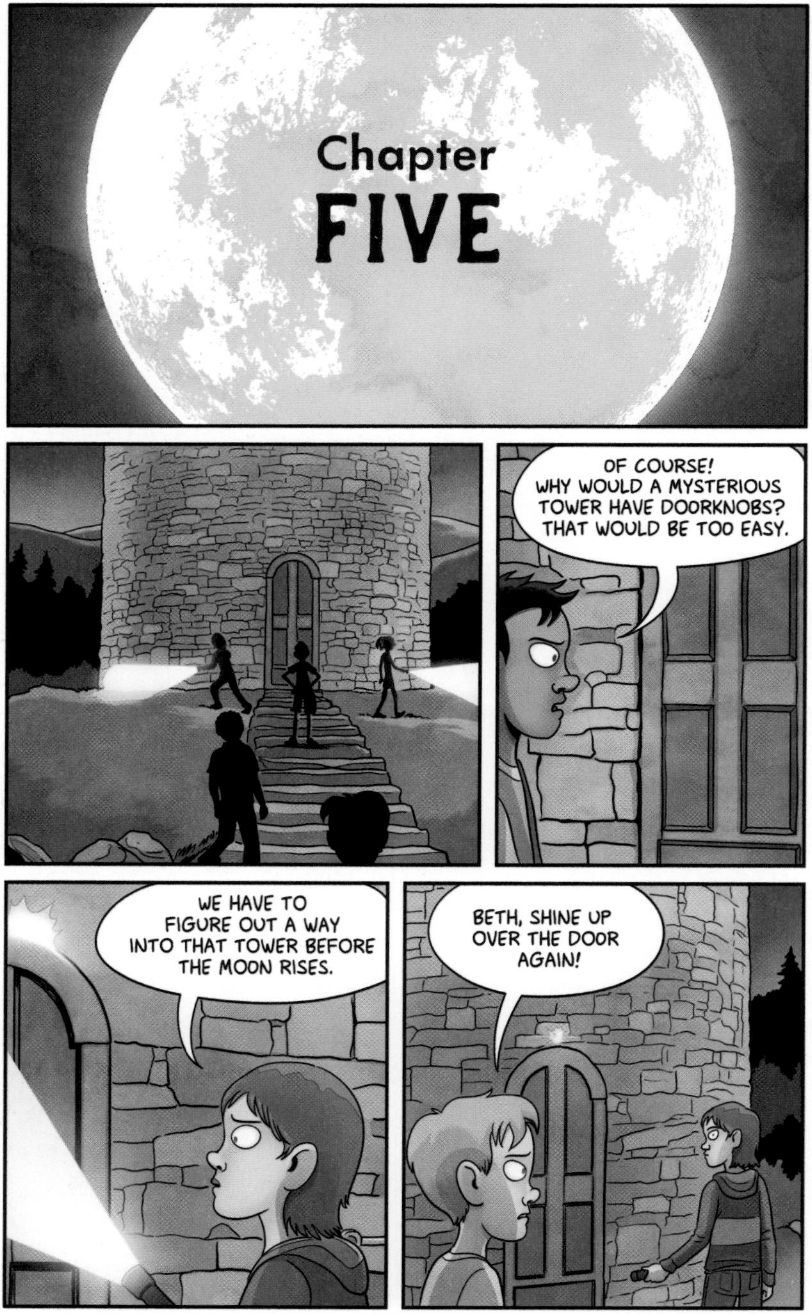

Chapter
FIVE
OF COURSE! WHY WOULD A MYSTERIOUS TOWER HAVE DOORKNOBS? THAT WOULD BE TOO EASY.
WE HAVE TO FIGURE OUT A WAY INTO THAT TOWER BEFORE THE MOON RISES.
BETH, SHINE UP OVER THE DOOR AGAIN!

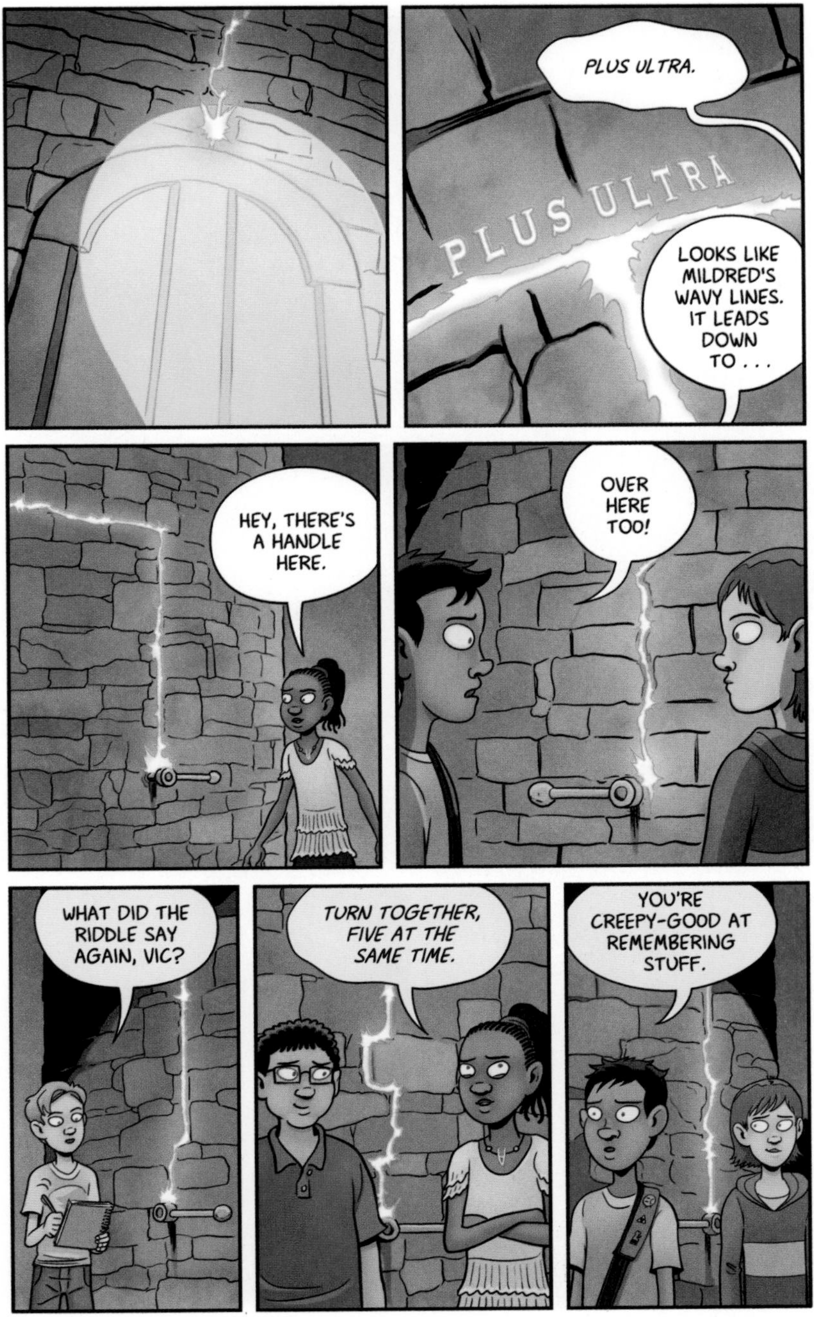
PLUS ULTRA.
PLUS ULTRA
LOOKS LIKE MILDRED'S WAVY LINES. IT LEADS DOWN TO . . .
HEY, THERE'S A HANDLE HERE.
OVER HERE TOO!
WHAT DID THE RIDDLE SAY AGAIN, VIC?
TURN TOGETHER, FIVE AT THE SAME TIME.
YOU'RE CREEPY-GOOD AT REMEMBERING STUFF.

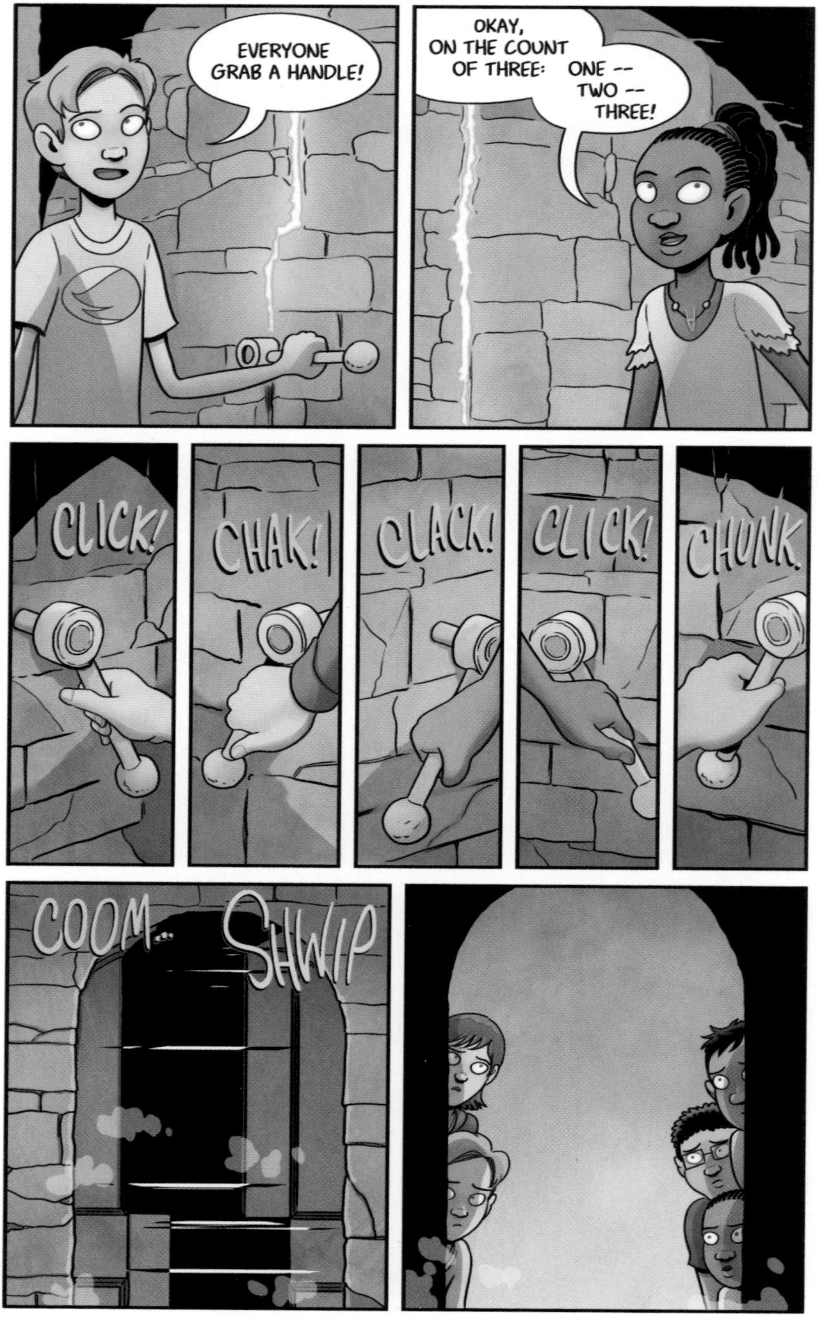
EVERYONE GRAB A HANDLE!
OKAY, ON THE COUNT OF THREE: ONE -- TWO -- THREE!
CLICK!
CHAK!
CLACK!
CLICK!
CHUNK.
COOM...
SHWIP

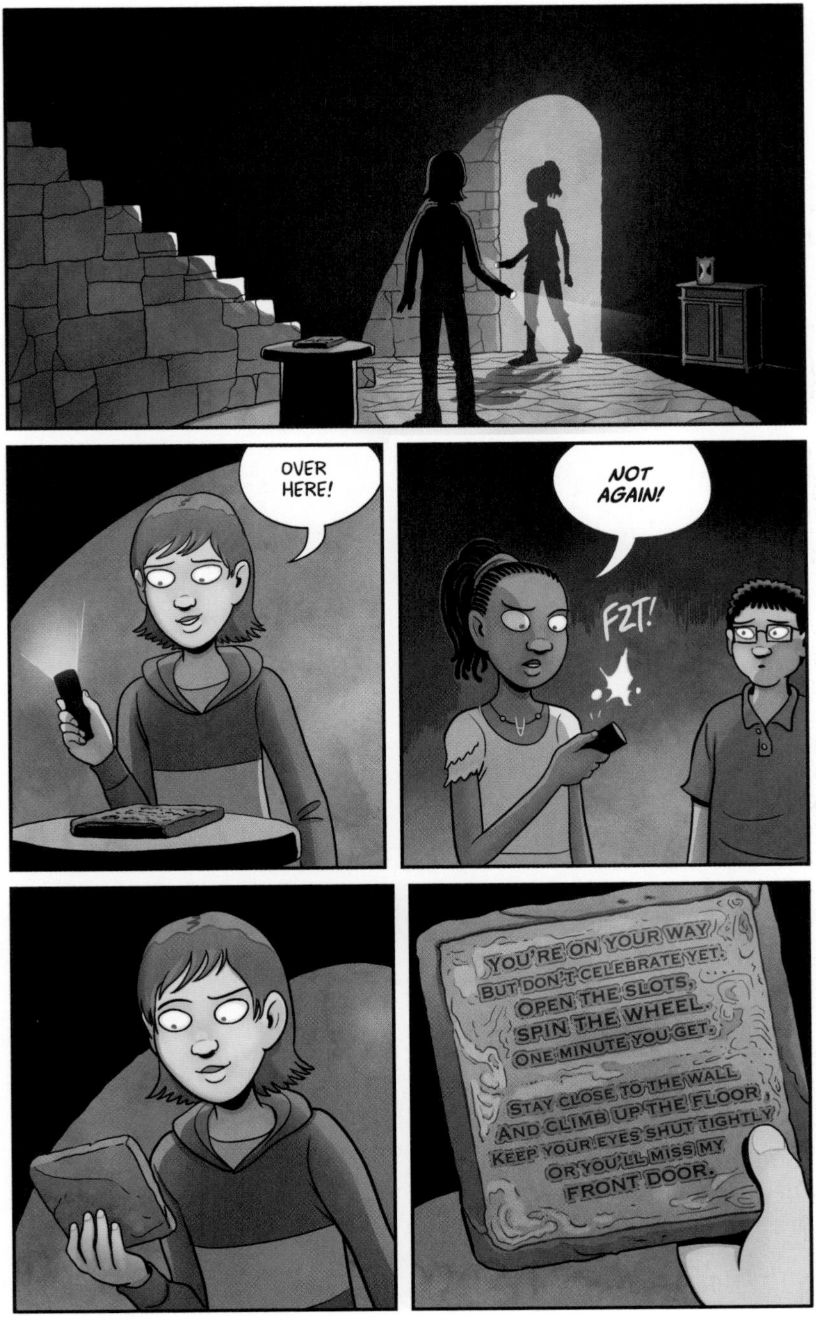
OVER HERE!
NOT AGAIN!
FZT!
YOU'RE ON YOUR WAY,
BUT DON'T CELEBRATE YET.
OPEN THE SLOTS,
SPIN THE WHEEL.
ONE MINUTE YOU GET.
STAY CLOSE TO THE WALL,
AND CLIMB UP THE FLOOR,
KEEP YOUR EYES SHUT TIGHTLY
OR YOU'LL MISS MY
FRONT DOOR.

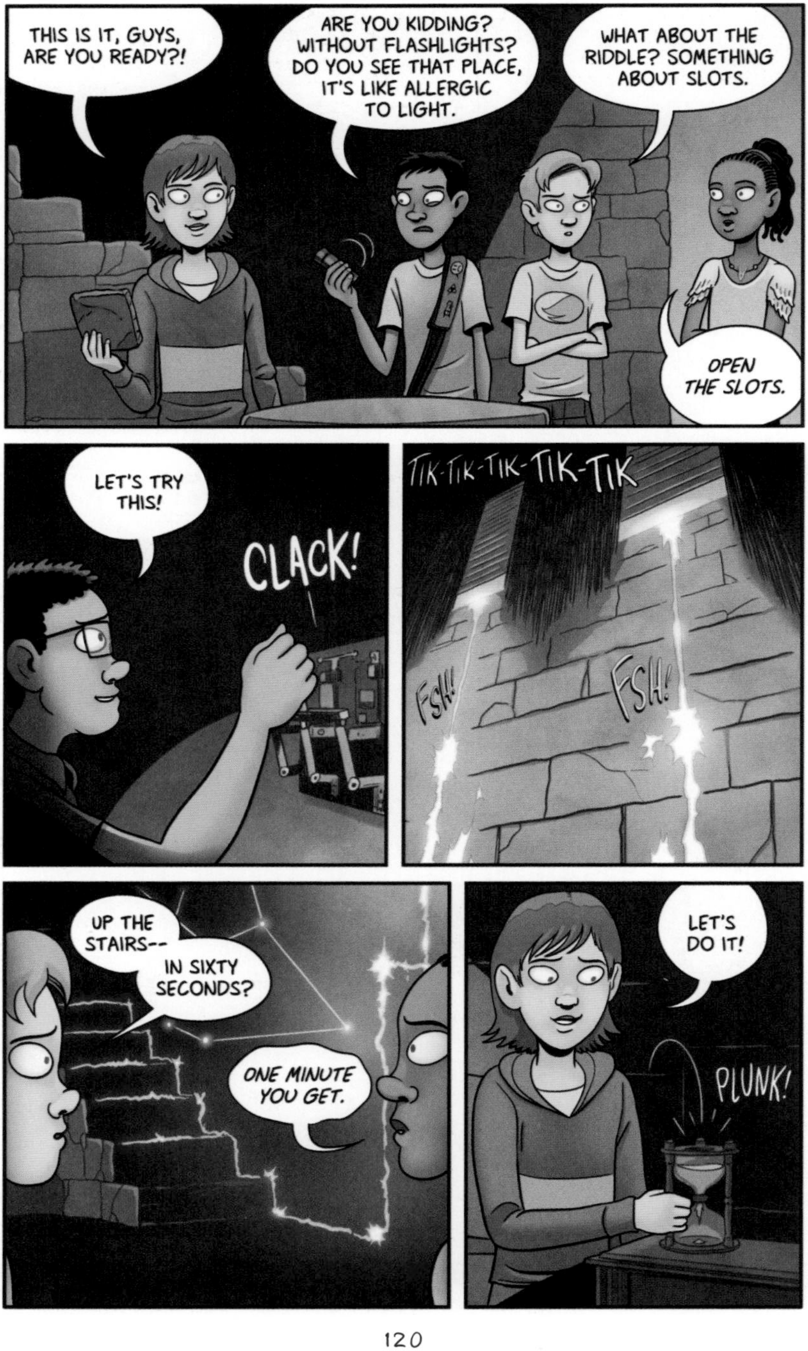
THIS IS IT, GUYS, ARE YOU READY?!
ARE YOU KIDDING? WITHOUT FLASHLIGHTS? DO YOU SEE THAT PLACE, IT'S LIKE ALLERGIC TO LIGHT.
WHAT ABOUT THE RIDDLE? SOMETHING ABOUT SLOTS.
OPEN THE SLOTS.
LET'S TRY THIS!
CLACK!
TIK-TIK-TIK-TIK-TIK
FSH!
FSH!
UP THE STAIRS--
IN SIXTY SECONDS?
ONE MINUTE YOU GET.
LET'S DO IT!
PLUNK!

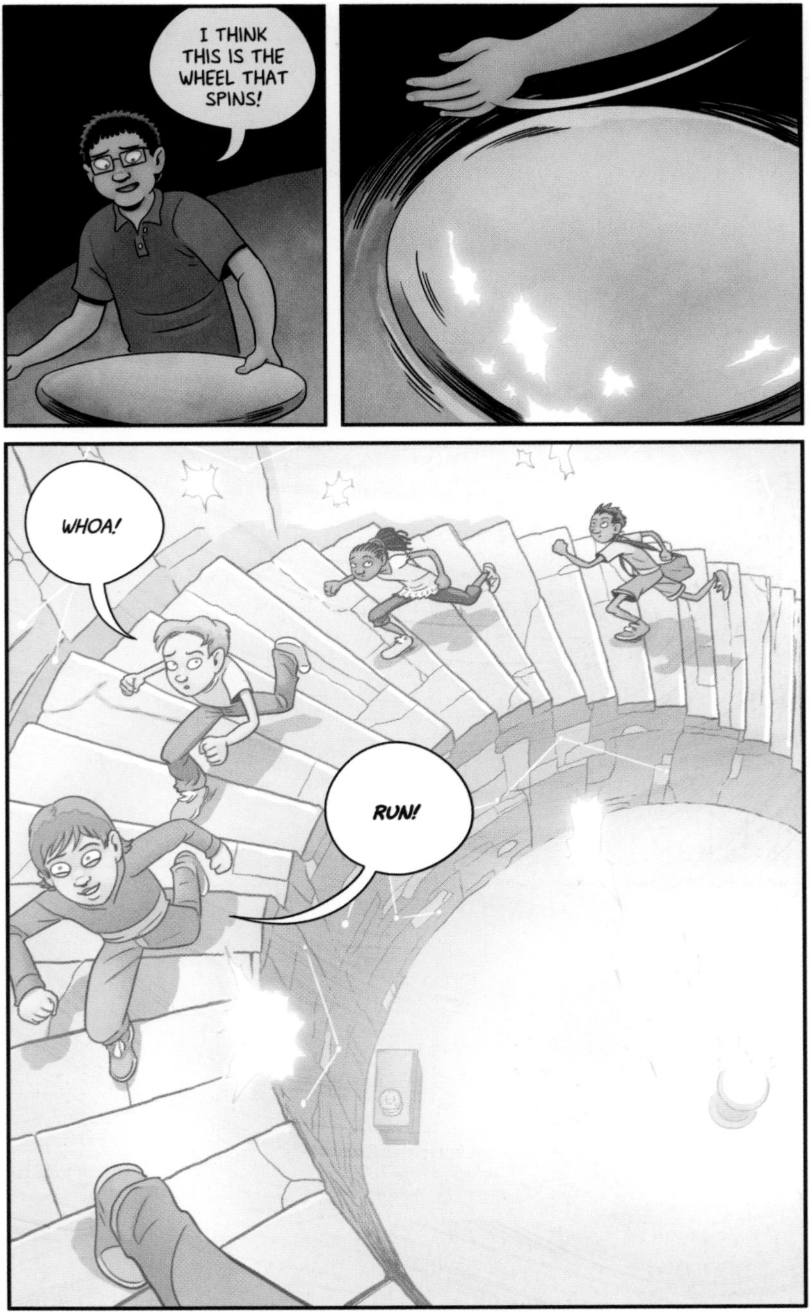
I THINK THIS IS THE WHEEL THAT SPINS!
WHOA!
RUN!

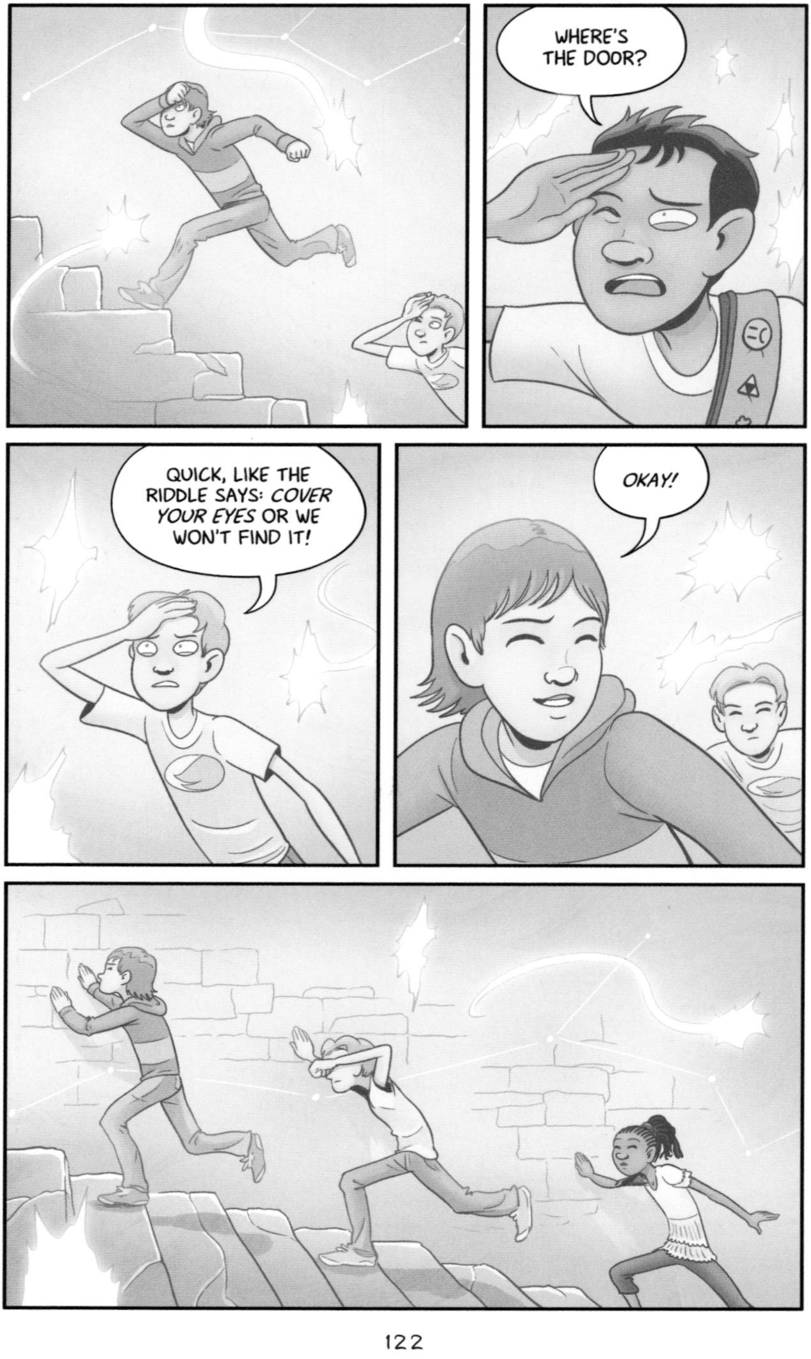
WHERE'S THE DOOR?
QUICK, LIKE THE RIDDLE SAYS: *COVER YOUR EYES* OR WE WON'T FIND IT!
OKAY!

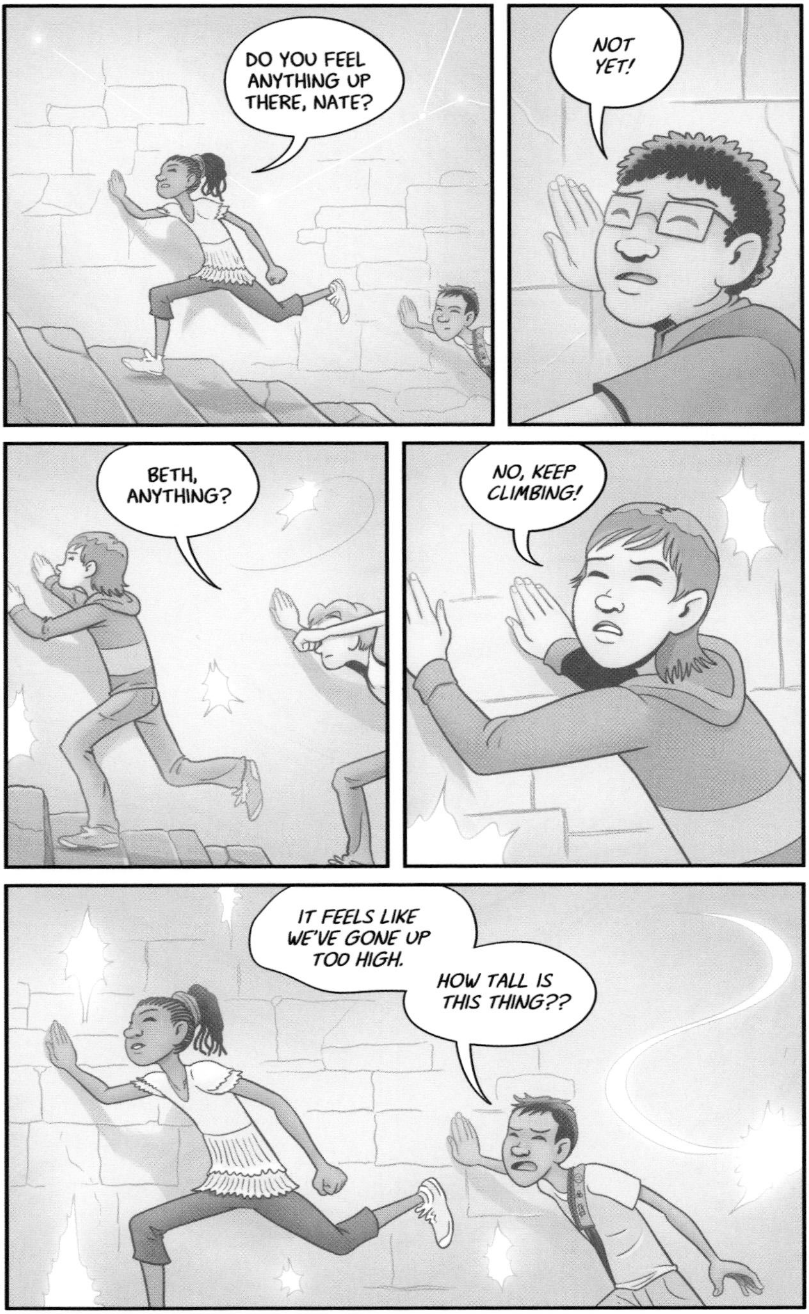
DO YOU FEEL ANYTHING UP THERE, NATE?
NOT YET!
BETH, ANYTHING?
NO, KEEP CLIMBING!
IT FEELS LIKE WE'VE GONE UP TOO HIGH.
HOW TALL IS THIS THING??

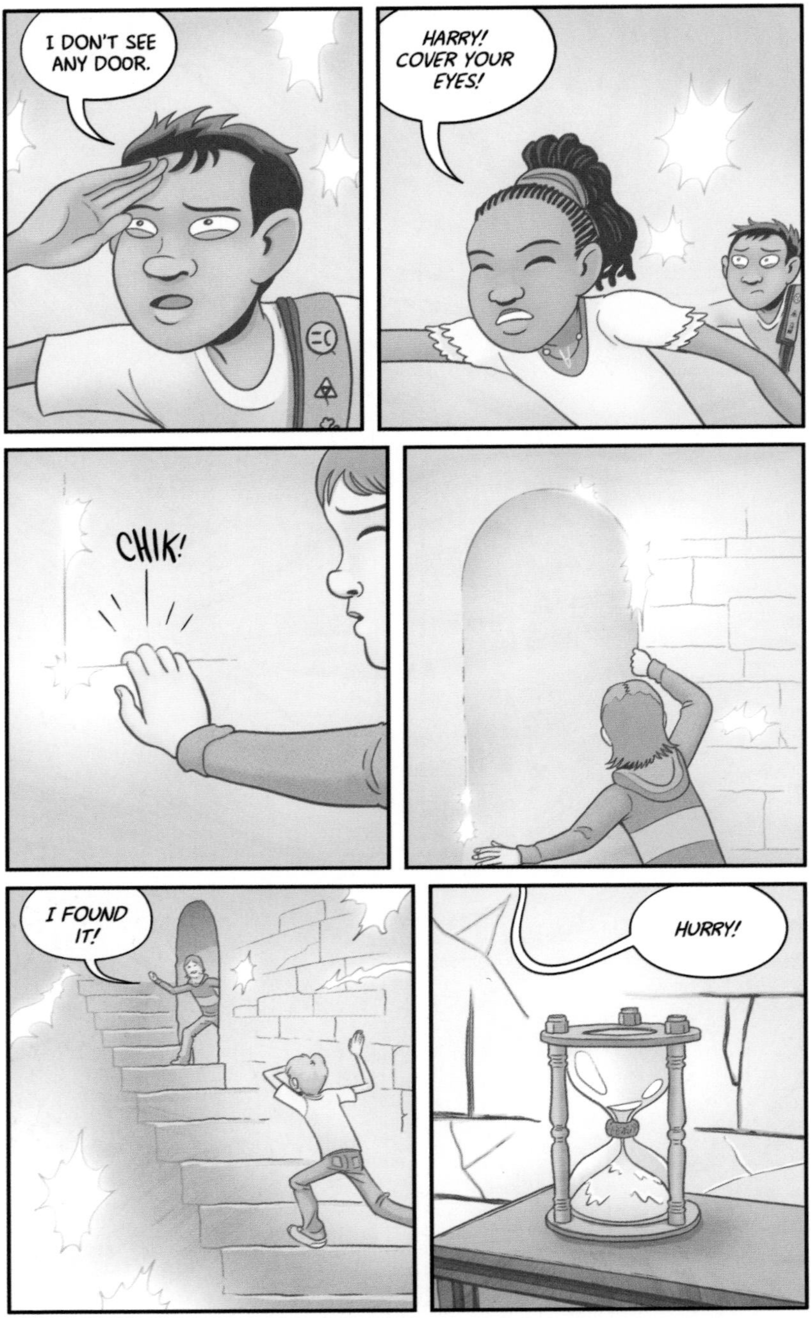
I DON'T SEE ANY DOOR.
HARRY! COVER YOUR EYES!
CHIK!
I FOUND IT!
HURRY!

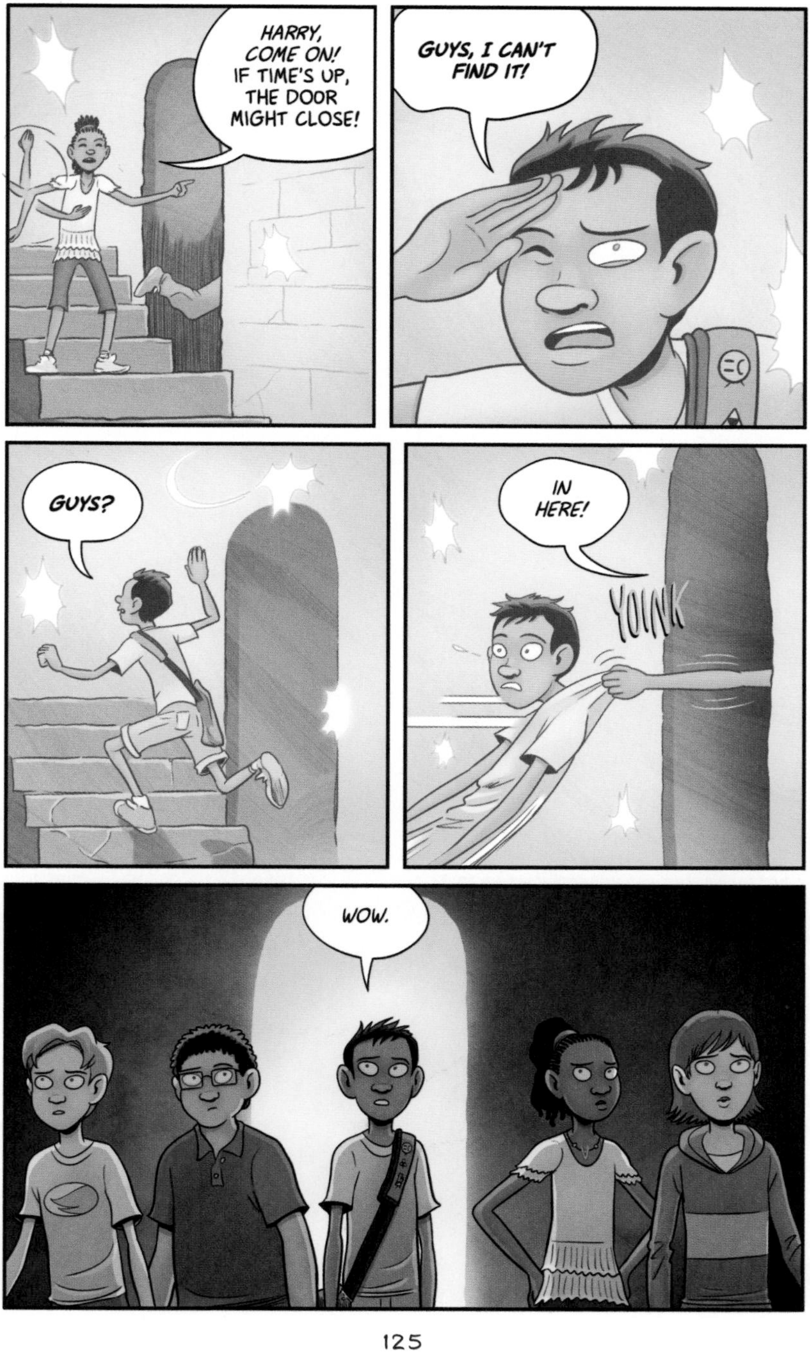
HARRY, COME ON! IF TIME'S UP, THE DOOR MIGHT CLOSE!
GUYS, I CAN'T FIND IT!
GUYS?
IN HERE!
YOINK
WOW.

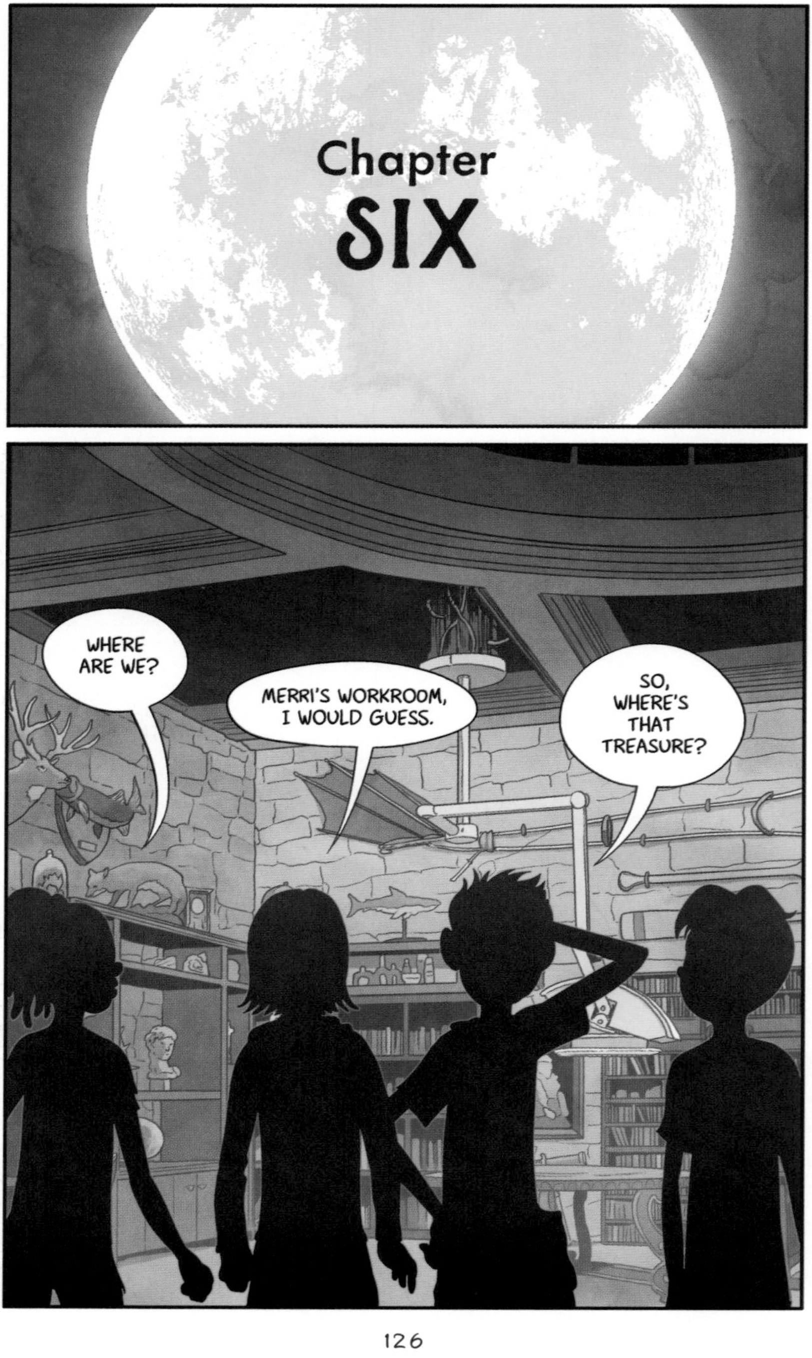
Chapter
SIX
WHERE ARE WE?
MERRI'S WORKROOM, I WOULD GUESS.
SO, WHERE'S THAT TREASURE?

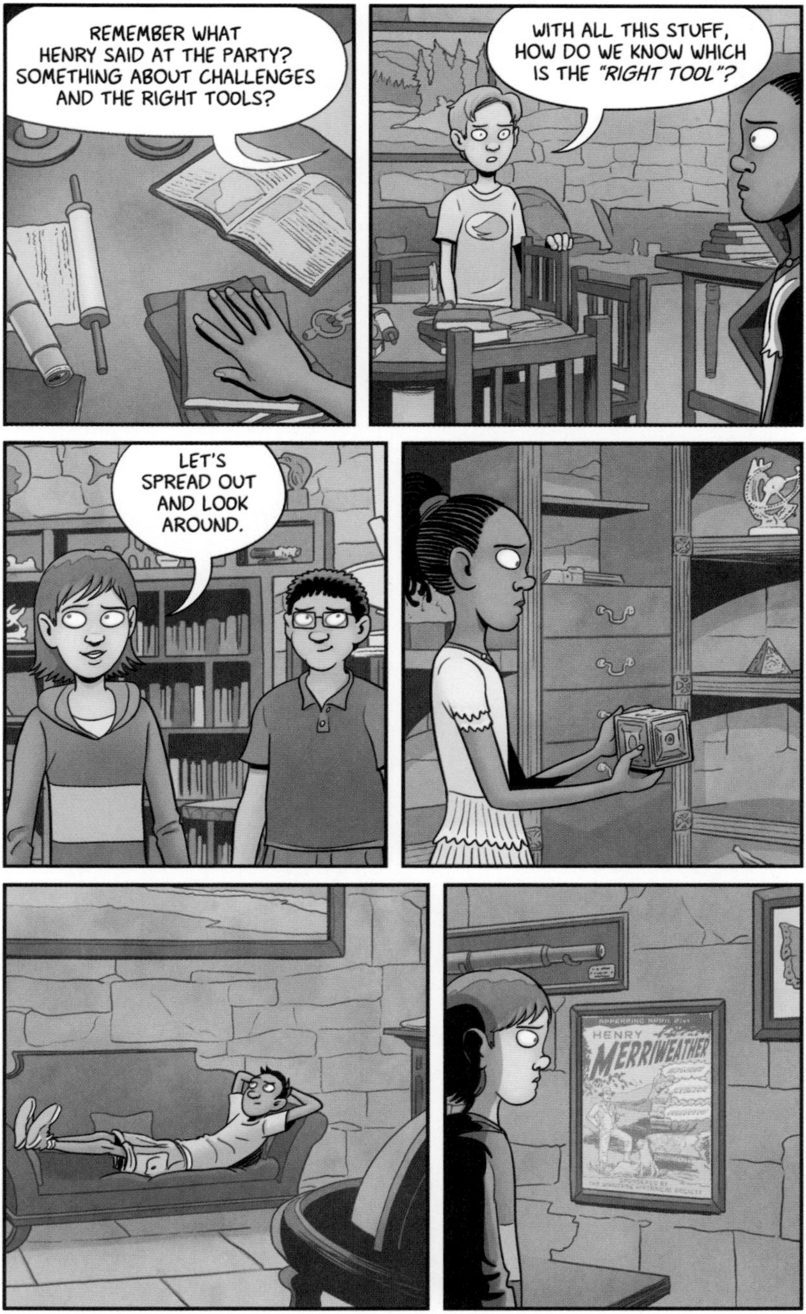
REMEMBER WHAT HENRY SAID AT THE PARTY? SOMETHING ABOUT CHALLENGES AND THE RIGHT TOOLS?
WITH ALL THIS STUFF, HOW DO WE KNOW WHICH IS THE *"RIGHT TOOL"*?
LET'S SPREAD OUT AND LOOK AROUND.
HENRY
MERRIWEATHER

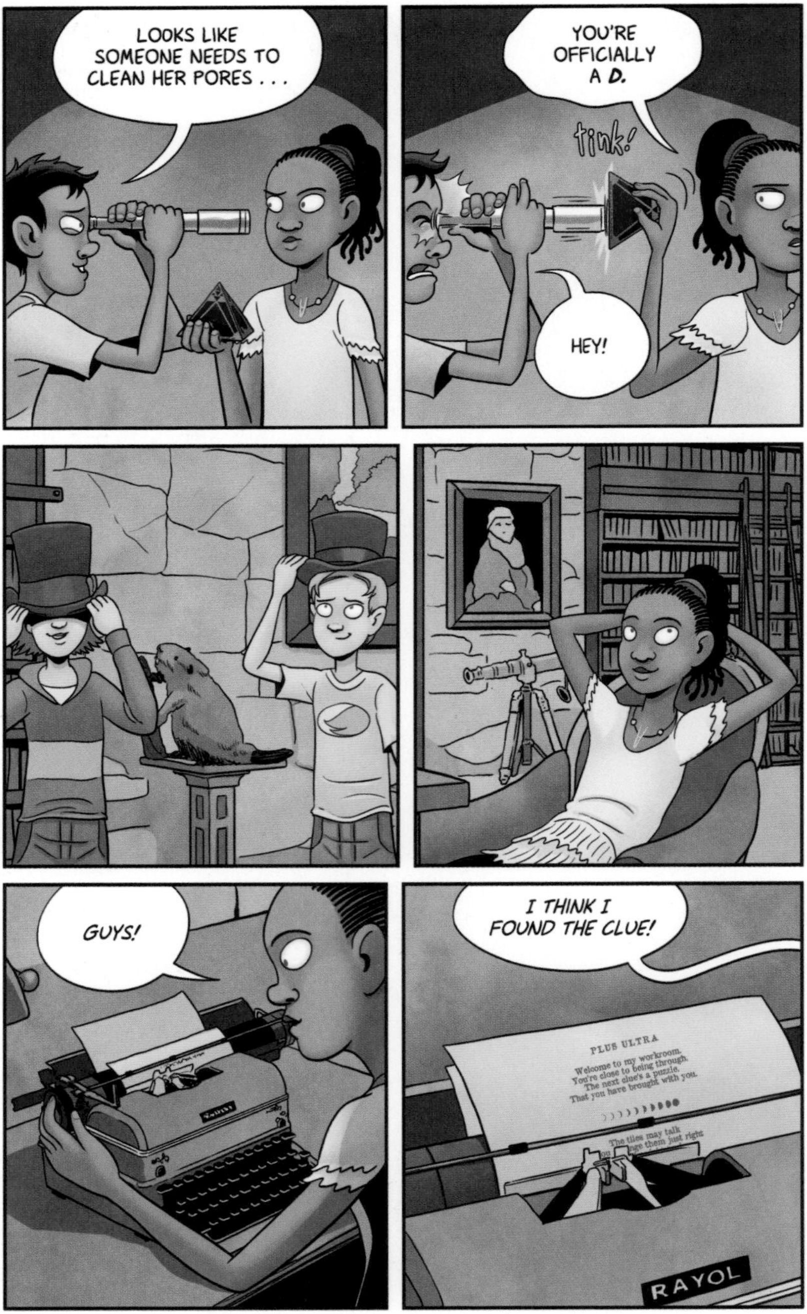
LOOKS LIKE SOMEONE NEEDS TO CLEAN HER PORES . . .
YOU'RE OFFICIALLY A *D.*
tink!
HEY!
GUYS!
I THINK I FOUND THE CLUE!
PLUS ULTRA
Welcome to my workroom.
You're close to being through.
The next clue's a puzzle.
That you have brought with you.
The tiles may talk
RAYOL

PLUS ULTRA

Welcome to my workroom.
You're close to being through.
The next clue's a puzzle
that you have brought with you.

The tiles may talk
If you arrange them just right

THE TILES MAY TALK IF YOU ARRANGE THEM JUST RIGHT. USE THE RIGHT TOOL FOR ANOTHER TIME SIGHT.

WHOA!

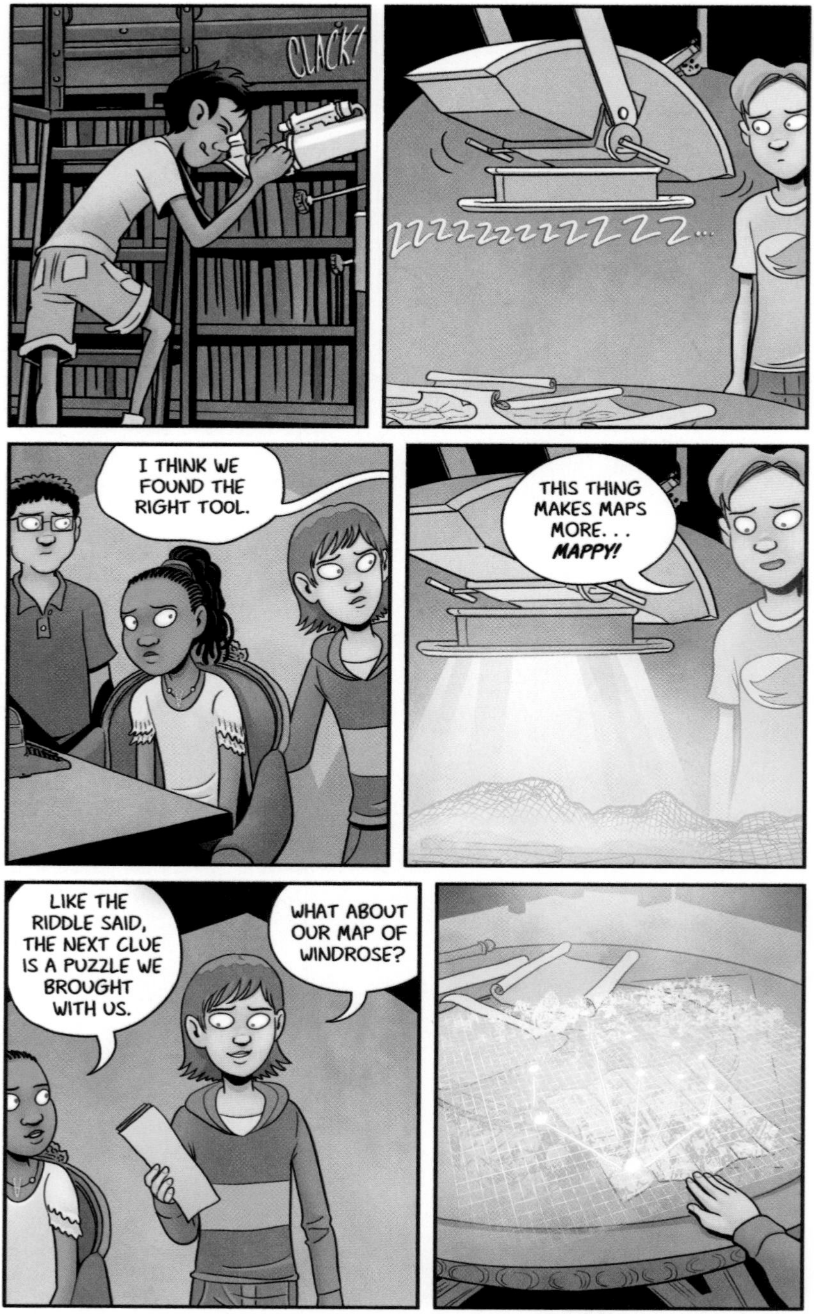
CLACK!
ZZZZZZZZZZZZZZ...
I THINK WE FOUND THE RIGHT TOOL.
THIS THING MAKES MAPS MORE. . . MAPPY!
LIKE THE RIDDLE SAID, THE NEXT CLUE IS A PUZZLE WE BROUGHT WITH US.
WHAT ABOUT OUR MAP OF WINDROSE?

OOOOSH...
IT'S GOING BACK IN TIME!
OOOOOSH

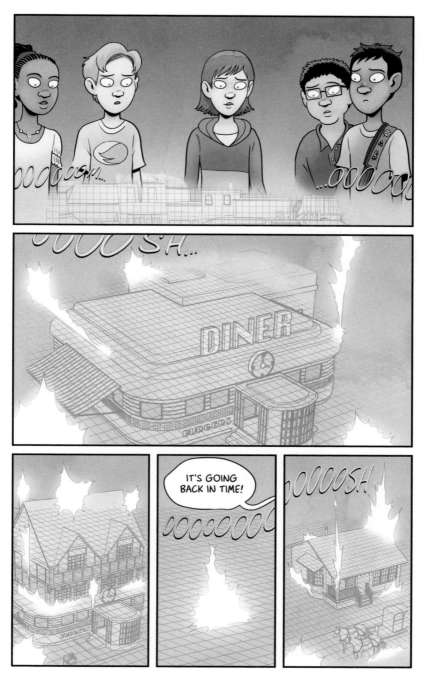

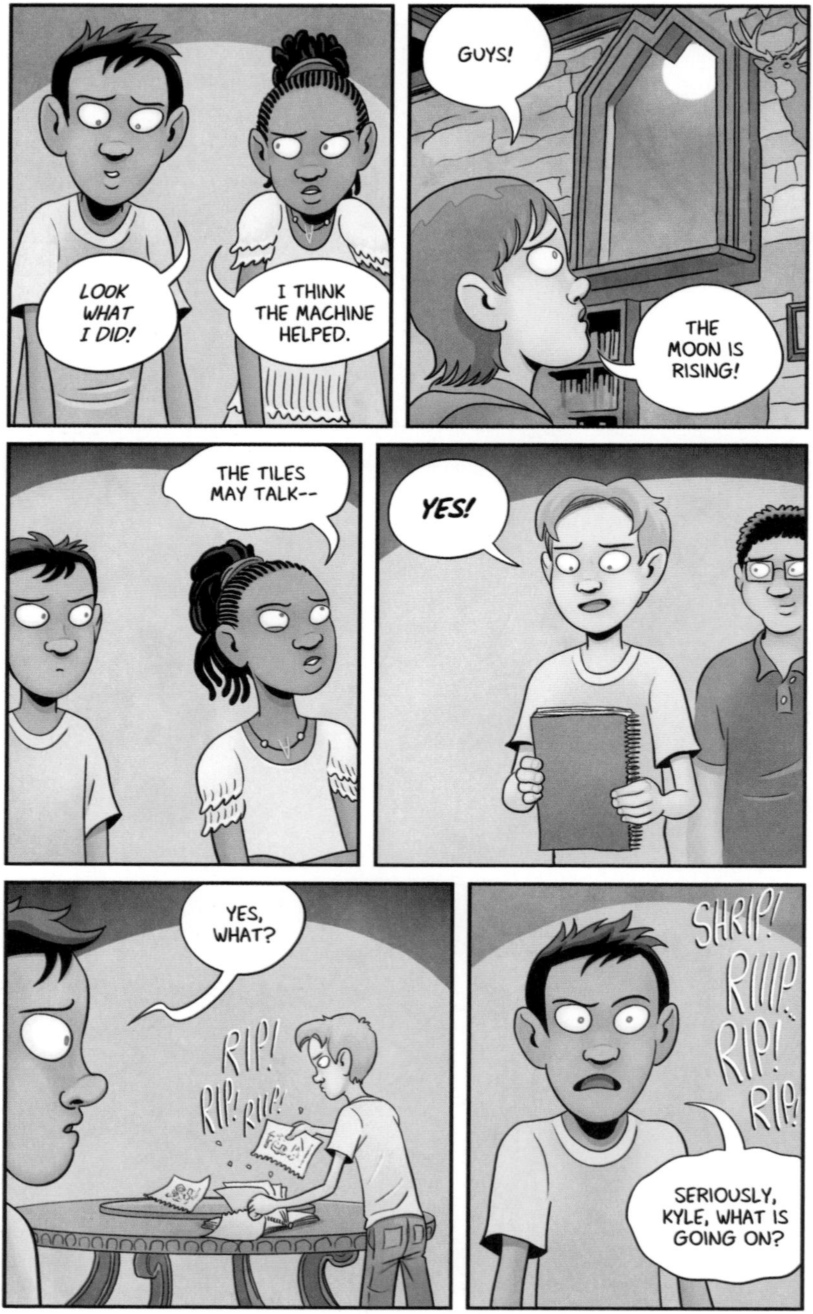
LOOK WHAT I DID!
I THINK THE MACHINE HELPED.
GUYS!
THE MOON IS RISING!
THE TILES MAY TALK--
YES!
YES, WHAT?
RIP! RIP! RIIP!
SHRIP! RIIIP... RIP! RIP!
SERIOUSLY, KYLE, WHAT IS GOING ON?

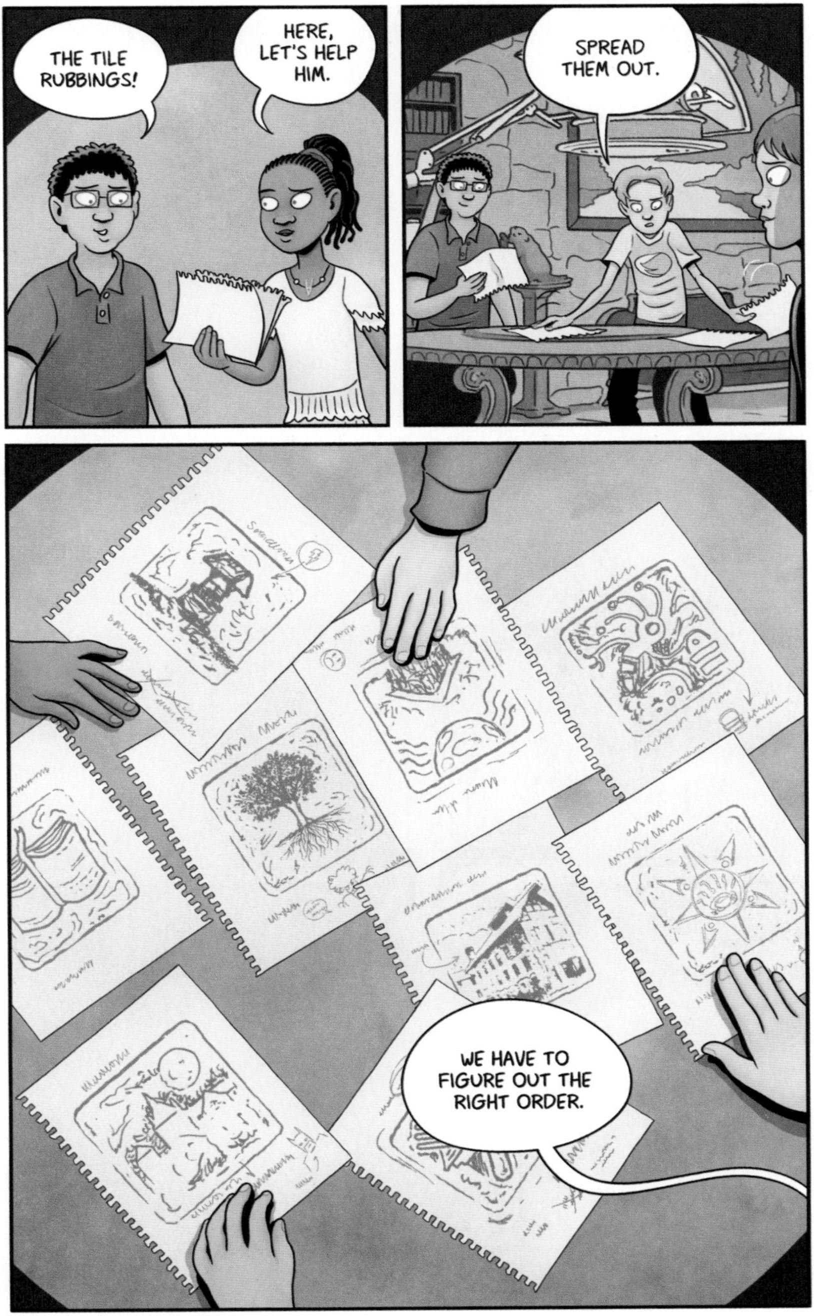
THE TILE RUBBINGS!
HERE, LET'S HELP HIM.
SPREAD THEM OUT.
WE HAVE TO FIGURE OUT THE RIGHT ORDER.

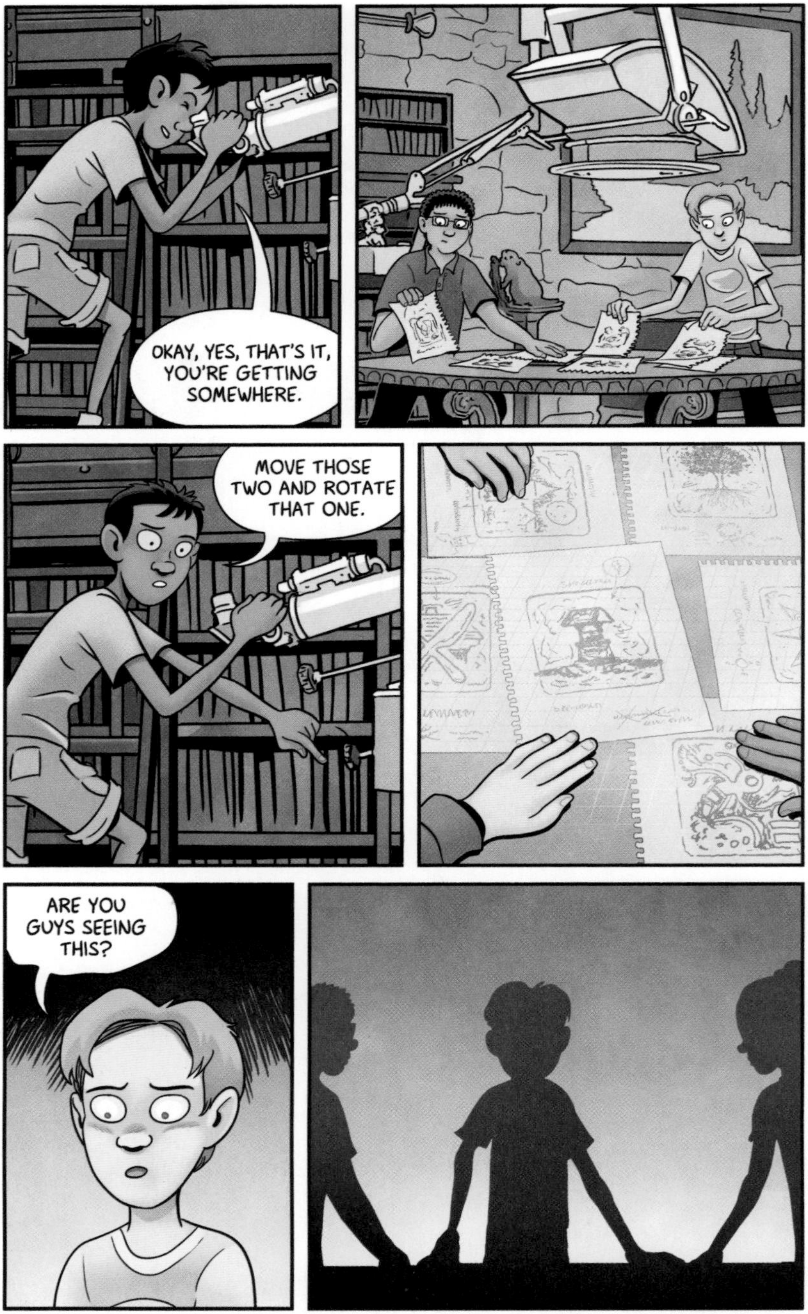
OKAY, YES, THAT'S IT, YOU'RE GETTING SOMEWHERE.
MOVE THOSE TWO AND ROTATE THAT ONE.
ARE YOU GUYS SEEING THIS?

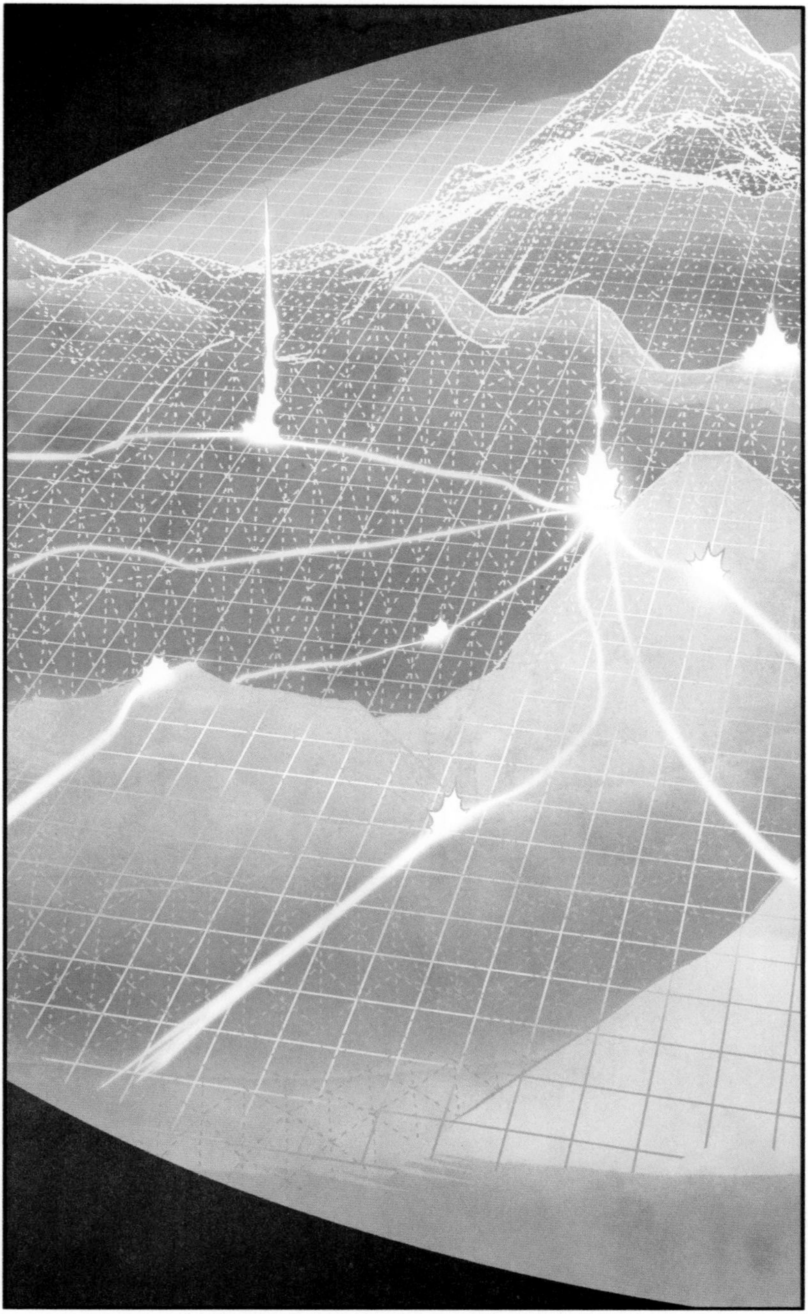

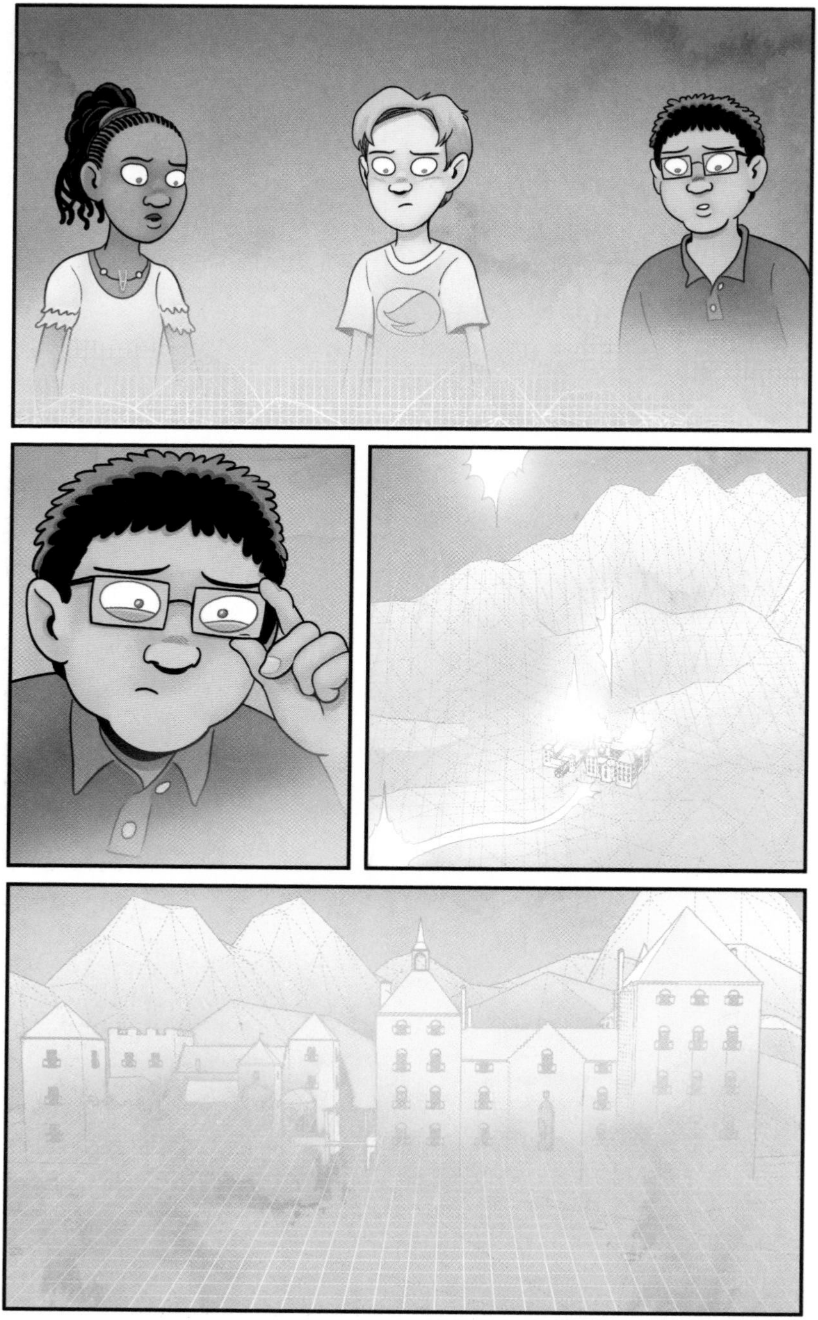

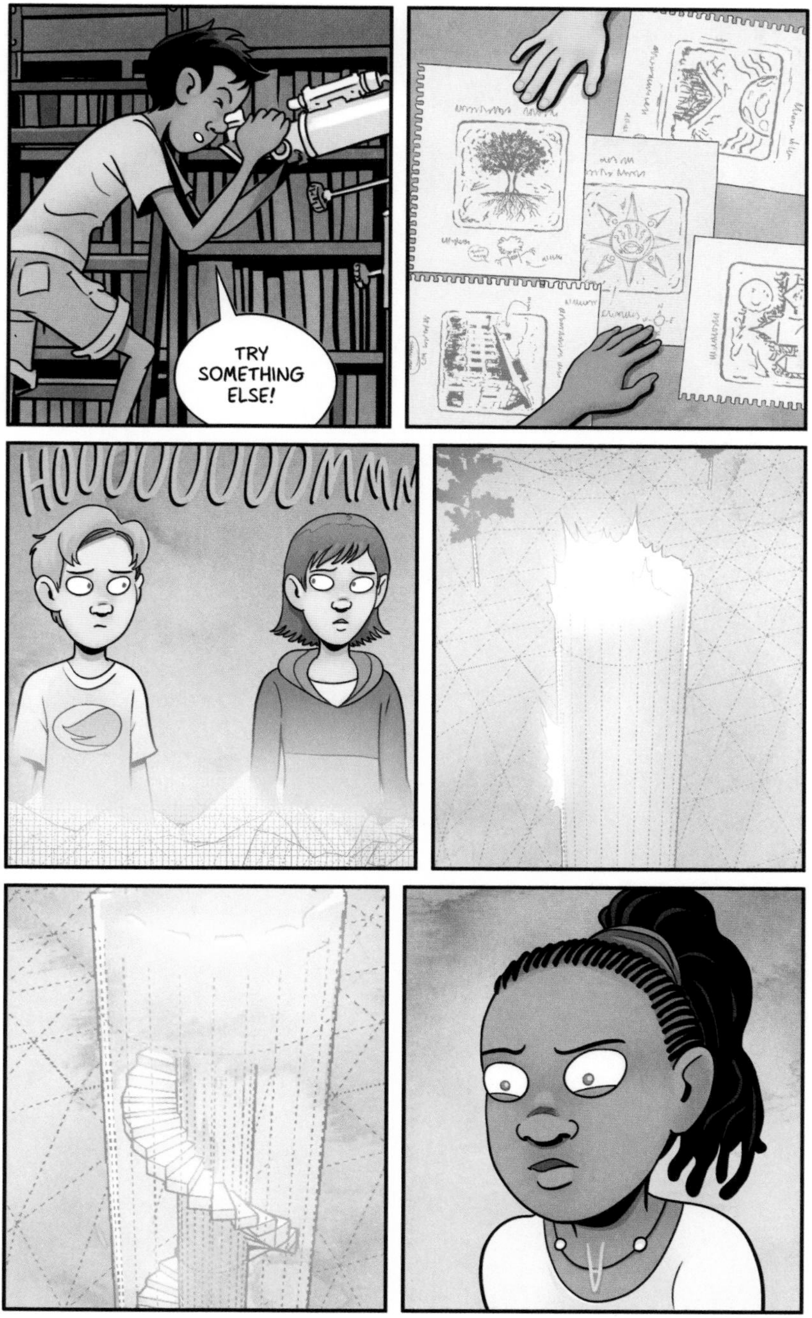
TRY SOMETHING ELSE!
HOOOOOOOOMMM

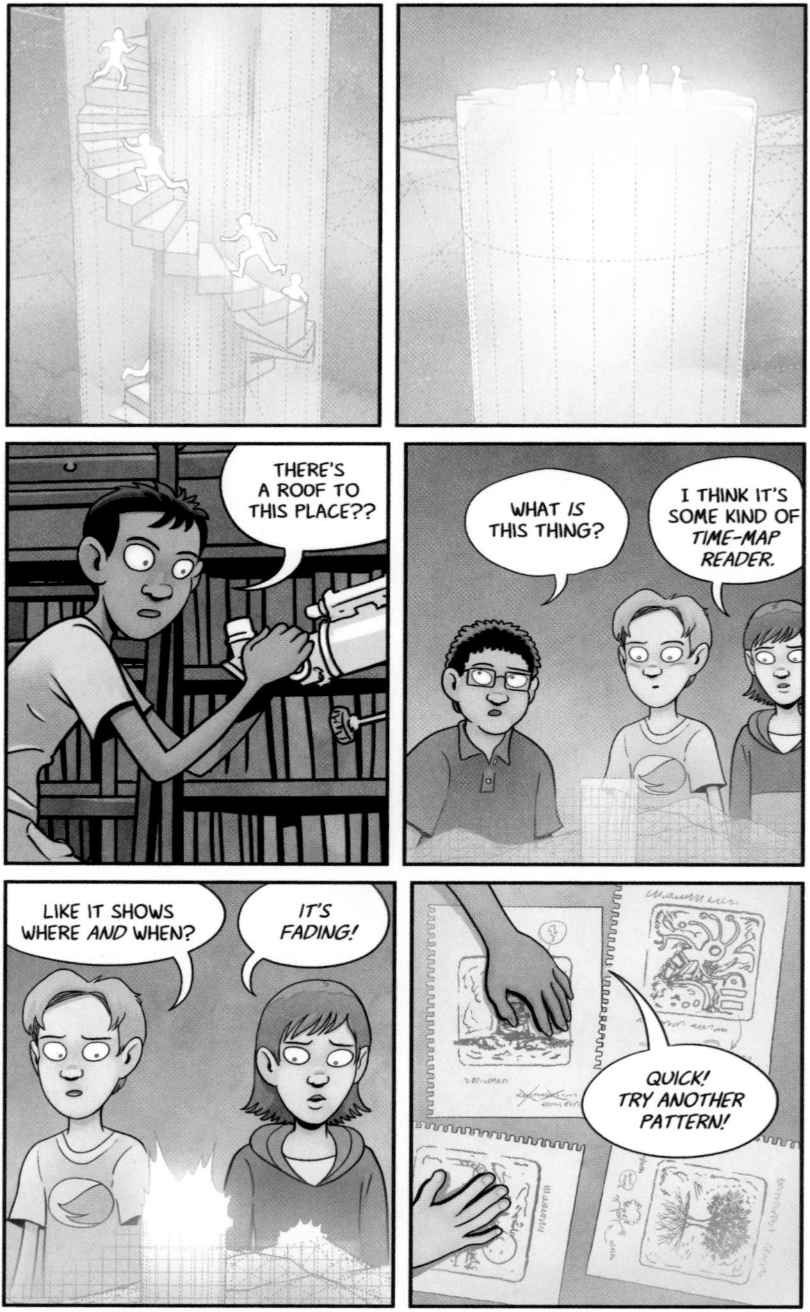
THERE'S A ROOF TO THIS PLACE??
WHAT *IS* THIS THING?
I THINK IT'S SOME KIND OF *TIME-MAP* READER.
LIKE IT SHOWS WHERE *AND* WHEN?
IT'S FADING!
QUICK! TRY ANOTHER PATTERN!

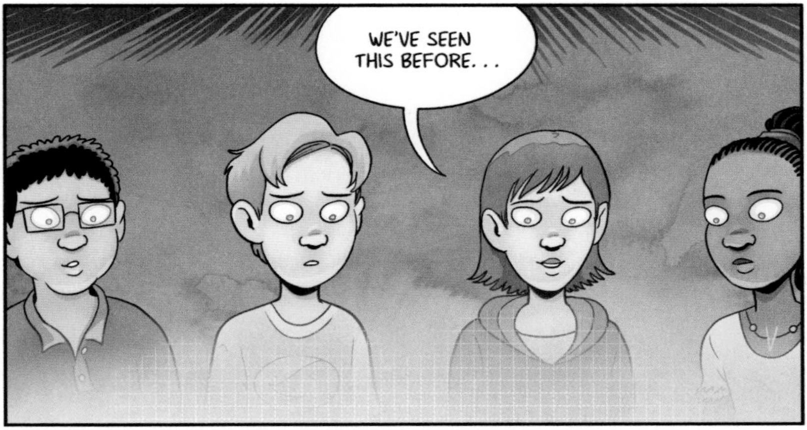
WE'VE SEEN THIS BEFORE. . .

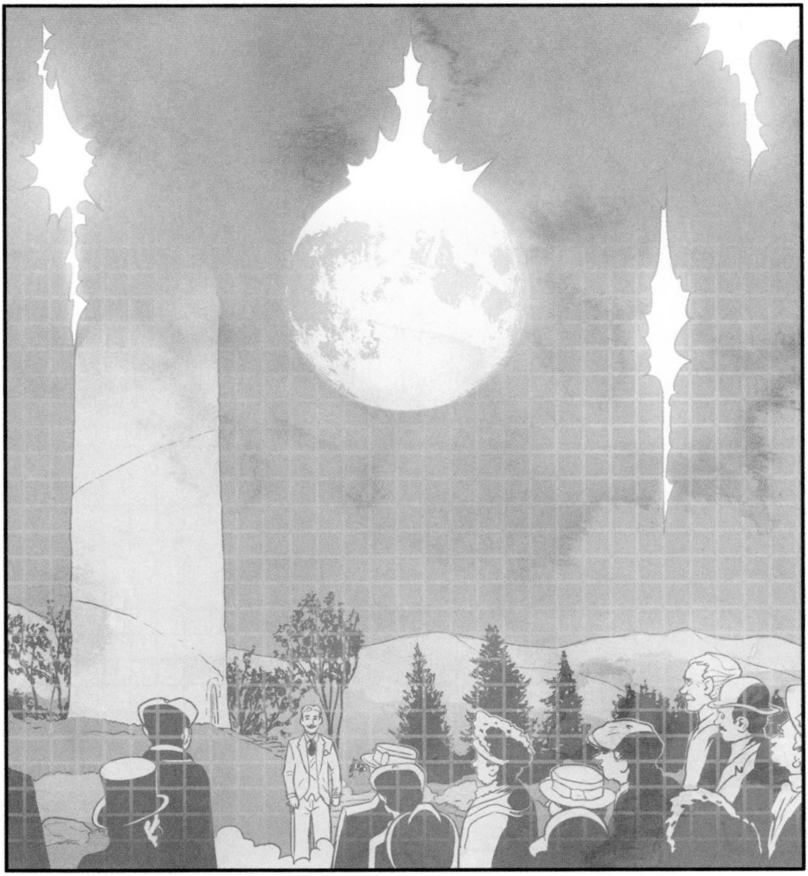

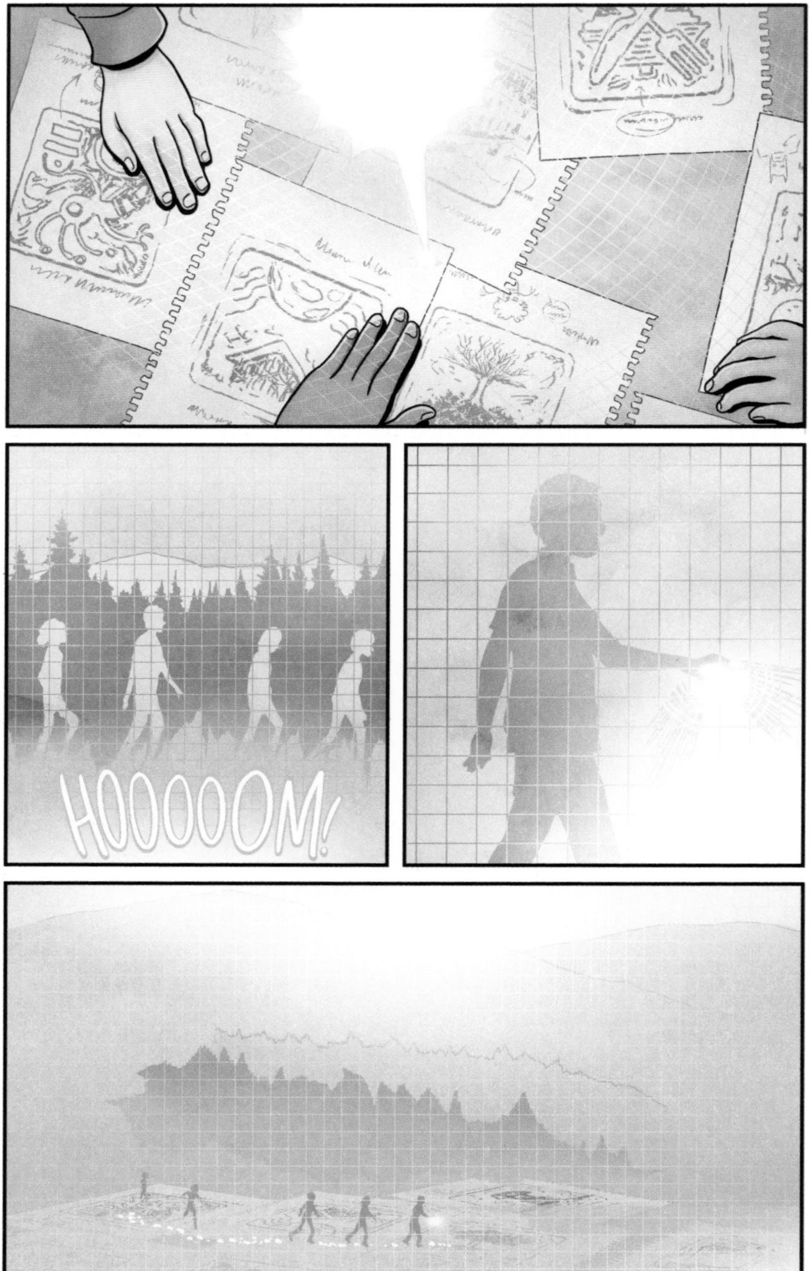
HOOOOOM!

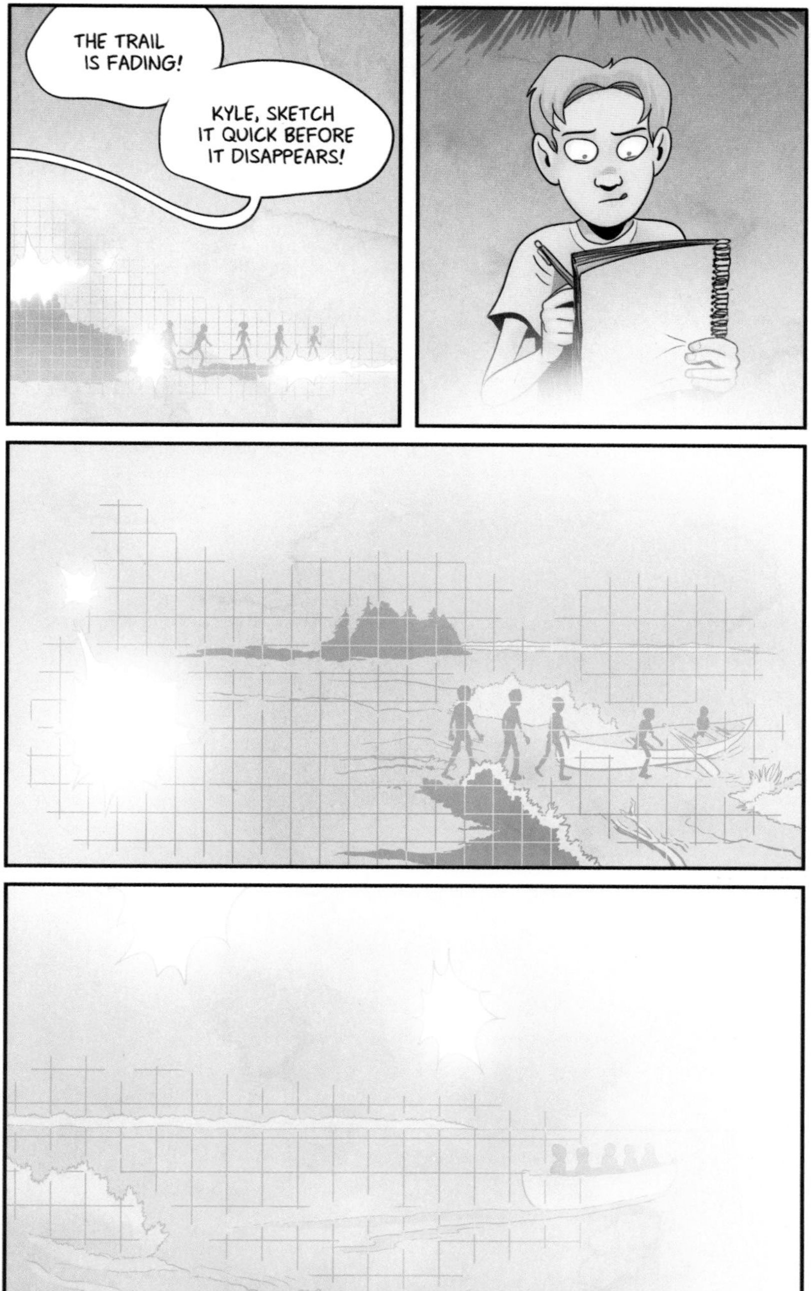
THE TRAIL IS FADING!
KYLE, SKETCH IT QUICK BEFORE IT DISAPPEARS!

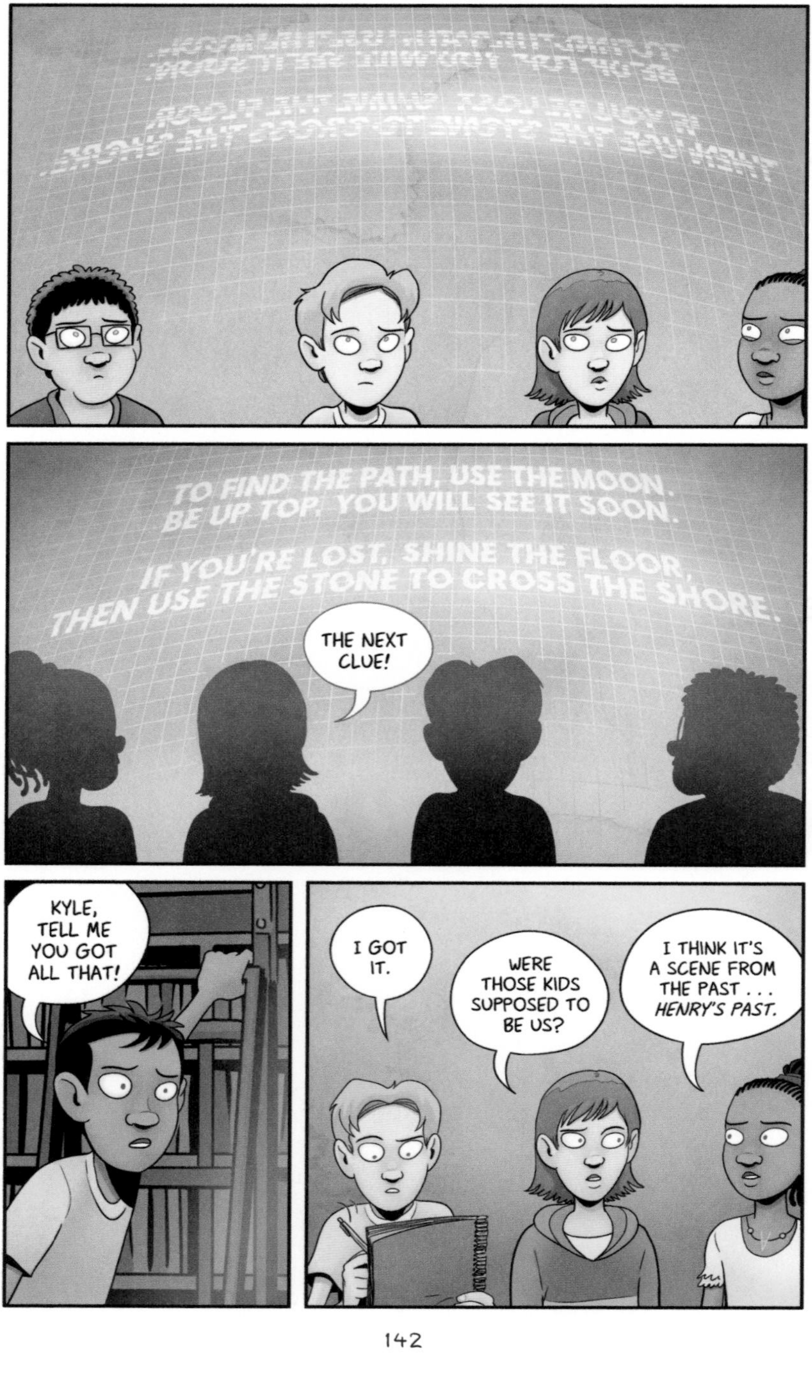

TO FIND THE PATH, USE THE MOON.
BE UP TOP, YOU WILL SEE IT SOON.
IF YOU'RE LOST, SHINE THE FLOOR,
THEN USE THE STONE TO CROSS THE SHORE.
THE NEXT CLUE!
KYLE, TELL ME YOU GOT ALL THAT!
I GOT IT.
WERE THOSE KIDS SUPPOSED TO BE US?
I THINK IT'S A SCENE FROM THE PAST . . . *HENRY'S PAST.*

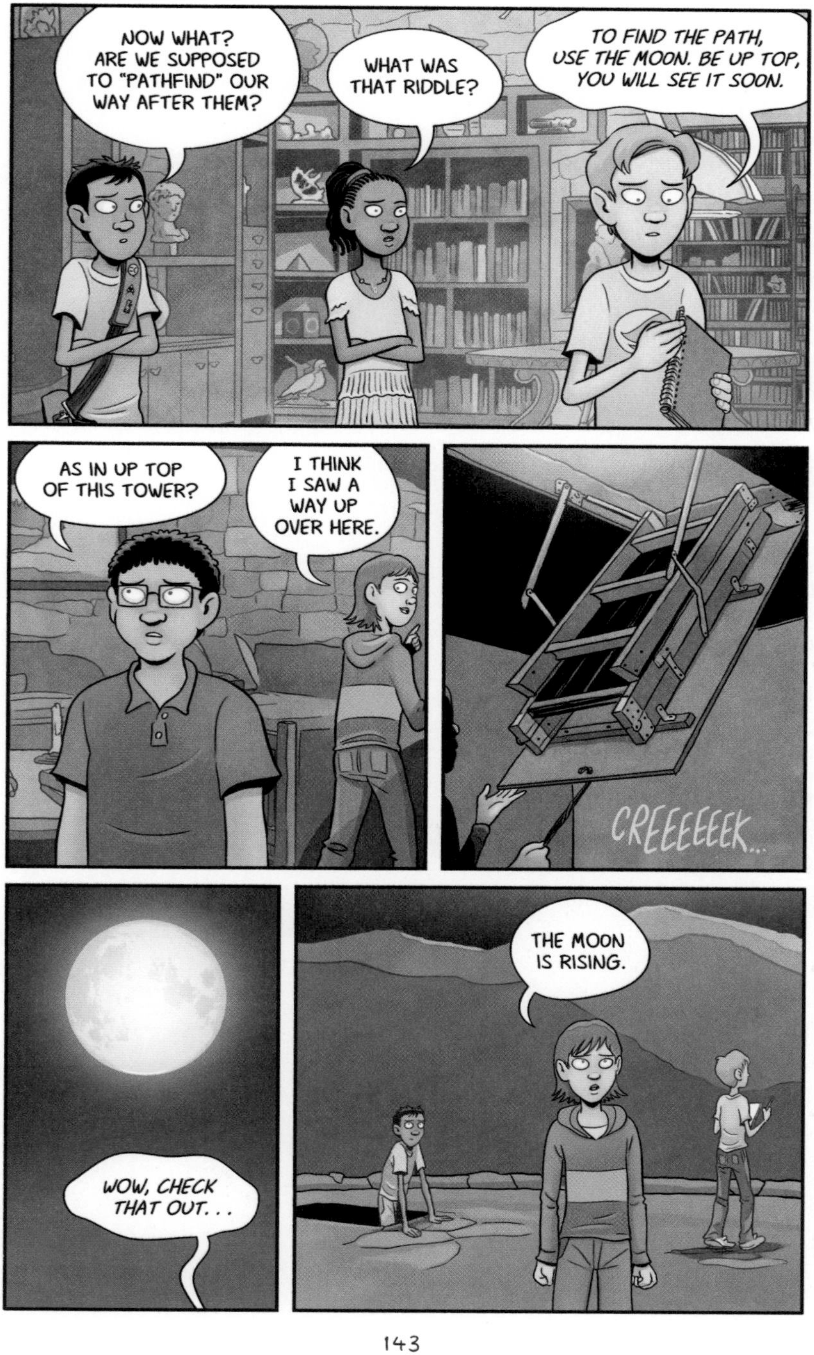
NOW WHAT? ARE WE SUPPOSED TO "PATHFIND" OUR WAY AFTER THEM?
WHAT WAS THAT RIDDLE?
TO FIND THE PATH, USE THE MOON. BE UP TOP, YOU WILL SEE IT SOON.
AS IN UP TOP OF THIS TOWER?
I THINK I SAW A WAY UP OVER HERE.
CREEEEEEK...
WOW, CHECK THAT OUT. . .
THE MOON IS RISING.

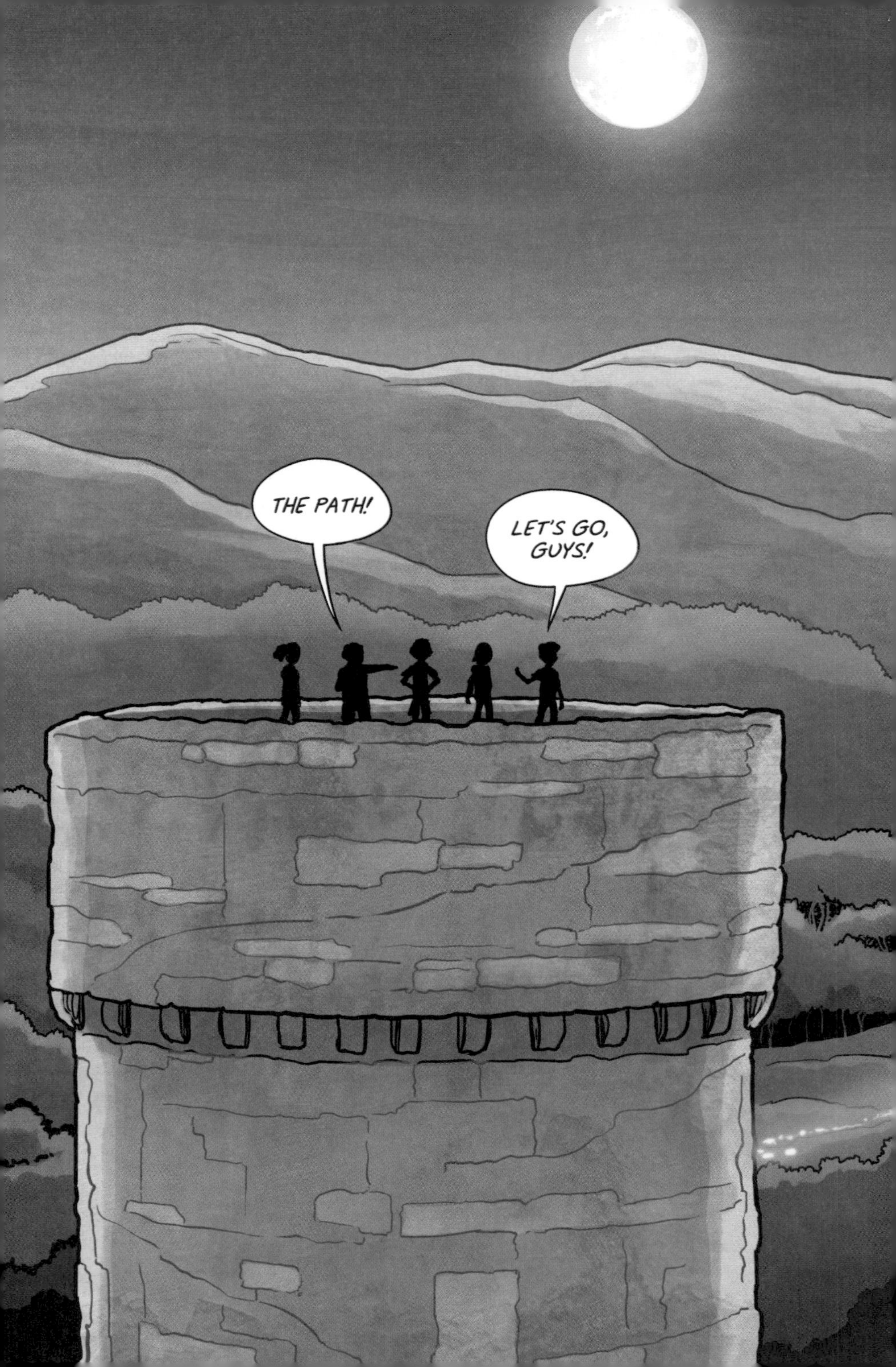
THE PATH!
LET'S GO, GUYS!

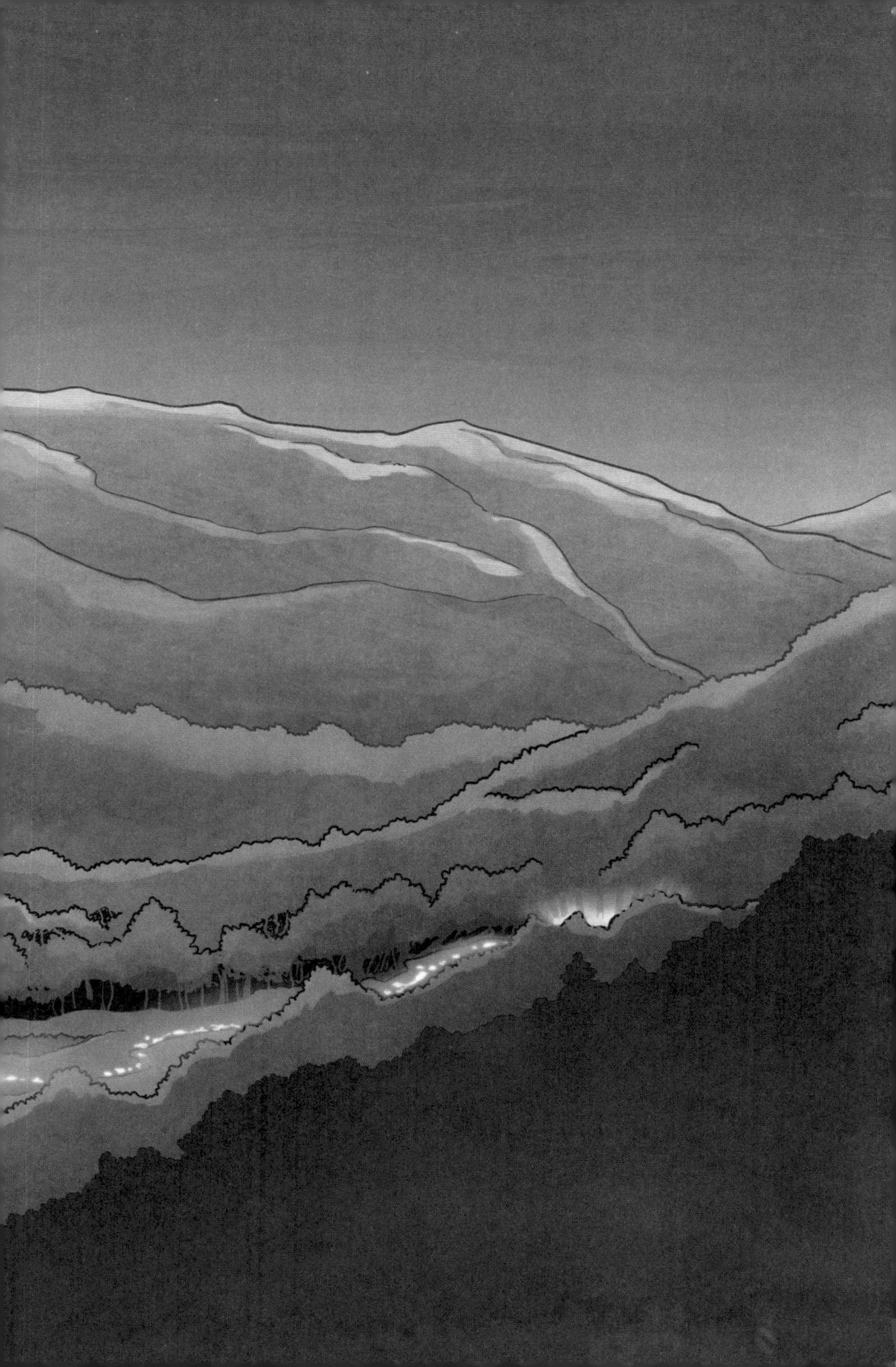

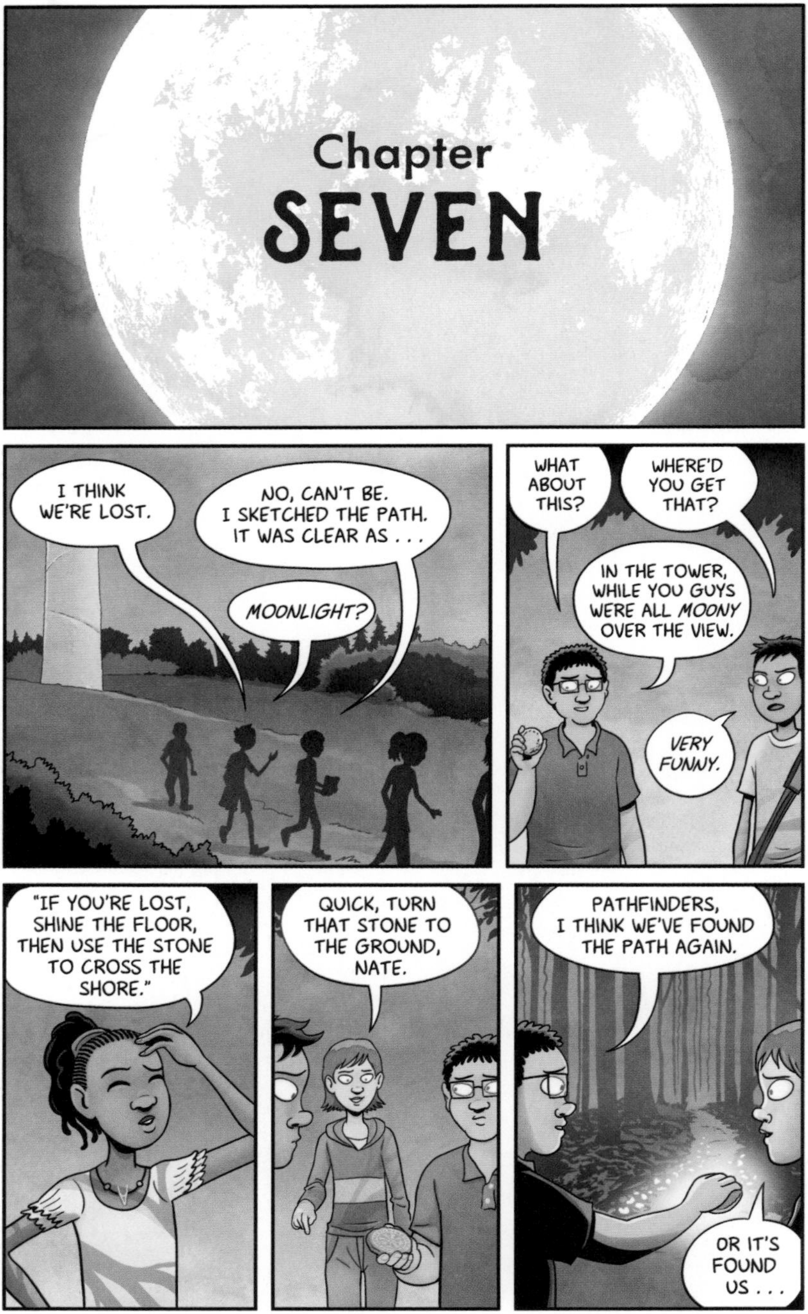
Chapter
SEVEN
I THINK WE'RE LOST.
NO, CAN'T BE. I SKETCHED THE PATH. IT WAS CLEAR AS . . .
MOONLIGHT?
WHAT ABOUT THIS?
WHERE'D YOU GET THAT?
IN THE TOWER, WHILE YOU GUYS WERE ALL MOONY OVER THE VIEW.
VERY FUNNY.
"IF YOU'RE LOST, SHINE THE FLOOR, THEN USE THE STONE TO CROSS THE SHORE."
QUICK, TURN THAT STONE TO THE GROUND, NATE.
PATHFINDERS, I THINK WE'VE FOUND THE PATH AGAIN.
OR IT'S FOUND US . . .

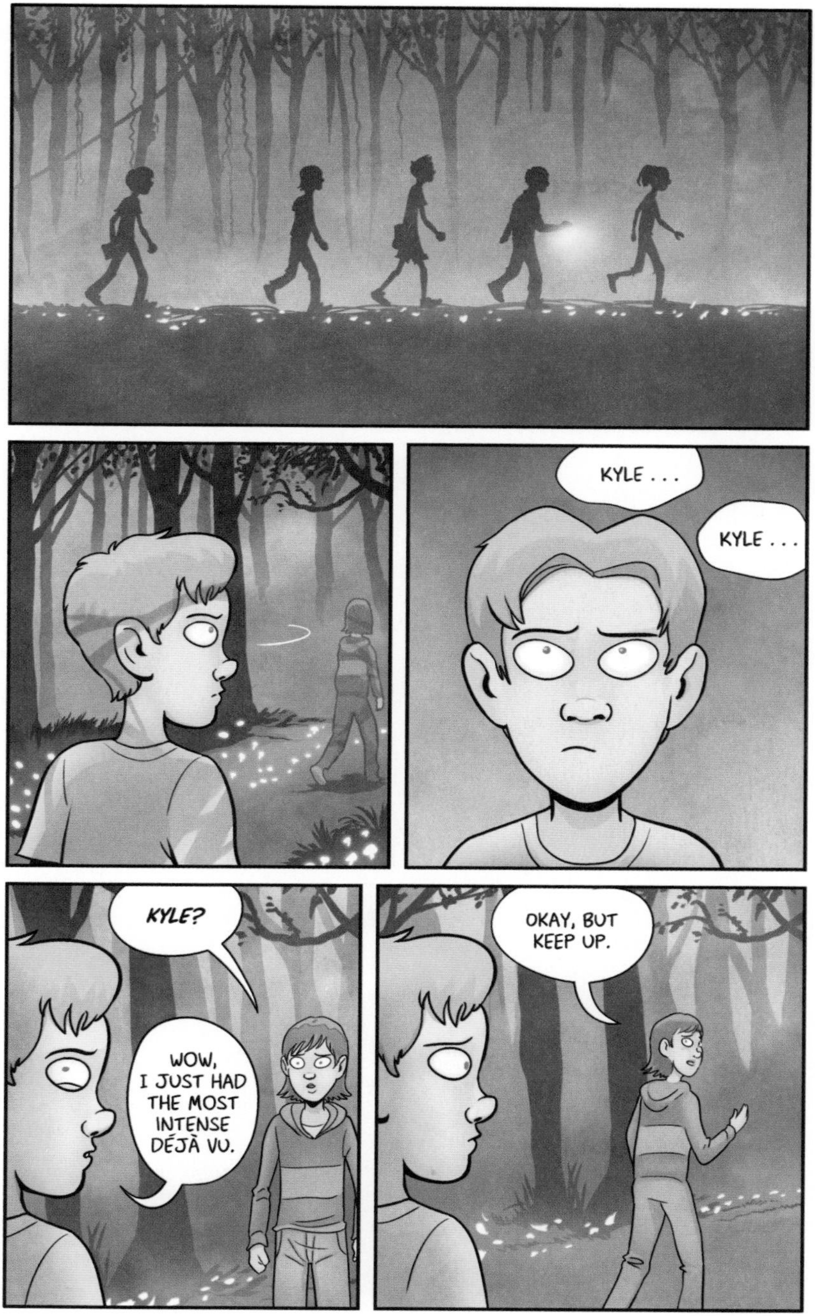
KYLE . . .
KYLE . . .
KYLE?
WOW, I JUST HAD THE MOST INTENSE DÉJÀ VU.
OKAY, BUT KEEP UP.

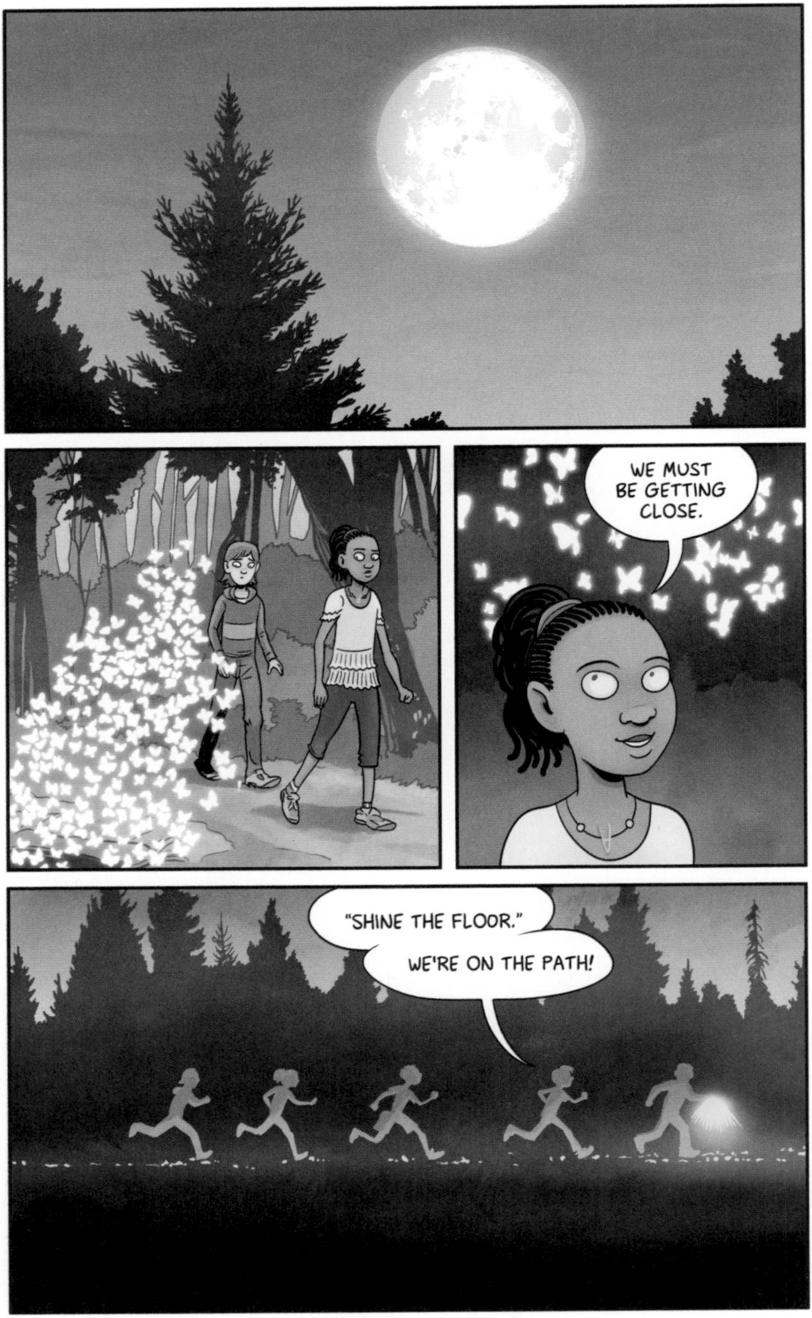
WE MUST BE GETTING CLOSE.
"SHINE THE FLOOR."
WE'RE ON THE PATH!

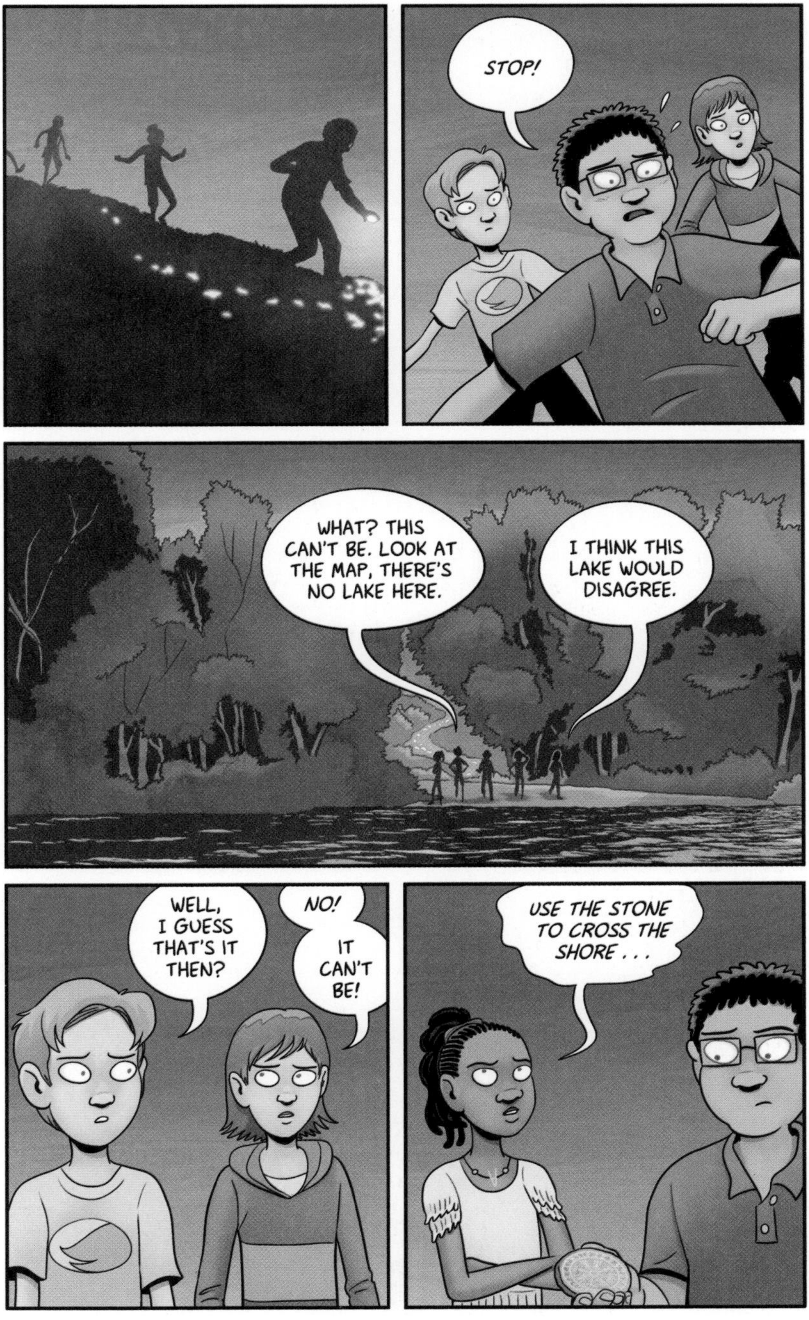
STOP!
WHAT? THIS CAN'T BE. LOOK AT THE MAP, THERE'S NO LAKE HERE.
I THINK THIS LAKE WOULD DISAGREE.
WELL, I GUESS THAT'S IT THEN?
NO!
IT CAN'T BE!
USE THE STONE TO CROSS THE SHORE . . .

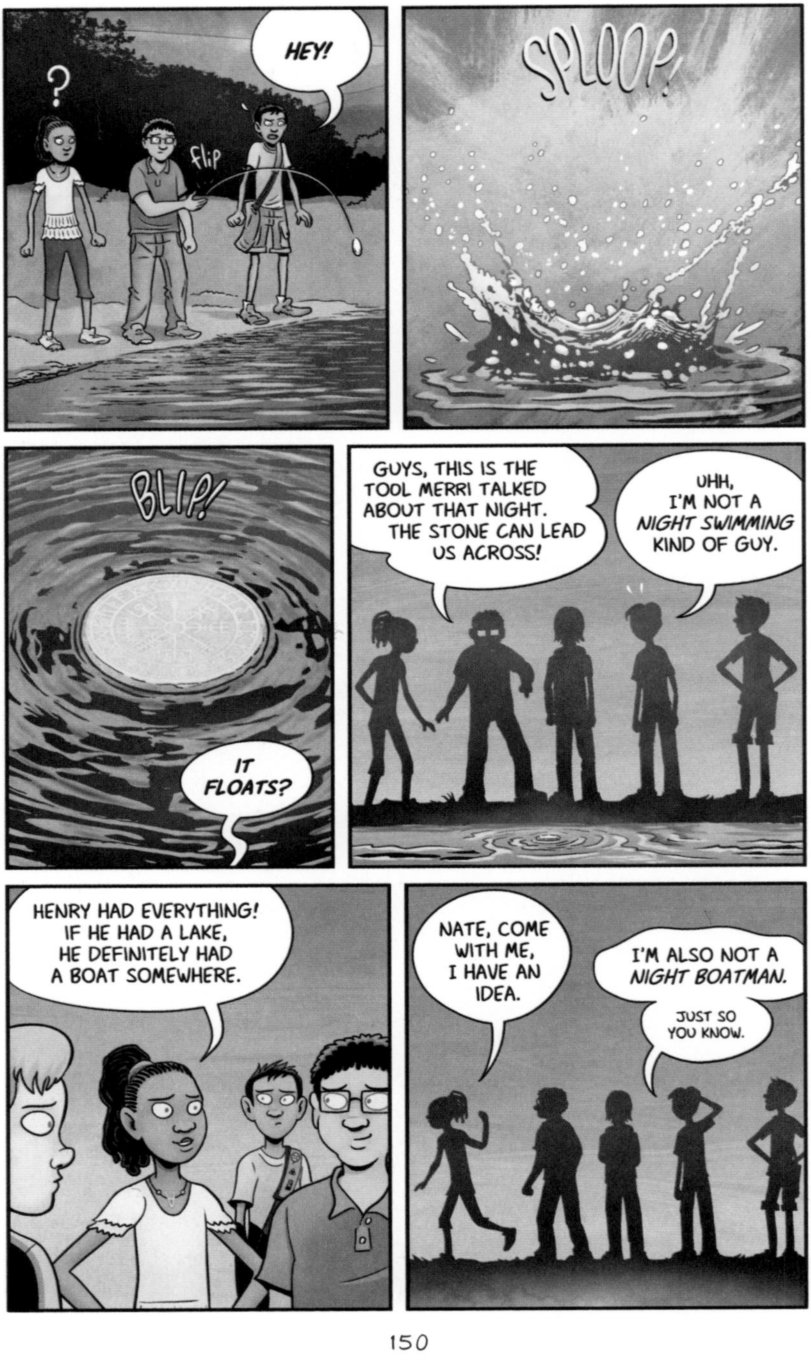

HEY!
?
flip
SPLOOP!
BLIP!
IT FLOATS?
GUYS, THIS IS THE TOOL MERRI TALKED ABOUT THAT NIGHT. THE STONE CAN LEAD US ACROSS!
UHH, I'M NOT A *NIGHT SWIMMING* KIND OF GUY.
HENRY HAD EVERYTHING! IF HE HAD A LAKE, HE DEFINITELY HAD A BOAT SOMEWHERE.
NATE, COME WITH ME, I HAVE AN IDEA.
I'M ALSO NOT A *NIGHT BOATMAN.*
JUST SO YOU KNOW.

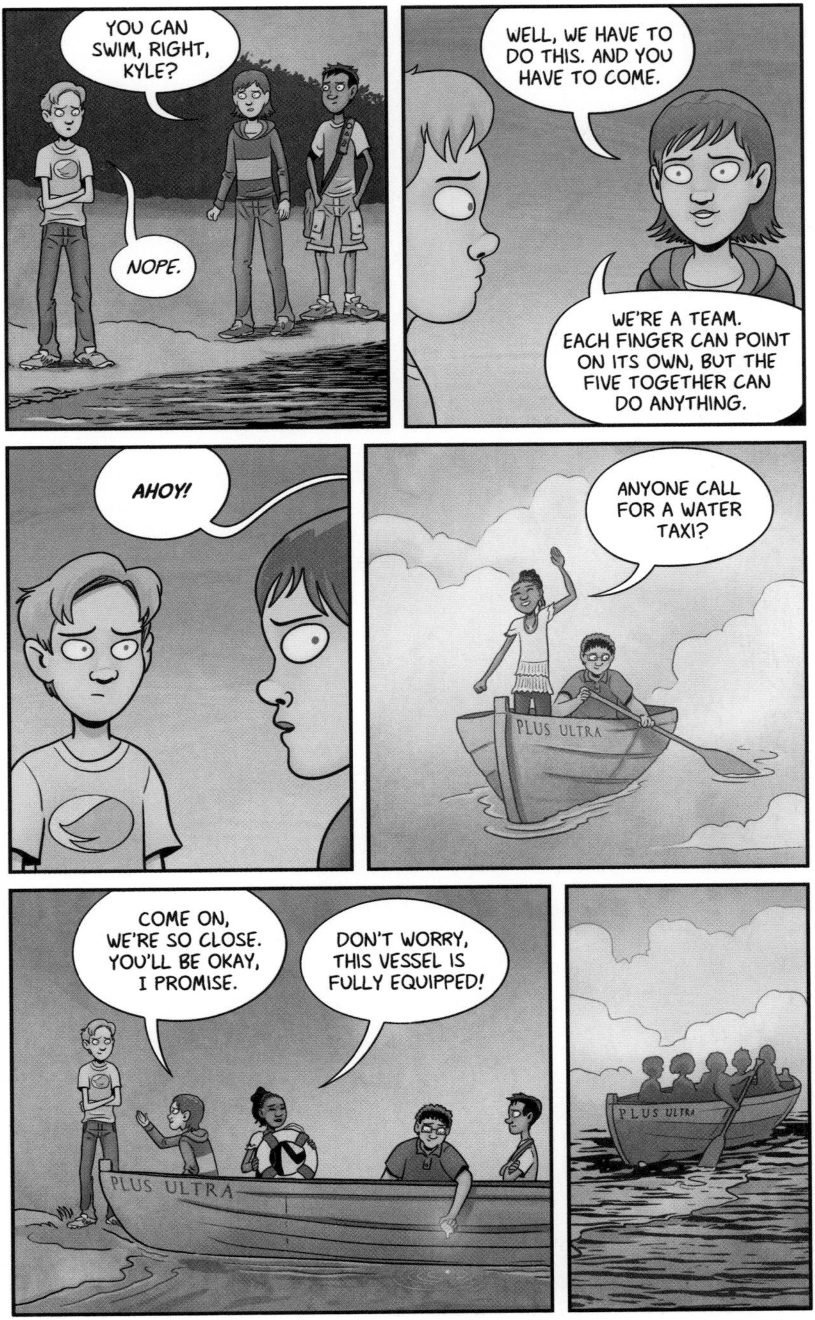
YOU CAN SWIM, RIGHT, KYLE?
NOPE.
WELL, WE HAVE TO DO THIS. AND YOU HAVE TO COME.
WE'RE A TEAM. EACH FINGER CAN POINT ON ITS OWN, BUT THE FIVE TOGETHER CAN DO ANYTHING.
AHOY!
ANYONE CALL FOR A WATER TAXI?
PLUS ULTRA
COME ON, WE'RE SO CLOSE. YOU'LL BE OKAY, I PROMISE.
DON'T WORRY, THIS VESSEL IS FULLY EQUIPPED!
PLUS ULTRA
PLUS ULTRA

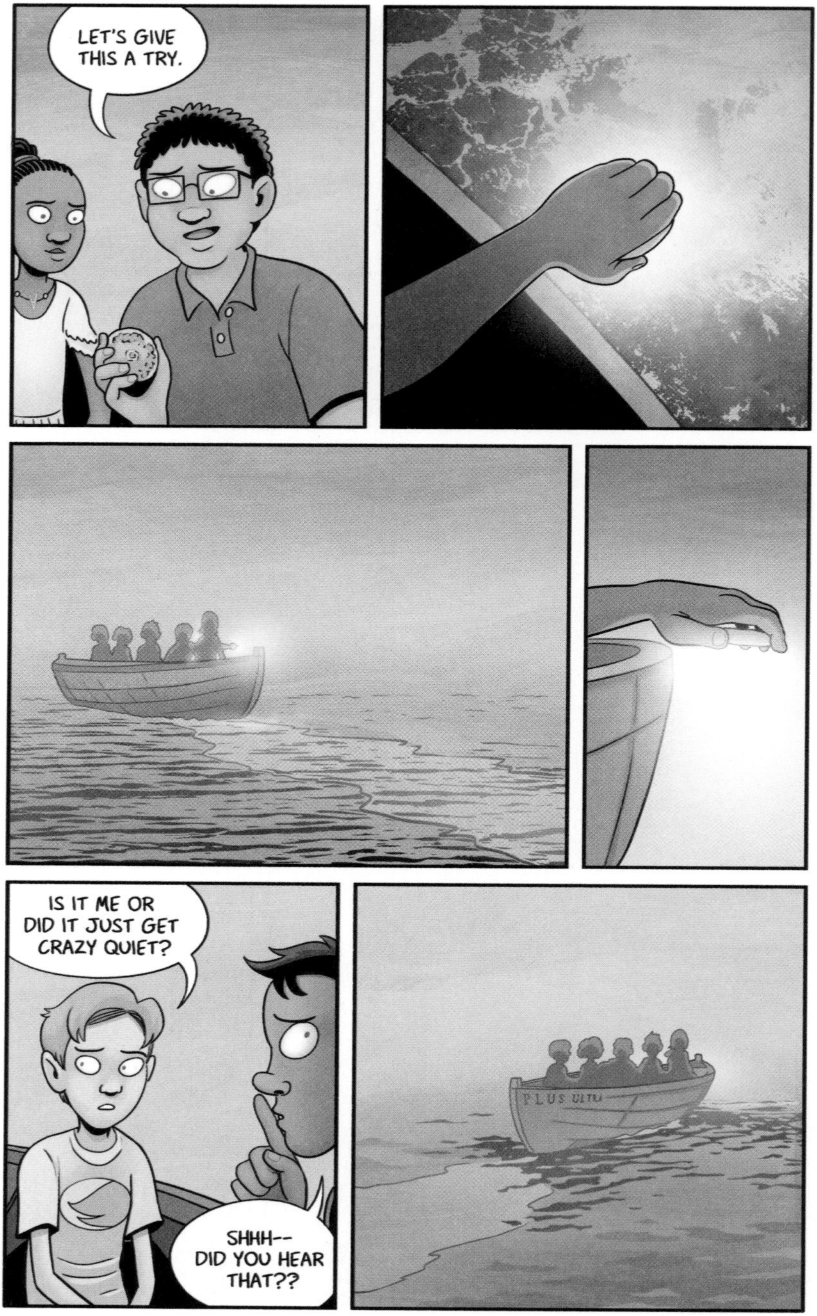
LET'S GIVE THIS A TRY.
IS IT ME OR DID IT JUST GET CRAZY QUIET?
SHHH-- DID YOU HEAR THAT??

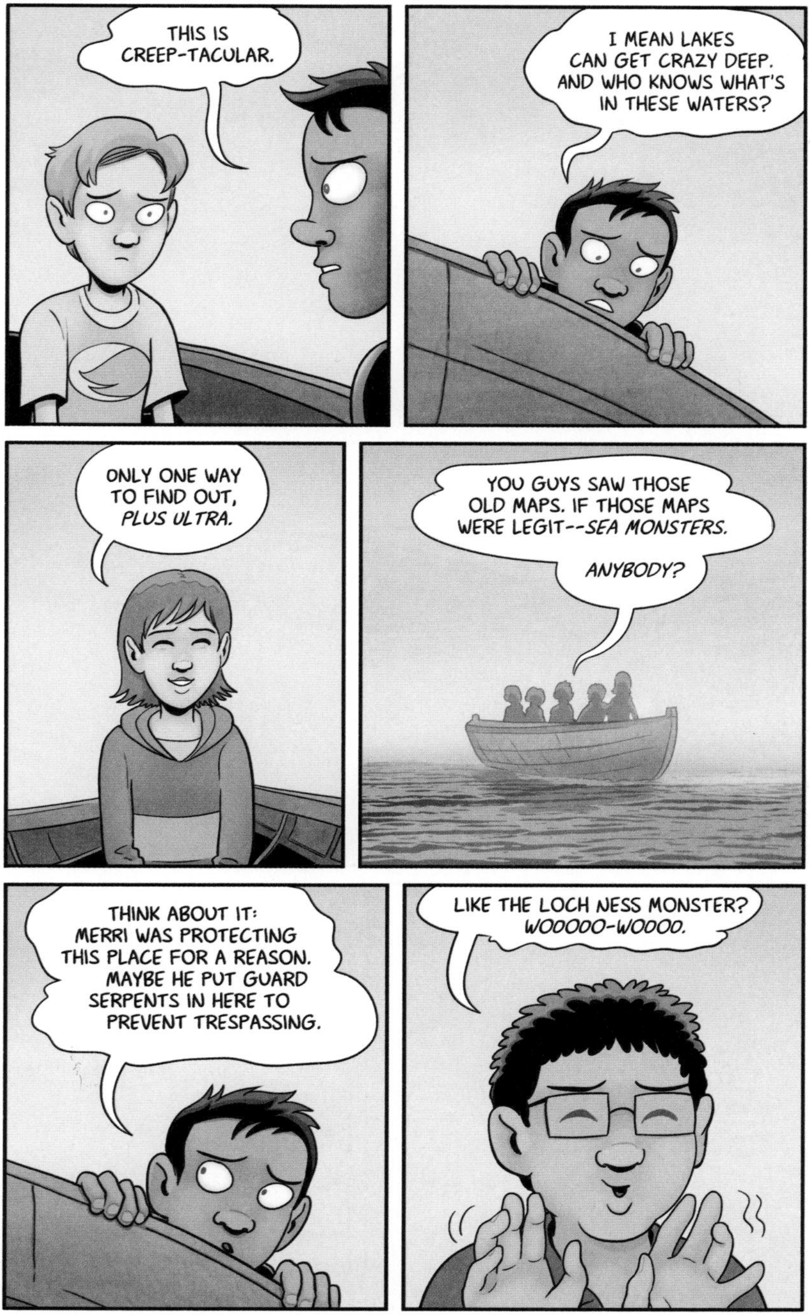
THIS IS CREEP-TACULAR.
I MEAN LAKES CAN GET CRAZY DEEP. AND WHO KNOWS WHAT'S IN THESE WATERS?
ONLY ONE WAY TO FIND OUT, *PLUS ULTRA.*
YOU GUYS SAW THOSE OLD MAPS. IF THOSE MAPS WERE LEGIT--*SEA MONSTERS.*
ANYBODY?
THINK ABOUT IT: MERRI WAS PROTECTING THIS PLACE FOR A REASON. MAYBE HE PUT GUARD SERPENTS IN HERE TO PREVENT TRESPASSING.
LIKE THE LOCH NESS MONSTER? *WOOOOO-WOOOO.*

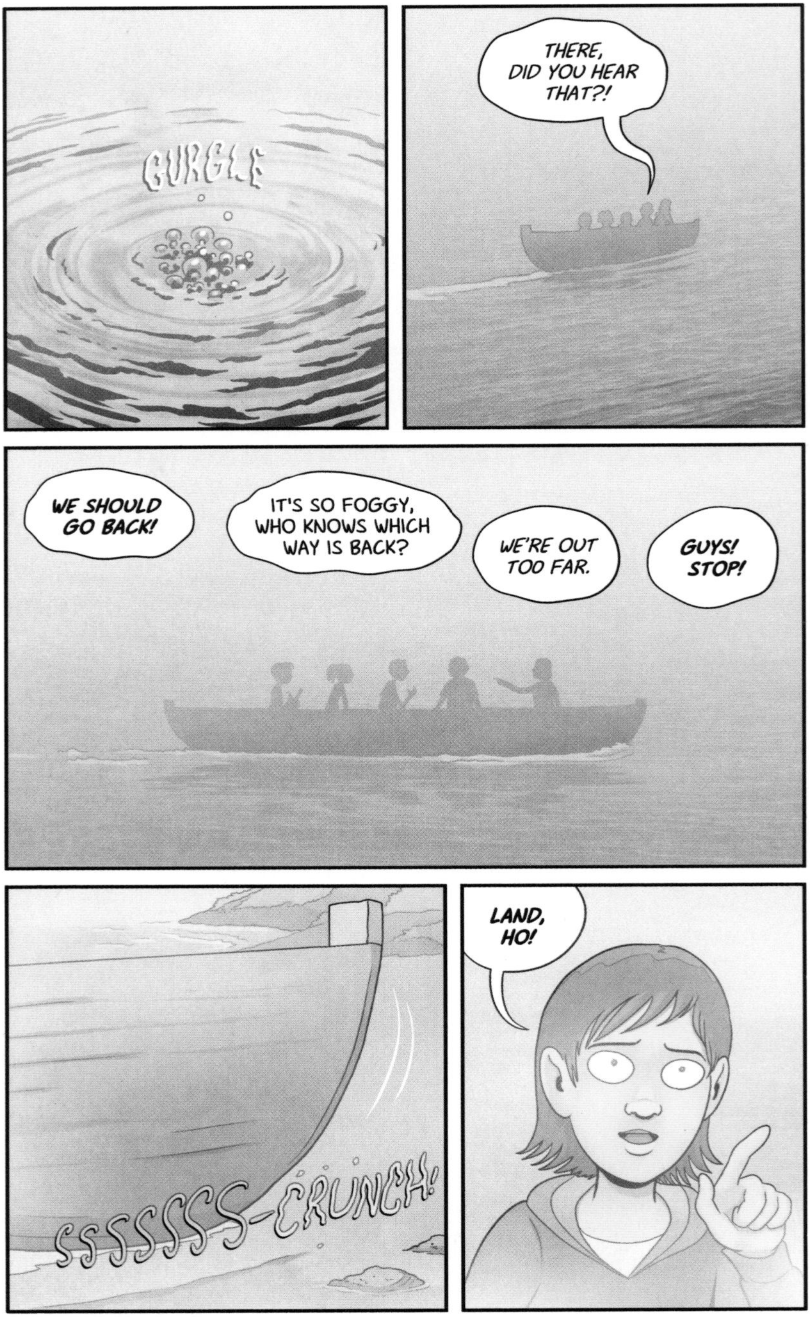
GURGLE
THERE, DID YOU HEAR THAT?!
WE SHOULD GO BACK!
IT'S SO FOGGY, WHO KNOWS WHICH WAY IS BACK?
WE'RE OUT TOO FAR.
GUYS! STOP!
SSSSSSS-CRUNCH!
LAND, HO!

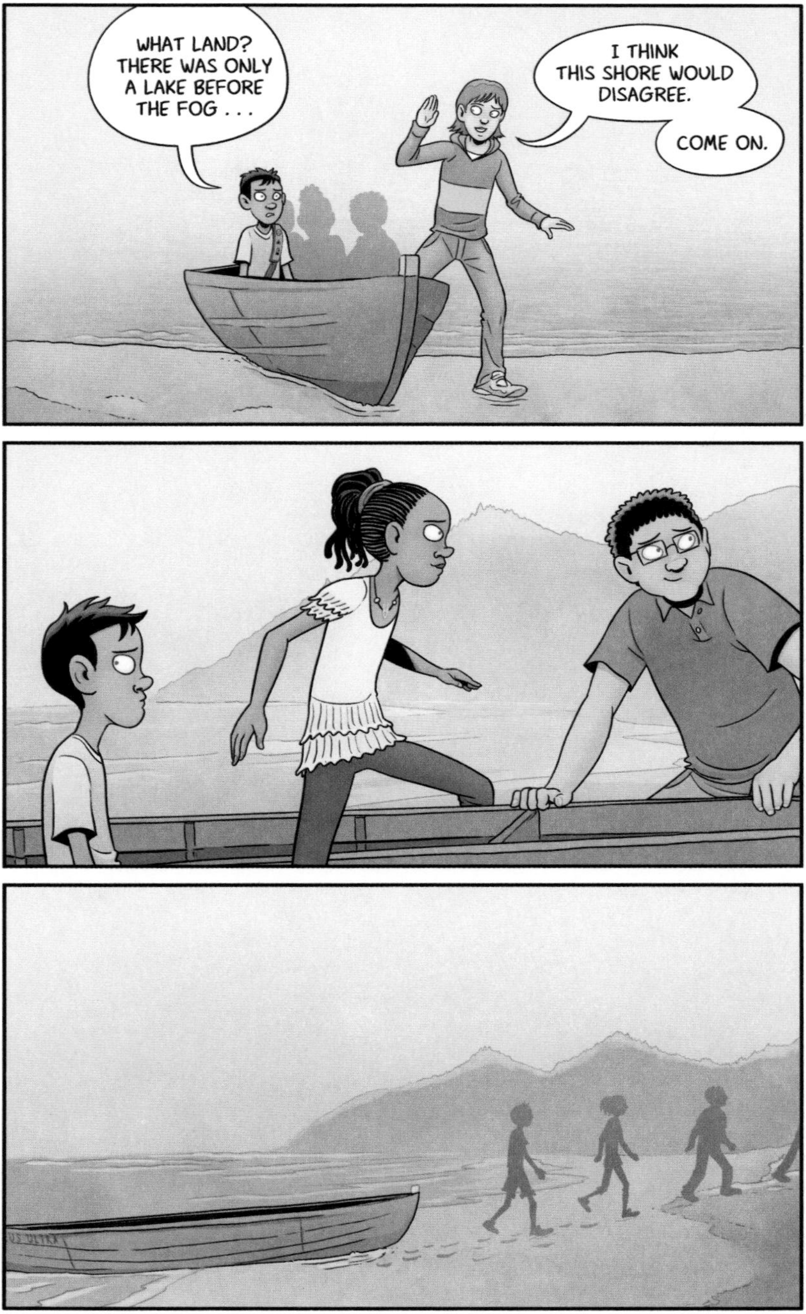
WHAT LAND? THERE WAS ONLY A LAKE BEFORE THE FOG . . .
I THINK THIS SHORE WOULD DISAGREE.
COME ON.

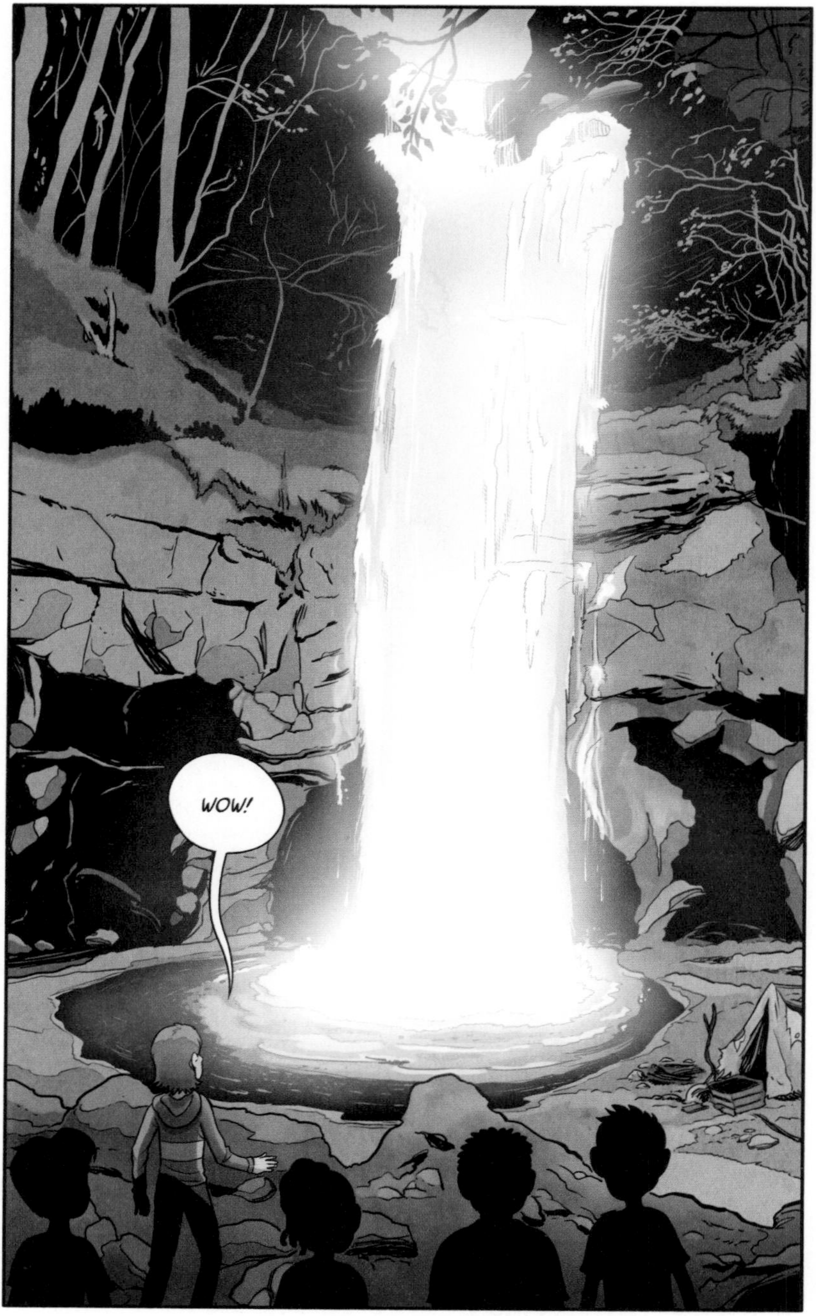
WOW!

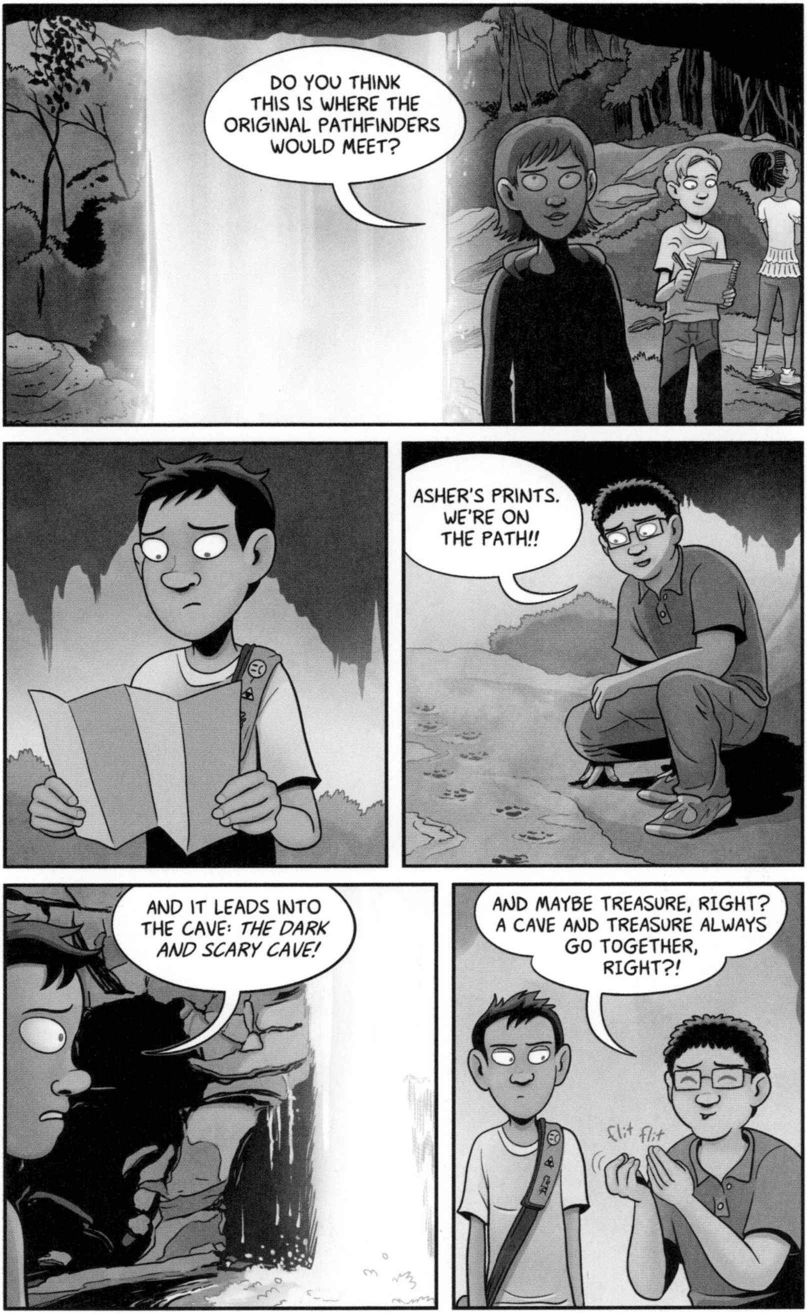
DO YOU THINK THIS IS WHERE THE ORIGINAL PATHFINDERS WOULD MEET?
ASHER'S PRINTS. WE'RE ON THE PATH!!
AND IT LEADS INTO THE CAVE: *THE DARK AND SCARY CAVE!*
AND MAYBE TREASURE, RIGHT? A CAVE AND TREASURE ALWAYS GO TOGETHER, RIGHT?!
flit flit

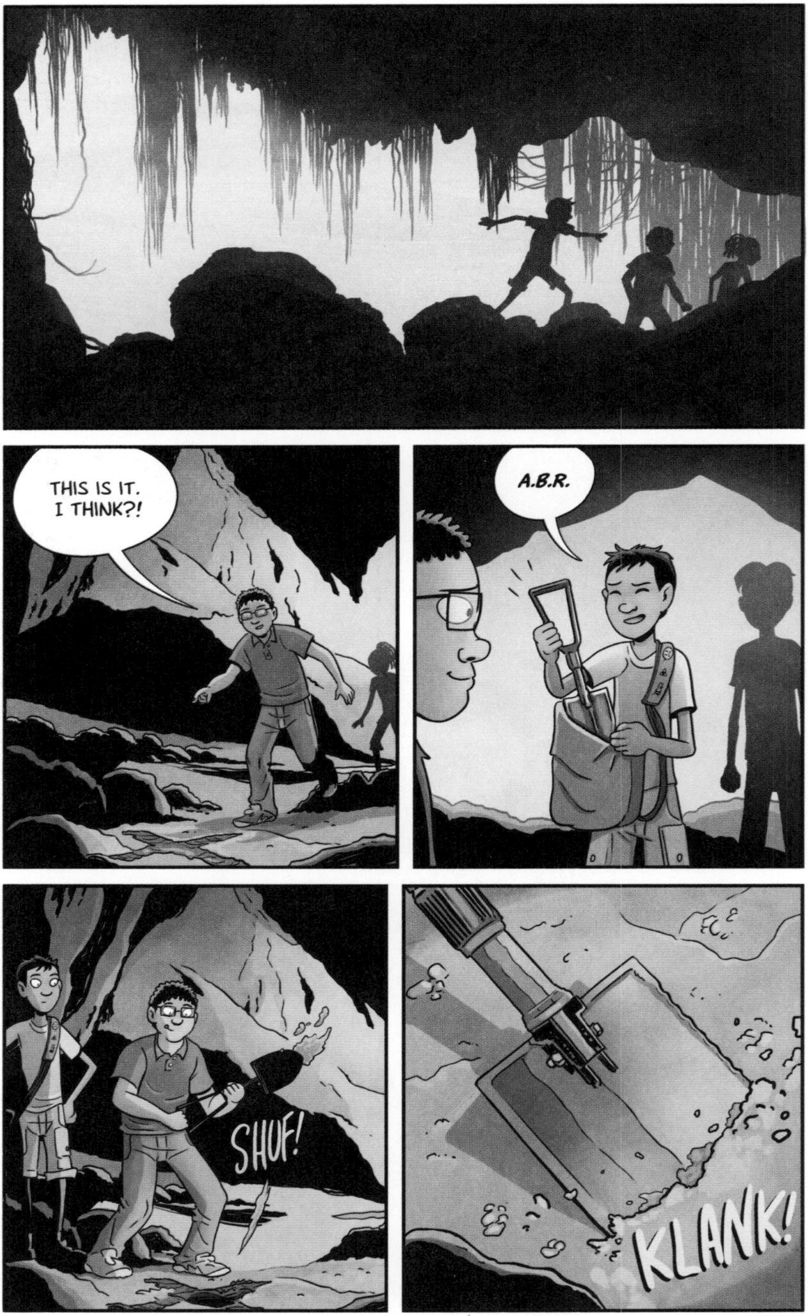
THIS IS IT.
I THINK?!
A.B.R.
SHUF!
KLANK!

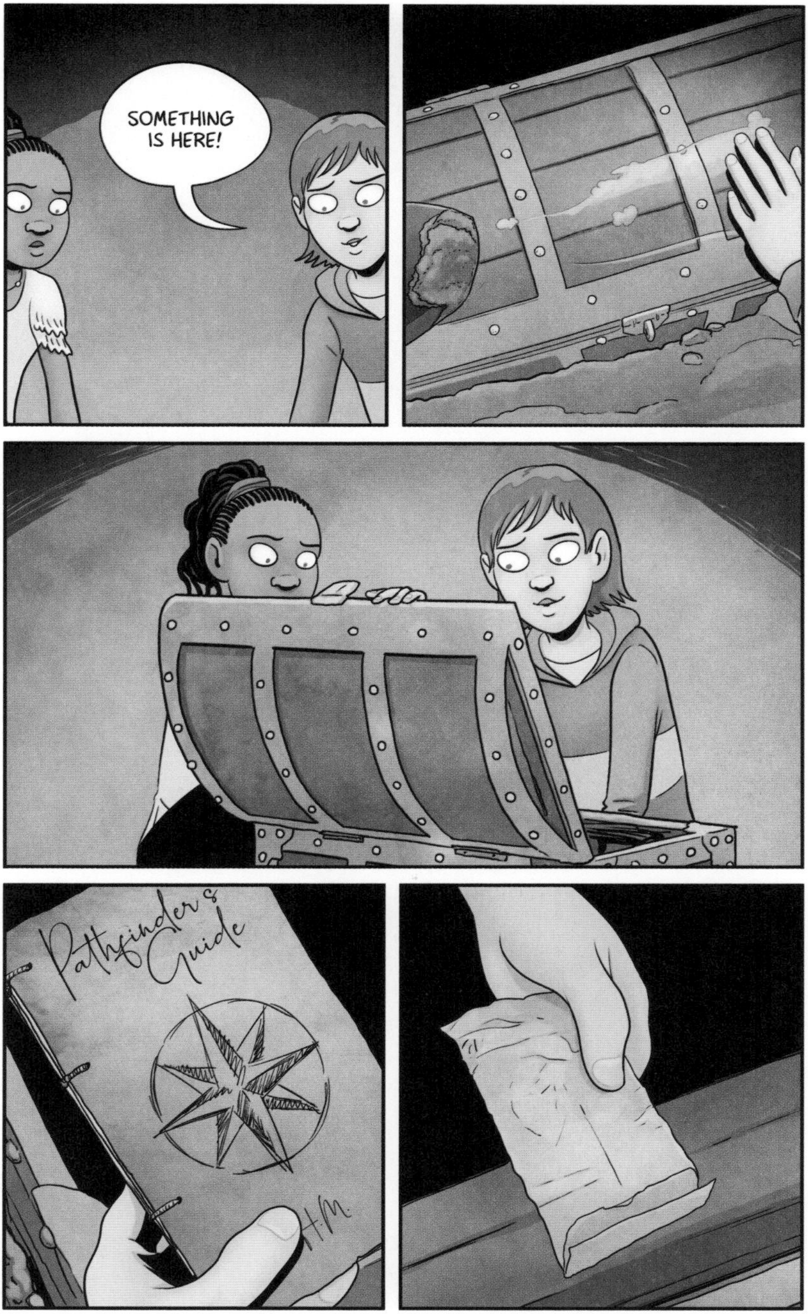
SOMETHING IS HERE!
Pathfinder's Guide
H.M.

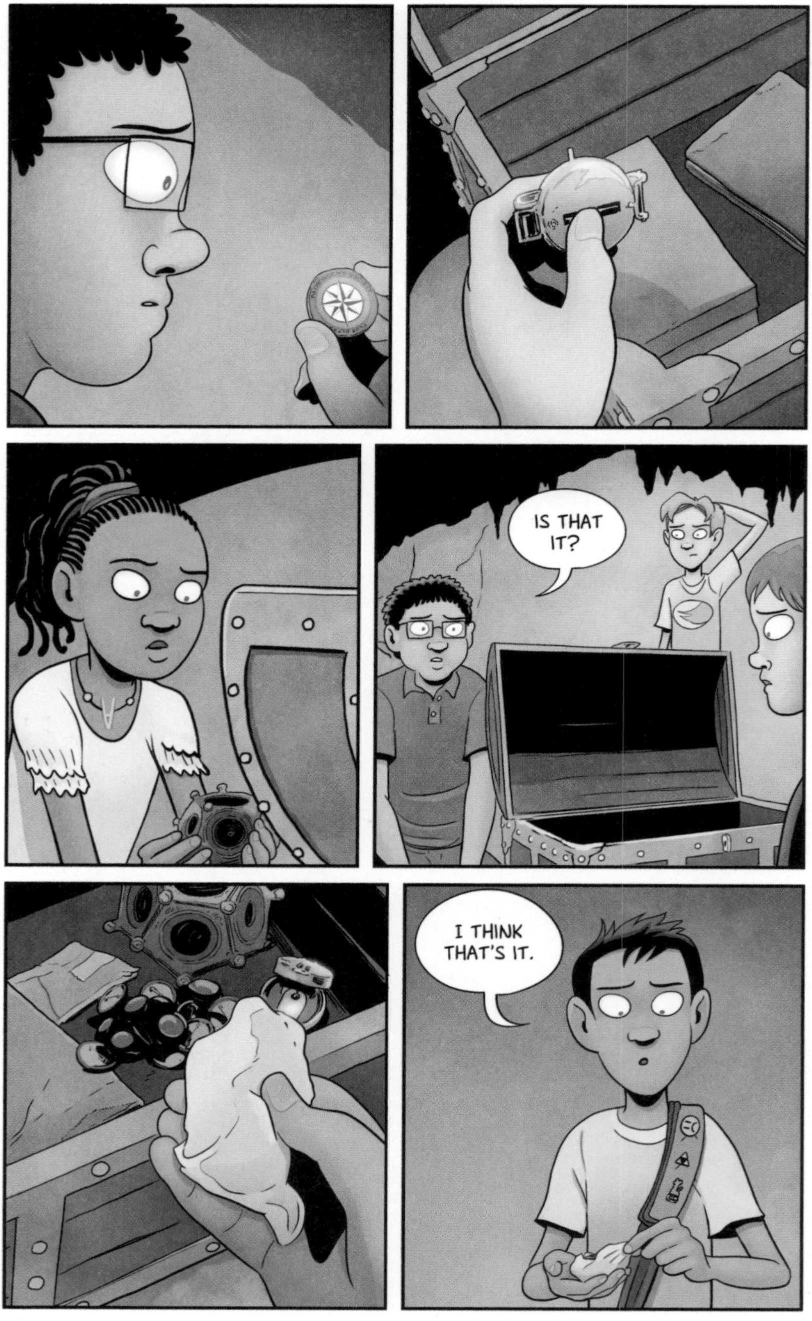
IS THAT IT?
I THINK THAT'S IT.

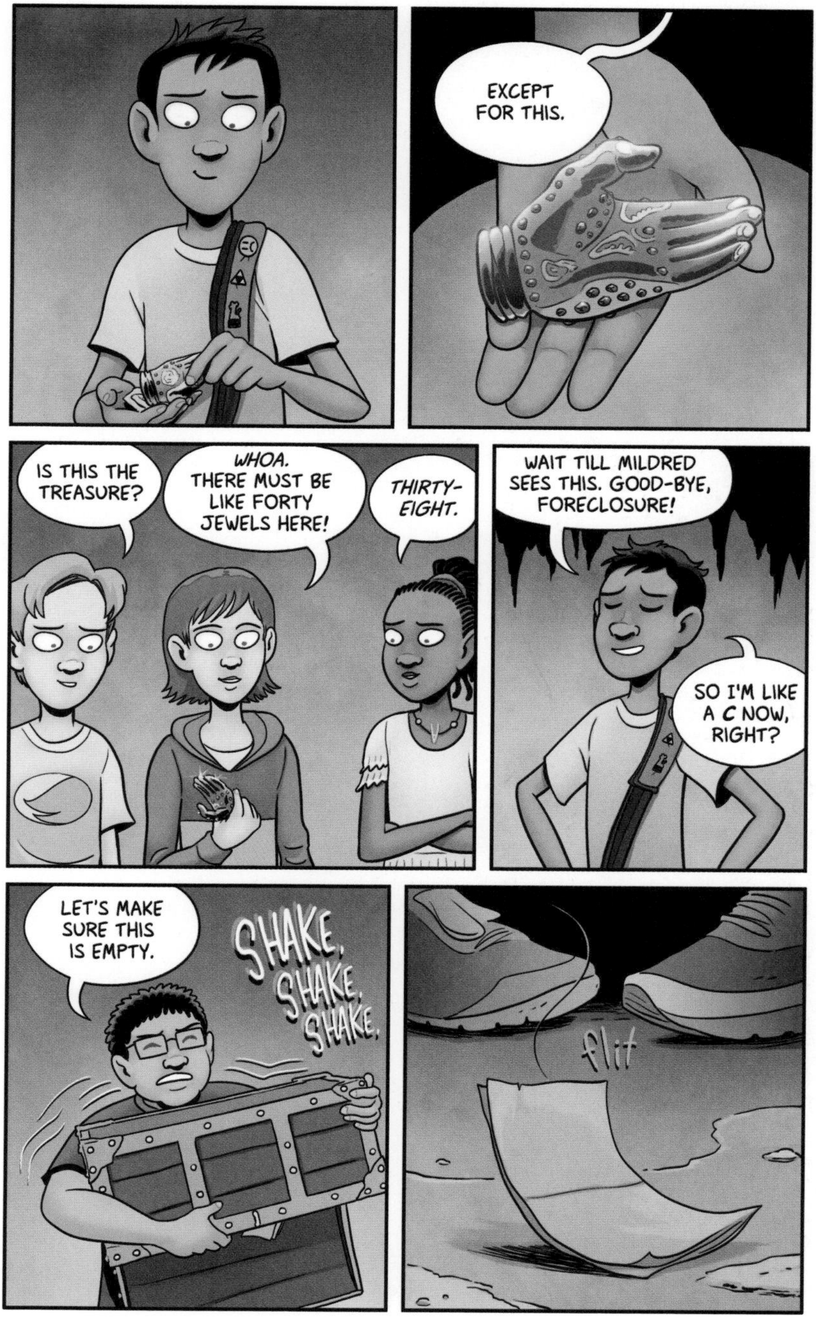
EXCEPT FOR THIS.
IS THIS THE TREASURE?
WHOA. THERE MUST BE LIKE FORTY JEWELS HERE!
THIRTY-EIGHT.
WAIT TILL MILDRED SEES THIS. GOOD-BYE, FORECLOSURE!
SO I'M LIKE A C NOW, RIGHT?
LET'S MAKE SURE THIS IS EMPTY.
SHAKE, SHAKE, SHAKE.
flit

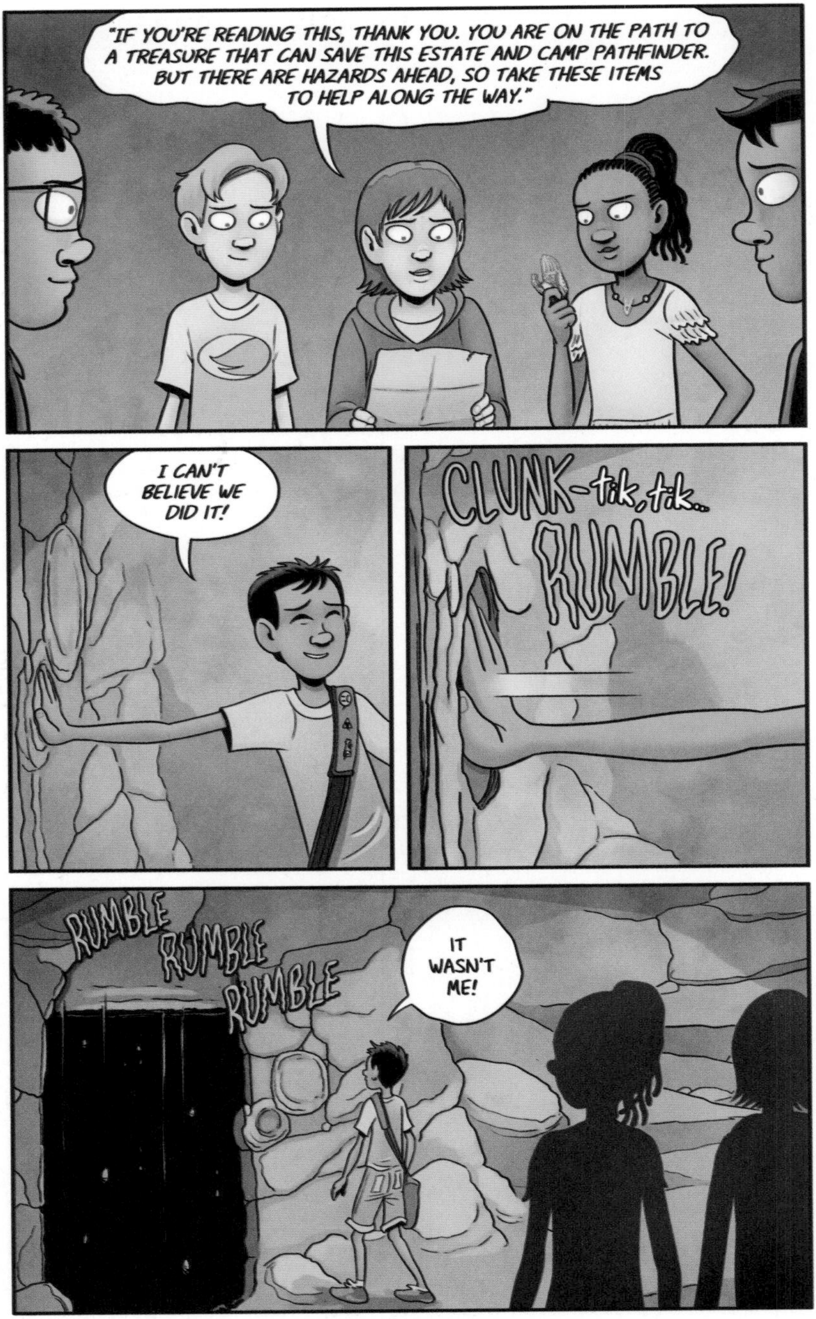
"IF YOU'RE READING THIS, THANK YOU. YOU ARE ON THE PATH TO A TREASURE THAT CAN SAVE THIS ESTATE AND CAMP PATHFINDER. BUT THERE ARE HAZARDS AHEAD, SO TAKE THESE ITEMS TO HELP ALONG THE WAY."
I CAN'T BELIEVE WE DID IT!
CLUNK-tik, tik...
RUMBLE!
RUMBLE
RUMBLE
RUMBLE
IT WASN'T ME!

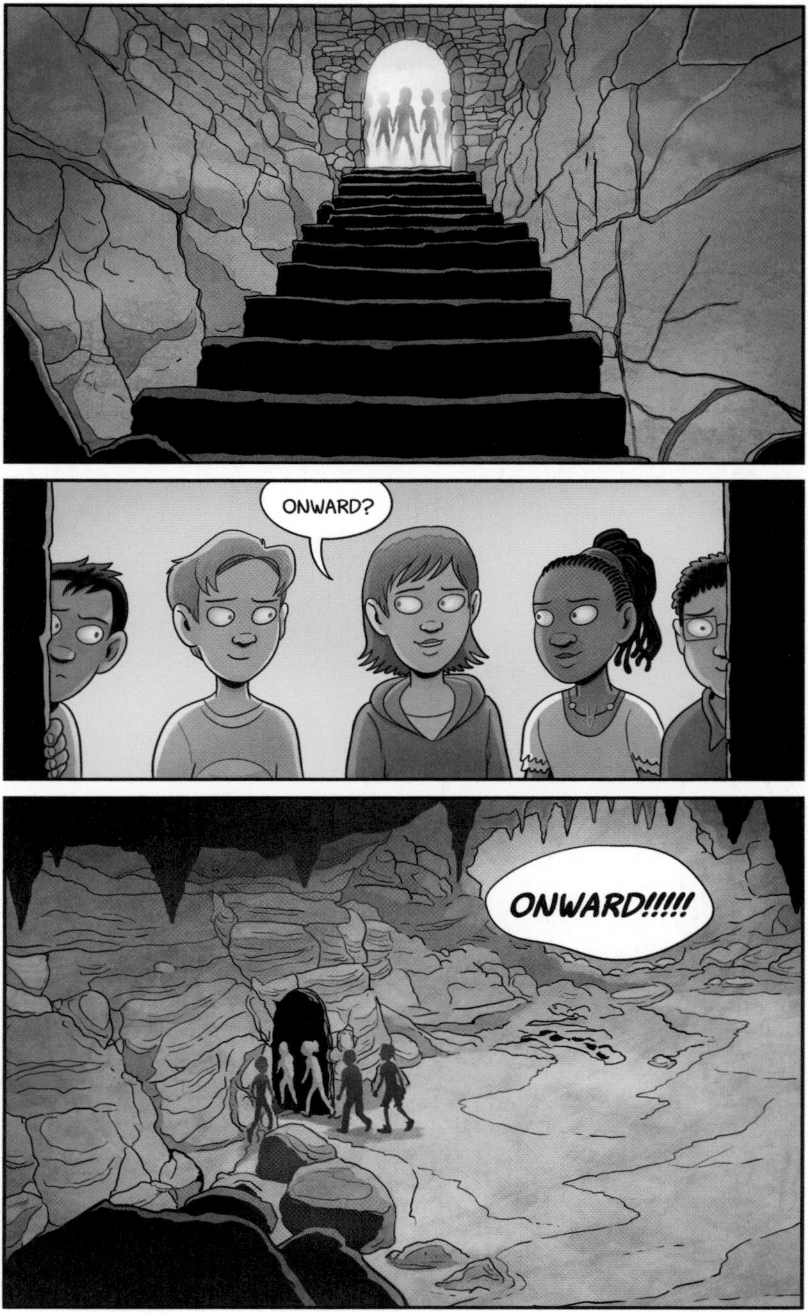
ONWARD?
ONWARD!!!!!

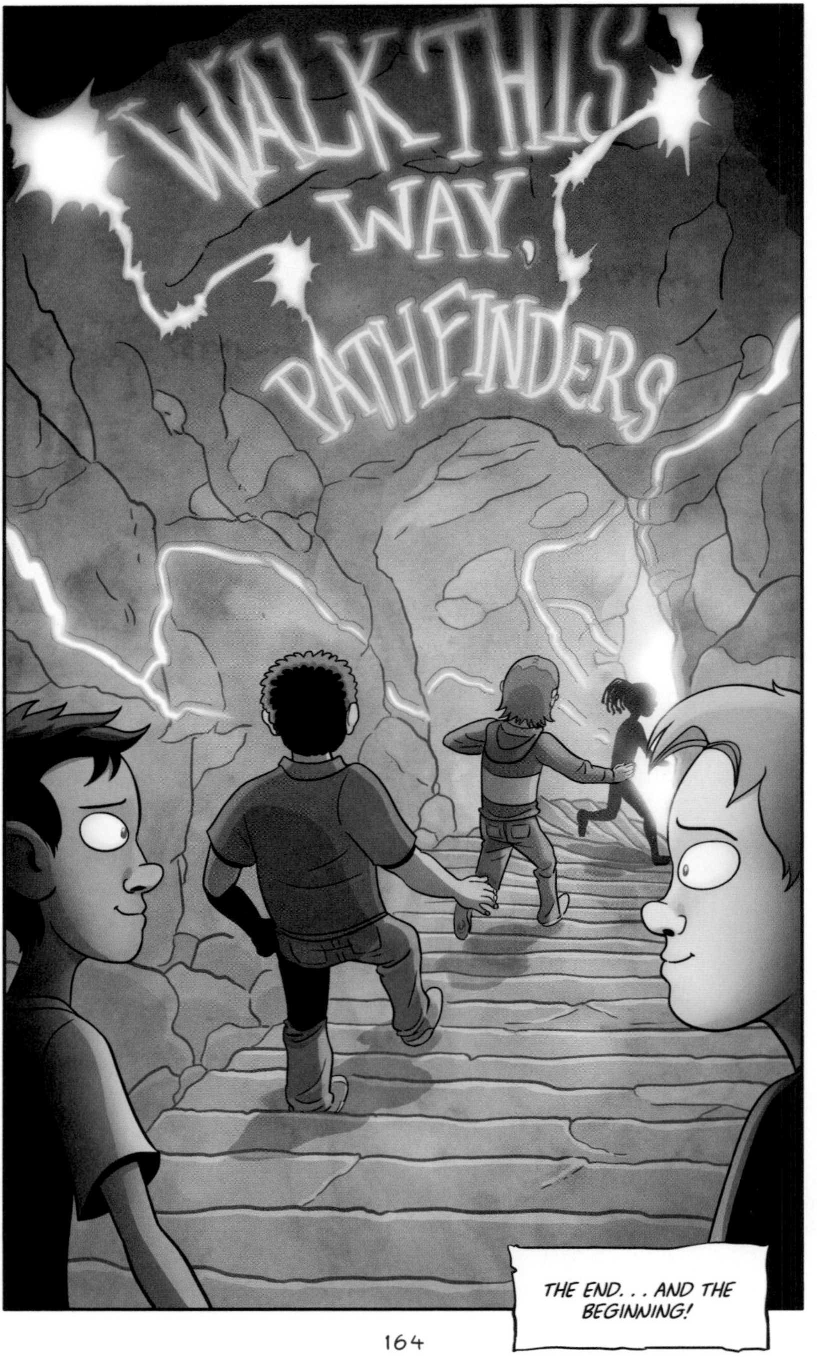
WALK THIS WAY, PATHFINDERS
THE END. . . AND THE BEGINNING!

*To Be
Continued…*

Meet the Author

FRANCESCO SEDITA likes to make lots of things: this book is one of them. Other things he has created are the Miss Popularity books series, the Emmy Award–winning *Who Was? Show* on Netflix (which he made with his co-author Prescott Seraydarian), as well as lots of other books in his job at Penguin Young Readers, like Mad Libs, WhoHQ bestsellers, and other books with amazing authors like Henry Winkler, Lin Oliver, Giada De Laurentiis, and even Dolly Parton.

When he isn't making stuff, Francesco is cooking in his apartment in New York City or binge-watching a series with his husband or playing with their cute cat, Alfredo. Visit him at francescosedita.com.

Meet the Author

PRESCOTT SERAYDARIAN loves stories, always has. When he was a kid, he wrote stories about himself (and his entire neighborhood!) in endless enchanted adventures. That led to *telling* stories as a grown-up with amazing partners like Disney, Penguin, NBC, and Netflix through his award-wining film company Lunch Productions.

Now he has the best job of all as a film teacher at George School, a Quaker boarding school in Newton, Pennsylvania. Every day he gets to teach students (just a little older than the Pathfinders!) skills to share their own stories. Prescott lives at his school with his lovely wife, dynamic daughters, and endearing dog named Asher. Check him out at prescottseraydarian.com.

A Note from Francesco

THE PATHFINDERS SOCIETY is a series that I really never thought I'd write. There's more of an ending to this sentence—but first, I want to tell you a quick story.

Prescott and I went to college together. We quickly realized that we liked to write as a team and had a lot of fun entering TV contests. We never won, but we still kept submitting ideas. We even had internships at NBC at the same time. I worked at *Saturday Night Live* in the writing department, and Scott was just a few floors below in the NBC promotions department.

One day, after we finished college, I watched the Adam Sandler movie *Click*, where the main character has a remote control that can stop, start, rewind, and fast-forward his life. I immediately called Scott and said, "We should write *Click Part 2*!" And I was serious.

What he came back with was not what I expected. "We *should* write something together . . . but what if we write a TV show about five kids who are discovering who they are and what they're good at?"

And so we did. We had one rule: There had to be no pressure on this writing process at all. It took us a few years, but eventually we had a script for a TV show! We called it *The Young Professionals*. Our show took place in a small town, modeled on Prescott's hometown in Pennsylvania. The story was about five characters who meet and become friends during their internships, just like Prescott and I had.

We liked what we wrote and nervously asked a few people to read it. One of the readers recommended that we turn our script into a graphic novel.

A graphic novel?!

At first, we both said no. We'd spent a long time on the TV idea and I think we just needed some space. And then one night, while eating dinner together in New York City, we changed our minds.

Francesco Sedita (right) and Prescott Seraydarian (left) at the Mercer Museum in Doylestown, Pennsylvania

We decided that the story should be a bit different, too. Scott often talks about where he grew up and brought me to a museum near there called the Mercer Museum and Fonthill Castle. Something sparked: a new setting! Windrose and Henry Merriweather were born in our imaginations! It was all very magical, and I hope we've captured that feeling in these pages.

Okay, I'm going to try that first sentence one more time: *The Pathfinders Society is a series that I really never thought I'd write . . . without Prescott.* As we've worked on this first book, the town of Windrose has become a second home to us, and these characters that you've met are like our lifelong friends.

And I would never have written this without one of mine!

A Note from Prescott

IT'S FUNNY TO THINK ABOUT the paths that led here. Looking back, although every step was important, some felt a little more magical then others.

One of those first magical moments happened very early in the Francescott story, when we were both interning at NBC. Francesco had the exciting assignment upstairs but I had the cool view over Rockefeller Center. So at Christmastime, my office party was the place to be. I was allowed to bring one person, so I invited Francesco. When I think back now, we were barely older than the Pathfinders, but looking down on the dazzling sparkle of the enormous Christmas tree in Rockfeller Center, it felt like anything was possible.

That moment proved to be the start of working on many creative projects together. On that journey, the most magical moment happened when we asked ourselves "What if someone like Henry Mercer left a trail in the past for kids to follow in the future?"

If you don't know the name Henry Mercer, don't worry. But if you've read our story it may sound familiar. We based parts of the Henry Merriweather character on Henry Mercer, a real-world person and a bit of a local legend in the part of Pennsylvania where I grew up.

Henry Mercer was a man of many interests, from science and archaeology, to history, folklore, writing, and art. He was constantly curious about the world and its many connections. But he didn't just talk about it, he put his interests into action and his legacy lives on even today.

Mercer was born in Doylestown, Pennsylvania, in 1856. He grew into an exceptional student who could speak six languages. Henry was encouraged to travel, and he took a special interest in castles along the Rhine River in Germany. These castles touched something deep inside him, and so Henry dedicated himself to building one of his own.

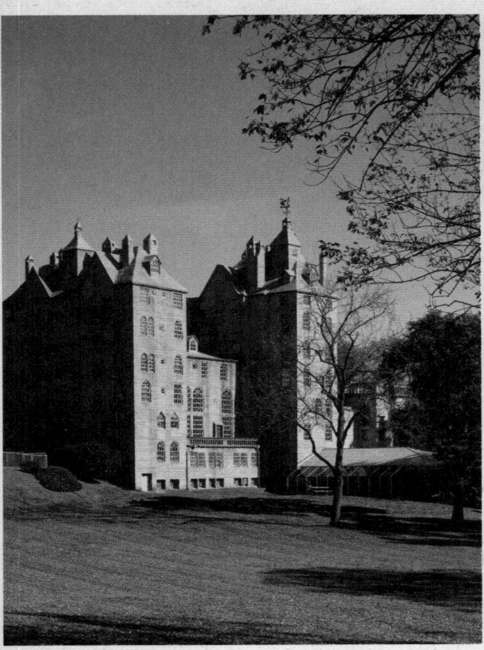 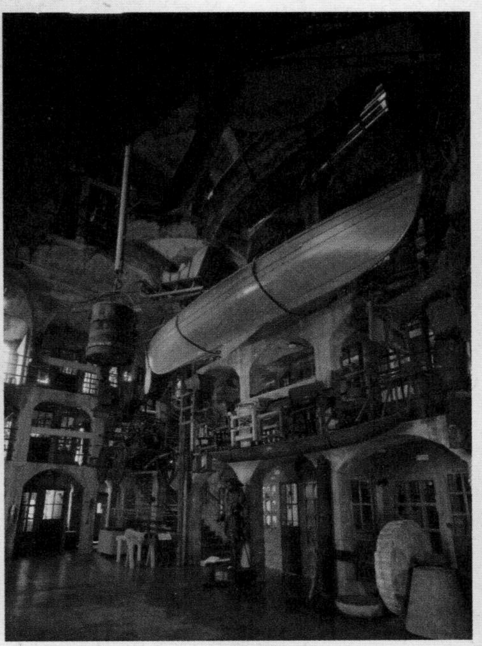

The Mercer Museum and Fonthill Castle, and the Central Court inside the Mercer Museum

The result of his hard work are two mysterious and beautiful concrete castles, as well as a tile factory where Mercer pioneered the creation of artistic tiles similar to those found in our book.

When Francesco and I discovered Henry Mercer, magic followed. We were intrigued by so many things about his life, from his dog's frozen paw prints in the cement castle, to his original keyboard, and thousands of unusual tools that he collected in his own museum. But it was Henry's love of exploration and interest in bringing history alive that inspired our fictional character Henry Merriweather.

We hope our story is a lasting tribute to Henry Mercer and all others who bravely set out to navigate the mystery, missteps, and perplexities of life in the spirit of "plus ultra!" Their courage has created a little more inspiration for each of us to find our own way.

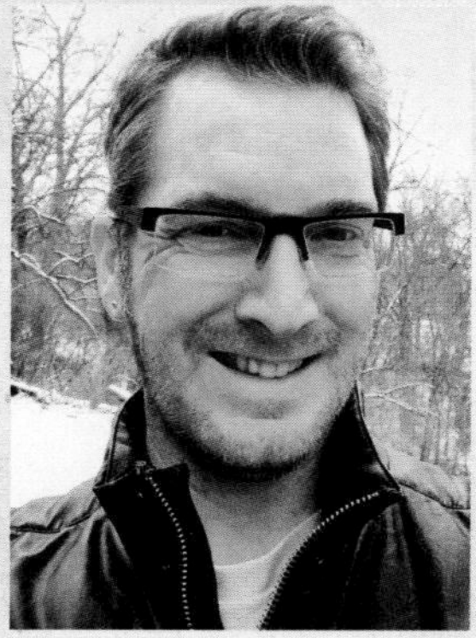

Meet the Artist

STEVE HAMAKER is the Eisner Award–winning colorist of bestselling graphic novel series such as Bone by Jeff Smith and Hilo by Judd Winick. He has also colored online comics series and created his own original web comic, PLOX. An avid tabletop and video gamer, Steve lives in Columbus, Ohio, with his wife and son.

Follow him on Twitter @SteveHamaker.

A Note About Steve's Process

1.

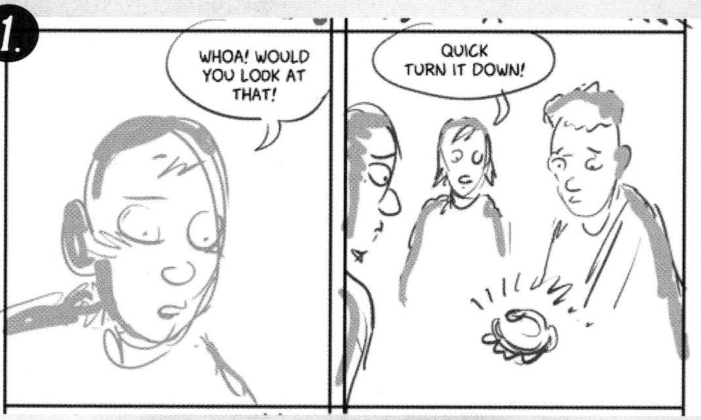
WHOA! WOULD YOU LOOK AT THAT!
QUICK TURN IT DOWN!

I get the authors' manuscript and sketch out the story so the look and the pacing are just right. The sketches go to the authors and editors. Sometimes we make changes.

2.

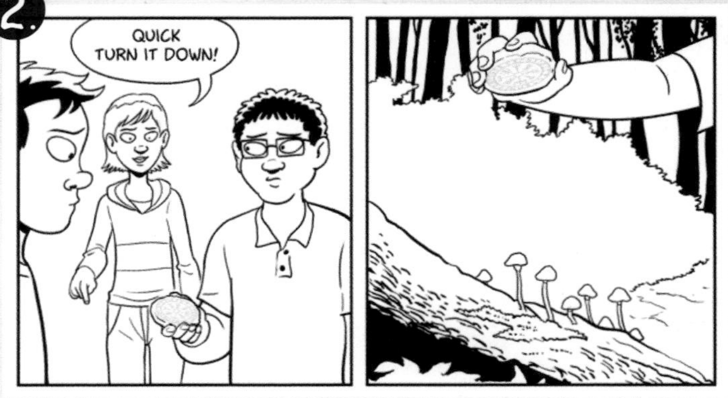
QUICK
TURN IT DOWN!

I redraw scenes if necessary and then trace over all the pencil lines in ink. I also do the final lettering.

3.

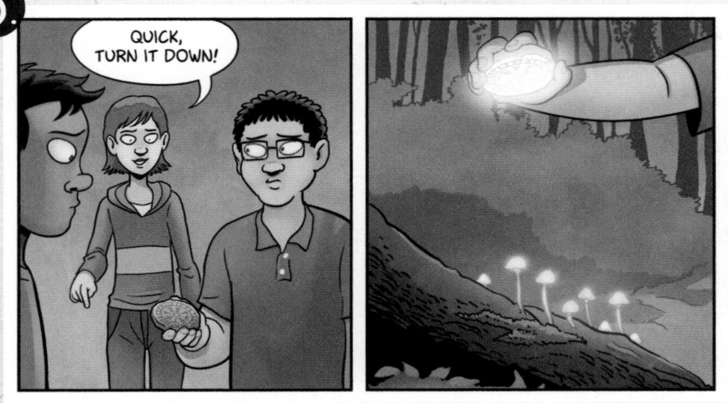
QUICK,
TURN IT DOWN!

Now the magic happens: I add the color. Check out how lighter colors can make the stone and mushrooms "glow."

P.S. I do this all on my computer: 1, 2, 3 and we have a book!